MAHTANTU

by Chris Kluge

WOODTHRUSH, LLC : NEWTON

1st edition - Woodthrush, LLC
ISBN# 978-0-9911803-1-8

for Cassius, Lina and Rocco

The blinding sunlight shimmered off the still, fetid water of the marsh, the sound of summer cicadas gently humming in the background. A solitary dragonfly pirouetted above the cattails at the end of the marsh, hovering for a moment before darting silently onto a lily pad. Its bulbous eyes swept the watery horizon and it took off again, levitating briefly before alighting onto a mossy rock among the lily pads. Dipping its head, the dragonfly sucked moisture from the spongy flora beneath its many feet.

From the far end of the marsh a warm breeze rattled the cattails, then fanned across the waters, bestirring the lily pads and ruffling the dry wings of the drinking dragonfly. A few yards away, a feeding sunfish flashed to the surface and slapped the water before returning to the marsh's muddy bottom.

Slowly, silently, the moss-covered rock began gliding toward the disturbance. The startled dragonfly leapt clear of the encroaching waters, moments before its feeding platform disappeared beneath the marsh's surface.

Chapter 1 — *Visitors From Another World*

The ship lolled offshore, its massive wooden hull alternately lifted and lowered by the gentle swells passing beneath it.

The sound of their eventual breaking on the shoreline came back to the man on deck, his telescope trained on the figures gathered on the white sands a few hundred meters away. Perhaps several dozen stood scattered along the beach, watching this strange wonder as it rolled with the incoming waves, its sun-bleached canvas sails listless in an almost windless sky.

A swarm of curious shore birds and gulls hovered and swooped around the becalmed vessel, their cries swallowed by the vast space.

The Dutch captain scanned the silent watchers enlarged by the glass, trying to assess their battle strength. A few carried lances, while others had wooden bows draped over their shoulders. There were no women or children among them, the Dutchman noted, reinforcing his assumption that these were warriors, and should be treated as hostile savages until proven otherwise.

Lowering his glass, he ordered the first mate to prepare the signal cannon, in order to establish dominance.

After packing a small amount of black powder and wadding down its barrel, the Mate swiveled the small brass cannon on its iron mount, and awaited the captain's order.

Raising his glass once again, he gave the order to fire when ready. The mate touched a smoking piece of rope to the fire hole, and a mighty roar belched forth, accompanied by a billowing cloud of thick white smoke.

The figures on the shore could be seen to flee back towards the low dunes and scrub, as the birds around the ship made hasty flight away from the explosion.

Satisfied that these people would pose no threat, the captain then ordered a boat to be lowered, and certain small gifts prepared to amend any harmed feelings. They would need to befriend those on the shore, as there was much to be done, and much to learn from them about the unexplored land beyond the dunes.

Chapter 2 — *Miltowagan   Gifts*

The Dutch captain and twelve of his crew had ascertained the village's whereabouts by following a well-worn trail through the marshlands that lay just beyond the dunes. Armed with muskets and sporting metal breastplates and helmets that reflected the sun's rays, they marched confidently through the tall grasses, toward the wall of oak forest, and the feathering columns of wood smoke that drifted skyward. Along with their armaments, they had a few score of double-headed axes, some patterned bolts of fabric, blankets, and a small cask of rum.

As they closed on the camp, they could hear dogs barking, and, soon enough, a few had bounded out of the forest to assess these strangely attired beings that shined like the very sun in the blue sky above.

The captain raised his hand and ordered the group to halt, as the dogs milled excitedly a few yards before them, barking furiously, but as yet unwilling to engage the glowing creatures.

Several Indian men emerged from the woods, armed with bows and quivered arrows. They approached the Dutch explorers cautiously, but without the terror they exhibited when the signal cannon routed them from the beach.

Reaching the pack of barking dogs, several of the Indians swatted at them with their bows, shouting commands and, in some cases, actually grabbing the curs by the fur on their backs and hurling them backward, where, upon landing, they were battered by other natives joining those in front. With the howling dogs subdued, one Indian stepped out further in front of those just assembled, and, making some sign with his hands, addressed the Dutchmen with several words.

The Dutch captain wasn't familiar with the Indian's language, but he believed that they must have formed a question, or questions.

While the Indian stood silently after his speech, the captain summoned those bearing the gifts to come forward, and told them to lay all on the ground between the Indians and themselves.

When the axes and other items had been arranged, the captain pointed to them and nodded his head first at them, and then at the individual and those arrayed behind him and to his sides.

"Gifts," he said.

The Indian who had addressed them stepped forward and bent down to retrieve one of the axes. Hefting it with one hand, he inspected the iron blades carefully, then handed his bow to one of his party.

Gripping the wooden handle just below the iron axe head, he ran his finger along one of the blades, bringing it away before it drew blood.

"*Pikschummen.*"

He turned to another and spoke several phrases, causing that Indian to trot back toward the village.

Several of his party crowded around him to inspect the axe, each in turn testing the sharp iron against a thumb.

Others stepped forward to pick up the fabrics and blankets, holding them aloft and blocking the sun, the better to study their weave.

The leader pointed to the jug of rum, miming lifting it to his mouth and upending it as if to drink, then pointed at the captain.

The Dutchman picked up the glazed vessel, pulled the cork from the spout, took a hearty drink, then extended it to the Indian.

14

Bringing it up to his nose, the Indian sniffed, then promptly lifted the jug and followed suit.

After a few seconds, he took another swig, then set it back on the ground with the other gifts.

"Good!"

By this time the runner had returned, bearing a rolled up blanket. With a nod from the Lead Indian, the runner unfurled the fabric on the ground next to the Dutch gifts, revealing animal skin pouches with beaded designs, twisted clumps of some sort of dried plant, several obsidian knives, and a smattering of metallic jewelry.

The captain stepped forward and retrieved several hoops of crudely fashioned metal.

"Copper," he noted, handing the glittering bracelets to one of his Mates.

Motioning with his hands to other trinkets on the blanket, then to bracelets, he raised his upturned hands, saying, "More?"

The Indian said "*Machkachsin*," then nodded in the affirmative.

The Dutch captain nodded his head, looked at his mates, a subtle smile on his face.

Turning to the Indian and hoisting the jug, he took a good draft, said "Good!" and extended the jug.

The Indian, upon taking the jug in both hands, spoke an approximation of this unknown word, then repeated the captain's action.

Chapter 3 — Machkachsin   Copper

The Dutch captain had no reason to conceal his interest in the copper amulets his Hosts had offered him and his crew. In fact, his interest seemed to please the Indians greatly. Using hand signs for digging, he held one of the shiny trinkets and, with a sweeping motion toward the surrounding forest, said "Where? Where is more?"

The Leader of the Indians spoke a few words with his second, who answered back, nodding affirmatively.

"*Machkachsin*"..... *Pechotschi*," pointing to the low ridges further inland.

"Take us there," said the captain, motioning toward the hills, a look of encouragement on his face.

The Indians motioned for them to follow, and both groups headed toward the ridges just a few miles westward.

Following a well-worn path that paralleled a stream, they soon arrived at the base of the mountains, where the stream disappeared into a break in the rock. This naturally formed opening had been widened over many years, to where a man could just pass through it.

Beckoning one of his smaller crew members, the captain ordered the man to hand off his musket to another and commence exploring what lay within the opening.

Removing his helmet and protective metal breastplate, he stepped forward and, straddling the small stream, followed the water into the cavern. He disappeared into the darkness of the fissure.

The Indian leader patted the rock wall just inside the fissure, and said "*Machkachsin*". Using his lance, he drew a wavering line in the wet mud at their feet.

"*Machkachsin*" .... Then made a breaking motion with both his hands, "*Talakat*," patting the rock once more.

After a few minutes, the crewman emerged from the hole, fairly covered with mud, but with a smile on his face.

"I found a likely seam only several leagues in" he breathlessly said. "There isn't much room to work, but if that seam is any indication, there'll be plenty reason to make more room, no doubt!"

Turning to the Indian. the captain smiled as well, saying "Good"... "very good" as he nodded his helmeted head approvingly.

Chapter 4 — *Mawewigawan   In the Meeting Lodge*

The wisps of smoke spiraled from the small fire, and up to a small opening in the thatched roof above. The dim light of the fire caused shadows to dance on the reed-bundle walls of the meeting lodge, as the flames wicked this way and that, gently fanned by the eagle feather in the Sachem's hand, as well as occasional drafts of cold air coming from without.

The forms of others, seated on the packed earth, encircled the fire and the Sachem. A soft chanting from all accompanied the gentle fanning of the feather; a song that seemed to fill the lodge without having any specific source.... like the call of a wood thrush at dusk.

Though a cadence, a slight rising and falling, gave a structure to this chanting, except for occasional words, the phrases within did not repeat.

The voice of the Sachem was only slightly louder than the accompanists arrayed, but there was a strength, a firmness to his utterances that set him apart from the whole.

Some of the others shook hollow gourds, the seeds trapped within making for a gentle washing pulse, like wind rattling dried corn stalks in autumn.

A few held small wooden hoops with stretched leather covers, and beat them lightly with the thighbones of deer.

Occasionally the Sachem would reach into a small leather pouch, and, with the slightest flick of his wrist, extend his fingers to the coals before him, like a viper spitting venom, causing a brief flaring of fire and an accompanying puff of blue white smoke to join the rising column.

While festive ceremonies were held in the lodge for many communal occasions, this was a somber affair.

The dreams of the Sachem had been fretful of late. While many of the People had the ability to remember their dreams, those of the Sachem were of particular importance to all. The ability to have and remember vivid dreams, and the special power to interpret those dreams and use as guides for the others, was in large part what caused one member to be chosen by all as a spiritual Leader... a Sachem.

The power to see the future fortunes of the family tribe through the Sachem's interpretation of his dreams was as important to the community's well-being, nay, survival, as growing crops, hunting for meat and skins, and defending from external threats, human and otherwise.

The Elders spoke of monsters that dwelt in the water, with horns and beards. These were known as real dangers for generations. But the Sachem had been seeing some new kind of sea monster.... one that came from the far horizon of the great sea, with many creatures on its back, and with its own clouds.

The fiery breath of this strange being brought sickness and pain to anyone it approached, and, as something unknown to the history of the People, the Sachem didn't know of any ready defense, spiritual or weapon-based, to repel it.

Without this necessary knowledge, the Sachem felt powerless to serve his function... to protect his People.

Chapter 5 — *Schawanammek   Month of the Shad*

The fish struggled to fight the downstream current, calling on its last reserves to reach some pool, away from the swift waters. Having reached this far up the wide waters, it had left many of its others behind; some too exhausted to continue, others felled by the varied predators that were as attuned to this annual ritual as the thousands upon thousands of shad that braved the watery gauntlet.

Just as the winter snowmelt added to the river's downward rush to the sea, the millions of shad began their rush to spawn; in effect creating a silvery counter river of life, pushing ever further up the powerful waters. The local People who joined the other numerous predators in this springtime bounty named this unvarying cycle as *"Schawanammek"... month of the shad.* It marked the end of the cold, and the beginning of the warming, and had so for as long as anyone could remember.

Sensing a break in the current, the almost spent fish moved toward the bank of the river, and a semi-becalmed pool that was sheltered by a huge fallen oak tree.

The bottom here was sandy, and suitable for the creation of a small fin-shaped nest to receive the eggs.

Resting on the bottom, the fish drew the sun-warmed water into its gasping mouth, and over and through its fanning gills, feeding needed oxygen to starved cells.

Suddenly, a thin wooden shaft pierced the water above it, and proceeded through the fish itself.

Stunned, the impaled shad was lifted up and out of the water, and into the air.

The boy held his catch aloft, then quickly deposited the flapping fish into a basket of woven branches at his feet.

He bent down to admire his catch, watching the bubbles of air and water rhythmically expelled from the dying shad's gills and mouth.

"A big one!" he said aloud, much pleased with his first catch of the season.

He imagined with pride how he would present this, and, if the *Monitos* favored him, more fresh meat to his family, encamped nearby.

A mangy dog that accompanied the boy in his forays beyond the village cautiously stretched its nose toward the still breathing fish in the basket.

"*HO!*" said the boy, waving his fish spear in the air. The dog quickly withdrew, knowing that it would share in whatever the People didn't eat. And a furtive snap at the fish was not worth the sting of the spear.

Checking the twin-sharpened wood prongs on the tip of the spear for damage, the boy renewed his stance on the partially submerged tree trunk, careful that his shadow did not fall on the water. The liquid surface beneath him reflected the warming sunlight up to the limbs of the alder trees that hung over the river, as well as the still silhouette poised, spear in hand. The dappled light on the limbs blended with the dappled light on the boy. He would be as invisible to anything below the water as a rail thin heron pursuing a similar meal.

Chapter 6 .... Papaisin   Sickness

The change of seasons often brought sickness to the encampments; the cold of winter to the wet of spring; the heat of summer to the chill of *kitschitachquock.*

An array of treatments existed, having been refined over many generations... such and such for the coughing.... another for fever...... this for rash........

But since the arrival of the foreigners, it seemed the severity and frequency of maladies had increased. Travelers from other villages brought accounts of strange outbreaks of sicknesses previously unknown. Some were fleeing from what had been their family group, after entire villages fell to these unseen forces.

The Sachem had at first welcomed some refugees, as was the custom of interlocking family groups. But as the number of incomers grew, and incidences of sickness among his own villagers followed, he realized that his own People's survival was at stake, and he took to turning many away.

The sickness had crept up on the people like an imperceptible predator; first one became ill, complaining of fatigue and dull pain. The sweat lodge hadn't slowed the fever, and then others succumbed. In a matter of days, half of the group were dead, the other half incapacitated with terror at this unseen malevolence.

Chris Kluge

Chapter 7 — Wihoman   Gift of Affection

The young man and the girl had taken to meeting furtively in a quiet glade beside the river, a short distance from the Quaker settlement. Several ancient beech trees, their massive limbs almost meeting high above, encircled a small clearing beneath. The slight rustle of the moving waters joined with the other forest noises, and the leaf filtered sunlight danced on the moss of the forest floor.

Even though the girl's Quaker parents intermingled well with the original settlers (even to the point of having learned to communicate with them in their native tongue, and to teach them the rudiments of their own Dutch in turn), the joining of their daughter in marriage to a Lenni Lenape would never be condoned; a sentiment carried equally by the boy's family.

For this special meeting, the boy had brought a gift, something worthy of the celebration of the new life growing inside the girl.

After embracing, the two sat on the moss facing each other, and the young man withdrew a small beaded leather bag from beneath his shirt. Placing it on the ground between them, he motioned with his smile for her to open it.

She loosened the rawhide drawstring and upended the bag, releasing two copper bracelets onto the moss. The shiny copper seemed to glow against the soft green of the moss, the shifting sunlight adding little sparkles of light.

Taking her hand in his, the boy then gently slid the first bracelet onto her left wrist, then repeated with the right. No words were spoken; none were needed. Rearranging themselves, they lay side by side on their moss bed, and held each other as a slight breeze made the leaves above them quiver, and the sunlight to dance around them.

Chapter 8 — *Lachsimuen   Dreamtime*

The cold wind had been battering the lodge house for several days, finding its way through every opening, and causing the bundled sapling walls to bend and creak, the deer hide coverings rattling with each gust.

Those within, huddling under fur robes, only stirred to tend the small fire, or scurry outside to relieve themselves in the snow-covered trees near by.

They had ample food to see them through the storm, but a few of them had developed fevers, and those not sick were anxious to get out and resume hunting.

The Sachem was worried about the sick ones; he'd tried all the cures and prayers known to him, without success.

Burrowing into his bedding, he decided he needed to coax wisdom from the dream world, and he shut his eyes and willed himself to sleep.

The firelight danced on his eyelids, and he let his thoughts wander, relinquishing himself to whatever path appeared to him.

Giant shadows loomed around him, and he was among others of his people. They seemed to be encircled by unknown forces, creatures..... Facing outward in a loosely formed circle, he and the others were afraid, though nothing tangible could be discerned in the surrounding darkness.

Soon, one after another of his group seemed to stumble, dropping to one knee, trying to get up again, lurching and falling. The Sachem felt the earth beneath him tremble, almost like a huge living being shivering from fever. Suddenly, strange pale shapes began emerging from the trembling ground, appendages thrusting up through the dark loam like lances, spiking through the reeling hunters, lifting their wriggling forms off the ground.

Strangest of all, the Sachem realized the emerging shapes were drawing together, coalescing into one giant monster that now began bellowing and stomping all around on the prostrate hunters beneath it.

The sound of a baby crying brought the Sachem back from the Dream World. The smoky interior of the lodge slowly replaced the vision of the giant. Huddled in his blankets, the Sachem realized what the dream was telling him.

Aside from the traditional medicines and cures for everyday ailments, there were still very powerful resources to be utilized; unearthed bones of monsters long extinct, originally extracted from brackish bogs and eroded riverbanks. These huge bones, some as tall as a man, had been handed down through generations, and were believed to have come from giant forbears, who stalked the monsters of their time. As such, these skeletal remains possessed great power; a power gifted to future generations of the People, to be used for their protection against powerful evil.

Small amounts of the bones, scraped, powdered and mixed with tobacco, could be smoked in shallow, ceramic pipes to protect against malevolent forces.

Minuscule effigies of Spirit Animals were carved, to be secreted in medicine bags, and hung around an individual's the neck, or from tree limbs and bushes around a village perimeter. Smaller diameter bones were fashioned as bracelets, charred from within to fit over a wearer's wrist. Wavering lines of copper, pounded thin with rounded rocks, entwined some of these bone bracelets, resembling the poisonous *Machqeuachgook* that lay on the sun-warm sand along the river in summer.

In desperation, even the hair and bits of clothing from the Dead were added, as if their *Mantowagan*, spiritual power, might somehow contain the pandemic.

Regrettably, many of those that faithfully embraced even these extreme rituals died, while some survivors ran away, leaving their cursed possessions behind, thinking a mid-winter trek into the wilderness preferable to fighting an omnipotent, invisible demon.

The old man knelt by the fire, his hands busily fashioning a little bundle of leather, bone, and hair. The air inside the hut was thick with heat and smoke; the sour smell of sweat and fever had sublimated into the woven mats and animal hides strewn around the dark interior. The ancient fingers, calloused and cracked, tied the thongs skillfully, although not as quickly as in years past.

Outside, the cold winds of winter pushed against the walls of the hut in icy gusts. The dried sticks and leather hides creaked in the sharp air, their summer flexibility frozen stiff. Shrouded bundles, stacked like firewood, lay silent in the thin snow, awaiting the dignity of a warm weather burial, or the indignity of being scavenged by animals emboldened by hunger.

Finally, after all known remedies had failed, the Sachem, himself beset by fever, had a vision; not of a cure for those already ill, but of a response to those forces that had caused his people to sicken and die. He now fashioned the bundle in his lap as a gift to those forces, to be offered as an appeasement to their whimsical cruelty. As he wrapped the thongs tightly around the scraps and bits of man and animal, he invoked words and thoughts to invest the offering with all the power he could summon. His prayers and tears would, hopefully, ensure the comfort of those already gone, and halt the return of the spirit to those not yet born.

They would also redirect some of the malevolent power from whence the old man believed it came; back to the pale people from across the water.

The little effigy would be sealed inside a cooking pot and buried in the lime pit by the wooded edge, joining the other such offerings already entombed there.

Chapter 9 — *Amatschipuis   Turkey Buzzard*

The turkey buzzard launched itself from its rocky perch atop Rattlesnake Ridge, catching the rising warm air from the valley below. The large wings beat several times, enough for the bird to begin its lazy ascent on the thermals that formed all along the *Kitahtëne*.

As the buzzard spiraled slowly upward, the creeks, ponds and river below reflected the energy of the sun back into the rapidly heating air, providing more lift to the scavenger's quest for altitude, and its search for food far below.

Relying on its keen site, as well as sense of smell, the buzzard was always dependent on predators for its nourishment; the rotting remains of prey deemed unworthy of further consumption by whoever caused their death, the leftovers from cyclical mass die-offs, like the shad that perished after spawning in the spring. An opportunist by necessity, the buzzard never let anything it could possibly digest go uneaten. Probably the only living food it consumed were the maggots and other insects that also relied on the dead.

Over time the sight of rising smoke had promised scraps of food, left over by the humans and their domesticated animals; offal so spoiled even the curs wouldn't touch it.

Rising ever higher, the scavenger could see several distinct wisps of cook fire smoke spread out along the silvery line of river far below. Tilting its bulk slightly, it let the warm air raise one wing, while dropping the other, and it headed slowly toward the nearest column of spindly smoke.

On the ground, several blanketed forms lay haphazardly around the dying fire. Clusters of saplings, stripped of their leaves, their tops lashed together with bark, belied abandoned shelters, the ground within the skeletal outlines packed hard, and clear of vegetation.

Most of the bundled figures had already been disturbed; by dogs and other ground mammals, judging by the scattered bones. A small group of Magpies stalked between or perched atop the bodies, quarreling over scraps of meat and gristle.

The sweet stench of death lay heavy in the air.

Up in the sky, the buzzard banked and circled above the deserted encampment, descending slightly with each circle. It finally came to rest on the top of a large beech tree, its large claws gripping the gently swaying branch.

After briefly surveying the ground below, it spread its huge wings, and swooped to a clumsy landing on one of the bundles.

The magpies scolded in unison, but the buzzard wasn't intimidated, and it began to pull flesh from the neck of the corpse it perched on.

Chapter 10 — A Vandalized Crypt

Jake Danley wrestled the bouncing '83 Ford pickup truck onto the rutted track of the Stokes Forest burial ground, the balding tires kicking up clouds of beige dust. The shuddering, creaking truck flushed three mourning doves from their midday roost in a juniper berry tree, giving Jake a start as they exploded across the truck's windshield.

As caretaker of the few buildings left in Stokes Forest, Jake never knew what he'd encounter on his rounds. That's why he liked the job, as a matter of fact; for that element of surprise, of discovery. Several years past his earned retirement, Jake continued his chosen career with happiness. Even after 47 years of prowling these backwoods meadows, forests, and mountains, he always saw something new, something unexpected.

The truck rounded an overgrown lilac hedge and passed through the rusted iron gates of the Stokes burial ground. Jake brought the truck to an abrupt stop, stepping down from the cab as the truck's dust wake caught up with him and passed him by, moving wraithlike across the tombstones and crypts spread around him. After the vibration and noise of the old Ford, the absence of sound had a suddenness, an overwhelming presence. He stood still and marveled at the quiet, the ticking of the hot engine mixing with the faint *"kerweeee"* of some redwing blackbirds nesting among the willows, down by the slow moving creek.

Jake stepped away from the truck, and walked toward the towering pines that formed a green wall between the northern boundary of the cemetery and the great marsh beyond. He meant to inspect a drainage pipe he had put in last year, in a never-ending attempt to keep the seeping moisture from permeating the cemetery grounds.

A small flash of color caught his eye; fluttering in the light breeze, a piece of maroon fabric, entangled in a wild rose bush, beckoned him. He stooped to pull the tiny banner from its tether, and held it gingerly, inspecting this odd fragment of litter.

"Looks like part of a dress," muttered Jake, "...looks like someone's Sunday Meeting dress, a fancy one, with tiny designs, stitched real close and fine, all around the collar... old fashioned-styled, too...."

Indeed, the swatch of finery brought evocative images to Jake's mind, visions of high-buttoned matrons, securely swaddled in cottons and velvets, with sun-browned faces, and work-weathered hands; faces from the past, from Jake's past; relatives long-forgotten.

"Wonder where this came from?" thought Jake, as he folded the antique cloth into his pocket and walked slowly down the road, his mind lingering somewhere long ago.

His reverie was broken as he noticed something peculiar about the Hardin Family crypt near the base of the pine trees.

The wrought iron doors, rusted shut for decades, were flung wide; one grate hung twisted from its broken hinge, and the inner metal doors were pushed inward, giving the crypt the look of a surprised Gothic jack-o'-lantern.

"Damn vandals!" swore Jake, as he walked hurriedly toward the moss-covered sepulcher, stepping between the asymmetrical gravestones and markers. As he got closer, Jake could see bits of rubbish around the open doors of the crypt, and still more litter within the dark confines.

Suddenly wary that the vandals might still be in the area, Jake stopped in his tracks and listened closely to the sounds around him... still only the light rustle of the breeze among the branches, the faint cry of summer birds. Nothing to suggest careless marauders or fleeing mischief-makers.

Cautiously, Jake stepped forward, close enough to smell the moist, musty odor so peculiar to all mausoleums; almost refreshing in its damp coolness except for the unavoidable realization of the source of that fecundity.

In the bright sunlight spilling through the pine trees beyond, some of the litter about the entrance to the crypt was suddenly identifiable as similar cloth to that which Jake had plucked from the bush; only here its identity was clearer; it was indeed clothing, clothing of a style from long ago; clothing which still shrouded its owner, or, at least, portions of its owner.

To his horror, Jake realized that the litter was comprised of bits and pieces of a human cadaver, along with what looked like shattered wooden planks and pieces of coffin hardware.

The long-dead corpse on the ground looked as horrified as Jake, with its head thrown back, jaw flung open, and long, grey hair splayed out. Its nearly skinless features seemed surprised at this rude awakening, after so many years of slumber. The torso was demurely clad in the same maroon fabric as was tucked away in Jake's pocket; once an elegant gown, now a tattered shroud. At once revulsed and curious, Jake stared intently at this dehydrated visitor from the past, put to rest with such care, and wrenched so abruptly into the light of the present.

Her once-folded arms were thrown open, like a doll's, with one actually cracked from the torso and laying like a broken branch a few feet away. The maroon sleeve of one arm, the one still attached to her torso, ended in a frayed tear, with a varnish-colored bone protruding beyond the torn cloth. The dismembered arm at her side had very little fabric on it. The forearm ended in a crushed break. There was no hand on either arm.

"Her hands," thought Jake, "where are her hands?" Stepping gingerly over the cadaver, Jake stood at the entrance to the crypt, and peered into the gloom. All four of the interior vaults had been violated. Their marble covers had been pried off, and the wooden caskets within dragged out and split open, leaving the grisly contents of three of them spread carelessly about the interior.

"Good Lord," whispered Jake "What happened here?" All the coffins were shattered, every corpse had been exhumed, and the entire assemblage tossed around like a dried salad.

As his eyes adjusted to the dark interior, Jake could clearly make out the withered features of the three Hardins, now so indecently displayed.

One male lay half-ejected from his broken bed, looking for all the world like a bobsled racer caught in mid-collision, just before being flung to a redundant death. He had on a black formal cloth coat, a cutaway, with a striped tie still tucked into a starched shirt, once white but now stained a blotchy yellow.

Another man, jammed under the first corpse, modeled a dove-grey waistcoat, trimmed with black velvet, a shriveled boutonniere still pinned in place. A tiny ray of sunlight pierced the one stained glass window, and illuminated a cracked pair of spectacles, peeking from beneath the shattered mahogany above him.

Propped in the far corner of the crypt, among still more broken rubble, sat the wizened mummy of a former lady of means... a leering skull, capped with a fright-wig of white hair, emerging from the remains of a powder-blue evening dress, inlaid with embroidered patterns and pearls, her still-folded arms partially covered by a bouquet of dried flowers.

While one part of Jake was thoroughly repulsed by this diorama of death, another part was fascinated. It wasn't everyone who came face to face with a real incarnation of their worst nightmare, and Jake couldn't stop studying, with great interest, the wealth of historical detail before him: the clothes, the hair, the attitudes of repose. After all, someday, thought Jake, that's what we all end as... a dried effigy of ourselves, a mummy in a box.

"I'd better call the ranger," muttered Jake, backing his way out of the cool shadows and into the bright sunlight. He felt an urge to compose the remains in a more orderly fashion, as if that might make them more comfortable somehow, but he shook the thought from his head. He realized he was viewing a crime scene, and the authorities would want nothing rearranged.

As he backed out of the darkness he noticed several grooved lines scratched deeply into the twisted, blackened metal of the ironwork of the gates. Stepping carefully over the poor soul splayed out in the dust in front of the crypt, Jake noticed indentations in the ground immediately in front of the crypt. "Like some kind of tracks," he thought, "but I can't quite make out of what...."

A growing sense of dread made him want to leave, and he turned toward his truck with quickened pace. It was time to get out of there, and fast. He was soon backing the truck around the narrow road and gunning the old Ford toward familiar, comforting sights to counter those which filled his mind.

Chapter 11 — Ranger Smith Visits the Resurrected

Ranger Smith looked up from the propane tank he was inspecting, as he heard his office phone ring. He laid the wrench on the tank, and strode quickly to the back porch of his cabin, letting the screen door slap the porch railing as he reached in the door to the wall phone.

"Ranger Smith, Stokes Station. May I help you?"

"Ranger Smith, this is Jake Danley, I'm calling from Bevin's Store. You better get out to the Stokes Cemetery right away. Somebody tore up the Hardin Crypt, and left a hell of a mess out there!"

"Whoa, Jake, slow down. What do you mean 'tore up'? Did someone break into the Hardin Crypt?"

"Frank, I mean somebody wrecked that crypt! There's bodies laying all over, and the gates are bent, and you better get out there right away!"

Ranger Smith knew that Jake was a little eccentric (who wouldn't be, he thought, living out in that remote forest) but that he was a reliable observer, and not one to exaggerate.

"I'll be right out there, Jake. Why don't I meet you at the store and we'll both go over in my car." No need for Jake to do any more driving while he was this excited, thought the ranger.

"And Jake... if you haven't already told anybody about this, let's you and I keep it to ourselves, at least until I can make up a first-hand report. We don't want the entire county out there taking pictures and disturbing the evidence."

"You bet, Ranger, I'll wait here for you at the pay phone. I won't tell nobody!"

Something this sensational would draw a bigger crowd than the annual Sussex Fair, and the ranger didn't want photographs of decomposed forebears showing up in any local Hardin relative's newspaper.

He grabbed his holster, his trooper-style hat, and his digital camera from the office desk, and headed out the back-door toward the Forest Service-issued sedan, parked in front of the utility shed.

He checked his two-way radio, turning the volume up and clicking it on (it hadn't been a hundred percent of late... nothing to bother fixing, just enough to have to adopt a new habit every time he got in his vehicle.)

Satisfied it was working, he started the car and spun gravel as he accelerated quickly out his driveway, heading for Stokes Forest and whatever awaited him at the Cemetery.

He spied Jake's Ford in front of Bevin's Country Store, and Old Jake standing in the shade of the front porch, alone.

"Hop in, Jake," Ranger Smith offered, opening the passenger door even before bringing the cruiser to a stop.

"I didn't talk to nobody, Frank," panted Jake, heaving himself into the car and slamming the door shut.

"I just told Jimmy Bevins I was going to leave my truck outside while I showed you a drainage ditch that needs fixing."

"Good work, Jake, I knew I could count on you. Let's get on out there before anybody happens onto the scene."

"Frank, I never saw anything like what I saw today! I've been trying to imagine who would do a thing so mean, and I can't come up with anybody."

A few weeks past, a group of local kids had tipped over thirty-five tombstones in the Johnson town cemetery, but they hadn't desecrated a crypt, or ravaged the sleeping dead. That incident had been written off to youthful vandalism, and had none of the markings of attempted grave robbing. With so-called satanic cults gaining in popularity of late, a black market in graveyard paraphernalia, especially human bones, had sprung up, and graveyard incidents were fairly commonplace.

If Jake's description was at all accurate, however, this wasn't the work of modern-day Druids. Why break into a crypt and leave the bodies? Ranger Smith swung the jeep through the gates of Stokes Forest Cemetery, and drove slowly toward the far green wall of pine trees. He parked the car on a grassy mound, between the dirt road and the tombstones. Grabbing his camera, he and Jake both got out and walked toward the crypt.

It was exactly as Jake had described it; the corpse in front of the opened iron gates, and the bits of coffin wood and interior fabric all around.

"Jake, I think it best if I proceed alone, so I can survey and document the crime scene as it is. Okay by you?"

"No, I don't mind one bit, Ranger Smith. I've seen enough for one day, thank you very much! I'll wait by the car. You call me if you need me, y'hear?"

"You bet, Jake. I appreciate it. I'll let you know if I need your help, don't worry."

Switching the camera on, Ranger Smith viewed the grisly scene before him through the lens, checked the light settings, then took two overall shots of the crypt, with its wide-open gates, and the human litter strewn all around.

Stepping closer, the Ranger bent to examine the rough indentations in the ground. Adjusting the lens, he walked to an angle that afforded a deep shadow, to get a good relief view of one of the markings in the dirt. It did look like some sort of print, but, like Jake, he couldn't quite figure what kind of tool or heavy object would yield such a mark in the rich earth.

The corpse in the sunlight was not that dissimilar to more recently-departed souls he had photographed; accident victims, old people who had died alone.... they almost always looked surprised in their final moment on earth.

This long-dead woman had that same look, even though some equally long-dead undertaker must have applied his utmost skill in giving her a countenance of ease and contentment, back when her people sent her off on her final outing, dressed in her best.

Ranger Smith took several close-cropped shots of her torso, with her handless arms flanking the torn maroon fabric. He studied the severed bones, trying to guess what force had separated the wrists and hands... maybe a bolt cutter? A little too frayed, he thought: a bolt cutter would have easily cut through dried, brittle calcium, and would have left a far cleaner cut. A hacksaw, with somebody in a hurry to finish the job, perhaps? No, the bone was crushed at the break, not sawn through. Some powerful devise had been used to snip the hands off, he concluded, though exactly what kind of cutting tool he couldn't for the moment imagine. He took several extreme close-ups of the severed wrists, then straightened up and moved to the opening of the tomb.

The coolness of crypts was remarkable, he thought, as he stepped between the twisted iron gates into the marbled interior of the vault. His eyes saw only blackness for a moment. As he adjusted to the change of light, he began to decipher the wreckage within.

He activated the camera's built-in flash to compensate for the darkness of the tomb. He shot each casket and corpse separately, then took in the lot of them for a macabre group shot. While the ranger had, of course, examined many cadavers, he had never seen unearthed corpses. The features of these long-dead Hardins were as he expected: wizened, dried masks, stretched tight over unyielding bone and horse-like teeth, with wispy tufts of hair shooting this way and that.

But the burial clothes.... Except for damage due to whatever violence had wrenched them from their slumber, the clothes were almost perfectly preserved; not a sign of wear, not a frayed collar or elbow.

And the cut of the cloth, the styling! It was as if images from an antique Sears Roebuck catalogue had emerged from a black &

white engraving and dropped themselves, in three dimensions, onto the floor of this crypt. He marveled at the fine details, the rich colors of the fabrics.

Now there was something to wonder about: the colors of the clothing. Not all black, or all white, as in old picture albums and velvet-layered frames. The upper corpse had on a purple necktie, and his coat was lined with a blue, satiny material. The woman was adorned in a peach-colored gown, with a pale green sash. With only black & white images to reference the past, the Ranger had never thought about all those faces framed in colorful attire. Funny, he thought, how people from long ago always look like they could only exist in that time. Was it the clothes? Their hairstyles? The sunken-eyed look of them, in daguerreotypes and coffins?

He refocused his concentration on the wreckage at hand. The marble slabs that had sealed the vaults had been pried off, the ornamental brass fasteners popped from the wall like tarnished buttons. The inner walls of the crypt, mildewed with age to a dark green, showed bright white markings around the corners of the vault covers; grooves cut into the untarnished marble beneath.

Looks too thin to be the end of a crowbar, thought the Ranger. "Maybe a pickaxe...." he muttered, his fingers following the parallel markings, etched into the border of each desecrated vault.

Pulling a cotton handkerchief from his pants pocket, he bent to retrieve a broken brass coffin handle, holding it, swaddled in the cloth, toward the open doors and sunlight. Twisted slightly from its original shape, the once-polished ornament had dulled in the airless vault. Except, noticed the ranger, where something had deeply scored it, in two distinct places, top and bottom, before ripping it from the aged mahogany coffin.

"The bolt-cutter, or whatever had been used to cut off the woman's hands outside?" mused the ranger? He decided that whatever tool had been used, there had to be some powerful hands using them.

Gingerly pocketing the heavy brass handle, wrapped in his handkerchief, he resumed his photographic documentation of the markings on the walls and the broken objects around him. After satisfying himself that he had taken enough pictures to recreate the crime scene for careful evaluation, Ranger Smith bid the residents a silent acknowledgement of respect, and picked his way carefully out of the gloom, back into the bright Stokes Forest sunlight.

He waved to Jake, sitting in the shade of the front seat, and walked quickly to the car. He knew he needed additional police coverage as soon as possible, to guard the gravesite from ghoulish souvenir hunters, and, more importantly, to stand vigil over the exposed dead, until they could be properly returned to their well-deserved rest.

He had already decided not to use his radio to call the State Police barracks at Culver's Gap. Like most rural areas, it seemed every family in Sussex County boasted a volunteer fire and/or rescue squad member. Social life revolved as much around the local fire company as around church. Consequently, just about every home in the area had a sophisticated police scanner turned on at all times.

The last thing he wanted at this point was the certain stampede of 4x4s, RVs, and pick-up trucks he would unleash, moments after radioing his findings to the troopers.

"Jake, thank you for calling me first. Let's get over to the State Trooper barracks and get their help."

As the car eased out of the cemetery, an inquisitive crow swooped from his high, pine perch, and stalked suspiciously the outstretched arm before him, unable to resist the mystery of the abalone sleeve-buttons, sparkling in the yellow summer sun.

Chapter 12 — Bobby and Randy at the Marsh

The sluggish, grey-blue waters flowed under the one lane wooden bridge, gathered momentum as they channeled into the rock-lined canal, and rushed, foaming and splashing, over the sluice gate and on down the raceway, where they would eventually lose their urgency and commingle with the marsh beyond.

Bulrushes— their feathered, flowering tops swaying in the evening breeze— congregated in the shallow water near the shore. On one, a red-wing blackbird gripped the gently rocking stalk, its claws and fanned-out tail holding its balance, as it descended, upside down, in search of food: an ink-black aerialist, with shoulder cape of crimson and yellow, poised for nourishment.

Its warbling, shrill cry sounded against the soft murmur of the flowing waters as it hopped to another cattail and hung out over the dense water plants below, its eyes searching for an insect morsel.

A young water snake swam furiously against the current, trying to slither into the safety of the cattails lest some airborne predator pluck it from the safety of the water.

Beneath the bridge, just under the rippling surface, hovered the long, stationary shadows of rainbow trout, their low-slung jaws kept pointed upstream by their gently fanning tails, waiting languidly to attack anything unfortunate enough to float within striking range of their tiny, sharp teeth.

Chris Kluge

The sound of narrow, skidding tires on gravel sent the blackbird reeling away, sounding a scolding cry.

Two ten year-old boys dropped their bikes and raced each other
to the edge of the bridge. "Look, Bobby, a water snake! Come on,
let's catch him!!" cried the taller of the two, as they ran around the
wooden railing, and slipped laughing down the grassy bank.

"Here, grab him with this stick," shouted the smaller boy,
handing a four-foot length of broken oak branch to the other. The
taller boy, leaning out over the water, one hand holding to the
boards of the railing base, the other fully extended over the water,
slapped the water with the stick end, as the snake swam into the
protective cover of bulrushes. Unknown to the boys, the long
shadows beneath the bridge had vanished moments after the first
one had leaned over the railing.

"Aw, he got away. Darn it, I almost had him! Well, we can try
for him after we check our bait traps."

Throwing the oak branch into the stream, the boys watched it
float under the bridge and gather speed heading into the raceway.
They tore up the bank, across the wooden floorboards, and down
the other incline, to witness the certain fate of the stick.

"It's a canoe, and the people in it are going to go over the
falls!" yelled Randy. Sure enough, the doomed vessel bobbed re-
lentlessly toward the sluice gate, then slipped over the glassy water
at the top and disappeared from view.

"*AAAAAAGHGHGH!!!!*" both boys screamed and laughed,
supplying the futile cries of the doomed, imaginary adventurers.

Their attention then shifted to the banks of the canal, where
they searched for the wire baskets they used for crayfish traps. No
small-mouth bass could resist a freshly skewered crayfish, and no
crayfish could resist half a sunfish, even one tethered inside a small
wire basket, among the grass and rocks of the canal bank.

"Hey, I got one!" yelled Randy, hauling his trap out of the water to display a four-inch iridescent crayfish, its claws still clinging
to the severed fish head.

Bobby tugged at their other trap, camouflaged with marsh grass, and pulled it free of the slowly moving water of the canal.

"Me too!," he cried with delight, dropping the dripping cage onto the muddy bank. The rear half of the sunfish was still tied securely to the wire mesh, and clinging to it were two small crayfish. As the cage hit the bank, the tiny beings backed up in alarm, waving their claws and stalk eyes at the giant above them.

"Hey, there's something else in here, Randy! It's a baby turtle!!"

Sure enough, halfway through the mesh was a tiny, struggling turtle, its little legs moving restlessly and tiny head stretched out toward the freedom of the water it had been wrenched from. As Bobby pried it from the wire, its movements became more frantic, and Bobby almost dropped it as its tiny claws tickled his fingertips. As he freed it from the wire mesh, the turtle managed to twist its head around and nip at his thumb.

"Whoa!!," he shrieked, dropping it onto the mud of the canal bank. "The little guy bit me!" Laughing, he grabbed for its minuscule shell, just before it reached the safety of the flowing water.

By this time, Randy had joined him to inspect this surprise catch. "Let's take him home and put him in the aquarium," suggested Randy. "There's plenty of room, and I'll bet he'll eat goldfish food. He'll really look cool with the skeleton and pirate chest!" The boys had saved their allowances for a joint venture aquarium, complete with colored pebbles, an oxygen pump, and various subterranean plastic props, through which emerged a perpetual fountain of air bubbles, fed by a cleverly concealed rubber hose.

The part about the pirate chest and skeleton clinched it for Bobby. The little turtle would complement their latest decoration perfectly.

"I'll get the jar!" said Randy, sprinting up the bank for the mayonnaise jar they used to transport their living treasures.

Returning to Bobby's side, he unscrewed the perforated lid, scooped the turtle into it, then dropped the three crayfish in as well.

Both boys then ladled handfuls of water into the mouth of the jar, until they had it half full. They added some marsh grass for good measure, then screwed the lid securely on for the bike ride to Bobby's house, where the aquarium was currently residing (they alternated principal ownership every other week, an arrangement their parents found perplexing, but the boys thought perfectly reasonable).

Submerging their empty, baited traps back into the water, the boys ran excitedly back to their bikes, not wanting to waste another minute before installing their latest prizes in their aquarium.

Soon after the sound of their bikes' tires on the gravel of the road had dissipated into the summer morning, the long, dark shadows of the trout had resumed their sentry beneath the cool shadow of the wooden bridge, waiting for whatever the gently flowing waters might bring their way.

Chapter 13 — Dr. Heckler Examines the Hardin Corpses

Dr. Heckler bent over the dried human husk before him, and pulled the adjustable light closer to the work at hand. Because of the mutilation of the female corpse, Dr. Heckler had been called on, as County Coroner, to examine the long-dead Hardin cadavers as if they were recently deceased members of the community whose causes of death were unknown. A crime had been committed, and, even though the "victims" had ceased living more than a century ago, the circumstances that brought them into the world of the living again warranted a formal investigation.

Flanked by Sergeant Justin of the State Police and Ranger Smith, Dr. Heckler moved the torn maroon fabric away from the exposed bone of the left wrist of the mummified woman.

"Your bolt-cutter idea wasn't so far fetched," he said absently, referring to Ranger Smith's graveside impression of the severed limb. "Except for the splintered lower half of the cut, I'd be inclined to agree with you. See here, where the bone looks as if it was torn off, after an initial cutting...." Dr. Heckler backed away some, to allow the Sergeant and the ranger to peer closer at the stump. "I'd venture to say that the limb was partially cut then snapped off or, perhaps, chewed off."

Both the trooper and the ranger looked up at the Doctor's remarkable statement, then back at the dried form on the table.

"The way the bone is compressed is uncharacteristic of the shearing action of a knife-like edge of a cutting tool, like pruning shears or a bolt cutter. Even a dulled cutting instrument would not have yielded precisely this type of result. I can't honestly speculate, at this time, on what exactly separated this woman's hands from her body, but I don't think we can dismiss it as solely instrument-related."

"So what you're saying, Doctor, is that we can't rule out some kind of animal attack on this corpse?" asked Sergeant Justin, looking first at the Doctor, then at Ranger Smith.

"I guess that's what I'm saying, gentlemen," replied the Doctor, bending again to examine closely the protruding brown bone of the arm on the table.

"Frank, what kind of animal could inflict that kind of wound? Bear? Coyote?" asked the Sergeant. The forests that bordered the Delaware River down from New York, New Jersey, and Pennsylvania, provided a vast haven for black bear, coyote, and bobcats. There had even been rumored sightings of mountain lions, which, while plentiful over a hundred years ago, had been thought extinct. Blaming the corpses' condition on a large predator wasn't without some merit.

"Well," mused Frank, "...even if an animal chewed this woman's hands off, that doesn't begin to explain how the gates of the crypt were twisted away, or how the sealed vault drawers were forced open and the coffins pulled out and plundered. Sure, once this one was out of the tomb, any number of local critters could have snacked on her... bear, coyote, bobcat, even a beaver could have done that. But no animal that I know of could have forced its way into the crypt, or broken open the vaults and shattered the heavy coffins.

"And, besides, why only this woman's hands? The other corpses were only roughed up. They weren't bitten into, their clothes weren't even torn. It doesn't appear that anything else was taken."

"Grave robbers wouldn't overlook jewelry," said Trooper Justin, "and all these corpses had some jewelry on: a stickpin, a watch and chain, Mason pendant, rings, whatever." He motioned to the enameled white table by the door, upon which were arrayed the various ornaments of the Hardin clan, carefully labeled as to what went where, for their eventual reburial. "And the most sought-after prizes for Satanist-type grave robbers are human heads, and none of our friends here lost theirs," Ranger Smith added, taking in the four examining tables and silent figures laying on them.

"As far as I can tell," Trooper Justin said, "besides the woman's hands, nothing else is missing. And as far as I'm concerned, we've got one hell of a problem here, and I'm going to look for a human cause for it, bolt-cutter, bear bite or whatever."

"Doctor," Trooper Justin continued, "I'd appreciate a written report for my investigation on all four of these bodies as soon as possible. I know that once the papers get a hold of this we're going to have more media coverage and politicians around here than ticks on a hound dog, and everybody is going to want to know who's doing what and how fast. I suggest we do everything exactly by the book, because a lot of people are going to want to get involved."

You're right, there," said Frank. "This isn't going to be a very quiet summer."

"According to the county burial records, and her probable place in the crypt, this woman is Tessie Hardin, aged 79 years, died July 13, 1912."

"I think Connie Mackay is a descendent of the Hardins," said Ranger Smith. "She's a friend of mine—we went to school together. She lives out on Plattsburg Road, near Balesville. If she's the closest relative to these, I guess she's going to have to make some decisions regarding reburial," said the doctor. "Can't just put them back in their marble shelves and weld the gates shut. They'll need to be either cremated or put in new coffins, and the vault will have to be properly resealed."

"I'll visit Connie this afternoon when she gets off work and let her know about this," said the ranger, thinking about the economic ramifications on his friend. As a single working mother in an underdeveloped part of an expensive state, Connie Mackay probably couldn't afford to spend money on herself and her ten year-old son, Bobby, let alone on four dead relatives who just happened to pop into the present after almost a century in the netherworld.

"Well, Doctor," Trooper Justin broke in, "I've got a lot of work to tidy up before getting my investigation of our friends here underway, so I'll be going now. I'll stop by for that report tomorrow, if you think it might be finished."

"No problem, Bill," the Dr. Heckler replied. "I'll have it ready for you."

"And Frank, let me know what Connie Mackay would like to do about our guests, here," continued the Doctor. "I'm not the busiest of coroners, but I'm afraid I'll need some of these tables before long, given the advanced average age of our fellow county residents, and I really wasn't expecting to have four patients this week."

"I'll have an answer for you by tomorrow, Doc. Thanks for your help in this." said Ranger Smith.

The Doctor nodded appreciatively as the two men saw their way out of the examining room, then bent back to the silent form on the slab. He cleared his throat, clicked on the microphone over his head, and began speaking in a measured, emotionless voice, describing the dehydrated attributes of the person before him:

"NAME: Tessie Hardin; Residence: former resident of Sussex County, New Jersey. Presently residing in a marble sepulcher in Stokes Forest Cemetery;

DATE OF DEATH: July 6, 1912;

CAUSE OF DEATH: ...Unknown at this time."

Chapter 14 — Connie Mackay at Home

Connie Mackay was kneeling on a foam pad, between rows of pumpkin vines and sunflowers, pulling weeds from among the pale green leaves pushing up through the dark earth of her backyard garden.

The hard-shelled sunflower seeds that her son Bobby had dropped into the thumb-sized holes in their garden earlier that spring had taken over two weeks to burst open. Free of their temporary interment, they re-emerged as dried caps, each protecting the pale green tendrils beneath from their first harsh exposure to the world of light and rain. Mounting cell upon cell, the tender shoots grew stronger and taller, splayed leaves marking their rapid upward climb. After only a few weeks, it was incomprehensible how the immense sunflower stalks could possibly have come from so tiny a striped seed. The transformation of rock-hard husk and granular, damp earth into a 9-foot pole of dinner-plate sized leaves seemed to Connie as miraculous as anything she had ever witnessed. Her son would spend many contemplative moments seated on the ground, staring at the gently bowing columns, mesmerized by their stately silence, bright yellow halo around huge podded head, leaves like stunted arms, swaying inscrutably in the summer air.

The two had never felt so eerie a connection to a plant before; these things just seemed more alive, somehow, than the other crops. Perhaps it was their shape, Connie thought. Someone had told her how the Minisink Indians had called them "People of the Fields," presumably in reference to the strong animistic attraction they held on people. It was said that sunflowers, along with pumpkins and corn, were among the first plants ever cultivated by the aboriginal settlers of North America, thus establishing their historical significance in rooting humans to a place, and beginning a process, still in motion, of changing people from opportunistic wanderers into agrarian societies; a startling event in human evolution.

For centuries, Indians had venerated sunflowers, reaping their seeds for nourishment, and glorying in their late summer yellow majesty.

Yes, Connie thought, it was easy to imagine why these monumental plants had captivated the Indians of this area.

Her thoughts were interrupted by the sound of the front door slamming.

Mom. I'm home!" yelled her son, Bobby.

"I'm out here, Bobby," she called, looking toward the white frame house.

The back porch door swung open, and Bobby flew down the stairs to where his mother was gardening.

"Randy and me caught three crayfish and a turtle and we're gonna put them in our aquarium now, okay?" he jabbered excitedly, already turning on his sneakers and starting to run back to the back door.

"Whoa, there, killer, slow down!" laughed his mother, tossing a handful of weeds onto the burlap cloth on the lawn. "What did you say you had?"

"Mom, Randy and me got three crayfish and a baby turtle from our traps at the canal! We're gonna put them in our aquarium right now!"

"OK, Bobby, but I want you to do your chores right after lunch, so make sure you don't make plans to play with Randy this afternoon."

"Yea, sure, Mom, okay.... Gotta go, now!" he said, flying back into the house to rejoin Randy, the crayfish and the turtle.

"Funny kid," thought Connie, smiling to herself as she resumed her weeding. Bobby was always so excited about everything, always rushing from one adventure to another. Kids, with their whole life ahead of them, always acted as if the next half hour in their life was their last so they had to pack every sensory experience, every emotion, into as compressed a time as possible. Connie thought it whimsically perverse how most adults she knew had lost that childhood excitement about living, and consequently acted almost bored, resigned— as if they had all the time in the world to experience things, and so didn't feel a need to rush to new experiences, to wonder, to embrace every moment as if it were their last on earth.

The few "grown-ups" that Connie had met and been really impressed with in her life had all shared this one common attribute: the simple capacity to be in awe of the very experience of living, of reacting to the sights, sounds, smells around them, of finding joy in the passage of a cloud's shadow over the ground, or of a bird's call— a common enough trait in most humans under the age of fifteen, but surprisingly rare, it seemed in anyone over the age of twenty-five.

She dug her trowel beneath the stalk of another milkweed, twisted the ragged plant out of the ground, and tossed it onto the growing green mound behind her. "Gardening sure brings out the philosopher in me," she thought, grinning ironically at her predictably introspective response to her son's unbridled happiness. "I Think, Therefore I'm Not," she paraphrased to herself, wishing, for a few nostalgic moments, that she were ten years old again, to feel as if every hour were her last, that every experience was full of wide-eyed wonder, that every day was absolutely, without a doubt, the best day ever lived.

She heard a car pull into the driveway at the front of the house, the sound of a car door slamming shut, and footsteps going up her front porch stairs. She pushed herself to her feet, took off the dirt-stained work gloves and walked around the side of the house to intercept whoever was expecting a response from within.

As she rounded the lilac bush at the corner of her house, she recognized Frank Smith's state-issued Ranger car parked in the cool of the big oak tree on her front lawn.

"Well, well, Ranger Smith, what brings you to these tame parts of our wild county?" Frank Smith and she had gone to grammar school together, and had remained good friends ever since. Frank was one of those few "grown-ups" that had somehow managed to keep part of his childhood wonder intact into adulthood. Frank's was well hidden, of course, given his solitary nature, and the necessary air of authority he had to cultivate to fulfill people's expectations of "Forest Rangers & Their Readiness To Serve & Protect." But to friends like Connie he opened up just a bit, and if you watched for it, one could detect a strong streak of humor in those shielded eyes.

"Just making my appointed rounds among the local citizenry, Mrs. Mackay, keeping the Peace between you all and the mighty wilderness beyond."

They laughed appreciatively at each other....it was a long-running verbal game for them to feign pretentiousness in the most mundane of events.

"Where have you been keeping yourself, Frank? I haven't seen you in a couple of weeks."

"We've had more than our usual allotment of summer visitors to the Parks this summer, so I've been pretty busy, Connie. It's good to see you. You're looking fit and trim as usual."

"Thanks, handsome, so are you..." she playfully flirted back. "So thanks for stopping by and saying 'howdy', but what are you really here for? You never visit during your work hours. Why aren't you out in the woods protecting the animals from all the hikers and other tourists?"

Frank smiled, and removed his hat. His demeanor shifted, almost imperceptibly, toward his "official" seriousness. "Connie, there was some vandalism out at the Stokes forest Cemetery, and the Hardin Family Crypt was affected."

Connie had visited that crypt several times in her youth with her great Aunt Netta, to tend the dogwood trees planted on either side of the entrance, and to listen to great Aunt Netta reminisce about the people inside the grey granite house. Connie always thought it strange that the people inside the crypt never came out to say hello, particularly since her great Aunt would carry on conversations with them, asking them did they remember such and such an event, or wasn't that great-aunt so-and-so that ran off and married a traveling evangelist, only to be captured by Pennsylvania Savages?

Connie hadn't visited that cemetery since she was fourteen or so. She just had never made much a connection with the strangers buried within.

"What happened, Frank? Did someone spray paint the door or something?"

"I'm afraid it was a bit more serious than that, Connie. Someone broke into the crypt, and broke open the vaults."

"Oh, lord! What a grisly thing to do! Who would want to do a thing like that? Did you catch them?"

"No, Connie, we don't have many leads at this point. The State Police are conducting an investigation, and the County Coroner is making up a report...."

"County Coroner? Frank, was anyone killed during this vandalism?"

"No, Connie, no one was killed.... Your relatives, however, those in the crypt— their bodies were roughed up a bit, so the State Police thought...."

"Oh, Frank, that's awful! Where are they, I mean, the bodies..., are they, are they all right? Did someone steal them or something?"

"Well, as I said, someone roughed them up a bit, and the caskets were pretty much destroyed, Connie. They will have to be reburied."

Connie stared silently at Frank Smith, a quizzical look on her face, as she tried to understand what her friend was trying to tell her.

"Oh, yes, I understand, Frank.... Of course. I'm the closest living relative, so I have to see to putting things, *ahhh,* back the way they were. The caskets were destroyed, you say?"

"Yes, Connie, I'm afraid they were. You will have to decide on whether you'd like them, your relatives, put back into the crypt in, ah, caskets, or if you'd prefer to have the remains cremated, and resealed in the crypt, or just kept, ah, somewhere else...." Frank's voice trailed off, as he groped for the proper way of conveying this unique situation to his friend. He thought that announcing a disinterment of someone's relatives was almost as hard as telling the next of kin that someone had only just recently had passed away.

"Well, my freezer's just jammed full right now, so I guess I might find room for them all in the root cellar...." she dead-panned.

Frank grinned, as his friend eased his embarrassment with her black humor.

"Boy, you don't hear from your relatives for a few life-times, and *whammo!!* They all of a sudden pop into your life, looking for a place to stay," she joked, as they both stood laughing in the sun.

"But seriously, Folks," Connie shifted the conversation back to a pragmatic approach to her problem. "I didn't know any of these people, so I don't really feel like I have to give them a nineteenth century send-off. I mean, I really hadn't budgeted the purchase of four coffins into this month's expenses! Frank, what do you think I should do?"

"Well, like you say, these aren't exactly next of kin. And they have been, uh, gone for a long while. I should think cremation of the remains, and re-sealing the vault would get the job done proper. Does that set well with you?"

"Yes, it does, Frank. Thank you for advice when I need it most."

"Hey, Mom!" cried Bobby from his second-story window. "Come up and look at my turtle!!"

Both adults looked up at the flash of movement in the open, empty window. Bobby had disappeared back inside before they had a chance to acknowledge him. "Well, Ranger, what say you to a look at a turtle?"

"Actually, it's just what I had hoped to do today," said Frank, smiling, as they both moved toward the house.

Upstairs, Bobby was standing at his dresser, his face inches from the glass wall of his and Randy's shared aquarium, watching the activities within the clear water. A small electric pump filled the room with a soothing, fluttering sound, and a special lamp, clamped to the aquarium's rim, provided a theatrical effect to the little world within. A small plastic skeleton lay on the colored gravel bottom of the aquarium, its legs and arms rhythmically waving as force-fed bubbles rushed through its rubber ribcage, and on up toward the silvery surface above. Clumps of marsh grass and small lily pads wavered in the water, mimicking a freshwater lake's environment for the assorted crayfish, snails, and tadpoles that scurried, floated and wriggled about.

One of the recently captured crayfish clambered onto an open pirate's treasure chest next to the submerged skeleton, fulfilling Bobby's wildest aesthetic expectations. "Alright... neat!" he said, almost reverentially, looking up at his mother and Frank as they entered his room.

"Hiya, Bobby, what have you added to your aquarium today?"

"Hi, Ranger Smith. Mom, lookit the crayfish on the treasure chest! Doesn't it look just like a movie?" he said, his words a mixture of pride and wonderment. "Hey, that is neat!" agreed Connie, bending down to peer at the crayfish perched on the treasure chest, its tiny legs moving restlessly on the colored plastic. The little claws were raised defensively, and its stalk eyes moved this way and that, assessing its new world.

Like most single parents, Connie did the job of two by doubling her enthusiastic interest in her child's activities... more like a friendship than a traditional "parent-child" relationship.

"Say, who's this little fellow?" asked Ranger Smith, his tapping finger one quarter of an inch of glass away from a very small turtle, which clung to a column of marsh grass, midway between the gravel bottom and the water's surface.

"That's my new turtle! Randy and I caught him and the crayfish today!" said Bobby proudly. The young reptile was no larger than an acorn. It had a flat, ridged shell, from which protruded four clawed feet, a minuscule tail, and a pea-sized head. As the ranger tapped his finger again, the turtle extended its neck and struck at the glass with its beak-like jaws; not once, but several times, trying for all it was worth to seize the giant object beyond the invisible glass barrier.

"Will you look at that little guy! He's trying to bite you, Frank!" laughed Connie in amazement. "Now, that's what I call innate aggression!"

"Bobby, from the way this fellow's greeting me, I'd say you've got yourself a brand new baby snapping turtle, Macrochelys Temminckii, or 'Gatortail' for short. There aren't many other creatures that come into the world with that mean a disposition."

It was an incongruous sight, this suspended, tiny creature, unabashedly trying to attack and devour something thousands of times its size. Without hesitation, the days-old turtle attempted time and again to bite the huge thing before it, seemingly unfazed by the glass obstruction between it and its intended meal.

"Better get some meat for your new friend," suggested the Ranger, "As you can see by his behavior, snappers aren't particular about what they eat, just as long as it swims, crawls, flies, or walks, or did at one time. They'll eat anything, dead or alive."

"You mean they feed on carrion?" asked Connie, her eyes riveted to the tiny creature.

"They play an important part in freshwater ecosystems, in that, like most predators, they weed out the weak, sick, and just plain unlucky, and they scour the bottom clean of any deceased matter, aquatic, animal or human."

"UGH! What do you mean by that ?" Connie asked, as she looked incredulously at the Ranger, then back at the turtle.

"Oh, there's a story that many years ago, a hunter got lost in the Great Marsh, and wasn't found for over a week. He finally popped up, or, at least part of him popped up, among some lily pads down by the wooden bridge at the south end. The story goes that there were five or six big ol' snappers dining on his torso when the search party finally located him."

"Wow!" cried Bobby, looking at his new pet with open admiration.

Connie gave Frank a bemused, sidelong glance, wondering if this were one of his slight embellishments on the truth. The Ranger's whimsical sense of humor was most often employed around Connie and Bobby, because they were so wonderfully gullible and trusting.

"Hey, I didn't make this story up, Connie," the Ranger protested, laughing. "Ask any of the old timers to tell you the story about the lost 'sport' out hunting from the city. They've even got more to say about it, believe me!"

"No thanks, Frank, I think we've got a pretty good picture of the event. I'm sure we'll cherish your imagery every night when we close our eyes, and try and imagine peaceful, happy thoughts."

By this time, the turtle had apparently decided the Ranger and the others were merely benign structures, or perhaps some sort of aquatic hallucination. It turned its reptilian attention to other things closer at hand. Pushing off from its green perch, it swam assuredly to the surface, where it exchanged old air for new, before submerging again and kicking and clawing its way toward the bottom. Although only days old, it was ready to take on all comers.

"From birth to adulthood in a few hours," said Connie, draping her arm over Bobby's shoulders. "How'd you like that, Bobby?"

"I'd like to be a turtle! All they have to do is swim around all day—no school, no homework!"

"Not a bad ambition, Bobby," offered the Ranger, "you'd also have a long time to enjoy swimming around. Some of these fellows live well over a hundred years".

"Really?" asked Connie.

"You bet," continued Frank, "if they can keep away from hungry pickerel and bass for their first few years, there aren't many things that can do them harm after that. Like most tortoises, their internal parts come with an extended guarantee. This little guy comes from a long, long line of evolutionary trial and error. I've even heard stories of some living to be over two hundred years."

"They aren't too pretty when they grow up. In fact, they're some of the ugliest things that ever took breath. But pretty doesn't mean much in its world. Longevity is what it's all about; outlasting your fellow foodchainers counts, and these ugly things never say never."

The subject under discussion had managed to push itself all the way to the bottom of the aquarium, and was attempting to counter the buoyant air in its new lungs by clinging to the plastic treasure chest. Unable to find a sufficient purchase, it grappled its needle claws onto the tail of the crayfish, which snapped away in surprise, yielding its berth to the struggling snapper.

Hovering momentarily above the treasure chest, the turtle began pursuing the movement of the crayfish, without any apparent regard to the lopsided odds at this larger creature becoming the turtle's next meal.

"Speaking of food chains, would you like to join Bobby and me for lunch, Frank?" asked Connie.

"Well, I'm officially on duty regarding the, uh, the incident," the ranger said, obliquely referring to the disinterment of the Hardin corpses.

"But perhaps you could tell me about your relative, Tessie Hardin, while we eat, and then I'd be gathering information essential to our investigation."

"Good suggestion, Mr. Ranger, quick thinking, there," laughed Connie. "Come on, Bobby, let's go downstairs and fix us all some soup and sandwiches."

"Okay!" agreed Bobby. He liked the Ranger, and was glad their visitor was staying for lunch. "Can we eat outside, Mom?"

"Sure, Bobby, good idea. It's such a beautiful day, it would be a shame to spend another moment inside. You and Frank go out on the front porch, and I'll rustle us up some grub."

"Sure thing, Mom! Come on, Ranger Frank. I'll show you a wasp's nest, right outside the porch!"

"Alright, Bobby, lead the way!" said the ranger, winking at Connie as he followed after the running boy down the stairs, out the front door, and onto the screened in porch.

"Make yourself comfortable, Frank. I'll be right along." said Connie, heading down the back stairs of the old frame house to the kitchen below.

Chapter 15 —Tessie's Story

After finishing their lunch on the porch, Connie began to tell Tessie Hardin's story.

"So, you want to know about Tessie Hardin...well, let's see what I can remember from my visits out to the graveyard, and Great Aunt Netta's meanderings...."

"Since Tessie died in 1912, let's see.... The coroner said seventy-nine years, so 1912 minus 79 is, hmmmm... 1833. She was born in 1833. That sounds right, because her mother was part Indian; Minisink, I think they were called."

"Yes, Connie," Frank answered "the local Indians were known as Minisink Indians, part of the a larger group named Leni Lenape by the Dutch and Swedish immigrant settlers. I didn't know your family tree went back that far! You've got those Mayflower snobs beat by about eleven thousand years!"

"Oh, sure, Frank, we're real blue bloods around these parts!" Connie laughed. "Can't you tell?"

"Hey, Mom, you never told me I was part Indian!" exclaimed Bobby excitedly. "Wow, wait'll I tell Randy!!"

"Actually, Bobby, you are about, oohhh... one-sixteenth Indian. That must be where you get all your love of the outdoors, I suppose," said Connie, patting her son's hand as they sat together on the porch swing.

"So, anyway, back to Great Aunt Tessie—where were we? Oh yes, I was talking of Tessie's Mama.... What was her name? It was one of those real Dutch names, like 'Hedda,' or 'Heidi,' or—oh, I forget just now. We've got some papers somewhere in my attic about all this. I'll dig them out later."

"Go on, Mom. This is neat!" said Bobby, prodding his mother to continue the tale.

"All right, so, as I was saying, Tessie's mother was part Minis-ink Indian because, so the story goes, her mother had run off with a handsome Indian prince!"

"Really?" asked Frank incredulously.

"That's what the 'unpublished' version of our family history says. Of course, any written records, family Bibles, county records, that kind of documentation, all have Tessie's mother having married a Dutch Trader who died soon after their 'union,' leaving a sorrowed widow with an infant daughter."

"Well, how do you know that isn't what really happened, Connie?" quizzed Frank, looking for some clue as to which story to take as the official history. Connie shifted her position on the porch swing, a sense of conspiratorial intrigue coming into her voice.

"Okay. While there are, obviously, no family snapshots from that far back, and the 'official' county records are unavailable, having been eaten by field mice or mold or used to wallpaper some-one's cabin, here are some tidbits passed along by my great Aunt Netta, about what may or may not have occurred to my forebears away back when....

"As I remember Netta telling it, Tessie's grandmother had been the recipient of a normal frontier upbringing. Her Dutch parents had come to New Amsterdam to live with relatives, but, for some reason, migrated to this part of the frontier wilderness. Perhaps they felt the need to make their own destiny, or they had a falling out with the in-laws. Who knows? Anyhow, Tessie's grandfather was your basic renaissance frontiersman—you had to be a carpen-ter, farmer, veterinarian, doctor, and hunter to survive back then—and set his wife and baby daughter up in a nice little 'one bedroom

with roof & no-hall colonial' on the outskirts of what is now Tranquility, New Jersey."

"Mom, where is Tranquility?" her son asked.

"Its that pretty little village we go through on our way to Hack-
ettstown, Bobby. You know— the one with the little bridge that the
Paulinskill River flows under, and there's a tall church steeple, a
bright white one, that rings out music in the evening?"

"Oh, okay, Mom, I know what you mean," said Bobby, resting
his head on the arm of the porch swing, settling in for more family
history.

"So, this little Dutch family worked hard to keep themselves
warm and fed, and managed to survive a few winters and growing
seasons, until their little farm was actually prospering. Nothing extraordinary, mind you, just enough to buy new cloth every so often,
or to afford a sturdy carriage, to take them over the dirt roads in
summer, and glide them over the snow in winter."

"I thought you didn't have much to go on about your distant
kin's doings, Connie," remarked Frank, amused at the wealth of
information Connie was drawing from.

"This is all coming to you courtesy of great aunt Netta, folks!
I'm surprised I am remembering so much, it's been so long..."

"Well," she continued, " their daughter grew up to be quite a
beauty, and the parents, naturally, kept her pretty close to home,
lest some muleskinner offer to take her through the Delaware Water Gap to a world of adventure beyond."

"So, during the summer growing season, most frontier families
packed up their produce, hitched up the family buggy, and jour-
neyed to their local marketplace. Tranquility served as my relative's town, and, so the story goes, on one summer Saturday, they
were in Tranquility, selling or trading their produce, and looking
over whatever others had to offer, and some of the local Minisink
Indians happened to be doing the same."

"Did they fight?" asked Bobby hopefully.

"No, Bobby. The Minisink Indians weren't fierce fighters, although they were very skilled with bows and arrows, and other hunting implements.

They were very peaceful people: farmers, and fishermen, hunters and gatherers of whatever the forests had to offer. Except for rare instances, they weren't in conflict with the European immigrants. Although the Europeans did, eventually, populate what had been the Minisinks' territory, calling it their own, and forcing the Minisinks to migrate west, to what eventually became Oklahoma."

"The Minisinks inhabited this area, where we live now. This whole area of New Jersey, New York, Pennsylvania, and Delaware was known as 'Lenapehoking.'" continued Connie.

"Why did they let the Europeans kick them out of their home without putting up a fight, like all the other Indians did?" asked Bobby.

"Well, the Europeans moved into the area very gradually, at first, and so it took a long time for the new people to predominate over the old inhabitants. And as the Europeans moved in, the Indians kept moving westward, deeper and deeper into the forest. Back then, the woods around us stretched, unbroken, all the way to the Mississippi River. The Indians you are talking about, the Plains Indians, the Comanche, the Blackfeet, didn't feel like they could move anywhere else when white settlers started to come into their land. Besides, those Indians were used to fighting with each other. They weren't farmers and berry pickers, like the Lenni Lenape. They were warriors. They were used to killing, both animals and people."

"What about this girl, Mom?"

"Okay, so back to our story. This one Saturday, a group of Minisinks were in Tranquility to barter, and one of their group, a handsome young man, as Netta used to tell it, took particular fancy to the Dutch daughter, and sought her out during the day's events."

"Apparently, he made a favorable impression on her, because, within the week, she had run off with him!"

"You mean she was kidnapped, Mom?"

64

"No, Bobby, your great-great aunt Netta distinctly said the girl ran away with him. Like the story says, he was handsome! And furthermore, he was some sort of Indian royalty, a prince or something."

"Wow, Mom— why didn't you ever tell this story before?" her son asked, incredulous that she could have kept silent about this fantastic addition to the family history.

"Well, Bobby, I figured I'd tell you all the family stories I knew sooner or later. I'm glad I'm telling you this one now, since you seem to like it so much."

"Like it? Mom, this is the best thing I've ever heard about our Family!"

"So, Connie, what happened to this relative of yours? Did she live happily ever after in a Quonset hut, gumming deer hides and smoking fish?" joked Frank, prodding his friend to continue her story.

"Actually, no. As you can well imagine, her parents were less than amused by her radical shift in lifestyle. They had pictured her, no doubt, bringing a modest yet reasonable dowry to some prosperous European landowner, thereby making the two families stronger and wealthier. In fact, the Indian boy's parents were apparently outraged that their noble son should choose a mate beneath his station, and they cast him out of their council lodge for bringing such shame on his community."

"So, what happened to the girl?" asked Frank, now as intrigued as Bobby.

"After a few weeks of living without either family's blessing, the two bereaved lovers returned to their separate cultures, older and wiser in the ways of familial expectations, and never spoke to each other again."

"Did her family welcome her back?" asked Bobby, hoping for a happy ending.

"Her family was happy to have her back, although their plans for a perfectly marriageable daughter were drastically altered, seeing as she gave birth to a beautiful baby girl nine months later, just at the end of the following winter."

"Was the baby an Indian?" asked Bobby.

"The baby was half Indian, and half Dutch; what was uncharitably called a half-breed in those less litigious times," said Connie.

"Did the Indian prince ever visit her and the baby?" her son asked.

"There is no record of them ever resuming contact, although they might have, at some time during the following months. Tragically, the boy died before he ever saw his daughter."

"What did he die of?" asked Bobby.

"No one knows for certain, but Netta spoke of some type of illness; a fever, I think."

"Why did he die from a fever?" Bobby asked, alarmed that something he himself had experience with could actually kill someone.

"Back then, there weren't that many medicines available, things like penicillin and vaccine. People could become very ill from diseases that we now ignore. And, yes Bobby, sometimes people died from those diseases. You have to remember that they didn't have hospitals, or even doctors close by. When something went wrong, when someone got hurt, or became ill, they just had to rely on whatever herbs, or poultices, or remedies they had right in the house. They actually had to make their own medicines."

"So, what about that girl?" persisted Bobby, his restless mind already bored with frontier medicine.

"She did, apparently, raise the baby with her parents' help, because the little girl grew up to have a baby girl of her own; your great-great-great aunt Tessie Hardin, born in 1833 in the village of Layton, who lived a long and happy life."

"Wow, Mom, that was a neat story! I can't wait to tell Randy! Can I tell him now?"

"Why don't you wait until after you've cleaned up your room and done your chores, Bobby. The story has lasted a few hundred years, and I'm sure it will last a few more hours without disappearing forever. Now, say good-bye to the Ranger, and get started on what you've got to do."

"Okay, Mom. Good-bye, Ranger Smith," he said, heading into the house and upstairs to his room.

"See you later, Bobby. Thanks for showing me your aquarium. I really enjoyed it." "You're welcome," came Bobby's voice, already upstairs.

Frank turned to Connie. "That's quite a tale, Connie. Did your great Aunt Netta ever say what Tessie died of?"

"No, not to my recollection, Frank. I do know that Tessie was never married, and that she lived with her parents until they died, and she then lived alone in the house she grew up in, until her death, in 1912. I think she was an artist, a painter...at least I think that's what Great Aunt Netta said. She had an interest in local Indian lore, too. She used to collect anything connected with the Minisinks; probably because of her maternal connection to them."

"I think she even gave some lectures about them, to ladies clubs, that sort of thing. Back then, if you had a hobby, chances are, you gave lectures on whatever it was that held your interest to others in your community. At least, that's what ladies used to do. God knows where they got the time, what with cooking, mending, hand laundering, farm chores, gardening....This little old' Dutch descendent will take the 'bad new days' over the 'good old days' anytime!"

"Why do you ask about Tessie's death, Frank?"

"Well, of all the occupants of the crypt, only Tessie was outside. And..." here Frank looked inside the front door momentarily, before lowering his voice, "...only Tessie's body was, ah, disturbed. Her hands were missing, Connie."

Franks' friend looked at him incredulously. "What did you say?" "Yes, Connie," Frank continued quietly, "her body was outside the crypt, on the ground, and both her hands had been removed somehow."

"Ughh! Somebody really sick must be out there, to do that kind of thing to a corpse."

67

"That's why we've involved the County Coroner and the State Police, Connie. We're not sure who we're dealing with here, but we sure as hell want to find out as quickly as possible."

"Connie, I'd like you to give me a call if you can offer any more information about your great Aunt Tessie, or why someone would want to get at her or any of the other Hardins. We don't have a lot to go on, so we're grateful for anything you might offer up."

"Sure, Frank, I'll give you a call if anything occurs to me. And Frank, thank you for coming by to tell me about this."

"Sure thing, Connie. Let me know if I can be of any help."

Frank picked up his hat from the table by the wicker chair, and let himself out through the screen door and down the porch steps to the front walk. Connie watched as he got into his car, started it up, and backed into the street. She waved as he rolled down the road, and stood there for a time, thinking about her childhood visits to the graveyard, her great Aunt Netta, and the assorted figures from her family's past that had come back into her present. She decided to go to the attic to dig out all the family documents she had, and try and sort out what she remembered about her relatives from what she might have dreamed, or just made up, as a little girl visiting a graveyard cottage for the dead.

Chapter 16 — *Thieves in the Forest*

The four-by-four truck cut off its headlights and lurched off County Road #617 and onto the broken macadam road that followed the Delaware River south, into the dark green heart of Stokes Forest.

The oversized tires of the pick-up hummed as they rolled over the unpatched ruts and potholes of the road beneath, the powerful engine rumbling quietly, just above idling speed. The two silent riders in the darkened cab peered anxiously ahead, trying to discern a still smaller dirt road among the looming silhouettes of trees, boulders, and brush.

"There, that's it! Up ahead about thirty yards, to the left... see it?" said one of the men, in a flat, heavy voice.

"Got it," muttered the driver, slowing the truck to a crawl, as he eased onto the turn off, and entered a pine corridor, the steady swishing sound of fir branches caressing both doors of the cab like an evergreen car wash.

The passenger added...."Its along here another fifty yards or so, off to the right."

The driver shut down the engine as they coasted to a stop in a small clearing among the tall pines, whose outlines were barely visible against the moonless, starlit summer sky.

"Follow me, and just do as I say." said the passenger, as he quietly opened his door, pulled on a medium sized back pack, lifted a pickaxe from behind the seat, and stepped to the ground. The driver got out of the truck, and, leaving the door ajar, stepped around the front of the cab to walk silently behind his partner, his hands gripping a small shovel. Both men walked for about fifty yards, following a crumbling rock wall, until coming to a mound of fern-covered earth.

Okay, here it is. Now, be careful... there isn't much more to break through since I was here last week."

The two men took up opposite positions from each other, both facing the mound, as they began picking and shoveling the surface with their tools. The crickets, silenced by the coming of the truck and its cargo, resumed their throbbing chorus into the cool, summer night air, and served as a steady melody line to the random crunch and thud of metal meeting earth as the two men worked silently.

After a few minutes, one hissed.... "Hold it! We're through!! Work with your hands, now." Both dropped their tools, and bent to the slowly growing opening in the top of the mound, pulling fragments of moss-covered earth back with their hands, like the shell of an enormous egg.

When the hole was large enough, one of the men affixed a climbing rope to the mountaineering harness he was wearing under his parka, handed the other end to his partner, and backed his legs into the black opening. The other man made the rope fast to a stout pine tree nearby, and, wrapping the rope around himself, nodded quickly to his partner, who slid himself into the cavern and disappeared from view.

The rope stretched tightly as the hanging man spun slowly within the hollow mound. The partner peered at the black hole, his eyes straining to see in the darkness. Suddenly, from the jagged opening of the subterranean cavern, there came a soft yellow light, illuminating the overhanging pine branches above, as the dangling explorer turned on his head-lamp, exposing, for the first time in centuries, the secrets of the prehistoric Indian storage cistern.

Chris Kluge

The man revolved on the braided nylon rope, his eyes following the lamp's cone of light down the clay-lined walls, to the litter-strewn floor below his suspended boots. The cistern held the cast off belongings of people dead since before the arrival of Europeans; pottery bowls and earthen jugs, some cracked and broken, a few still intact, encircled with faint geometric designs, carefully applied and painted by hands that never knew coins or calculators.

"*Pssst!!* Gimme some more rope! About five feet, but take it slow," hissed the hanging man to his partner above. Bracing himself, the man above ground jerked out small lengths of rope, his feet digging into the pine needles on the ground, as the man below slowly turned, like a spider dangling from its web, onto the floor of the cistern. At the bottom of the pit, he undid the rope from the climbing harness, and quickly set to his appointed task of assessing the ancient refuse around him.

Taking the backpack from his shoulders and placing it on the ground, the man opened its drawstring wide, and took out several swatches of terry cloth. Selecting the unbroken pottery vessels, he carefully wrapped each in a cushion of towel, and gently placed the cocoons inside the backpack.

When he had a full load, he tied off the top flap of the knapsack, attached the shoulder straps to the braided rope, and called to his partner to hoist the treasure aloft. He watched anxiously as the bundle pirouetted above him, up and out of the hole, into the blackness beyond.

Four times the pack rose from the lighted hole, until only scattered pieces of broken clay marked lives long dead.

The robber reattached the rope to his harness, gave a soft call, and the man above began hauling him up, slowly and steadily, using a small, hand-held winch to wind up the rope between the man and the tree.

After a few minutes, the man groped his way out of the jagged rim of the cistern. Gathering up their tools and booty, the two returned to their truck and wordlessly packed everything away in the storage bins in the open bed of the truck. When all was secure,

71

they took a last look around the area to assure themselves that nothing had been forgotten. They climbed into the cab, started the engine, and maneuvered the 4x4 around in the cramped clearing.

Finally, the darkened vehicle pointed its way out of the pine-walled forest, and the truck rocked and lurched its way along the time-rutted road, heading first north, then east, carrying its toweled cargo to anonymous collectors, greedy to possess a piece of the past.

Chapter 17 — An Unexpected Find

The steel teeth of the back hoe bit deeply into the moist earth, then swung the dirt onto the growing pile next to the hole before it. The union of the operator and the machine was such that it was impossible to tell if he were operating the back hoe, or the back hoe was operating him; his arms and legs were seemingly connected to the levers and foot pedals, as the throbbing diesel engine revved now and again, and the hydraulically-powered arm reached smoothly out and down to dig into the earth, again and again.

It looked almost delicate, the oiled metal movements so repetitive, the operator's motions rhythmically trance-like... a 4-ton praying mantis digging in the sand, flicking hundreds of pounds of earth with each casual motion of its triple-jointed arm.

Every so often, a loud "bang" would signify the presence of another unyielding rock, and the operator would pull the steel teeth away, then gently fondle the obstruction, like a chef ladling a boiled potato out of a stew with a giant spoon. Tentatively moving the rock first one way, then another, to and fro, he would cradle the stone in the steel bucket, and slowly swing the prize onto the growing mountain of debris.

Maneuvering a large, oval-shaped slab of red-brown rock in the hole, the operator noticed some unusual scratches covering its surface. From his elevated perch atop the backhoe, he didn't think the

steel teeth of the shovel had made them. They looked too— too
regular, as if they were almost a design of some kind.

Needing to take a break anyhow, he put the throbbing machine
in neutral, set the throttle, and swung down from the cab, stretching his cramped back as he ambled closer to the large, flat rock.

The entire surface of red-brown stone was etched with what
looked like stick figures: little beings in various poses of agitation,
with arms held high, arms thrown wide, arms holding...what? A
spear?....all surrounding some sort of form that had what appeared
to be four sticks emerging from a semi-circular dome, with a blob
of something at one end, and another stick figure straddling the
dome, pointing a short object over the assemblage around him.

"What the heck is that supposed to be," wondered the operator,
as he wiped some dirt away that obscured part of the curious
grouping.

These weren't random markings made by his backhoe during
excavation; they were drawings of some kind, sure enough.

The slab had to weigh over a hundred pounds, thought the man.
It was positioned too deep in the hole for someone to have recently
buried it.

Not wanting to disfigure the markings by moving the rock with
the machine, the operator decided he'd better phone his supervisor
at the County Road Works right away, and let him get in touch with
people who might be interested in this kind of find. Besides, it was
almost lunchtime.

He strode back to the idling machine, swung himself up to the
cab, and shut the throbbing beast down. He hopped to the ground,
wiped his forehead with a bandanna, and headed to his car, parked
off the side of the road in the shade of some birch trees.

He suddenly grinned to himself, realizing his good fortune
connected to his unusual find. He'd drive to the country store, call
in, and get himself a sandwich and a cold beer, and await whatever
else the day had in store for him. Hell, if he was lucky, this
scratched up old rock just might keep him from doing any more
digging for the rest of the day.

Chapter 18 — Notes From the Past

The air in the attic had been dry, hot and close, and Connie had bumped her head, twice, on the wooden beams that supported her one hundred year-old slate roof. Her search for the collection of family photo albums, deeds, wills, and assorted letters and precious objects had taken longer than she'd expected.

Except for a few boxes of winter and summer clothes that she and Bobby reshuffled with the changing of the seasons, Connie didn't venture much beyond the top of the attic stairs, and so had lost track of which cardboard box held the few remaining objects of the previous generations' special occasions.

Since her husband's death four years previously, Connie had avoided the attic whenever possible, with its collection of painful reminders of their brief life together. She had unwittingly opened up several containers that held purposely forgotten vestiges of her recent married life, thus releasing a flood of repressed feelings and memories. Still not ready to incorporate that lost chapter of her life into her present, she had hurriedly closed the boxes, and shoved them far under the eaves, lest she open them up accidentally again sometime.

Finally, behind a trunk, in a stained cardboard box, its edges frayed from several previous moves, Connie located her ancestors' things.

There was a big black Family bible with records of Births, Weddings, and Deaths. Its vellum pages were thinner than any paper Connie had ever turned, and the inscriptions in the front were written in a beautiful, flowing hand, from a time when penmanship was as important as properly spelled words.

There were also several leather bound photograph albums with ornate, gold-leaf borders around the delicate cameos within: most were formal portraits of frozen-featured men and women, looking about as relaxed as someone in a Dentist's chair, their anxiety at posing for a daguerreotype immortalized on photo-sensitized metal plates.

Some of the pictures were more informal, however: one was of a young man, standing by a horse drawn wagon in front of an open barn door. Smiling at the camera, the bottom of his face was weathered a dark tan, his hatless forehead in sharp white contrast, uncharacteristically exposed to the sun. Another featured three round-faced women in long-sleeved dresses, all with white aprons, flanking a very young girl in high-buttoned shoes. The four of them stood in a row, as if just called out from the kitchen, into a front yard scratched bare by chickens, a clothes line visible behind and to the left of them, festooned with several hanging pairs of overalls, the grey legs blurred in a previous century's summer breeze. Still another photo showed a scenic panorama of a two story clapboard farmhouse, a barn, and a country road, running straight as a rail bed, through a field dotted by giant loaves of stacked hay, toward a distant horizon of low hills.

Beside the Bible and old photo albums, there were bundles of letters, still tied with the fancy ribbon of some general store's "notions" counter, and some thin, ledger-type volumes, containing faded brown entries.

Lost in the wonder of these old documents, Connie had pulled herself out of a hypnotic reverie of time travel, crouched in the hot, stuffy attic. She had made herself close the old books, so that she might transport the lot downstairs where she and Bobby could dwell on them at leisure and in far greater comfort.

Connie brought the box down to her living room, where she had ample space to lay out everything on the low coffee table in front of the sofa. The afternoon sun provided a warm, cheery light by which to study the words and pictures, and, fixing herself a pot of tea, she proceeded to lose herself in the dusty volumes.

Settling herself comfortably on the sofa, her family history arrayed before her, Connie picked up the family bible, and opened the dried leather cover to the handwritten entries within.

The ink was a faint brown, and the elegantly penned lines varied slightly from the pressure of the hand on the quill. The earliest entry, appearing under the heading "MARRIAGE," was 1769 and announced the wedding of one Ezekiel Van Hoordin to an Emily Troost. The next entry, under the heading "BIRTH," heralded the birth of a seven-pound girl, Eugenia, to the newlyweds. But cholera claimed the young girl only five years later, so noted under "DEATHS," in 1774. The little life seemed so brief, thought Connie; only two dates, and a few words, and a human had come into the world and gone out of it.

A packet of letters, brittle with age, had been inserted in one of the photo albums. Their outline was embedded in the silk liner of the gilt-edged cover. Connie gently held the small bundle before loosening the faded satin ribbon that held them together. Laying the papers next to her on the sofa, Connie picked up the top one and delicately opened the mildew spotted parchment. It was a newspaper clipping, and very old, she thought, judging from the style of type and the way the words crowded the surface of the newspaper, with every sentence demanding equal attention.

"SUSSEX COUNTY MAN STILL MISSING," proclaimed the bold headline, with "RELATIVES WILL NOT GIVE UP HOPE" in equally bold typeface, printed immediately below. Connie moved the fragile paper into a patch of afternoon sunlight on the sofa, and continued to read. "Despite the brave and unfaltering hopes of assembled relatives, authorities in the county of Sussex are fearful that a local man, missing since Tuesday last, may be Gone forever."

"John W. Hardin, of the town of Layton, was last seen riding toward Buttermilk Falls, on the Mountain road, on his Sorrel Mare "Fair Princess," more than one week ago. According to relatives, Mr. Hardin was embarking on his annual spring fishing expedition to the falls, and was expected back that evening. No sign of horseman or mount having been reported during the past week, Mr. Hardin's relatives have combed the trail to and from Buttermilk Falls without rest since Wednesday last, but have found nothing to indicate the whereabouts of Mr. Hardin or his Mare."

The newspaper story ended at a torn edge of paper. Connie couldn't really tell whether the tale had continued beyond the tear, or whether the editors had decided, long ago, that the local readership would lose interest after four fact-filled paragraphs.

No one would ever know, she realized, staring down at the almost translucent scrap of paper. There was no date on the paper, so Connie turned it over, hoping to get some clue about the age of the story. Unfortunately, no date was evident. The two columns of print on the reverse dealt with Farmer's Almanac-type information: the weather conditions that might be expected during the coming summer months, a brief description of a cure for whooping cough (Mix 1 part alum with 3 parts molasses, bring to a boil. Simmer for 1 hour, then drink entire batch when cooled) and a schedule of the next several full moons.

Connie lifted another document from the packet in the Bible, and laid it carefully next to the story about John Hardin. This turned out to be several pages of some sort of legal document, written in a beautiful, flowing hand. At the top of the front page, there emerged a one-inch wide red satin ribbon, which actually bound the three pages of the document together. The ancient cloth continued down the side of the front page, and was affixed to the bottom, beneath an official looking circular wax seal. Turning over the pages, Connie saw that this document was dated January 13, 1838, and that it was the Last Will and Testament of the missing man.

Excited, Connie began reading the document. It said, in effect, that all the worldly possessions of John Hardin were bequeathed to his loving daughter Tessie Hardin, aged four years and five months. Connie quickly read through the listed possessions of the missing John Hardin: a sixteen-acre farm in what was then the area of *Wahlpeck.*

The farm came complete with a one-story stone farmhouse (including all furnishings within), a stone cooling house, three wooden outbuildings and all farm tools therein; two workhorses and a plow; a Pennsylvania Long Rifle, with powder horn, a bullet mold, four pounds lead and a ten pound keg of black powder; a spinning wheel; and three ornamental bracelets.

Well, Miss Tessie Hardin, you had yourself quite a dowry for a backwoods country girl, thought Connie. Peculiar that there was no mention of a mother, or anyone else, for that matter— just a four year-old girl... no guardian, no uncles, or aunts, or best friends, nobody except a tiny child, out in the New Jersey wilderness.

Along with the photo albums and Bible was a flat, tin box, about eight inches long by six inches tall, and one inch deep. The box was hinged along the back, with a faded advertisement for some long-extinct product on the lid's surface: "Halsey's Restorative Liniment." The name was scripted in flowing type, hovering above two fashionably dressed ladies from what looked to be the civil war era, each with a serene countenance, their arms intertwined, a stately oak tree forming a leafy border around them and the product name. Connie gently pried the tin box open with her fingertips, the top slightly hesitant after so many years' neglect. The light corrosion yielded to Connie's steady pressure, and the lid swung open.

Inside were two folded documents: yet another newspaper clipping, and a primitive, hand-drawn map. The newspaper clipping concerned itself with some repairs being done to the canal at the base of the great marsh, and detailed the work required. It also provided a brief history of the dam and canal as of 1873. Connie read with interest how the dam had been engineered sometime before the revolutionary war by a collection of local Dutch entrepreneurs, who were seeking to harness the water's power for several lumber and grist mills, and to enlarge the marsh itself for a cranberry bog. The article went on to describe how the original dam had increased the marsh's size considerably, causing its waters to cover what had been a large tract of farmland known as "Voorland's Field," as well as a small limestone pit, believed to have been in use for many centuries previously by the local Minisink Indian tribes as a source of crop fertilizer.

Connie had never really given much thought to the age of the dam, or the land beneath the marsh's waters. She just figured that the marsh had always occupied the space it now claimed. She lay down the newspaper article, and unfolded the brittle parchment of the map, laying it out in the afternoon sunlight on the couch. The area featured was not immediately evident. The map seemed to have been drawn by hand, given the elegantly cramped style of lettering. The letters were identifiable, but the words were not. They seemed to be names of places: farms, rock outcroppings, streams, and sounded either of Dutch or Indian origin. The center portion of the map depicted a large, irregular shape, its interior a blank on the ancient paper.

"A body of water," thought Connie, "...this is a large pond, or lake." The word "Buttermilk" revealed itself to her, off to the right of the water. "Buttermilk Falls," she said aloud.

The marsh seemed more round in this primitive depiction, Connie thought. She looked to the southern shore of the marsh, and didn't see a dam or canal referenced; only a blank space, bisected by a meandering pen stroke, and the inscription "lime works" a few inches south. "Vorsted's Road" identified a bolder line, which ran east to west across the bottom of the map. Connie was fairly certain that that road currently marked the southern border of the marsh itself.

Connie looked closer at the map, now starting to recognize previously unfamiliar names: "*Paulen's Kill*" scribed along the black squiggle of what must be the Paulenskill River. *"Wahlpeck"* was penned microscopically at the convergence of two indicated trails. Connie was looking at what appeared to be a very old map of the great marsh and environs of what was now called Stokes Forest. Concentric lines rippled along the left side of the map, from bottom to top: The Kittatinny Mountains.

At the left side of the parchment, along a thick pen line running southeast to northwest, the word "Sussex." To the left and above, the great marsh, and the forests, fields and meadows of the colonial wilderness.

The map wasn't titled, and there wasn't a legend or date any-where, but it was obviously older than the dam and canal. How old might it be? Connie focused anew on the previous border of the marsh, trying to estimate the actual distance between what it was when this map had been drawn up, and what it was now. Half a mile? Three-quarters of a mile? It would seem that the building of the dam by the "local Dutch entrepreneurs" had added upwards of a square mile of water to that area several hundred years ago, cov-ering "Voorland's Field," an old lime pit, and who knows what else.

The notion of several Dutch Elders compulsively damming the waters of an obscure marsh in the primeval interior of New Jersey, all in the name of progress and cranberries, brought to Connie's mind modern day Chamber of Commerce boosters, grinning for posterity, shiny shovels at the ready, immortalized in the act of breaking ground for some new mall, highway, or fast food restau-rant. She smiled at the thought of the faceless Dutch ghosts, stand-ing in a semicircle, wooden shovels at the ready, somewhere back in chamber of commerce history.

Connie looked closer at the blank area between the previous marsh boundary and the present, following the line down through "Voorland's Field" and through a little drawing of what might have been a hill with "flat rock" scripted on it, to the area marked "lime pit." Immediately to the right of the words "lime pit," there appeared, in a different style of handwriting and in fainter lettering, the words: "Hendrika's Gift."

"What gift?," Connie muttered aloud, recognizing a name repeated by Great Aunt Netta during their graveside visits. Could it have signified an actual object bequeathed to her relative of long ago? And if so, from whom? A Dutch merchant? Perhaps it meant a tract of land, a grove of fruit trees, a stone bench to rest on and view whatever there was to view several hundred years ago.

There were no other markings or words nearby on the ancient map, no other clues as to the precise nature of this mysterious "gift." Connie looked into the empty tin box, in the hope that some other scrap of information would appear, and throw light on this puzzle from the past.

Nothing. Not a clue to be had.

Perhaps there was some other corroborating evidence, somewhere among this treasure trove of pictures and papers, thought Connie, viewing the objects all about her on the sofa. She carefully folded up the map, and placed it and the newspaper clipping back into the tin box, and closed the lid. She didn't want to risk the fading effects of the sunlight on these fragile documents.

Chris Kluge

Chapter 19 —The Old Man and Blackie Check Traps

The wooden oars, frayed by years of fending off rocks, fighting marsh grass, and pushing through mud, moved rhythmically, making a soft, gurgling sound as they propelled the old aluminum dingy along. A large, black dog stood poised in the bow, like a hood ornament, its eyes set straight ahead, tensed for the sudden flight of a swan, or the fly-catching leap of a trout. Every now and then, it would turn its big head around to look at the old man bent to the oars, as if to offer encouragement to him, to keep him pumping the wooden sticks, and continue the excitement and thrill of gliding over the smooth waters of the marsh.

For his part, the old man, his straining back to the dog, occasionally stopped rowing, the dripping oars suspended momentarily in mid-stroke, and looked over his shoulder to assure himself they were still on course, his eyes honing in on the pine-covered island three hundred yards beyond the bow of the dingy. Once reassured, he turned back to face where they'd been, resuming his steady, silent ritual.

The bottom of the boat held a small, oscillating pool of stagnant water, and in the water, sloshing forward and back, were several painted cork spheres, each attached by several yards of monofilament to a fifteen pound weight, to which was attached in turn about a yard of 1/8" braided steel cable. A slab of raw, putrefying meat camouflaged the thick, barbed fishing hook at the end of each metallic strand.

An early morning fog still hung above the smooth waters of the marsh. It would be another hour before the summer sun climbed above the tall pine trees, evaporating the dancing mist with its insect-filled light. From deep within the encircling evergreen curtain of forest came the cacophonous twittering, chirping, and trilling of dozens of songbirds: blue jays, robins, wood thrushes, catbirds and crows. At the top of one towering pine, a great horned owl took swooping flight, its huge wings silently beating the morning air as it slowly gained speed over the waters below, disappearing into the cool woods across the marsh to wait out the daylight.

The dog swiveled his head in the direction of this sudden movement, following the heavy flight of the big predator for a moment before dismissing the bird with a dismissive "woof," and resuming its steady forward gaze.

The squat boat moved through the grey-green water in spurts, pushing ahead as the oars dug through the heavy water, then losing momentum, until the two yellow oars fanned up and then down, propelling the boat forward again.

"Won't be long now, Blackie...." murmured the man, timing the effort of his words to the rhythm of his backstroke. Hearing its name, the big dog looked back at him for a moment, then shifted its attention to the clear water flowing under the bow, on the alert for subterranean shadows. "No sirreee, won't be long now, my fine canine companion..." continued the old man, his pace picking up a beat as they drew nearer to the island, now only fifty yards off their bow.

The sound of lily pads, gliding underneath the dinghy's aluminum hull, alerted the old man that they were very near their destination; the north side of the small island, the northernmost point of the marsh, where underwater plants proliferated, providing sub-merged canyons, tunnels, and escape routes for the creatures that fed there, and were in turn fed upon.

The friction of the huge, dinner plate-sized lily pads underneath the hull slowed the boat down, and the old man reduced the pace of his rowing. The small island slipped by their port side, and the old man quietly shipped the oars, as they drifted around the tip of the island and entered a cove between the land and a boggy area that gave way to a wall of green forest.

The old man gathered up a fifteen pound weight, a cork ball, and the lines that connected them to the meat-covered hook, and sorted them in his hands, like a cowboy readying his lariat, as he peered over the side of the boat, into the clear waters beneath. The dog had repositioned itself so that it could monitor the old man's activities, and so looked down into the waters as well.

The foliage beneath the water formed a miniature universe in various shades of browns, greens and purples: long thin strands of grass, and dense, close shoals of tiny leaves, all rocking, gently, in the waters' shifting currents; plateaus and mesas of broad-brimmed plants, just below the marsh's surface, dropping off, suddenly, dramatically, into deep, dark ravines, some more than ten feet straight down, the green walls broken by ledges and outcroppings of different shaped underwater plants, or submerged tree trunks, their water-logged branches draped now with tangled lily pad stems, rather than maple leaves.

As the aluminum boat drifted over one of these underwater chasms, the old man gently placed the fifteen-pound weight be-neath the placid surface, and released it from his grasp. The black metal disc slipped through the water like an autumn leaf, its flat surface causing it to slide one way, then another, until it came to rest on the marsh's bed of rotten vegetation, ten feet below. The monofilament line, invisible underwater, rose from the flat anchor to the orange cork ball, now tethered to the marsh's surface, serv-ing as a marker buoy. A greasy, floating film outlined the spot where the putrid meat had entered the water, and followed the black weight down. It now hovered lazily in the underwater current, suspended a few inches above the bottom, and ten feet below the surface, a half-pound of dull grey beef, the glittering metal leader connecting it to the immovable weight.

Satisfied with the placement of the rig, the old man put the oars back in the oarlocks, and proceeded to row the boat several yards further along, repeating the entire ritual at another spot, and so on, until he had deposited all six of his eccentric fishing rigs in a semi-circle around the northern edge of the island.

By the time he had placed the last hook, the sun was peeking over the pines, and the grey waters around him were becoming bluer in the morning light. The black dog, attentive at first, had since lost interest in the old man's predictable activities, and was searching the rock-lined shores of the forest for more interesting things to look at.

"Well, Blackie, let's us go see what came to dinner last night!" laughed the old man, amused at his little joke. The dog didn't even bother to respond to the sound of his name.

The old man swung the bow around toward the south of the marsh and the other side of the island. He rowed for a few moments, until the island was about forty yards off their starboard side. He scanned the marsh's sunlit surface for the orange corks he and Blackie had placed this time yesterday. Spotting one tangled among some lily pads only a few yards away, he propelled the boat skillfully toward the orange marker. As the boat slid alongside, he hooked the bobber with a small boat hook, pulling it from the lily pads and into his outstretched hand. Hauling up the strong monofilament, he smiled and said to his mute companion, "Well, well, we've got a dinner guest, Blackie! Someone responded to our invitation, and just couldn't resist the main course."

The dog watched the man's hands closely, like a bird dog watching a pheasant, anticipating what was undoubtedly attached to the wet, clear line being pulled from the marsh. Leaning out over the side of the boat, the old man continued to pull the line from the water, until a dripping fifteen-pound weight emerged, followed by a length of braided steel line. Pausing to place the weight in the bottom of the boat, the old man peered at the water beneath him, and very slowly, with great care, hauled the final length of cable straight up.

The silvery steel line disappeared into the clamped jaws of a hideous looking creature, whose baseball-sized head looked like a cross between a drowned parrot and a dinosaur: the flesh was the color of mottled grey-brown mold, but with the seeming texture of sandpaper; the serrated, sealed jaws ended in a fierce-looking beak, and the glazed, dead eyes stared reproachfully up into those of the old man. Beneath the head stretched a long neck, which disappeared into a squat, ridged shell, hanging just under the water's surface.

"Ah, yes, this will run a good ten pounds, this little snapper will," said the old man appreciatively, as he supported the weight of the turtle by placing his other hand under the limp hind legs and long reptilian tail and hauled the dead, ugly thing into the boat, dropping it on its belly, in a mocking pose of life. "He's a good 2 feet long, with his neck stretched," said the old man. The dog, still perched in the bow, warily sniffed at the fierce gargoyle lying prone in the bilge water, not fully trusting its demise.

"Oh, he's dead, alright, Blackie! Come and have a good sniff at this gruesome corpse." To illustrate his point, the old man grabbed the long tail and shook the creature, causing it to slide from side to side in the bottom of the boat, the inch-long claws on all four feet making a loud scraping noise on the aluminum hull, the heavy head lolling on the end of the limber neck.

The dog recoiled at this unnatural movement, but then, cautiously, stepped closer, inching its nose to within a foot of the inanimate head. Satisfied the creature was, in fact, dead, the dog warily stepped back up on the bow seat. It was never entirely comfortable with sharing the cramped space of the boat with a snapping turtle, even one that appeared to be dead.

"That's one down, Blackie, and 3 to go! Let's see what else we've caught today.

Slipping the oars back in their locks, the old man rowed a few yards to the next float. Hauling up the line, a slightly larger turtle was attached to the metal line, having swallowed the hooked, putrid meat and drowned, unable to surface for air.

"Ah, my lovely monster of the deep, bit off more than you could chew, eh? And what's this extra prize hanging off your prehistoric rump?"

A large crayfish, a good 5 inches in length, held onto the dead reptile's alligator-like tail, temporarily oblivious to its situation. After a moment, it released its grip and dropped back into the water, where it propelled itself swiftly toward the bottom.

"Did you see that, Blackie? We almost got a side order with our soup!" He dropped the big turtle on top of the other one, and set about hauling up the rest of the rig. The next trap yielded a still-living eel that had just managed to get its mouth around the barbed point of the hook. The old man broke its neck and took it off the half-eaten meat, adding it to the catch at his feet.

At the final trap, the old man's mood changed, for the braided metal line had been cut. There was nothing at its end; not turtle, not meat, not hook.

"What the hell" he growled, peering closely at the shredded metal fibers. He swore under his breath, trying to figure what type of creature could have chopped through the braided metal leader. "Have to be a powerful snapper to bite through this. Weren't no turtle.... have to be a man!" He riffled through a mental inventory of enemies of the past. He really didn't have any current ones that he was aware of, and those from long ago were all either dead or had moved on. Maybe it was somebody that didn't know him, but had found his traps. Or maybe the line was defective, some hidden flaw that gave out under the force of a big snapper's bite.

Yes, he decided, defective line sounded like the best bet. After all, why take one and not the others? "One goddamn thing's for certain, Blackie. Whatever turtle is walking around on the bottom

88

with a quarter pound of meat and a three inch hook in its throat is going to float up sometime!"

Smiling at this eventuality, he hauled up the rest of the rig and dumped it in the bottom of his boat. "Let's head for home, fella. We did good for one morning."

Chapter 20 — *Professor Van Zandt*

Professor Van Zandt returned from the afternoon lecture series to his cluttered office, high in the Romanesque tower of the Museum of Natural History's North Wing. The dark, imposing edifice was not everyone's idea of the perfect office building, but its time-yellowed plaster walls, oak banister stairways, and secluded, unpretentious office spaces suited the professor perfectly. The bookshelves were built into the walls, and former gas light fixtures now held wall sconces lending a warm, womblike atmosphere to the space. Just what any self-respecting scholar would give half a tenure for.

Without prior knowledge of the professor's field of scholarship, a visitor would be hard pressed to guess at his particular expertise, solely relying on the objects placed haphazardly about, among the pamphlets, books, and papers: a human skull, with a map of what appeared to be Greenland scrimshawed into its lacquered forehead; a very old photograph featuring a mezzo tinted line of bathing beauties, smiling, arm in arm, on a beach before a huge, Victorian hotel; a collection of novelty postcards, all featuring oversized vegetables or fruit in various quasi-humorous modes of transportation (a typical one had a giant ear of corn atop a flatbed truck, somewhere in the heartland of a 1940's America, with "We're All Ears in Iowa" scripted across the hand-tinted azure sky....).

However, wedged among the iconoclastic effluvia of popular American culture, lurked a few remnants of an even older "New World": delicately decorated clay vessels, beautifully carved stone figurines of animals and people, wooden masks, and bone flutes.

These things, almost lost among the sublimely ridiculous effects of the more recent European invasion of North America, were what the professor lavished most of his interest and time on; mementos of a vanished era....

A good deal of his fifty-eight years had been devoted to scraping traces of pottery shards from brick-red clay in the Pine Barrens of New Jersey, or crouching in dripping, underground caverns, sifting millennia-old detritus for scraps of lives long dead. Professor Van Zandt's passionate sleuthing into the pastimes of the first settlers of America's northeast had earned him, over the years, the deserved reputation of "Expert," and many fellow enthusiasts sought out his assistance in evaluating their own archeological efforts and finds. Like all true scholars, Professor Van Zandt shared his acquired knowledge enthusiastically and selflessly. He didn't hoard bits of information, trivia, or Indian lore, and use them, like poker chips, in some ridiculous academic competition with his peers. He absorbed information because he was excited about the subject matter, and loved sharing that excitement with anyone who showed the slightest interest; in short, a natural teacher.

Some of his fellow academicians thought him naive in the "no holds barred arena" of higher education politics. Instead of honing his professional image, of focusing at least some energy on ensuring his professional advancement, Van Zandt followed his interests for their own sake. He really didn't devote much thought to how others might perceive him; not from any sense of superiority.... he just wasn't wired that way.

The Professor dropped his briefcase onto a chair, as he noticed a bright pink telephone message sheet propped conspicuously in the middle of his cluttered desk blotter, placed there, most likely, by his summer intern, Fran.

"Sussex County Community College called, regarding reported find of large stone with pictures, call Bob Ambrose at 973-579-1546."

The professor's interest in local archeological treasures had led him several times to the northwestern corner of New Jersey, sometimes to guest lecture in the Sussex County College's Science Department, but also to just pot around with the local "bone detectives," enjoying the quiet, natural beauty of the area.

Bob Ambrose taught Computer Sciences at the college, but Van Zandt considered Bob a peer, although Bob held no formal degrees in the strange avocation of rooting around the dirt for signs of other peoples' cultural remnants.

However brief the message was, the words "stone with pictures found" were the only words he needed to make him reach for his phone. Local prehistoric residents hadn't often committed their doings to so durable a bulletin board as rock, and, if this find were authentic, it would make for very interesting reading indeed.

Balancing the receiver on his shoulder, the professor shrugged off his windbreaker and sat down at his desk, swiveling his chair around to gaze at the green treetops of Central Park, across 8th Avenue.

"Good afternoon, this is Sussex Community College. How may I help you?"

"Good afternoon, Sussex Community College....may I speak with Bob Ambrose, please? This is John Van Zandt, calling.

"One moment, and I'll connect you.... please hold."

"Hello, Bob Ambrose speaking."

"Robert, this is John. I'm responding to your intriguing and somewhat cryptic message! How are you?"

"Hey, the Professor lives! Long time no talk, Amigo! Nothing like a 13,000 year-old scratch pad to grab your attention, eh?"

"Enough of your B.S., Ambrose...what about that rock?"

Laughing, Bob continued..."Okay, John, here's the deal. Our Science Dean, Ben Haubrich, got a call from the Sussex County Roads Department yesterday. One of their backhoes had unearthed a large, flat rock with markings across its surface, describing a definite pattern. So, knowing of my interest in local archeology, Haubrich calls me up before he heads out there to investigate."

"I wasn't sure what to expect, since some people out here consider a glass Coke bottle a prehistoric find, but when we arrived at the scene and looked the rock over, I knew we were looking at something interesting. The markings were etched into the surface, with stick-like figures arrayed around a central form."

Professor Van Zandt was staring at the green trees out his window, but not seeing them anymore. He was trying to imagine what the rock looked like, what the figures were saying...

"John, are you there?" asked Bob, not hearing anything from the receiver...

"Yes, yes, of course I'm here, Bob! Sorry, I was just thinking.... Say, is the rock still out at the discovery site? I mean, is it anywhere safe?" The professor was all too aware of the high prices being commanded by rather inferior examples of early American Indian artifacts by private collectors, as well as some greedy curators of established Museum collections. His expertise in the evaluation of the authenticity of such artifacts had made him the unwanted correspondent of several "enthusiasts" of late— shady characters who had mysteriously come into the possession of rare and valuable examples of Indian artistry, and who sought the professor's imprimatur on the worth of their antiquity. The black market value of the rock in question, if it were authentic, would be substantial.

"Ben and I took his pickup," continued Bob, "and the two of us wrestled it onto the bed, and we brought it back to the college. That thing must weigh over a hundred pounds, John. We've got it in a wheelbarrow outside the cafeteria supply room. Tomorrow we figure to roll it into the science lab, where we can do some serious speculating. Care to join us?"

"Fantastic! I sure as hell would! I've only got one lecture in the morning tomorrow, so I can be out there by, say, twelve-thirty or one o'clock. "

"Listen, Bob, about that rock.... If at all possible, I think you ought to try and get it into the science lab today. I'm sure your backhoe operator's going to be telling everybody in his fire company about what made his day unique, and, as wise men oft say, 'possession is nine-tenths of the law.' I think if some of your friends and neighbors out there knew that they could trade an authentic piece of prehistoric pottery for a new bass boat, you would have a lot more help out there in your archeological digs. Know what I mean?"

"Yeah, maybe you're right, John. I'll see if Haubrich can help me. I'm pretty sure he's still in the lab, preparing for next week's summer session."

"We'll see you tomorrow, John"

Professor Van Zandt hung up the phone, and sat motionless in his chair, staring out the window, trying to visualize the markings that Bob had described. If this rock was authentic, there would be a lot more people interested in it than a few New Jersey rock hounds. It might add to the fragmented knowledge of the original human settlers of the eastern North American continent.

Professor Van Zandt opened his briefcase, took out the day's lecture notes, and reached for a reference book on Indian Iconography, as well as a book on the Geology of the Delaware Region of New Jersey, New York, and Pennsylvania. He would need these and a few other reference materials for his trip tomorrow. He always looked forward to archaeological digs with an excited anticipation. Something felt different about this one...

He threw the books into his briefcase, snapped it shut, and strode out of his office. He could beat the evening commuters fleeing the city, be home by 5:30, and get organized for his adventure tomorrow. Following his morning class, he could be on Route 80 West by 11:00-11:15, and after another hour and a half he'd be reading a message scratched in stone, a carved record from a long, long time ago, when people lived in dread of the night and all it might bring to the rim of their campfires.....

Chapter 21 — Something Awakens

Whoosh....
Silence....
Whooosh!
Silence....
Whoooosh! The sound of blood, pushing through its huge body, pumped by a mass of heart muscle that contracted once every minute.

Silence....

Whooosh! The contractions came closer together...

Whooosh! The massive limbs sought to move against the imprisoning mass of cold mud... first one great claw, then another, pushing, then pulling, in and out, like an awakening newborn baby.

The movements were spasmodic, the brain not functioning fully, the neural messages clipped, incomplete.

Whooosh! ....Whooosh!

Eyes closed, the big head pushed out against the cold clay, turning and twisting, like a subterranean root seeking light, and warmth, and air.

Whooosh!

The large heart contracted quicker still, and the blood-fed limbs moved with greater urgency... pushing and pulling, forward and back, in and out... like a four cylinder engine slowly turning over on a cold morning, the heart pumping rhythmically now, the limbs jerking one..., two..., three..., four..., one.., two.., three.., four.., one, two, three, four, ...the womb of mud yielded, ever so slightly, giving a little here, a little there... the beating heart sending a steady current of blood through the muscles, the tissues, the organs... everything coming alive, working to free the Thing from its black, cold tomb.

Whooosh!

The Thing's brain started to coordinate the efforts of the long dormant limbs, and they began to work together, pushing against the mud, the huge body shifting within the black cocoon. The sound of the Thing's blood pumping through its body was now joined by a sucking, gurgling sound, as spaces opened between the cloak of muck and the heaving form.

Its head continued to grope upward, pushing hard against an unyielding mantle of mud, even as its limbs heaved its body upward and side to side, gaining a little more freedom each time.

Suddenly, the weight above its flat head gave way, and a cold rush of water spilled between its body and the cavities in the mud its movements had created. The inrushing water mixed with the enshrouding clay, emulsifying it further, acting as a lubricant for the struggling limbs.

The long neck stretched upward through the cold water, the eyes cautiously blinked open, and beheld shafts of sunlight piercing a murky gloom. All four appendages pushed hard against the mud below, and the Thing heaved its massive body against the water-softened mud above it, once, then again. Sensing its imminent freedom, it gave a mighty push, finally exploding from its subterranean tomb, a mushroom cloud of silt spreading out around it, as it propelled its massive form upward, toward the glittering world above, the world of light, of color, of air...

As its head broke through the marsh's surface, and into the oxygen-filled world above, the Thing opened its mouth wide, gasping in a lungful of air, thereby reactivating its long-dormant respiratory system. Its limbs paddled hard to support the great weight, allowing the gaping jaws to hold above water long enough for the lungs to pump out and in and out again, re-patterning the rhythm of breathing into the primitive nervous system.

The inflated lungs forced the sun-warmed oxygen into the pumping blood, which fed, in turn, brain, organs, and muscles. Its movements became more coordinated, more assured. Portions of the brain, asleep for so long, began to come alive. The Thing grew stronger by the minute, its gaping jaws above the marsh's surface, the huge body floating just below, silently treading water, as its central nervous system remembered how to function in a world of oxygen.

After a time, the Thing's bodily functions had reoriented completely from inactive dormancy to oxygen-breathing, heart-thumping life. Sucking in a huge volume of air, the Thing closed its cruel-looking beak, and sank beneath the surface. The overwhelming need for air had served its purpose of rousing the Thing from its sleep beneath the marsh's bottom. Temporarily satisfied, that desire was now being quickly replaced by another; the desire for food.

Suspended in the buoyant water beneath the surface, the Thing paddled its limbs slowly, swiveling its flat, ugly head in a semi-circle, the hooded eyes taking in the aquatic jungle around. It had emerged near the center of the Marsh, where the water reached twenty feet. Curtains of underwater grasses swayed slowly along with scattered concentrations of algae, lily pads, and other colorful underwater vegetation. Sunken logs, spongy with age, littered the marsh bottom, their surfaces dotted with gelatinous aquatic growth.

The Thing hung amidst this underwater forest like some prehistoric dirigible, its four appendages paddling slowly, sunlight glinting off the seven-inch long claws at the end of each limb. A thick, scalloped shell encased its broad torso, with two long spiked ridges running front to back. At the rear of the gray-green shell, an alligator-like tail, more than two meters long, waved slowly from side to side, acting as a rudder. From beneath the front of the carapace emerged the closest living representation of a dinosaur anyone was ever likely to see: a cross between a stegosaurus and a medieval image of Satan. It's massive head, too large to retreat into the protective shell, was covered in leathery flesh. Serpentine brow ridges formed a shallow roof over the small, expressionless eyes. The unblinking iris of each eye formed a star pattern, radiating out from a tiny, iridescent pupil. From the eyes forward, the unwieldy head tapered to a gargoyle's pouting beak, flanked by slit nostrils. The large mandibles of the Thing were bulging with muscle, leaving no doubt as to the vicious potential of the creature's serrated jaws. Its expression was at the same time dull, disinterested, and deadly. There was nothing of mercy in this demon from beneath the mud.

The sunlight rippled through the waters, dancing off the vertical columns of lily pad stalks, making the clouds of microorganisms glow a fluorescent green. A school of sunfish flashed into view, then scattered into the vegetation. Heeding its hunger, the Thing began moving forward, slowly, through the murky water, in search of meat, living or dead.

It hadn't eaten in a very long time.

Chapter 22 — *A Dog Goes Missing*

"Heeeeere, CJ! Come on home now, CJ..."

The call went out over the marsh waters, bounced off the shale rocks of Rattler Mountain, and echoed back. Maudie Ellsworth stood on the small deck off her kitchen, listening for the familiar sound of her Irish setter crashing through the undergrowth, or splashing down by the water's edge.

She had been calling his name for over five minutes now, and she hadn't heard anything, other than the mocking cry of some blue jays.

Not like him at all, she thought, her eyes scanning the willows and forsythia shrubs that separated her fifteen acres from the woods and marsh beyond.

With few neighbors about, she always let CJ have his freedom. He never went far, and he always came running when she called him home. Other than a summer cottage across the cove, and the Bevans family a hundred yards down the road, Maudie, her twin sister Ruth and CJ had the southern edge of the Great Marsh to themselves. A self-employed illustrator, Maudie enjoyed the privacy. While gregarious by nature, she made productive use of her self-imposed solitude, spending long hours sketching and painting the New Jersey wilderness around her. Her sister, a semi-retired schoolteacher, still substituted for the local public schools, giving

her a reasonable balance of intellectual stimulation and respite
from the unbroken demands of a full time teacher's life.

The sisters shared ownership and chores of their fifteen-acre
farm, along with five Hereford cows, one Hereford bull, two goats,
thirteen chickens, and a rooster. And, of course, CJ. The farm had
been in their family for over three hundred years. Since both
women were spinsters in their late fifties, with no direct heirs, they
represented the last direct link to the original owners.

A deed, on record at the county courthouse, listed the original
acreage at seven hundred and fifty acres. It had spread over the
surrounding rolling meadows and hardwood forests seemingly as
far as the eye could see. Back then, before the marsh had been
dammed and expanded, the tilled earth would have run unbroken
all the way across the valley to Rattlesnake Mountain, with row
after row of bright green corn stalks waving in the midsummer air,
thrusting their way up from the dark, rich earth. Now, the marsh
lapped at five of the remaining fifteen acres, the waters having
claimed over five hundred acres of the original farm, and the rest
having been sold off during the preceding centuries, piece by
piece, to keep the family going.

With no mortgage payments to make, one fully-paid car between them, and modest living habits, the sisters managed to survive by selling some farm produce, Maudie's illustration jobs, and
Ruth's teaching checks. Like most old-timers out here, the sisters
had no "lifestyle" to keep up, other than keeping the house warm,
the utility bills paid, and the animals fed. The cows paid their way,
albeit marginally, by the milk they produced. The bull, a windfall
inheritance from their Uncle Fred's estate, had been leased out as a
breeder to several local farmers, and a large garden kept a nearby
vegetable stand in business during the summer months.

When not tending to farm chores, Maudie devoted most of her
hard-earned time to capturing the beauty around her with sable
brush and watercolor. She sold some of her work to several nature-
oriented magazines, and sold a few original landscape paintings
each year, through local art galleries, to the well-heeled tourists

that drove out from more densely-populated areas of the state, for an afternoon of Antiquing and fresh air.

While not possessed of visual artistic talent, her sister Ruth had been born with a musical ability that almost secured for her, as a very young woman, a position with the Newark Symphony. Trained as a harpist, Ruth had actually performed with the symphony as a summer intern, but the death of their parents in a freak boating accident had cut short her budding career. Ruth had returned home to live with her sister, and redirected her talents to teaching music in the local grammar schools. While she never resumed a performing career, she held onto her vintage Lyon & Healy concert harp, practicing regularly. Occasionally, weather permitting, she hauled the gilded instrument out to the milking barn, performing for the cows in their stalls. They seemed to enjoy the soothing music, especially the French impressionists, and it satisfied some lingering desire in Ruth for public approbation. She was glad to have performed with a professional symphony orchestra, but was happy just to continue playing whenever the spirit moved her.

Maudie called out into the heavy summer air "CJ... come on, CJ.... Where are you, boy?" She stepped from the deck and headed down to the water's edge, which was about seventy feet from their two-bedroom farmhouse. She hugged her sweater closer around her, feeling a fresh breeze blowing from the North. Her eyes scanned the thunderheads forming over the Kittatinny Mountains, and she quickened her pace.

"Heeeere, CJ, come on home, boy!"

She walked to the end of their small dock, and looked up and down the cattail-fringed shoreline, but saw no sign of the dog. Up on the meadow above their house, five black and white cows stood, the sound of the mouthfuls of grass being pulled from the ground audible in the still air. Off to the side of the fenced in meadow, under the huge old oak tree that marked the far corner of their farm, lay their big bull, Luther. When he wasn't mounting a cow or threatening trespassers, Luther was generally immobile. He posed no danger to the sisters or CJ, or any of the other farm animals, since he accepted them as an inevitable, subservient part of his domain. But anything else, on four legs or two, he considered a challenge to his rightful monarchy, and subject to whatever punishment he felt like meting out.

The breeze was picking up now, kicking up small waves that splashed the lichen-covered rocks of the shore. A dull "thump" of thunder sounded in the distance, moments before raindrops as big as marbles started slapping the green oak leaves overhanging the water and the birch railing of the dock.

Frowning with concern, Maudie lingered at the water's edge for a few more moments, as the rain drops came closer together, the sound of their fall now drowning out the other ambient marsh and forest sounds of birds, insects, and other furtively-moving creatures.

"I'll put his dinner out on the deck, and he'll be in by and by," she half-heartedly assured herself, as she turned from the water and strode back up the lawn to her home, her arms still folded protectively across her chest.

Beneath the rain-dimpled surface of the marsh at the end of the dock, among the gently-waving stalks of marsh grass and lily pads, a crayfish picked delicately at the head of a sunfish, its dull eyes staring, its dead mouth open, rocking to and fro on the rotted leaves of the marsh bottom.

Chapter 23 — A Plan is Hatched

The two men in the 4x4 truck had checked into the Deerfoot Motel after midnight. The desk clerk, awakened from a light sleep in front of his office TV by the sharp ring of the desk bell, had blinked his eyes open to some incomprehensible activity on the small tv screen. Another ring reminded him that he was obligated to attend to some travelers in his lobby.

He shuffled sleepily from his tiny office, and stepped into the fluorescent light of the motel lobby. Picking up the Register from beneath the desk, he looked up for the first time at the two customers before him.

Both men had the nondescript look of truck drivers, burned out from too many sleepless miles and too many cups of coffee. In their middle to late thirties, they were dressed like hunters in heavy protective clothing. The clerk thought this somewhat peculiar, given the balmy summer night air. One man did the talking, while the other, his tired eyes unfocused, leaned against the soft drink machine by the door.

"We need a room, for tonight and tomorrow night. Give us something away from the highway, and away from any ice machines or vending machines. Second floor." The man gave these terse instructions without making any eye contact with the night clerk. As he spoke, he fished in the various pockets of his jacket for what turned out to be his wallet, from which he pulled a rolled a wad of twenty dollar bills.

"How much?" he mumbled, his eyes on the guest ledger being opened on the counter top.

"Sixty dollars a night, payable in full at time of check in. We take Visa and American Express cards, Travelers checks, and..."

"Here," the man stopped him, dropping six twenty dollar bills onto the metal-flaked linoleum counter top. Collecting the crumpled bills with one hand and offering a pen with the other, the night clerk pressed on with his prepared welcome.

"Check out time is at twelve o'clock sharp, and all phone calls must be credit card or collect. Are you fellows interested in anything in the way of..."

"We'll take our key now," said the man, scribbling two names in the guest ledger, lifting his head to stare, for the first time, into the eyes of the desk clerk.

"Certainly, you bet. I'm sure you two are very tired and anxious to get to sleep," the clerk rattled on nervously, sensing a danger to these two that he'd carelessly overlooked. He reached under the counter and retracted a key attached to a large plastic oval marked "153," and handed it to the man, who had resumed filling in the guest book.

"Room 153 is around back, second floor, the corner of the building, facing the industrial park behind us. Would you want a wake-up call?"

"No thanks," said the man, already turning to walk out the door. His partner, who had remained propped against the soft drink machine, now lifted himself from his reclining pose and followed the other one outside.

The clerk watched them stroll across the parking lot to a midnight blue 4x4. The constant hum of traffic, heading into and out of New York City only 30 miles east, increased in volume while the motel lobby door was open, then dropped off suddenly as the glass door hissed shut. A muffled roar sounded briefly, and the big truck rolled across the floodlit lot and disappeared around the corner of the two-story building.

The clerk swung the register around and looked down at the scribbled names; Bob Smith and Craig Johnson. The sound of late night TV laughter issued from his office. No, he thought smugly to himself, those guys weren't who they said they were. He was a pretty astute observer of humankind, given his many years of motel management, and he knew these two weren't on the up and up. Still, he had no intention of pursuing the matter of their real identities. He figured they'd be gone by the day after tomorrow, and the absentee owners of the Deerfoot Motel didn't pay him enough to pry too far into the customers' doings.

The truck stopped at the back of the motel, and the two men retrieved several duffel bags from the bed of the truck and made their way up to the second level. The man who had signed the register opened the door and turned on the light, followed closely by the second traveler.

Once inside, they drew the accordion plastic curtain, closed and locked the door, and settled their belongings onto each of the twin beds. Shucking their jackets, one man went to the bathroom and retrieved two cellophane-wrapped plastic drinking cups, setting them on the simulated wood dressing table that ran the length of the wall facing the beds, as the other man carefully set a knapsack onto the bed nearest the bathroom.

The standing man had by this time uncorked a bottle of bourbon from among the other duffel bags and filled each plastic cup halfway to the top with the amber liquid. The other man opened the knapsack and carefully removed the towel-swaddled contents from within, placing each delicately on the green and blue bedspread.

There were four pots in all, each slightly different in size from the other. The smallest looked to be the size of an orange, and the largest was the size of a large grapefruit. All four were pale yellow in color, with faded red stripes running around the widest circumference. Assorted animal-like figures ringed the area immediately above the bands where the vessels narrowed at the neck. The little drawings, glazed into the clay, were crudely rendered but recognizable; a bird, a snake, a turtle, and a wolf. The same figures decorated each of the jugs, with only slight variation in the design. Two of the pots had open mouths, like bowls. The other two, the largest of the collection, had slender necks that narrowed down to a small opening. The bigger of these was sealed shut.

"Here, give me one of those," said the man on the bed, motioning for a plastic cup.

"Looks like a good set." the standing man said, handing a drink to his partner as he surveyed the pottery laying like pale pumpkins on top of the checkered coverlet. "I'll bet these little ones go for fifteen hundred, maybe two thousand each. The big ones, eight, maybe ten thousand."

"Ten grand? No way!," protested the man on the bed. "Ray, we've never seen that much for this stuff."

The standing man, identified as Ray, emptied his plastic cup in a few swallows and smiled at his partner. "Come to think of it, Nick, I'll bet we're looking at twenty-five, thirty thousand for the lot of them. I doubt anybody's ever seen a matched set like these before." He arranged the four gleaming pots in ascending order on the bedspread, a few inches between each one, to underscore his newly developed marketing plan.

The man named Nick, skeptical of his partner's appraisal of the artifacts, silently sipped at his bourbon. He had no real idea of the value of these clay relics, his expertise being more in the line of stolen jewelry and designer drugs.

"When are we supposed to call Sacks?" he asked Ray.

"I told him nine-thirty a.m., sharp." Ray checked the watch on his wrist. It was twelve-fifteen. "Don't worry, Andrew J. Sacks is always cooperative when it comes to Indian artifacts. He's just happy to get his manicured hands on new product. All his competitors are out scuffling for retreads; dusty old crap that everybody already knows about. Nobody's seen this shit for a couple thousand years and he knows it. Makes him feel like a hotshot to all his society museum friends, offering never seen stuff. Believe me, he puts a premium on showing those assholes up, and he's willing to pay for it."

"I don't really trust him." said Nick, looking down into the golden liquor in his plastic cup, before tossing it back in one gulp.

Ray laughed sharply. "Look who doesn't trust who! Hey, my friend, last time I looked, it was you who got two years for aiding and abetting a criminal conspiracy. We didn't study Art at Harvard with Andy Sacks, and we don't rub tan shoulders and talk tax shelters with celebrities in the Hamptons. We're not talking trust, here, Nick; we're talking cash and carry, no credit cards, payment in full for services rendered. All he's gotta do is flash the green, and he walks with whatever he wants. So far, he's paid up in full. He's just a money machine to us, an ATM with an attitude. Enjoy it!" Ray laughed some more, shaking his head in amusement. Nick poured another few fingers into his cup, keeping his thoughts to himself.

Ray picked up the largest of the vessels and rolled it slowly in his hands. A muffled, rattling sound came from within.

"There's something in this one" he said, holding it closer to his ear, shaking it gently. Putting his plastic tumbler on a nightstand, he hefted the next smaller pot in his hand, comparing the weight of one to the other. "Not much heavier, though, so whatever it is in here can't weigh much." Nick moved closer to the bed, his worried expression changing to one of curiosity.

The sound of something rolling and sliding against the interior wall of the pot held the two men's interest, each trying to deduce the nature of whatever was entombed within the hardened clay.

Nick finished the bourbon in his cup and reached for the bottle. "Might be something valuable in there. Can you break the top open without shattering the rest of the pot?"

"I say we keep it as is, and try and entice some bonus money out of our dealer friend."

"But what if whatever is in there is a jewel or something! It might be worth more than all the pots together!"

"Yeah, and what if it's a five thousand year-old turd," said Ray. "What then? We've got a broken pot, and we're a few grand poorer. Let the dealer worry about whatever it is, not us." Ray's voice was tinged with anger, implying the end to any further discussion.

Nick backed off; he'd seen others press Ray beyond this point, and he didn't want to set his partner off.

"Want another drink, Ray?" Nick wanted to move away from the discussion, and quickly.

His partner didn't speak for a moment, but then answered quietly "No, no thanks. It's late; let's get some sleep. 9:30 will come soon enough, and we want to be sharp for Mr. Andrew J. Sacks. These yuppie types will steal your balls if you don't keep your hands on them."

He slowly rolled the largest pot in his hands, the movement of the invisible contents audible above the soft whine of the air conditioner.

Chapter 24 — Transfer of Goods

The four pots, perfectly matched, were arrayed on the glass coffee table, smallest on the left, largest on the right. The morning sunlight, streaming in the open window, illuminated them, making them look like they'd been newly varnished. The faint sound of traffic wafted up from the crowded city street thirty stories below, carried on a breeze that smelled faintly of exhaust. Ray had come over from New Jersey only an hour before. He looked at his watch for the second time since he'd checked into the room a half hour ago. It was 11:15. As per their arrangement, he'd called Andrew Sacks at 9:30, directing him to this midtown address. Keeping the location of meetings a flexible secret was an old habit of Ray's. It had served him well in the past and there was no reason to stop doing it. He had no intention of relaxing his guard, even if he was dealing with upper class culture-types instead of career criminals.

He knew the antiquities dealer would arrive precisely at 11:30. Like most Manhattan power types, Andrew J. Sacks was punctual; time to a New Yorker seemed to be the only commodity as precious as space. People took their meetings very seriously on this big island, thought Ray. No harm in that, though. It was one of the few things he liked about doing business in the City. People didn't waste your time; once you got past the inevitable hondeling and displays of dominance, you either had a deal or you didn't.

This would be his third transaction with this antiquities dealer since being introduced to him via a mutual friend several months ago. The initial association had been pharmaceutical; you met the nicest class of people buying and selling drugs; stockbrokers snorted from coke lines with well heeled ex cons, everybody sharing the same respect for money and the tangibles it bought. If you dressed sharp, sported a good watch and a nice set of capped teeth, there weren't many places you couldn't get access to in New York's varied social strata.

After a certain rapport had been established courtesy of the coca connection, a little skilled probing had enlightened Ray to the risk-free opportunities to be had in the world of antiquities and archaeological collectibles. While not as lucrative as peddling high grade cocaine, the hours were great, there was plenty of outdoor exercise, and beautiful college-educated women with horn rim glasses fell all over you if you professed to be both an amateur archaeologist and a practicing heterosexual. Most importantly, the people you were involved with were more apt to carry a New York Yacht Club membership card than a gun; you never had to worry about getting shot while conducting business.

Ray had paid his dues, outrunning Coast Guard boats, ingesting drug-filled condoms to beat customs searches, and bluffing his way through countless dangerous situations and hostile encounters. This was the easiest scam he'd ever fallen into, and he intended to keep it working for as long as he could. A quick learner, Ray had already mastered the finer points of assessing Native American pottery. He had devoted many hours to studying various public and private collections, and had read all he could get his hands on concerning local aboriginal antiquities. So far, he'd been able to fulfill the requests of Andrew Sacks with little risk to himself. He wanted to use this one connection to branch out to other people, to other opportunities. Filling the pipeline was not a problem for Ray. He was very resourceful, and once he learned what people were willing to pay for, he never had difficulty supplying them with whatever it was they wanted. He knew the key to success was maximizing opportunities while minimizing risk. Ray looked at Andrew Sacks as just the first measured step toward a very lucrative future.

Ray walked to the open sash window and looked down at the colorful parade of vehicles and pedestrians scuttling over the tarred and cemented surface below. No matter what time of day or night, there always seemed to be people moving somewhere, engaged in some scam, pursuing some vision of wealth, of a better situation. New York was eight plus million individuals packed one on top of another, speaking different languages, sharing nothing in common, really, except their ability to dream of making a big score, winning one lottery or another; each one just trying to rise above and away from the congestion and inhumanity all around. An island of dreams, thought Ray.

The phone next to the bed rang, and Ray caught it on the second ring. "Good morning, Room 3012, this is your wake up call." It was Andrew Sack's cheerfully arrogant voice.

"Yes, come right up." Ray spoke in a flat, emotionless voice, not caring to engage in any further conversation over the phone.

"Be right up." responded the upbeat voice, unfazed by Ray's cold tone. Several minutes later, three soft raps sounded beyond the door. A glance through the peephole revealed an elegantly dressed, properly tanned white man in his late thirties, standing nonchalantly a few feet back from the door, one hand casually hidden in the side pocket of a cream silk suit jacket. Ray opened the door, beckoned the man inside, and quickly reclosed it. Andy Sacks had extended his hand to Ray as he walked through the door, but it hadn't been taken. He now stood in the middle of the hotel room, a bemused look on his handsome face, the hand still proffered.

"Good morning, Ray, good to see you."

Ray belatedly shook Andy's hand, slightly annoyed at the man's persistence in maintaining this facade of good fellowship. Ray's previous business experience rarely included such intimate rituals as handshaking. Armed men generally preferred to keep their hands to themselves.

Unfazed by Ray's aloofness, Andy pressed on. "So, Ray, what have we today?" Rubbing his hands together, his eyes swept the hotel room, locking onto the sunlit forms arranged on the coffee table.

"Beautiful, Ray, really beautiful." Andy strode over to the ceramic pieces, seating himself on the sofa before them, like a man sitting down to a gourmet meal. "May I?" he asked of Ray, arms already reaching forward, fingers caressing the glazed surface of the largest sealed urn. Walking to the open window and taking a seat on the small ledge, Ray nodded his assent.

Andy raised the flawless pot from the table, and drew it toward him like a newborn child. He turned the sphere slowly, admiring the way the sunlight moved across the textured surface, highlighting each glazed design in turn.

"Turtle, Wolf, and Bird. Water, Earth and Air." The slight sound of something sliding within the sealed urn could be heard above the murmur of traffic from outside. "What have we here, Ray? A treasure within a treasure? A prehistoric crackerjack surprise?" Andy beamed with delight, both at the beauty of the object in his hands and unabashed pleasure at his witticism.

He held the pot closer to his ear and rolled it side to side, his eyes round with happy wonder. Ray thought he looked like a kid on Christmas morning, trying to guess the contents of a beautifully wrapped gift. Andy carefully replaced the large pot and examined each of the others in turn. His initial excitement was still evident as he slowly set the last and smallest of the matched crockery on the glass table. He looked at them in silence for a few moments, palms on his knees. There was no question that he was impressed with these latest offerings. From the look on his face, Ray doubted the man would be able to walk out of the hotel room without them.

Andy slapped his knees with his hands, as if to break his reverie, and looked up at Ray.

"Okay, Ray, you've really outdone yourself this time. These pieces are just the kind of specimens I'm looking for. Which are you interested in selling?"

Chris Kluge

Ray had been waiting for the ritual to begin, and he smiled in-
wardly at Andy's coy question, as if Ray had any desire to keep
this outmoded cookware. But he played the game, keeping his disdain well hidden. These museum types had a whole different way
of negotiating, and Ray was anxious to learn their unique protocol;
he wanted to become adept in this new market arena, and besides,
these formalities were a lot easier to deal with than the dangerous
unpredictability of drug dealers.

"I'm interested in selling them all, Andy; as a set."

The man on the sofa nodded, an understanding smile on his
face. "I'm glad you feel that way, Ray. They belong together, with
someone who appreciates their beauty and who will care for them
properly. What amount were you looking for?" The dealer looked
up at Ray, an innocent, questioning look on his face.

Ray sat impassively on the windowsill, arms folded. "What are
you prepared to pay for them?" he asked back, not a trace of expression in his voice or eyes. Andy folded his hands over his knees,
his head cocked slightly to one side, gazing at the four clay forms
arrayed on the sunlit glass table. He was silent for a moment, then
looked directly at Ray, the carefree tone gone.

"Twenty thousand for all, in cash."

"Thirty" responded Ray, his voice conversational, relaxed.
Andy raised his eyebrows a little, shaking his head slightly, as if
he'd just heard something utterly incredible. He looked at the pots,
a pensive look on his face, then met Ray's blank eyes.

"Twenty-five, Ray, and please consider that my final offer."

There was no sense in making an issue on this one, thought
Ray. There would be other opportunities to negotiate, time still to
learn the subtleties of this new bartering forum. Besides, twenty
five thousand was more than he thought he'd realize from this deal.

"Done" said Ray, standing from the window seat and walking
to the sofa, extending his hand to the still-seated man. It was
Andy's turn to leave a hand hanging in space, but he rose from the
sofa and shook on the deal, a bemused grin on his face.

"Will you take a check?" He broke into a sardonic smile, being well aware of Ray's insistence on cash. He reached inside his linen coat and withdrew a tan leather billfold, from which he extracted a stack of currency. He carefully counted out fifty crisp five hundred dollar bills, fanning them out next to the largest of the pots on the sparkling glass of the coffee table.

Both men noted that he had counted out all the money he had in the billfold. The price had been set before their meeting.

Ray reached down to gather up the bills, sweeping them together like a stack of cards, and secreted them into a zippered interior pocket of his windbreaker, which was folded over a chair. He then retrieved a large gym bag from the closet by the bathroom door, and set it, open, on the sofa. He withdrew four plush towels, and proceeded to wrap up the smallest of the clay pieces. Andy silently joined him, taking the largest urn in his hands, briefly noting the sound coming from within before gently enclosing the clay within the terry cloth. Ray packed away the bundled pot, and started on the next.

"What do you suppose is in there?" he said, nodding at the large wad that Andy was placing in the bag.

"I've really no idea, but it's a fascinating mystery, isn't it? Might be a pebble or a dried piece of food; a dehydrated fish, perhaps, or a four thousand year-old summer squash. I suppose I'll have it x-rayed at some point. I think it gives the piece an exciting dimension, don't you?" Andy looked down at the soft packet, a serene look on his face. Ray nodded briefly, handing the next pot to him. He guessed that Andy would dispense this collection too quickly to probe the unknown contents of the urn. He knew he wasn't planning to keep these treasures for himself; he couldn't afford it. What the hell, thought Ray, he had his twenty-five thousand; he didn't give a damn if Andy lobbed it all out the open window and down onto the crowded streets below.

Having securely packed the last bundle in amongst the others, Andy zipped the gym bag shut. He hoisted the webbed shoulder strap over his shoulder, and adjusted the bag comfortably under his arm. He looked like any of the thousands of well-dressed business people seen every day on New York's streets, on their way from a business meeting to their daily workout, or vice versa. No one would give a second glance to yet another white man with a gym bag hanging off a well-tailored shoulder. He extended his hand once again, and this time Ray took it without pause.

"Nice doing business with you, Ray. Please call me if you have anything further to discuss. I'm sure you know I'm most interested in anything that may come your way."

"Sure thing, Andy, its a pleasure doing business with you, too. I'll give you a call as soon as something else comes along."

"I'm sure you will, Ray, I'm sure you will. Well, I've got some other appointments this morning, so I'll be going. Have a nice day."

Ray moved forward and opened the door to the hall, swinging the door wide as he stepped aside. "You have a nice day, too, Andy. I'll be in touch."

Andrew Sacks stepped out into the 30th floor hallway, looking first one way then another, as if he'd forgotten where the elevators were. He strode off down the hall without a backward glance, his footsteps silent on the heavy patterned carpeting, his walk confident and assured. Ray watched him for a moment, scanning all doors up and down before withdrawing into the room and shutting the door. Ray locked the door and threw the extra deadbolt, then went to the large, old-fashioned tile bathroom. Taking the fifty bills from the secret pocket of his windbreaker, he switched on the vanity light over the large porcelain sink and held each up to the bulb. He then turned one of the thick white faucet handles, the hot water one, and let a generous amount flow into the sink. He took two of the new bills, held them under the hot water, and then rubbed them briskly together. Holding them aloft, there was no smudging evident on either.

Apparently his friend Andy wasn't in the counterfeit business ... yet. Ray smiled at the irony of him and this upper class wimp gradually changing rolls; Ray learning the rituals and manners of this rarefied, cleaner world, and Andy moving toward the danger-ous side of things.

Gathering up the bills, Ray zipped them into the windbreaker, put the jacket on, and switched off the sink light. Walking out of the bathroom, he closed the window, returned and rearranged the slick magazines across the coffee table, and looked briefly around the spotless room. Seeing that all was in order, he touched the gun secreted in the small of his back, undid the locks on the door and let himself out into the hall. Looking up and down the empty corri-dor, he closed and locked the door, and walked briskly to the bank of elevators several doors away. He planned to be out of Manhattan before the noon rush hour. He wanted to get working on the next delivery. He knew Andy would be happy to see him again, and soon

Chapter 25 — *Market Day*

There was a stillness to the air, as if all things had suspended their activity, for just a moment, listening for something just over the horizon, just out of view: an imminent change in the atmosphere, a midsummer thunderstorm, perhaps. The sunlight was bright and flashed between the overhanging boughs, heavy with green leaves, that enclosed the wide, dirt road rolling beneath the wagon's wheels. The wooden carriage creaked as the wheels jolted over pebbles and dropped into the ruts and potholes of the well-traveled road. The two draft horses pulling the heavy load of people and hay kept their movements at a steady pace, their great heads focused on the road immediately ahead, lest they break the forward momentum established over the last few miles, and have to summon strength they might not possess to get the great weight moving again.

The three people perched high on the wooden bench lurched silently with each swaying motion of the wagon, covered heads lolling side to side, their faces impassive with fatigue. The driver, a man in a black frock coat and a broad-brimmed brown felt hat, fixed his expressionless gaze on the nodding ears of the draft horses, his large hands holding the reins loosely in his lap, one boot up on the foot break to ease the stiffness of the unyielding plank against his back. Next to him, a woman, her shoulders covered by a linen shawl, her shadowed face hooded by a large, white bonnet, sat with her hands crossed over a burlap sack of recently woven fabrics. At the end of the bench sat a young girl, bonneted like the older woman, but with a face less touched by shadow and fatigue. She, too, held a sack in her lap, but hers contained several slabs of homemade cheese, wrapped in an additional wet layer of fabric to ensure coolness from evaporation, even after an hour ride in the midsummer sun. The three hadn't exchanged any words for several miles. Like most families who worked, ate, cleaned, and slept together, they generally used language as a strategic method to coordinate their labors, and not as a source of entertainment. Their silence wasn't to be interpreted as anything approaching anger or boredom or insensitivity; they were simply too tired to make idle talk.

Up ahead, in a sky blue break in the oak leaf canopy, a white church spire slid into view, like a shingled mast on a schooner, a beacon of rest and rekindled hope to the surrounding farm families. The periodic tolling of its cast bronze bells cut through the loneliness and nightmares that occasionally festered among the isolated humans out in the wilderness, away from the more populated centers of commerce some miles to the east. Here, the community church signified a lot more than a weekly obligation to give thanks; to some, it was the only manifestation of "civilization," of order, and of good. Each week, its steadily chiming bells drew farmers and their families like moths to a light.

The young girl lifted her head to the passing branches above and let herself be mesmerized by the steady flickering of the sunlight piercing the leaves. That, combined with the gentle rocking motion of the wagon, seduced her into a nodding hypnosis. Her eyes drooped shut, and the sunlight continued to dance through them, drawing her deeper into slumber. All things swooned together for an instant, or an hour, until one leaf fluttered across her cheek, then one brushed her forehead, then another across her neck. She raised a desultory hand to swish them aside, only to intercept more in their downward spiral. Her sleep-numbed mind couldn't accept the thought of falling leaves in late July, and her eyes opened slightly to bear witness to this strange phenomena.

She beheld a blizzard of leaves, of varying shades of green and brown and orange, all in random flight between the blue sky and her eyes, blown as if by a thousand separate winds, with no apparent overriding direction. As more and more swirled by her, and some continued hitting her softly on her face and hands and hair, she realized they each were comprised of moving parts, and were, in fact, propelling themselves hither and yon, as there was no breeze to move them.

Her mind suddenly shifting into sharp focus by a surge of adrenaline, Connie's eyes opened wide to thousands of butterflies, swirling like confetti in a parade above, to the side, and under her. She gripped the sides of the hammock she was lying in, and quickly scanned her backyard, and saw that the air was filled with fluttering butterflies, in greens, and browns, and yellows and oranges. Never had she witnessed such a profusion of them before, and in all these colors! Afraid to move—and afraid to lie still— her heart raced at the benign terror of these thousands upon thousands of harmless insects, covering her plants, and trees and sky, causing the sunlight to flash through their translucent wings with a sickening frequency.

Finally, after some interminable time that might have been seconds or minutes, the intensity of the insect activity seemed to abate, the strobing of the sunlight became less frequent, and the oppressive sense of chaos less threatening. A few moments more, and the pulsating, flickering wave was definitely moving on, like a luminous, colorful cloud, although Connie could not ascertain if there was one overriding direction in which these thousands of creatures were moving toward or away from.

Her hands still gripping the woven rope sides of the hammock, her neck stiff with the unnoticed effort of holding her head, rock still, halfway off the pillow she had been asleep on, her whole body shaking with delayed fear.

"Jesus, Mary, and *JOSEPH!!*" she uttered with equal terror and relief, now that only a few lingering butterflies darted through the afternoon air. Swinging her feet to the ground, Connie pulled herself upright on the edge of the hammock, let out a long, slow breath, and allowed herself to break into loud, hysterical laughter, with tears of some strange cross between joy and sorrow cleansing the places just caressed by the insects.

Chapter 26 — *Unexpected Company*

A few hundred feet from the marsh's edge, up on a grassy rise, stood the Old Man's shack. A ramshackle, one-story, weather beaten hovel that blended, almost invisibly, into the surrounding landscape of unkempt honeysuckle, lilac, and juniper berry bushes, rusting farm implements and broken tools.

To one side of the house, disappearing in a tangle of tall grass and poison ivy, sat the skeletal remains of a 1955 "Vista-cruiser" two-door Mercury, its former shell pink paint job rusted to a red brown patina, giving the car the look of a discarded cicada husk. The passenger door was rusted shut for eternity, while the driver's door lay in the weeds. The fabric interior of the car had mildewed to a neutral gray color after years of rain, snow, and sun, and hung in tattered strips from the ceiling. The floorboards were covered with dead leaves, except where new, green grass sprouted from beneath the corroded metal body. This once-grand vehicle served as Blackie's doghouse; the front seat during the warm evenings of late spring and summer, and the more protected back seat during the frosty nights of late fall, and the freezing nights of winter.

On the opposite side of the house was a slant-roofed wooden shed, its gray, warped walls seemingly held together by a leafy coat of wild roses.

Inside the open door could be glimpsed a tangle of rakes, scythes, rope, and canvas. An old cane chair was placed directly inside the shed's opening, facing out; a workingman's gazebo, a rain watcher's paradise.

Between the car, the shed, the house, and the shoreline, scattered at random, were assorted projects, in various stages of development or abandonment: a cement mixer on its side, its spilled, hardened cargo permanently affixing it in that position; 2 whitewall tires, their wavering tread almost gone; a pile of rotting lumber, half-covered by a greasy tarp; a wicker baby carriage, with no wheels. Since no effort had been made during recent time to hold back the encroaching forest, these objects emerged from the tall grass and weeds like modern day Easter Island effigies. They looked more like sculpture than junk. At least that's what the old Man thought, whenever he remembered to look at them.

The house itself had once been the proud summer fishing camp for some "sport" from somewhere else, come out here to relive the American frontier dream for a few weeks each year. Like most fishing cabins, this one had been solidly constructed of rough-hewn lumber, with thick, insular log walls, a large, fieldstone fireplace, and a wide front porch to survey the surrounding countryside from. When the Old Man had claimed it, some 35 years ago, it had been home to a family of raccoons, and an occasional visiting black bear. Only slightly the worse for wear, the cabin had proved sound enough to require a minimum of patching and minor repair, before the Old Man was ready to move into his new home. The raccoons left immediately, though grudgingly, returning occasionally at night to harass the Old Man with their nocturnal acrobatics and chattering. The bear returned sporadically, hoping the new resident had given up life in the wild, but stopped coming after a few purposeful near misses from the Old Man's twelve-gauge, fired off at point blank range.

For the last thirty-five years, the cabin had slowly filled, inside and out, with whatever the Old Man decided had enough value to haul home. Its weathered exterior boasted several sets of bone-white deer antlers, a moldered bear hide, and several turtle shells, all nailed haphazardly to the dried wood. The cramped interior now resembled some strange museum of discarded cultural droppings, encompassing pretty much the previous ninety years of American Rural life.

One man's trash was another man's treasure, and the Old Man was happy in his home, surrounded by thirty-five years' accumulation of other people's cast-off possessions. There was a cotton mattress on a wooden bunk frame, dining table with seating for two (though one of the chairs could barely hold the weight of the books and magazines piled on the seat), a large wooden hutch, filled with yellowing SATURDAY EVENING POST magazines, and an ancient pot-bellied stove.

No one knew for certain where the Old Man came from. It just seemed he'd always been around, a familiar feature of the landscape, with his checked hunting shirt, long billed cap, and crooked grin. He made his way in the world by doing odd jobs for people, hauling trash, or clearing brush, mending old machinery. During the winter, he cut wood and poached enough game to keep himself fed. When the spring thaw melted the ice from the marsh's surface, he harvested fish, otters and turtles from its waters. As a solitary person, he was the subject of all kinds of wild gossip and speculation. All children assumed he was a cannibal at best, and gave him a wide berth. Those who took the time to converse with him found him eccentric but harmless. Like most shy people, the Old Man was most comfortable keeping his own company. Besides, a big, black dog, with the uninspired but functional name of "Blackie" always accompanied him.

Blackie was some unknown hybrid of Labrador, Mastiff, and whatever else was mating at the time. He had wandered out of the forest one day into the Old Man's camp, a lost puppy, with bleeding paws and deep scratches on his face. The Old Man had cleaned and mended him, and the two had been inseparable companions ever since. With years of running through the dense New Jersey woods, and swimming in the weed-choked marsh waters, Blackie had developed into a very strong animal, and was a dependable hunter and fighter. As far as the Old Man could tell, Blackie didn't know the meaning of the word retreat; regardless of the task or opponent, the dog would push forward, over, or through whatever was between it and what it had to do at that time. It bore several scars attesting to its fearlessness; a long, grey line running from under its left eye to the bridge of its nose, several calloused grooves along its neck, and a cross-hatch of scars along its lower rear left leg. This latter wound gave Blackie a nagging discomfort, especially when rain was imminent, and caused him to limp slightly after a full day of padding over the countryside.

The scar on Blackie's face was inflicted by the Ellsworth Sisters' Hereford bull, which had objected to the dog's presence in what it considered its private meadow. To Blackie's mind, the open field was a convenient way to bypass the county road en route to the forest, and was the private property of no one, certainly not that of an oversized dog with horns. After several snorting, dirt-tossing threats went unheeded by the massive creature, the bull had charged, but the dog had side-stepped at the last moment, and had managed a snapping bite at the enraged bull's hooves in the process. Turning swiftly, the huge animal had caught the dog's face with one of its twisted horns, and Blackie had had one more swipe at the beast's legs before deciding that whatever this big thing was, it was time to move on, and regroup for a later rematch. Of course, Blackie made it a point ever after to walk through the great bull's meadow when his business took him to the forest, and the huge creature would eye him sullenly from beneath the shade of a large oak, mindful of the dog's ability to evade its horns. Neither animal would admit defeat, and neither would dignify the other's presence with an open challenge. It was a standoff of mutual consent.

The fierce lacerations on Blackie's rear left leg were the signature of a particularly ornery snapping turtle that had become entangled in one of the Old Man's muskrat traps. Blackie had never seen a snapper up close before, and was curious about the hissing, flat, grey lump in the shallow waters of the marsh, tethered by the clamped jaws of the spring metal trap on one of its leathery claws. As the dog stepped around the partially submerged thing to sniff its backside, the ugly head shot out, snake-like, and seized Blackie's left rear leg in its jaws. Yelping in surprise and pain, Blackie tried to jump straight up in the air, but couldn't twist himself out of the viselike grip of the snapper. After floundering ineffectually in the water, Blackie decided to give what he'd got, and clamped his jaws around the turtle's out-stretched neck. For a long moment, both animals held each other, like some interlocking, angry puzzle, neither one able to move nor breath, the dog's snout being underwater, and the turtle's esophagus squeezed shut between Blackie's teeth. The two formed a bizarre frieze, motionless, except for the underwater movement of Blackie's blood mixing with the marsh water. The turtle tried to get a deeper bite on Blackie's leg, and in the moment it shifted its jaws, the dog withdrew its leg, released its grip from the thing's neck, and jumped well back from the beaked jaws before they could whip around and find something new to grip. Blackie withdrew to the water's edge with a profound understanding for the hitherto unknown creature hissing in the water. The vicious bite had almost crippled him, and thus served as a powerful lesson. Blackie had limped home, and had his wound bound up by the Old Man, who backtracked the dog's bloody trail to the snapper, dispatching it with one .22 long rifle slug through the back of its ugly head. Later that evening, Blackie was seated in the Old Man's cabin, sharing a candlelit feast of snapping turtle stew and sweet New Jersey corn, since the Old Man thought it amusing to have the dog dine on his tormentor, in regal backwoods style.

After that, Blackie never missed a chance to eat snapping turtle, though he retained his caution of living ones. Whenever he and the Old Man were floating on the marsh's waters, Blackie would look carefully for round, gray shapes beneath the water's surface, and when he saw them, he would grow excited with a mixture of hatred and hunger.

Down where the rock-strewn grass and weeds merged with the muck and cattails, two twisted, sun-warped planks joined land and water, meandering across this netherworld for twenty feet or so, held aloft by a series of rotting posts. This derelict set up served as the Old Man's dock, and he was just making his final approach from a morning's hunt, Blackie at his usual post in the bow, and the Old Man bent to the oars.

As the aluminum bow scraped against the side of one of the wooden posts, the whole catwalk shuddered. Blackie leapt confidently from the bow onto the walk, and padded his way across the boards and up on the sloping land, heading straight for some previously planned rendezvous in the woods behind the tool shed.

The Old Man, steadying himself with a dock post, gathered up the wet halyard and made the boat fast to the dock with a few half-hitches. He then collected the two dead snappers from the bottom of the boat and swung them gently onto the wooden plank. Hoisting himself from the boat, he bent down and tied the two nylon lines protruding from the turtles' hooked beaks together. He lifted the joined turtles, draped them over his right shoulder, like a pair of armored saddlebags, and walked over the trembling boards toward his home.

Just as he stepped from the wooden walkway onto the grassy embankment, he noticed something shiny to the left of his house, back behind some birches, just off the road; it looked like, yes, it was... a chromed roll bar, behind the cab of a midnight blue 4x4 pickup truck.

The Old Man froze in his tracks, motionless except for his eyes, which quickly scanned the breadth of his property, searching for something else out of order. He stood still, the dead turtles dripping marsh water down his shirt and growing heavier with each passing moment. He didn't recognize the truck, and never expected visitors. He cursed the distance between himself and his side by side twelve-gauge, propped just inside the front door. He stepped forward and was striding quickly toward his house when a bearded man stepped out of the Old Man's tool shed, and stood looking at him.

The Old Man slowed his walk, then turned to face the stranger. His grip tightened on the nylon line, and he felt his extremities grow light with adrenalin, readying himself for anything.

"Hello. Are you lost?" he asked of the stranger.

The man said nothing, just continued staring. From out of the corner of his eye, the Old Man now caught movement from the back of his house, and another white man stepped into a patch of sunlight just off the front porch.

Neither of the strangers spoke.

"Where are you fellows from?" continued the Old Man, his fear well concealed. The positions of the two made him feel too vulnerable, too exposed. They were over thirty feet apart, stood on higher ground, and were both strong looking men; add their years together and they were still younger than me, he thought.

"Nice turtles you got there, mister." said the one near the porch. He took a few steps forward after he spoke, and the one in front of the tool shed mimicked his movements. "You gonna make soup out of them?" he continued, now standing still, his arms at his sides, palms open.

The Old Man figured to swing the turtles at Porch Man, and hopefully get some serious punches and kicks in before Tool shed Man covered the distance between them. Damn— if only he had brought his gun with him!

"Yep, gonna boil these beauties for a day or so, add some carrots and potatoes, and make the best damn snapper stew any man ever sipped," he said, his smile not matching the dead cold of his eyes. He hoped they thought him a harmless fool, and would move on to wherever they came from or wherever they were going. He didn't care, just so long as they went.

"Say, Pop, we're looking for old Indian things. You know, like arrowheads, and carvings, and pottery... that kind of stuff. You ever see that kind of stuff around here?" asked the man near the porch, putting his hands nonchalantly in his back pockets, beginning to move again, circling slowly to the side, away from his silent partner.

"Indian things? There aren't any Indians around here." countered the Old Man, his grin still plastered protectively on his face. He knew by Porch Man's rehearsed movements that these two were as dangerous as he suspected. He put one foot slightly forward, shifting his weight to the back foot, readying himself to swing out the dead snappers like bolos. It was a long shot, but it was the only one he had, and he planned to make the most of it.

The other man, as if reading his mind, started to close the distance between them, moving steadily toward him from the shed. The Old Man was just beginning to lift the nylon cord off his shoulder when Porch Man's gaze shifted abruptly to the left of the Old Man, where Blackie had silently materialized from the brambles near the first black mud of the marsh. The big dog trotted over to the Old Man's side, and turned to face the two men, his head held high, his broad black face expressionless. The two intruders stopped dead in their tracks.

The Old Man silently exhaled his tension, and felt his whole body relax, as the balance of power swung back his way. He allowed his outward grimace to become a real smile, and continued the motion he had begun by lifting the turtles off his shoulder and lowering them to the ground.

"No, I don't think I've ever seen any Indian things like you're talking about. What made you think you'd find that sort of thing out here?"

Porch Man, standing motionless with his eyes fixed on the big dog, looked to his partner, then back at the Old Man.

"Oh, we heard there might be, you know, relics and things, out here by the marsh. A friend of ours found something out in these parts once. Right around here, as a matter of fact."

"You don't say? What did he find?" asked the Old Man, his head cocked slightly to one side.

"It was a pot, a clay pot, with red bands on it. He said there was lots more out this way, too."

The man near the tool shed stepped forward tentatively, and the black dog instantly countered by stepping out in front of the Old

Man a few feet, before resuming his impassive vigil. The man didn't advance any further.

"No, I'm sure your friend was mistaken about the location. He didn't find anything like that around here. All you'll find out here are snappers, snakes, and us two." The Old Man grinned as he spoke, motioning to the turtles, Blackie, and the marsh behind with a sweep of his arm.

"Well, I'd better get these into some boiling water or they won't be fit for anything but crayfish bait." He stooped slowly to pick up the two limp turtles from the grass, then straightened up with them hanging from his hand, a weapon once again. He started to walk slowly toward his house, and Blackie fell silently in step, walking beside him and slightly to the rear. The dog kept both men in view.

The two men, realizing their temporary advantage was lost, decided to withdraw gracefully. There was always tomorrow, or some moonless night.

"Maybe our friend was mistaken," offered Porch Man, backing up a few steps toward the parked truck in the birch shadows. "Maybe he meant somewhere else."

Tool shed Man had also tracked away from the Old Man and the big black dog, and was picking his way uncomfortably through some brambles toward the back of the house. He had undoubtedly decided that the tearing of the thorns was preferable to the teeth of the big dog.

The Old Man continued unopposed to his house, where he mounted his wooden steps, draped the turtles over the rough-barked porch railing, and stepped quickly through the screen door, to wrap his hands, finally, around the blued metal of his shotgun. In the darkness of his living room, he broke open the gun, saw the two brass casings protruding from the open barrels, "REMING-TON EXPRESS #OO BUCKSHOT" stamped in each, then snapped the metal together with a solid *thunk*. He didn't wish to confront them now. They hadn't, in fact, overtly threatened him. He just wanted them gone.

Holding the heavy shotgun at his side, he looked out through the screen door at Blackie, who hadn't moved from his designated stand at the bottom of the porch steps. The dog was looking off to the left, and the Old Man heard a truck engine crank over and rumble to life. After a moment, he heard the whine of the 4x4 backing its way through the thick brush that overgrew the road, until it found a turnaround clearing a ways back, stopped for a moment, clunked into first, accelerated slowly, into second, then faster, third, slightly faster still, until the sound of the engine was swallowed into the dense forest.

The Old Man opened the screen door, shotgun in hand, and stepped out on his porch. He stood for a moment, looking in the direction of the now imperceptible sound of the truck, then looked down at Blackie, who still sat at the ready, an onyx sphinx.

"Blackie, you are the best damn creature I've ever had the pleasure to meet! Tonight, my fine friend, you are going to dine on turtle stew by candlelight."

The big dog, alert to the exuberant tone of the Old Man's words, turned and looked at him. The Old Man could swear that Blackie had the slightest curl to his lips... as close to a smile as any dog could manage.

Chapter 27 — *A Gift From the Marsh*

Bobby always liked to pretend he was flying when he rode his bike alone, with the rushing air hitting his face, making his eyes squint, tugging at his shirt and pants, the summer bugs occasionally slapping him on the forehead. He pretended to fly now, as he flew along the Vorsted Road, gliding over the heat-smoothed tar, then bouncing over pebbles and potholes, his hands gripping the handlebars tightly whenever the bike took a hard jolt, then relaxing again, barely touching the rubber grips, keeping a light hold to let the bike's momentum steer itself down the familiar road.

The leaf-filled branches crosshatched the road with shadow, and Bobby pretended to smash through each black band, as if they were force fields of lurking evil that could not match his speed and power. He loved to ride like this, master of his own universe in the world he knew so well.

Up ahead was the bridge, and canal, and whatever incredible thing his traps had held for him. Bobby swung off his moving bike before it had stopped, hit the ground running, and came to stop with it just where the edge of the wooden bridge disappeared into the grassy earth of the road and bank. Propping his bike against the railing of the bridge, he stood suddenly still, thrilling in the change from rushing movement, wind and noise, to static silence. Silence, that is, except for the subdued noises of the forest and marsh all around. Beneath the bridge, the softly swirling water, stealing away from the vast, silent marsh, then bubbling and gurgling into the rushing canal; high up in the evergreens that marked the border of the forest, a solitary catbird sang its heart out, fending off its loneliness with staccato trills, melodious whistles, and beautiful cascading notes. Bobby marveled at all the bird calls in the catbird's repertoire: the scolding call of a blue jay, the mournful song of a whip-poor-will, a robin, even something sounding vaguely like a woodpecker drilling for grubs. Every so often, the mimic would begin its cycle of impersonations again. Bobby had always liked these grey cousins to the mockingbirds; he thought them underrated as true talents, given the clarity and beauty of their calls.

Somewhere, from deeper in the forest, a wood thrush delivered its unique song. The sound seemed to come from everywhere at the same time, filling the air with its subtle perfection. Bobby listened attentively, and so, apparently, did the catbird, for it had cut its recitation in mid-trill, yielding to the distinct musical phrases that emanated from the dark woods beyond. A brief cadence, a pause, a variation on the first phrase, silence, then a lilting, haunting string of notes, sounding as if the wood-thrush was giving a musical answer to its own question. It was a song as old as time, and it seemed to Bobby that he'd known that song even before he was born, so familiar did it sound. For a moment, that sequence of melodies was the only sound in the world. It was at once both beautiful and sad, plaintive and hopeful, a little song with no beginning, or middle, or end.

The wood thrush's soliloquy was suddenly interrupted as the catbird let forth an unbroken string of calls, one right after another—blue jay, starling, robin, warbler—without a pause for breath. Bobby couldn't imagine how so tiny a body could let loose with so much sound and air. The catbird's call brought Bobby back to the bridge, and the canal, and his waiting traps.

He leapt down the grassy bank to the stone blocks of the canal walls, slippery with moss and moisture, and gazed into the dark, clear, water. Light green grasses, rooted into the crevices of the stone blocks, waved gently beneath the flowing water, undulating in the steady current. Bobby could see light pebbles all the way down on the bottom of the canal channel, reflecting the sunlight that ricocheted through the moving water. Must be six feet deep, thought Bobby, looking for some object on the grassy bank to test his theory. He located a fist-sized rock, and, holding it briefly over the water, let it drop with a plop into the canal. He followed its gentle tumbling motion as it wavered toward the bottom. Suddenly, a shadowy form appeared, as if from nowhere, and struck at the tumbling sphere, knocking it off its meandering course a few inches. The form backed off, then followed the rock as it continued its fall through the water, finally coming to rest on the bottom.

As Bobby stared at the shadowy figure, he finally realized he was looking down at a good-sized bass, maybe a three or four-pounder that had mistaken his falling rock for a potential meal. The big fish hovered inches above the now dormant rock, its fins and gills fanning, making sure it was indeed inedible, before slowly cruising away from the decoy, and disappearing into the water's gloom.

Bobby followed the fish's movement until he could see it no more. His eyes then tracked back to something else that had caught his attention. There on the bottom, maybe one foot away from the rock he'd just dropped, lay a curiously shaped object that didn't look like the other rocks and vegetation on the bottom of the canal. Too many lumpy things to be a rock, thought Bobby, and its color didn't fit in either; it was light in parts, then dark, then light again...kind of layered. It seemed to be about the size of a toy horse...in fact, it looked kind of like a toy horse, or cow, or something. Bobby's curiosity was growing, and he now looked about the banks of the canal for a stick or vine or anything with which he could try and retrieve this submerged treasure. Unfortunately, he and Randy had used up almost all buoyant branches and deadfall during their frequent visits to this special place, the boys having used anything that could be turned by their imaginations into speedboats, barges, or ocean liners, careening down the swiftly flowing waters to the certain death waiting at the waterfall below.

Bobby looked once more into the deep, flowing water, down at the intriguing object, winking up at him from the canal bottom. With a little bit of fear, and a lot of excitement, Bobby decided that he had to have whatever that was down there, and that he had to dive down there to get it. He immediately started taking off his tee shirt, then his sneakers, socks, and dungarees. Hesitating for only a moment on the mossy rock, he closed his eyes and dove head first into the water.

The cold water shocked him, and he opened his eyes to try and pick out his submerged target. The fuzzy images beneath the water's surface were just barely identifiable to Bobby, and he could see the area he was interested in right below him. Kicking his legs furiously, he made for the bottom, his arms outstretched before him. The current was stronger than he'd expected, and he had to work his arms and legs harder than he'd imagined, just to stay near the bottom in the area he wanted to explore. His lungs were starting to feel tight, and he realized he'd have to find that thing soon or break for the surface without it. The sunlight danced crazily down there, off the stone walls of the canal, and off the multi-color pebbles on the bottom. There were other shadows down there, too, but Bobby didn't let himself think about those for now, about what those shadows might be, or what they might do to him. He grasped the bottom with both hands now, and kicked his legs for all he was worth, propelling himself along the bottom, grabbing things and discarding them if they felt too round, too small, or too large. His lungs were ready to burst, but he had to keep going, he couldn't give up and break away now. He was right near the thing, he was sure of it!

His hands closed on something that looked lighter than the surrounding objects, and he brought his other hand around the thing, feeling its shape. He brought whatever it was close to his wide open eyes, and thought he could see bands of color. This is it!!, he thought, swinging his legs under him, and kicking off from the bottom with all his might. He shot through the water's surface and exhaled, all in the same instant, and he filled his lungs with air, exhaled, and gulped in another lungful, before side-stroking toward the stone wall of the canal. He grabbed the slippery rock with one hand, and carefully deposited the object on top of the wall with the other, and hung there for a moment, too tired even to inspect his prize. After a few more measured breaths, Bobby struggled to swing himself up onto the rough-hewn rock, and finally lay on top of the wall, exhausted, his head resting inches from the object.

He was surprised to discover that what had looked like a small horse under water was, in fact, some kind of carved or hand-molded figurine, in the form of some kind of animal. It was about 5 inches long, had a rounded torso, and five protrusions: what appeared to be four arms or legs, and a round knob on a stalk, a head perhaps. The figurine was cream-yellow in color, with three dull red bands encircling it. Bobby noticed several small holes along the object's front, arranged in a wavering line. There was another hole on the opposite side of the torso.

Having recovered his breath, Bobby sat up on the wall, and hurriedly put on his shirt and dungarees. He then carefully picked up his sunken treasure, holding it close to his face. As he lifted it, water ran in tiny rivulets out of the holes, and Bobby shook it gently to empty it completely of canal water. Turning it over in his hands, he thought it resembled a very fat clown, with short, stubby arms and legs, and a tiny, pointed head. Since a little water remained inside the figurine, Bobby put one of the holes to his lips and blew into it, thinking to force any remaining water out of the remaining holes. A watery, piercing whistle exploded into the silent air, surprising Bobby so much it almost caused him to drop the object back into the canal. He abruptly pulled the little figurine away from his mouth and held it at arm's length, eyeing it with alarm. Bringing it tentatively back to his mouth, he blew a sharp breath into the hole again, and again a sharp whistle emitted from the stone.

More curious than ever, Bobby experimented with the other holes, covering them with his fingers, and piping short notes out of the little musical creature. The hollow figure was like an ocarina, capable of several, distinct tones. Bobby didn't hear a recognizable pattern to the tones his breath produced, nothing he could arrange into a familiar melody, like "Home on the Range," or "Jingle Bells." Bobby thought the notes sounded like they belonged together, but somewhat plaintive.

"Sounds like a whip-poor-will, grieving for its mate."

Bobby froze in mid-song, the figurine seemingly stuck to his mouth, his elbows locked in fear. So sudden and unexpected was the voice that, for a moment, Bobby didn't even think about the meaning of what was said. Slowly, he turned his head around to locate the source of the words. There, not ten feet away and halfway up the embankment, sat a large black dog, staring unabashedly at him.

Bobby's scalp puckered with fear. A sudden chill swept over his whole body as he realized how vulnerable he was to this unblinking, self-possessed animal that had managed to steal up on him silently, and who certainly could have attacked him without any forewarning. Bobby never felt so helpless in his whole life. Had this fierce-looking animal been the source of those spoken words? Bobby was thoroughly confused and frightened.

"Don't worry, he won't fuss with you. Just don't make any sudden moves toward him. If he thinks you're threatening him, he won't hesitate to threaten you right back. His name's 'Blackie,' and he's the best damn dog a man ever had the privilege to walk with."

Bobby's eyes shifted upward toward the source of these latest words. There, with arms crossed over the wooden railing of the bridge, stood a white-haired old man with a green and black checked hunting shirt, a long-billed baseball cap, and a crooked grin set among grey whiskers.

Bobby, still uncomfortable at being the unannounced object of two sets of alien eyes, was slightly relieved to find the human source for the spoken words. The black dog was plenty ominous enough without being possessed of human speech. It hadn't moved a muscle, and continued to eye Bobby with a detached calm, like a lion looking at a kitten. Unlike most other dogs that Bobby had ever seen, this one didn't wag its tail, or fawn, or loll its tongue in canine contentment. It possessed a confidence, a total lack of fear that precluded any show of dependency or submission. This dog exuded an almost human sense of self-possession that made it seem most un-doglike.

"Whatcha find there? Looks like an Indian whistle. Sounds like one, too. You don't play half bad, son. What's your name, if you don't mind my knowing."

Bobby had been counseled about talking to strangers, but, given the awkward circumstances, he decided that courtesy should prevail over caution.

"Bobby Mackay. What's yours?"

"Michael Van Door, but most people just call me 'Old Man.' I live over by the east cove, just a few hundred yards from here. I like to listen to the sound of the water moving under the bridge."

He wasn't sure why, but Bobby decided he could trust this grey-haired stranger. He relaxed a tiny bit.

"Will your dog come if I call him?" he asked tentatively.

"Only if he wants to," laughed the old man. "Go ahead, see if he's in a sociable frame of mind."

"Here, Blackie. Come here boy. I like dogs. I have one named 'Skipper', and we get along fine."

The big dog continued to look at Bobby, then abruptly stood up on all fours and began moving slowly down the embankment. Still feeling vulnerable, Bobby held out one arm, open palm up, offering himself for inspection. The dog came close enough to sniff the small hand, then moved closer to inspect the boy's face. Bobby felt the fear returning slightly, having the big, round, scarred face inches from his own. The dog's head was actually larger than Bobby's, and the animal must have outweighed him by forty to fifty pounds of solid muscle as well. Both Bobby and the dog knew who would have prevailed if a fight broke out. After a moment, however, the dog pushed his black face still closer, and licked Bobby squarely on the lips. So surprised and relieved was the boy that he broke out laughing and the man on the bridge joined right in.

"Oh, Blackie likes you, he does. He doesn't usually greet people like that. I'd say you've made yourself a friend, and believe me, that's a good friend to have."

Bobby slowly raised his arm and patted the big dog's head. Blackie tolerated this for a few seconds, then shifted its attention to the flowing waters of the canal, looking for something to snap from the water.

"How old is Blackie?" Bobby asked.

"Round about eight years. That's how long I've known him, anyhow."

"He's not like most other dogs, is he?"

"No son, Blackie's special. He's master of his own life, a slave to no one. He only tolerates me, I think, because I don't expect anything of him. If I go fishing or hunting, he might come along, and he might not. Sometimes, he goes into the woods, and doesn't come out for a few days, and looking none the worse for wear. Sometimes, I have to admit, I think he's the smartest person I ever met. And I've met a few. "Did you get your Indian whistle from the water, Bobby?"

"Yes, I just found it today."

"Well, there's plenty more old Indian treasure around here, believe me. Just keep your eyes open, and you'll find more than you'll know what to do with. If you practice blowing that whistle, you'll be able to imitate any bird you ever heard around these parts, and some you'll never hear anywhere."

"I've found me a few over the years, and I got so I could call in owls and crows at the same time, and have them fighting the hell out of each other as they met right over my head. I imagine the Indian that made that whistle could imitate the whole damn forest if he felt like it."

"Sometimes. late at night, especially in the deep cold of winter, I hear sounds that I can't tell if they're real or Indian-made. But that's what living alone will do to you."

Bobby listened to the old man with a trust he rarely felt with strangers. It seemed he already knew the old man from somewhere. There was something familiar about him, although he couldn't tell what. Anyhow, he enjoyed the sound of the old man's words.

"Well, I think I'll be moving along. I've got some traps to set out by the island. Do you have traps, Bobby?"

"Yes, I've got some for crayfish right over there" he pointed toward the cattails bending in the morning breeze a few yards down the canal. "My friend Randy and I caught three crayfish and a baby snapping turtle just last week" he said with obvious pride.

"Well, well, that's mighty good hunting, Bobby, mighty good indeed. I don't think I've caught three of anything in the thirty plus years I've survived out here. Well, son, you have a good day, and practice on that Indian whistle, now. I'll be listening for you. So long!"

"Good-bye, Mr. Van Door."

The old man had slipped from view. The big dog, having surveyed the entire length of the canal wall, continued past Bobby, walked purposefully up the embankment, and soon disappeared from view beyond the bridge.

Bobby looked at the place where it had topped the rise and vanished, not sure that all he had just seen and heard had been real or some kind of mirage. The only sound now was the soft movement of the water flowing past his feet, and the wood thrush singing its beautiful song from deep within the forest. Bobby didn't even try to mimic it on his Indian whistle.

Chapter 28 — Bobby's Dream

Bobby had pedaled home directly from the canal, his treasure wrapped securely in his rolled up shirt, strapped into the wire basket over his front wheel. He didn't stop for anything or anybody, not daring to risk losing or breaking the treasure he now possessed. When he got home, he ran into the house, dashed upstairs, and deposited his mysterious find under his pillow. He had then taken all his damp clothing and put them in the laundry hamper in his closet, and changed into dry clothes. Satisfied that no one had followed him home, and pleased that his mother was still at her job, Bobby retrieved the little ceramic creature from beneath his pillow, and laid it carefully on his bed. Still out of breath from his mad rush to get home from the marsh, Bobby sat with his chest heaving and his brow perspiring, looking down at the little object before him.

Picking it up and placing it to his lips, he blew softly into the hole on the thing's back, and produced a sustained, wavering tone. Placing his fingers alternately over the other holes, he continued to experiment with the range of sounds, piping little strings of notes into the quiet of his bedroom. At first the songs were soothing to him, as he followed the afternoon shadows across his bedroom wall, but restless images and thoughts distracted him after a time, and he began to feel a little feverish and achy. He stopped playing, and placed the stone whistle down on his bed stand. He was feeling increasingly sleepy and uncomfortable, and he decided to lay down

140

and close his eyes. Fully dressed, he pulled back the bedspread and curled up beneath it, feeling a chill.

He wasn't sure how long his eyes were closed, but he had the sensation of someone else in the room with him. The air seemed very warm and moist, and the far reaches of the room were cloaked in darkness. Things seemed at once far away and very close, like looking through the wrong end of a telescope, and perceiving things as tiny, although you knew they were right there next to you. The light was a golden orange, and flickered on the uneven ceiling. There seemed to be a subdued rhythmic clicking or rattling noise, just out of his field of vision. His limbs felt incredibly heavy, so heavy he couldn't move them, as was his head, which was steadily aching from within. Rivulets of perspiration flowed off his forehead, neck and chest, and his breathing was shallow and labored. The clicking had defined itself into a low chanting, which came from the area behind his head. A large shadow loomed on the rumpled wall to his left, and swayed slightly to the chanting noise. The outline of the shape wasn't familiar, although parts reminded Bobby of certain things; tree branches seemed to sprout from the top of the shadow, while the lower part looked like the silhouette of a person. Two sail-like shapes protruded from behind, and spiked points bristled from the area directly below the outline of sharp chin and beaked nose. The pirouetting, dancing shape, revealed on the ochre-red leathery wall, was performing something for Bobby's benefit, although his fevered mind couldn't hold any thought long enough to define what the thing was doing, other than bobbing in place.

The air was becoming very hot and damp, and actually burned as Bobby drew in short, gasping breaths. He tried to throw back the bedcover, but couldn't get his leaden arms to respond. His chest felt as if a great, wet weight had been placed on it, and he couldn't dislodge it. The shadow's movements became more agitated, and the chanting grew louder. The subdued, warm light started to flicker from darkness to light and back again, and a peculiar, smoky odor pervaded the close atmosphere. Bobby was drenched in his own sweat, and the salty water continued to flow off his body and collect beneath him where he lay. His mind was becoming more confused, with the dancing shadow, the chanting, the oppressive heat and wet. The very walls began to spin, and Bobby's eyes fluttered shut. A wave of black closed over him.

His shoulder was shaking, disturbing his sleep, reminding him how exhausted he felt. His hair was plastered wetly to his forehead, and the bedspread stank of his sweat.

"Bobby honey, wake up. Come on honey, wake up now. It's mommy, I'm home. You're having a bad dream, honey. It's okay now. I'm here."

He carefully opened his eyes to peek out from beneath the bedspread, into the twilight of his bedroom. He had no idea what time of day or night it was. The walls of his room were almost invisible, and he could see the sky out his window, a few stars emerging from the deep darkness beyond the black tree limbs. His mother's face was barely distinguishable in the gloom, perched on the edge of his bed like a vaguely familiar portrait. One hand was gently gripping his shoulder, and the other was resting on his stomach.

"Hmmm?" Bobby said, stirring slightly.

"Honey, you seem to have a fever. I got home about an hour ago, and came up here to check on your room and found you curled up in the dark, sound asleep. Just now I heard you cry out in your sleep....what happened, dear?"

Bobby looked at his mother vacantly, trying to remember what day it was, and why he was feeling so exhausted. His mind was drugged with sleep and fever, and his thoughts wouldn't stay still long enough to make words.

"Mom? What's going on....what did you say?"

"When did you go to bed, Bobby? I thought you were going to be at Randy's today. You seemed alright this morning when I left."

Bobby thought back, through the dream, to whenever it was he and Randy were meeting....no, he was at the canal alone this time, he had been on his bike, riding home fast, with something in his basket, something special....

He looked to his bedside, at the light-colored object resting on its side in the dim light. His hand reached out from under the bedspread, groping for the little figurine. His fingers closed around it, and he drew it to him under the covers.

"Bobby, what have you got there? May I see?" He hesitantly brought his hand out from under the cover, and offered the stone whistle to his mother. She took it gingerly in her hand, holding it where the hall light fell across it. "Where did you get this, Bobby?" she asked, turning it this way and that in the dim light.

"Its a whistle, Mom. Go ahead and make a noise."

She smiled tentatively, and brought it to her mouth. She gave a little puff, and the little creature chirped in the darkness.

"Well, well, so it is indeed, son. Where did this come from?"

Reconstructing the events of the day, Bobby remembered how he had ridden alone to the canal, and had seen the whistle glimmering from beneath the water.

"I found it, Mom. It was in the water, down at the canal, below the bridge." His mother looked from him to the object, then back at him again.

"How did you get it out of the water, Bobby?"

"I, well...." Bobby hesitated, realizing he had broken a cardinal rule of his mother's. He was never to go in the water without a grownup nearby.

"I kind of fell in the water, Mom, and then I saw this, and I just sort of reached down and got it."

Connie looked impassively at her son. She knew he was lying to her. But she also didn't want to make an issue of it at this time, while Bobby was obviously sick with some sort of flu.

"Bobby, you know I don't allow you to go swimming alone. Its very dangerous, and I couldn't help you if something happened to you. You know how that would make me feel, if you needed my help, and I couldn't help you, because I didn't know you needed my help?"

Bobby looked remorseful. "I'm sorry, Mom."

"I know you're sorry, dear, and I know you'll never go swimming without an adult present again. So let's forget it this time."

"Yeah, I won't ever go swimming without an adult again, Mom. I promise!"

"Thank you, dear. You are more important than anything, and I don't want anything to happen to you." She reached down and gave him a hug.

"Mom, do you still miss Dad?"

Her son's question caught her completely off guard, and she didn't reply for a moment. "Yes, of course I miss him, Bobby. Do you?"

"I guess so. I mean, I kind of remember him."

Connie let herself remember her husband's last months: how she had urged him to go to the doctor after his cough wouldn't go away, and how he had resisted for a few weeks. Then the tests, and the tests to confirm the first tests, and the finality of the results. It seemed like only a few weeks passed before her husband had ceased to be the person she had dated and married and shared a life with. So sudden, and unexpected, and irrevocable. Yes, she still missed him; there had been no time to say good-bye. One month they were a happily married couple, with only minor financial matters to occasionally worry about, and then their lives were turned upside down and inside out, and he was gone; a withered flower, never to bloom again.

"I guess you were just a bit too little to remember a lot about your Father, Bobby. He loved you very much. He spent all his free time with you. I think you two have a lot in common."

Connie patted her son's head, and smiled appreciatively at him. "I miss your Father very much, Bobby, but I've got you to remember him by, and that's enough for me. Now go back to sleep, my son, and let's see if you aren't all better by morning."

"Okay, Mom. Will you keep the door open?"

"Sure, son. We'll keep the door open and the hall light on all night."

"Good night, Mom."

"Good night, Bobby. Love you."

"Love you too, Mom."

Connie placed the little whistle on Bobby's nightstand, and quietly let herself out of his room. From the dresser came the soft bubbling of the aquarium pump, and the little shapes could be seen within, moving silently about their enclosed universe.

Chapter 29 — Driving West

The drive out from the city the following morning went pretty much as Professor Van Zandt had planned. By mid-morning, he had squared away all responsibilities for the next few days, and had no one else to account to. He had awakened to a radio weather report that called for light precipitation during the next few hours. By the time his aging Jeep was through the Lincoln Tunnel and heading west, the skies were dark, and the rains had begun.

Northwestern New Jersey, only forty miles from New York City, was, in many pleasant ways, forty years away from the densely populated metropolis ...still predominantly an area of small towns: tranquil islands of General Stores, churches, and backyard gardens among a sea of rolling farmland and forest.

With higher elevation than the lowlands to the east, the air was scrubbed by winds coming from the west, the skies a stunning blue. Bordered on its western boundary by the Delaware River, the vast hardwood forests of New Jersey merge with those of Eastern Pennsylvania, providing a seventy thousand square acre haven to countless whitetail deer, timber rattlers, beaver, coyote, and black bear.

With so much untouched by the modern world, the rich history of the area, both Indian and colonial, is very much alive, its past very much present; stone foundations of way stations and taverns were still visible along the Old Mine Road running through Stokes Forest, marking an early thruway for intrepid settlers, fearlessly pushing into the American wilderness.

Between some parts of the Kittatinny Mountains and the Poconos, a person might walk for several days with only the faint hum of an occasional passing aircraft to bring one back from the 17th century.

Many of the residents of the area were distant descendants of those early interlopers, and maintained a wary view of whatever mental fads were currently in vogue. Without being naïve to the rapid movement of the present, they weren't harnessed to it. While some landowners were cashing in on the housing needs fostered by the increasingly intrusive masses of people to the east, most "locals" chose to live their lives pretty much as their parents did.....keeping close to home, enjoying the space and quiet beauty around them....not feeling a need to keep pace with an ever-fast paced world.

After about an hour, the professor turned his jeep off Route 80, and onto Route 206 North. Another 25 minutes, and the wet road was winding through fields of corn and meadows dotted with black & white cows. He had read somewhere that, as recently as 50 years ago, dairy cows had outnumbered people in Sussex County. It wasn't hard to imagine, even with all the obvious home-building going on. There was still a lot of open space between those new, expensive homes, all in clusters, with typical development names like "Pheasant's Walk," and "Orchard Views"; Ironic, thought the professor, how developers always had to be so damn obvious with their feeble attempts at preserving in name what they had subdivided and destroyed in practice. He couldn't blame the farmers who had cashed in on the recent explosion in expensive housing demand. After a lifetime of pre-dawn chores, 16 hour work days, and unpredictable milk prices, who wouldn't jump at the chance to trade your address for a million dollar grub stake, and a well-earned retirement to Pennsylvania, Florida, or the golf courses of North Carolina?

Every few miles, another fresh produce stand would hiss by his open window in the rain, and the professor wondered, again, if he shouldn't stop and see what they had to offer. Finally, after passing by the fourth or fifth one (he'd really lost count by now...) he saw one up ahead through the rhythmically slapping wiper-blades of the jeep, and he down-shifted on the wet macadam to pull over.

A solitary figure, shapeless under a dark green rain poncho, stood within a frail wooden structure that looked to have served many years through every type of weather; pumpkins and cider in autumn, Christmas trees and wreathes in winter, vegetables in spring and summer. As the jeep rolled to a halt on the wet gravel in front of the stand, the hooded figure remained motionless behind rows of tomatoes, summer corn, and heads of lettuce. The professor swung open the door of the jeep, and walked over to the stand.

"Good morning. A real wet one, today, huh?" he called out cheerfully. The silent figure didn't return the greeting, but stood mute behind the rows of produce.

As the professor ducked under the wet wooden overhang of the stand, he noticed that the person within the poncho was a young woman, dark-complexioned, with long black hair. A beautifully fashioned woven bracelet around the youngster's right wrist marked her as a distant descendent of the region's earliest settlers, the Lenni Lenape.

"I would have thought it too early for corn," the professor bantered, admiring the plump, green ears arranged on the table.

"We've had a wet spring, and some crops have come up early," the young woman offered, her reserve dissipating a little.

"I'll take these six ears, please." The professor pointed out a half dozen large cornhusks on top of the mound as he withdrew his wallet from his denim coat. "That's quite a bracelet. Did you make it yourself?"

The young woman looked at him quizzically, assessing if the man was sincere in his praise, or just some old guy coming on to her. Deciding that the professor was sincere, the girl put the ears of corn in a brown paper bag and mumbled "I made it. That'll be three dollars, please."

"A friend of mine made me a bracelet like that once. He told me it was the same design that had been passed down through his family for as long as anybody could remember, and that people would recognize me for a member of his extended family, albeit a pale one, whenever I wore that bracelet."

The girl looked at the professor with interest now, first at his face, then down his arms to his wrists, one of which sported a woven bracelet. The youth looked back up at the professor's face, no longer with an aloof disdain, but with a guarded acceptance.

"My friend was right about the bracelet. Whenever I wear it, wherever I find myself, someone recognizes me by it. Thanks for the corn. Have a good day."

"Thank you. Hope you enjoy the corn," said the girl, as the professor walked back to his jeep, swung himself into the cab, and started the engine. He waved at her before accelerating onto the highway. As he headed up Route 206, he looked in his rearview at the hooded figure, standing motionless in the rain. The momentary feeling of familiarity he had enjoyed had vanished, and he was reminded of how insular these people were, and how little any outsider knew about them.

As the shiny black road snaked over the undulating earth before him, he marveled at the profusion of foliage all around. After several weeks or months of city existence, it was a wonderful experience to be surrounded by countless shades of greenery. The growth seemed to push in from all sides, crowding the thin ribbon of tar. And while the edges of the road were free of paper litter, all types of dead animals lay in various broken poses: skunks, ground hogs, birds, turtles, deer. Their twisted and squashed forms appeared on the horizon and passed by the rolling tires as predictably as mile markers, the smaller animals in the middle of the road and the bigger ones off to the side. Those that had perished a few days ago were bloated by decay, their limbs protruding straight out from their swollen bellies, laying on their sides or backs like grotesque parade floats fallen to earth. The smell of death lingered around the larger road kills, and swirled along with the professor's car for some distance after he passed them by.

Chapter 30 — A Message in Stone

After passing through several collections of antique stores, general stores, and gas stations that marked the centers of the small hamlets of Sussex County, Van Zandt sighted the low buildings of the community college up ahead. Pulling into the parking lot behind the science building, he got out and stretched his cramped limbs, before heading into the cool interior. Bob Ambrose's office was empty, so he headed directly to the lab at the end of the long cinderblock corridor.

Ben Haubrich and Bob Ambrose were at the far end of the lab, a large, red-brown slab of rock before them on one of the slate examining tables.

"You're early!" exclaimed Bob, looking up at his friend and the large clock on the wall. "I didn't expect you for another hour. How was the ride?"

"Fine, gentlemen, just fine." The professor smiled and nodded at Professor Haubrich, who returned his greeting with a wave. "Hello, John. Come inspect our puzzle."

Taking off his rain parka and placing it on an empty table, the professor joined the two men. He took off his glasses, wiped the moisture from them with his handkerchief, then put them back on and peered closely at the markings that covered the rock's surface.

"We took the liberty of doing a little preliminary house-cleaning, John. The markings were somewhat filled by packed earth. I think we've got all of them pretty well delineated."

The surface of the rock had been brushed free of dirt, and the carefully carved lines exposed. Van Zandt was excited. A dozen or so small figures, each about three inches high, were inscribed in a circle. The figures seemed to be running or dancing, and most were depicted holding a stick, or lance, in one hand. They were arranged symmetrically like numbers on a dial around a central decoration.

Bob pointed to the design at the center of the rock. "This item seems to be the featured attraction. What do you think?"

The professor's fingers traced the grooves at the stone's center.

"You're right, Bob. That's definitely the star of the show." The form looked like a child's drawing of a ladybug, with a high-domed body and four stick legs dropping straight down, and a circular head protruding from one end, and a stick tail emerging from the other. Scored into the rock among the figures and central form were various other short, squiggly lines, circles, and other shapes. Depicting .... what? thought the professor.

"Well, John, what do you think?" Bob asked, leaning on the table next to his friend. "Are we looking at a 10,000 year-old edition of the National Enquirer?"

Van Zandt laughed. "Well, I'm not sure whether it's a primitive scandal sheet, Bob, but I'd bet my Ph.D. that it's the real thing. Whatever the specific message is, it's safe to say it predates anything we'd be familiar with. This might have been somebody's way of whiling away the long winters of the last ice age, for all I know. I wouldn't suppose this rock was carried by glacier from somewhere else; the grinding motion would have obliterated the carving. I'd presume it was inscribed locally. You say it was unearthed not far from here?"

"Just about five miles north and west of here," said Haubrich. "Under about three feet of earth and stone."

"I'd like to have a look at the site. We might be able to discern if this thing was carved at that location, or was brought from elsewhere and buried. From your account of the unearthing of this thing, I'd be inclined to think it was carved while partially exposed, then covered with other rocks and earth."

"Who inscribed it?" asked Haubrich

"The people who inhabited this region before Scandinavian or European settlers are believed to have been migratory aborigines, thought to be originally from what is now Siberia. They wandered this way ahead of the last polar ice flow, following the herds of bison, mastodon, and other animals escaping the endless winter. As the ice flows retreated and the earth warmed up, those that migrated all the way to the eastern shores of our continent stayed on, gradually supplementing their hunted food with vegetables and other cultivated crops."

"There were various large cultures of peoples, known collectively, at least by Europeans, as the Lenapehoking. Within that general group, there were subgroups: Unami, Munsee, Unalachtigo. The names referred more to geographic location than to characteristics of these people. The group that predominated in this area, encompassing northwestern New Jersey, eastern Pennsylvania, and lower New York, were the Minisink Indians. If this petroglyph was created here, then I'd say our author was Minisink."

Professor Haubrich asked both men, "What is —was— this for"

Van Zandt nodded at his friend, inviting him to provide an answer.

"Well, the original settlers of this region didn't leave too many historical footprints for us, so it's difficult to know exactly why this was created. Except for some copper ornaments and pottery, most of their possessions were carved from wood, or sewn from animal skins, and so they decomposed back into the earth after a fairly short time. A carved, permanent document like this is very rare. My guess would be that this petroglyph is a record of a real or mythological event of some importance, and that, as such, it took on a totemic importance of its own... sort of like the tablets given to Moses with the ten commandments, or the Egyptian book of the Dead."

"So...," Professor Haubrich proposed, "...This stone might have been an object of worship to these Minisink Indians?"

Bob Ambrose nodded affirmatively. "Yes, its quite possible. Something this large, and this permanent, must have been quite important. These people hauled everything of value around with them. They didn't keep anything nonessential, and most of the tools they used probably needed replacing every few years. Before the Europeans introduced methods of working with raw iron to this continent, they relied on sharpened flint for arrow heads, shaped rocks for axes, animal bone for agricultural and other digging tools. Inevitably the flint would break, the wooden handles would decay, the leather bindings rot. They usually buried the possessions of a dead person with the corpse, thinking they'd need their things in the afterlife rather than passing a deceased's possessions on to the next of kin or whoever else might benefit from them. Except for very special totemic objects that might have been preserved in special circumstances, things weren't expected to outlast their original owner."

"Whatever inspired someone to record this event, or myth, must have had pretty powerful significance to the author of these markings. The carrying out and completion of the scribing invested this rock with a lot of totemic power.

Ben looked at the two other men. "So how rare a find is this rock?"

Picking up the history discussion from his friend, Professor Van Zandt continued..

"As far as archaeological records of early New Jersey wood-land Indians, I'd say very rare indeed. Given its scholarly significance, I'm sure there would be a healthy bidding war for posses-sion of it by any number of Native American museums, not to mention the fatter purses of private collectors."

Professor Haubrich looked down at the rock with a new re-spect.

"So, John, what do the drawings mean?" asked Ben.

"Lenni Lenape believed certain animals had special significance and power; the wolves, representing the power of the earth; the eagles, for their mastery of the air; turtles, for their ability to live in water, as well as on land. I think this central figure represents some sort of turtle....."

"The Lenape creation myth has a great flood engulfing the entire world, with a turtle rising to provide safety for many living things...... Their historical term for the North American Continent is 'turtle island'.... Many of the Minisink occupying what we know as New Jersey, parts of Pennsylvania, New York and Delaware, constituted the Turtle Clan."

"Ok, so this figure might represent a turtle....... so how might it interact with those surrounding it?"

"To the Lenni Lenape, every thing... every rock, every tree, every being, possessed a spirit, and every individual spirit was linked to the greater spirit of all by an intermediary... called *Manito*........ These *Manitos* might be nurturing, loving, playful.... or, just as likely.... they could be disruptive, a bringer of misfortune; malevolent.. a trickster. So a being of special powers, like a turtle, might manifest beauty, orderliness...... or... ugliness and disruption; chaos....

"Different sides of the same coin?" added Bob...

"Good luck.... bad luck........ fortune... misfortune....... same beliefs held by most of us so-called 'civilized' people," replied John.

"The overriding spirit of beauty and order was known as '*Kishelemukong*'. Its "'evil twin,' so to speak, the spirit behind those things vexing to humans... sickness, stinging insects, poisonous snakes and plants....was known as '*Mahtantu*'"....

"Ha!" exclaimed Prof Haubrich........ *Stinging Insects...Flies* as in ancient Hebrews' *Beelzebub*... also known as 'lord of the flies'! Fascinating parallel, John...."

"Really something, how these seemingly unconnected creation myths have so many common threads...." mused Professor Van Zandt.

"We all like to think of ourselves as 'The People'.... and all others as, well.... 'others,' as in 'not quite people'........

"Ok,.." interjected Bob Ambrose, "... so back to our stone here........ this central figure, which might be a turtle, could be a source of positive force, or an equally malevolent force..... the surrounding figures ... are they beckoning this force to provide them with power for their betterment... or are they keeping bad forces at bay?"

"Or," suggested Professor Haubrich, "are they beseeching a malevolent ally to help them prevail or fight off an enemy?"

"Complicated, isn't it?" remarked Van Zandt.

"The Lenni Lenape were well-respected among their fellow native American tribes. They were proud, fierce warriors when that was required, but also good mediators when conflicts arose between neighbors. They were referred to by others as *'the grandfathers'*... in part for their history and influence, but also for their deserved reputation as people of honor... *'Wulapeju.'*"

"Between the ancient time when they arrived on the eastern coast of the North American continent until the arrival of the first Europeans in the early 1600's, they had enjoyed a long time of stability and plentiful resources."

"They didn't need Sachems skilled in warfare as their past had sometimes required. They were more attuned to hunting meat than taking human slaves, and the woodlands they inhabited were rich in game, and fertile lands provided abundant crops of corn, squash, tobacco and berries. The seacoast held unlimited stocks of fish and mussels, and shells for making *Wampum*.

"However, certain European settlers saw them as a barrier to the settlement of the New World, and openly called for eradicating them, in any way possible. One early Dutch Governor of New Netherland, Willem Kieft, openly called for their extinction. During his administration around 1637, he levied a tax on them, en-

156

couraged Dutch settlers to let their domestic livestock feed on Indian crops, and finally sent an armed force into a Hackensack Indian settlement on Manhattan Island, in an area then called Pavonia, and slaughtered Indian women and children. Another Dutch group attacked an Indian plantation at Corlaer's Hook, bringing the heads of some of their victims back to their settlement at New Amsterdam. Actions like these provoked several local bands of Lenape Indians to retaliate by burning Dutch homes and killing livestock. The cycle of violence would then feed on itself, as the European settlers who coveted the Indian lands would then call for retaliation for these 'atrocities'. The inevitable dominance of the area by rapidly growing European settlements was accelerated by the introduction of various European diseases, such as small pox and syphilis, against which the Indians had no natural immunity. It is said that some Europeans purposefully infected Indian settlements with these and other infectious viruses, although no positive evidence exists to support these rumors. Call it homicide or accidental infection, once these European bacteria were passed to Indian settlements, the results were swift and catastrophic: whole villages sickened and died, the living unable to even bury their dead. The unburied corpses, fed on by wild animals and domesticated dogs, spread the plague to other animals and settlements, and the deadly bacterial links of infectious chain stretched further and further into the American wilderness."

"As much as 90% of the indigenous native population had been wiped out by the early 1800's... estimates of from 3 to 30 million souls gone after a little over a century of interaction with European immigrants."

"Depressingly familiar scenario in many parts of the world." observed Professor Haubrich.

Van Zandt continued... "If you'll permit me a wild guess, I'd say this petroglyph documents a prophesy, or perhaps a calling forth. of some Powerful Force, a Spirit, in a time of crisis."

Bob studied the central figure "Do you think this rock was carved during the last few centuries, then, in reaction to the Dutch and Swedish settlement of this area?"

"The rock might have been carved a few hundred years ago, or a few thousand years ago.," said Van Zandt. "I really can't say. If we go with my little scenario for the moment, we could have a Lenni Lenape Sachem recreating a formula and carving a new prescription into a found rock to call forth spiritual help. And I, for one, would like to get out into the fresh air, and go look at the site from whence our mysterious rock came."

"I'll pass," said Haubrich. "I've got a lot of work to do, and I've had enough of Evil-doers for one day."

"Suit yourself," replied Bob, as he and the professor headed out of the lab toward the parking lot, and a look backward in time.

Chapter 31 — *At the Digging Site*

After a brief car ride through the countryside, the Professor and Bob Ambrose arrived at the roadside excavation site where the petroglyph had recently been unearthed. As they came over a small rise, they saw a car with a US Forestry seal painted on the driver's door. A man in a park ranger's regulation pants, shirt and hat was standing by a recently dug mound of earth, his arms crossed, his face shrouded in concentration. He looked up briefly as the professor's jeep braked alongside his vehicle, but resumed his downward gaze almost immediately.

Bob and the professor walked toward the construction site. Bob greeted the Ranger.

"Hello Frank, hot enough for you?"

"Hello Bob. What brings you out in the sun on a day like today."

"Ranger Frank Smith, this is Professor John Van Zandt, a friend of mine." The Ranger nodded a greeting.

"I understand you're another 'rock detective' like my friend Bob, here."

"Yes, you could call us that. Bob invited me out to see a very interesting rock that was just unearthed from around here."

"So, there was something removed from here" nodded the ranger with a look of bemused skepticism, as he glanced at Bob, then down at the hole in the ground. "I'd heard from a friend at the county roads department that something interesting had been dug up, but by the time I was able to break off from my other obligations, someone had already made off with it."

Bob smiled sheepishly. "Ben Haubrich and I were worried somebody might want the rock for their trophy room, so we hightailed the trophy back to the community college for safe-keeping. Judging from what John here says, I'm glad we did."

The Ranger looked at Professor Van Zandt for a further explanation.

"Bob suspected he had an important geological record of our Sussex County predecessors, and he was right. The petroglyph appears to be genuine. If it is, it's an important find. We were hoping we could talk to the backhoe operator about his discovery. Is he around today?"

The Ranger answered. "I'm afraid you're a little too late to interview him. He was seriously injured this morning, right here."

"Injured?" exclaimed Bob. "How?"

"Snakebite," said the Ranger.

"Where did it occur?" asked Bob Ambrose.

"Right here." The Ranger pointed to the unearthed glacial boulders, shale and smaller stones, surrounding the hole in the ground.

"He was working his backhoe, and stopped to move something, and got bit by a large copperhead. He managed to get to his car, and drove himself to Newton Memorial Hospital. He about collapsed at the nurse's admitting station. Luckily for him he still had enough wits about him to tell them what happened. They keep plenty of antitoxin serum for timber rattler and copperhead bites at the hospital, especially during the summer and fall tourist season. I think he's going to make it. Damn lucky he was wearing his heavy leather work gloves, or that snake would have pumped more venom into him.

"Did anyone find the snake?' asked Bob.

"Don't ask me how, but he managed to kill the thing after it bit him on the hand. Its right there." The Ranger pointed to a spot only a few feet from the men's feet.

There on the ground, crumpled like a colorful bit of thick, twisted rope, was a four to five-foot copperhead, its pale mouth still open. Both men instinctively backed away, as they realized how well camouflaged the large, dusky-orange viper was, even in plain sight. Had it been alive, one of the men would surely have been bitten. The size of the reptile left little doubt about how severe the effect of a bite would have been.

"Wow, that is a big devil!" exclaimed Bob. "I didn't realize they could grow that long." The dead serpent's middle was as thick as the top of a Louisville Slugger, tapering to a blunt tail on one end and a flat, triangular-shaped head at the other.

Giving the copperhead a respectfully wide berth, Professor Van Zandt walked closer to the recently dug earth and peered down into the hole.

"How long ago you figure it was put there?" asked Bob, looking at the layers of sediment.

Van Zandt answered, all the while surveying the newly dug pit. "The last glacial sheets retreated some twelve thousand years ago, leaving these rounded boulders behind. Crushed earth was left behind to form a base for still more wind-blown dirt and seed to accumulate. The petroglyph could have been placed among these rocks before the end of the last ice age, or well after it."

The three men looked at the deep hole, and at the dark earth and light boulders that were reclaiming the void, even as they watched. Little cones of talus were sifting downward, and an occasional rock tumbled downward into the center of the depression.

Bob Ambrose broke the silence as he simultaneously slapped at the back of his leg and yelled, "Hey!" A large black horsefly, having taken a good bite out of the tender flesh behind Bob's knee, eluded his victim's flailing arm and buzzed confidently around to try the flesh of the man's back.

"This bastard's persistent!" Bob yelled, as he danced away from the pursuing fly, coming precariously near the deep hole.

"Damn, that S.O.B. must have some big choppers," said Bob, massaging the back of his leg, a bloody trickle beginning to travel down toward his shoe.

Even as he spoke, more horseflies had materialized, in search of any exposed flesh they could find. Professor Van Zandt was the next victim, as several large flies attached themselves to his head and neck, despite his attempts to slap them away with his hands.

The Ranger yelled for all to retreat to his car, as he swatted at several on his arm and chest.

The three men bolted for the vehicle, slamming the doors behind them and cranking up the windows at the same time.

Several large flies had already gathered on the windshield and the side windows, drawn to the warm food just within the glass.

Professor Van Zandt took his hand away from the bloodied side of his neck where one of the flies had enjoyed a quick meal.

The Ranger inspected several bloody spots on his khaki shirt. Apparently a mere cotton barrier didn't dissuade these particular horseflies.

"Very early for horseflies, and where did they come from so suddenly?" he wondered aloud.

Professor Van Zandt gingerly felt the wound on his neck, "Maybe they heard that some out-of-state meat was part of the buffet today."

Bob Ambrose looked at the hungry insects assembled on the car's windows. "I've never seen such aggressive ones... And, like Frank said, where in hell did they come from all of a sudden?"

"You aren't wearing some special cologne, are you John?" joked Bob.

"It's called Au de Horse Manure, Bob... I wanted to make sure I'd smell like you rural hicks."

Frank laughed, as he looked at the newly dug hole several yards from their temporary sanctuary. Van Zandt followed his gaze.

"Bob tells me there have been other discoveries of archeological interest of late."

"You mean stones, or Indian artifacts?" asked Frank.

"Indian artifacts" said the professor.

"Well, a fellow that lives out on the marsh, Mike Van Door, has come across a fair amount of arrowheads, pottery and even some ornaments over the years. And a friend of mine's ten year-old boy pulled a clay whistle out of the canal at the base of the marsh just the other day."

"Really? Would it be possible for me to get a look at the whistle while I'm here?" asked the professor. "Just to look at it, mind you. I'm not a collector or a dealer or anything."

Frank looked at Bob for reassurance of this stranger's intentions.

"I'll vouch for my friend's behavior, Frank." said Bob, smiling. "He gets out of line, I'll leave him tied up out here with these horseflies for a few hours."

The three men laughed.

"I'll talk to the boy's mother. If she doesn't mind, I imagine we can arrange something."

"Thank you, I'd really appreciate that."

The three looked at the hungry insects gathered beyond the car's windows.

Frank broke the silence.

"Well, gentlemen, horseflies or no horseflies, I've got to collect that big snake for safekeeping. That old copperhead can still do serious damage to anything unfortunate enough to step on it. I imagine the Police will want to know of its whereabouts as well, once they are notified by the Hospital about the backhoe operator."

From the rear seat, Professor Van Zandt spoke to his friend.

"Bob, I've seen enough for today. I'll race you to your car."

"You're on, John!" laughed Ambrose, his hand on the interior passenger door handle.

"Nice meeting you" said John, extending his hand from the back seat to the Ranger.

"Likewise. I'll let you know about the Indian whistle. Are you staying at Bob's?"

"Yes, at least until he throws me out."

"Okay, then.... Every man for himself!" shouted Bob, as the two men dashed into the warm afternoon air

Chris Kluge

Chapter 32 — Milking Time

The late afternoon sun still had more than hour before it would dip below the treetops, and it continued to warm the hillside where the Ellsworth sisters' cows grazed. The large creatures stood in a loose cluster, long necks descending, their great heads working restlessly over the grassy meadow. The distinct sound of clumps of grass being ripped from the ground filled the air, as each cow grabbed a mouthful and pulled, before shifting the green mass back to the grinding motion of their wide molars. It seemed they only chewed three or four times before dipping their heads again and cropping another few inches of fresh vegetation from the ground.

As they sheared away the grass directly in front of them, each cow would take a step or two, and begin clearing a new area. Small birds, fluttering among their shifting hooves, feasted on whatever insects had been evicted from the safety of the just-shorn grass. Beetles, cicadas, and grasshoppers scurried for safety, and the birds pounced, all the while dodging the cloven hooves and occasional torrent of waste from above.

The cows flicked their large ears and long tails at the countless gnats and other flying insects that swarmed like a twinkling cloud around them, back lit by the setting sun across the marsh's still surface.

One cow's grazing had taken her to the bottom of the hill, where the long grasses became cattails and marsh weed, and the

brown dirt liquefied to black mud. She always enjoyed the succu-
lent grass that shot up from the fertile shoreline, and her eager
mouth had pulled her to the very edge of the marsh.

The birds that grazed with her suddenly took flight.

A flash of movement under the marsh's surface hadn't quite
registered in her mind when the water in front of her suddenly exploded, and something grabbed her face, painfully clamping her
mouth shut. The bewildered cow tried to rear back, but whatever
had emerged from the marsh held her fast; her legs, scrambling for
purchase on the bank, slipped on the long, wet grass, and she felt
herself being drawn closer to the water. Her bulging eyes beheld
other eyes, inches from her own, and beyond them, something
broad and dark, merging with the water. The terrified cow tried to
bawl, but her sealed jaws wouldn't release her cry. She flopped
wildly on the sloping shoreline, and her legs buckled beneath her.
Despite her frantic efforts, she found herself being drawn closer
and closer to the muddied, roiling water. The pressure on her face
was increasing, and blood filled her eyes, blocking her vision. Her
muffled, impotent cries had her gasping for air. The splashing
muck now covered her jaw, now her clamped mouth and nose; now
her eyes. The foul water burned her throat and lungs as it was
gulped in between her smothered cries, and the panic-stricken animal redoubled its thrashings, desperately fighting to free itself
from the thing that held her down. The harder she fought, the
tighter the grip on her head, and a profound weakness was stealing
over her, and a black cloud gathered within her, becoming darker
and deeper, dulling her senses, and pain, and terror.

The cows grazing on the hill had been startled at the commotion at the water's edge, and had moved away and watched for a
time, their mouths working the grass, their tails and ears still flicking at the insects in the air. It was a curious sight for them to see;
the mud-covered cow, submerged save for her shuddering hind-
quarters, as if she were trying to drink the entire marsh dry. But
when she had stopped moving, and the waters became still, they
hardly noticed her slip gradually beneath the muddy, blood-swirled

water. It had all played out so quickly that they hardly had time to register her disappearance.

Warily, one by one, they were soon working their way back up the hill, in search of fresh grass, moving themselves closer to the buildings on the other side of the meadow. They could tell by the sun's slanting rays it would soon be milking time.

Chapter 33 — Van Zandt Visits Connie

The sound of two car doors slamming brought Connie from her kitchen to the front hall.

"Hello Frank" she called out, as she held the front screen door open to greet her friend and the archaeologist he had spoken about. The two men walked quickly across the grass and up onto the porch.

"Connie Mackay, I'd like you to meet Professor John Van Zandt."

"How do you do, Mrs. Mackay. Its kind of you to allow me to visit."

"Its just Connie Mackay, Professor. And I'm happy to meet you, too. Won't you please come in. It's much cooler, believe me!"

"Yes, thank you very much."

The two men followed Connie into the darkness of the front hall. It was significantly cooler inside the wainscoted walls of the old house. The professor took in the tastefully sparse furnishings that decorated the central hall. Connie led them through sliding pocket doors into a Victorian sitting room.

"Would either of you like anything to drink? Tea, coffee, a beer perhaps?"

"I'm off duty for the day, so I'd love a beer." said Frank, taking a seat by the front window.

"Professor?"

"John will do, and yes, I'll have a beer, too, thank you," said the Professor, still standing in the middle of the room.

"Please take a seat!" Connie laughed. I'll be right back with your beers."

"Nice place, huh?" offered Frank.

"Beautiful place. Very beautiful." agreed Van Zandt, looking all around the cozily appointed room. He walked over to a bookcase, its upper shelves filled with various objects that must have had special significance to Connie. On the top shelf stood a glass decanter, with a Dutch windmill etched into its polished side, a dark burgundy liquid within. A tiny pewter man, holding a long stemmed pipe and perched on a cork, smiled from the top of the decanter. A stuffed baby alligator, the sort that used to be for sale at every tacky roadside souvenir stand, stood uncertainly to one side, balancing precariously on its crooked legs and stuffed tail, its lips sewn forever in a toothy sneer.

The professor's eye went to a small yellow and ocher vessel alongside the other treasures. It was barely three inches tall, and only two inches in diameter. A blue jay feather protruded wistfully from the opening at the top. His hands behind his back, he leaned forward to peer closely at the little stone pot.

"I was given that by a relative some years back. She said it was made around here, many years ago."

The professor stood up and abruptly moved a few paces away from the bookcase, embarrassed to be seen inspecting a stranger's possessions so closely.

"Please, look all you want. I'm glad you're interested in it. My great aunt Netta would be pleased, too."

Connie walked across the floor and handed Van Zandt a tall glass of cold beer, then handed Frank one.

"Thank you, Connie," said the professor, taking his glass carefully, and turning to admire the small pot again. "This is a very lovely example of Minisink pottery, and I'm inclined to agree with your relative that it was made around here, perhaps several hundred or several thousand years ago."

"How can you tell?" asked Connie, standing next to him at the bookcase.

"These three reddish bands encircling the bowl were very characteristic decorations of the Minisinks. They favored the color red. They took iron scrapings from the abundant ore deposits around here, and ground them into a paste for coloring their earthenware. This subtle reddish tone resulted from the firing they subjected their pottery to."

"Did they use kilns?" asked Frank.

"Yes, though not the above-ground type that we're familiar with. They would dig out a deep pit in the earth, line it with hardened clay blocks, fill it with dried brush, and fire the entire lot. They would then add coals and recently molded clay vessels, ornaments, and what have you, and dump in more coals and wood fuel. They might continue for several days. After whatever amount of time suited them, they would grope within the smoldering heap and extract their now-glazed finery. After several years of hard use, they would use the cistern for storage of certain goods, or for the burial of one or more tribal members."

"My great aunt Netta used to talk about the 'Indian Holes' all around these parts. She talked about them almost as if they were alive, full of mystery and treasure."

"She wasn't far off the truth, Connie. This area was home to so many interconnected familial groups for so many thousands of years that there probably are many of these old cisterns, or "Indian Holes" as your great aunt called them, still undisturbed underneath a few feet or inches of topsoil and pine needles. And most of them would certainly be filled with what I would consider archaeological treasure, although you might think of it as prehistoric rubbish."

"Frank told me about the rock that was found. Was that from a cistern?"

"Not from what we could tell. There didn't seem to be any remnant of a collapsed cistern at the backhoe site, just naturally occurring glacial refuse, and some even older shale outcroppings. That's what makes the rock so intriguing, Connie. It's an unusual

Indian artifact, and it was buried in an unusual way. We really have a lot to learn from it, if we can decipher all it has to tell us."

"What do you think it means?" Connie moved to the sofa and sat down.

The Professor sipped reflectively at his beer, then continued. "From our preliminary study, I'd venture to say it tells about a particular spiritual being of Minisink mythology, a protective spirit, that was summoned to help the Indians in a time of crisis. Like most aboriginals, the Minisink believed the world was made up of good and bad energy, and that most of what we perceived in our daily lives was the result of the inevitable conflict of these forces, pushing back and forth. As is true for us modern types, things can go very well for a time, and then go awry, for no apparent reason. The Minisinks had a name for all the out-of-sync, negative happenings that could befall an otherwise honorable human.... *Mahtantu*. Poison plants, disease, accidents...."

"...And horseflies!" added Frank from the sofa.

"Yes, definitely horseflies!!" laughed the professor.

"Horseflies?" queried Connie, smiling at their laughter.

"Our investigation of the site where the big rock was found was curtailed because of some incredibly ferocious horseflies," explained Frank. "I've never seen so many so early in the summer."

"And with such big teeth," the professor grinned, rubbing the wound on his neck. "So anyhow," he continued, "*Mahtantu* was the personification of evil, of imbalance, and was often thought to take the form of a large animal."

"What type of large animals were there around here?" asked Connie.

"During the last Ice Age, there were wooly mammoths, giant cave bear, saber tooth cats, all kinds of large beasts. But during what we have taken to call the woodland period, the time that lasted right up to the European settlement, there were black bear, elk, panthers, and wolves. This *Mahtantu* force might manifest itself in anything big, strong and threatening.

"Weren't these Indians skilled hunters? Why would a big animal put dread in their hearts?" asked Connie.

"Have you ever camped out under the stars, far out in the wilderness, away from roads and telephone wires, where bears have the run of the land?"

"No, not really." Connie smiled, enjoying the mental imagery the professor shared.

"Well, after the campfire dies down, and the star-filled cold air has pushed you deep into your sleeping bag, and you hear something moving beyond the flickering shadows cast by the embers, that's when you will remember the fear of a big animal, no matter how many you've killed in the light of day."

"Why, Professor, you just about had me reaching for my six-shooter! Another second, and I would have been blasting bullet holes in my imitation Victorian wallpaper." The laughter of the three filled the room.

"Interestingly enough, of the little animistic imagery that has survived from the Minisink, a fair amount is of reptiles: serpents, toads, and turtles. It might be the inherent shape of these things was suggestive of the bowls, spoons, and long sticks they carved and cast. There was certainly as much abundant reptile life in this area one thousand to four hundred years ago as there is today."

"What would this spirit be protecting the Indians from?" asked Connie.

"Whatever they found threatening to their survival, their way of life: violent weather, incursions by alien nomadic tribes, lack of game or crop failures, sickness. We have to assume that there were occasional outbreaks of contagious disease in primeval America, unexplained illness, rashes, fever. The Indians had to make some sense of these mysterious contagions, and they might have called on their guardians to help them vanquish these invisible and powerful enemies. They were particularly unprepared to deal with European diseases, brought over by the Dutch and Swedish explorers... small pox, syphilis...."

"I thought that only the Plains Indians —the Sioux, the Comanche, those tribes— were infected by white diseases." said
Connie.

"You think that because you've been told that," suggested Van
Zandt. "Try and tell me everything you were ever told about the
Indians that lived among these very forests and lakes."

Connie began to speak, then stopped herself, her left hand held
in mid air, about to make a point. "Hmmm, let's see... I know! The
sale of Manhattan Island for twenty-four dollars!"

"Very good," encouraged Van Zandt, "What else?"

"Around here? In New Jersey?"

"Yes, right here, in New Jersey."

"Besides my little bit of family history, not much at all."

"Then you have heard more than most." continued Van Zandt.

"History is a very subjective scholarly art. Each age has its
champions, its dutiful reporters, who decide what will be talked
about, and passed along, and remembered of its time. Every subsequent age picks and chooses what it collectively decides to remember of those previous memories, and forgets what it wishes to
forget.

"In a perverse way, history is as much the product of what is
forgotten as much as the sum of what is remembered. There has
been very little information collected or disseminated about the
earliest Aboriginal settlers that preceded us in this area. For some
reason, our collective American imagination leap-frogged over the
Appalachian mountains a few generations ago, and focused on the
Sioux, the Blackfoot, and the Apache. Of course, by the time
Europeans were pouring into the vast regions of the western frontier of America, the Indians they encountered had nowhere else to
wander or escape to. And so they fought us, and harassed us, and
became forever embedded in our cultural consciousness as "savages," worthy of annihilation.

"The woodland Indians who greeted us from the dunes of
Sandy Hook, who had lived and died on this land for thousands of
years, soon became disenchanted with the avaricious ways of the

newcomers, and ceded what had been their "promised land," gradually moving westward, away from the intruders."

"That's a grim story, Professor." said Connie.

Frank spoke up from his seat by the fading sunlight. "Connie, tell the professor about your great-great-great in laws. I'll bet he'd be interested."

Connie smiled at Frank, but said nothing.

"If you'd like to tell me, I'm sure I'd be interested," assured Van Zandt.

"Well, I'll give you the ten-cent summary." agreed Connie, settling herself on the sofa, and reaching for the stack of documents on the floor.

"My relatives mingled pretty intimately with at least one native of these parts" began Connie. "In fact, I'm carrying a few Minisink genes myself."

"Really!" said the professor, genuinely interested.

"Yes. My great-great-great- or thereabouts grandmother had a child by an Indian prince, or so the story has been handed down."

"The Minisinks did recognize certain tribal members much as Europeans have Royalty. Did your great-great-and etcetera grandmother join an Indian tribe?" asked the Professor.

"I think it was more like 'Romeo and Juliet' than 'Priscilla Smith goes Native'," Connie joked. "The couple ran away together, but their parents interceded and split them apart. The Indian prince died soon after; a fever of some kind. The young girl, my great etcetera grandmother, bore a daughter out of wedlock. I don't think the young man lived to see his daughter.

And that's the story." concluded Connie.

"Tell John about 'The Gift', Connie," urged Frank.

"Of course! That's the best part," agreed Connie. "Well, the young Indian Prince was so smitten with this vision of Dutch virginity that he braved the wrath of his tribal elders, and procured for her some very special bracelets as a token of his Indian love."

"Why were they special?" asked John, settling onto the sofa.

"Apparently they were not your run-of-the-woods Indian trinkets, these bracelets. They were more like sacred talismans than decorative jewelry, and they were not the young Indian's to give; especially to some blond-haired, fair-skinned heathen! Had they known about it, The Tribal Oldsters would not have been amused."

"They didn't know about the amulets?"

"Apparently not," continued Connie. "The girl returned to her home, where her parents, to their mortification, soon realized she was pregnant,... and by a savage, to boot! So they kept her as secluded as possible, until she had her baby.

"Somehow, they learned of the young Indian's death. Perhaps the young mother tried to make contact with him, to let him know of their daughter, who knows.... Anyhow, she learned of her lover's death, by fever, some kind of disease, and she then and there vowed to never remove the bracelets he had given her, and never to love another man. And so, she raised her daughter with her parents' help, and never married, and never removed the bracelets. Until, so the story goes, she bequeathed them to her daughter on her deathbed, seventy years later.

"The bracelets made their way down through about five successive generations, until they were buried with my great aunt Tessie Hardin, back in 1912. At least, that's what various family documents lead me to believe."

"This is incredible!" enthused the Professor. "You should write this down."

"I've been thinking about doing just that" agreed Connie. "I've just recently been going through a lot of bits and pieces of my family's past, trying to make sense of some recent events in light of some things that happened long ago. It sure is fascinating to me, though I doubt that others would find it very interesting."

"Oh, I disagree!" countered Van Zandt. "I'm sure a lot of people would be fascinated by a recounting of the history of this area, as told through one family's point of view. There just isn't that much information available about the first encounters between the native Americans and the early settlers. So, the Indians never got their sacred amulets back?"

"Not until recently," Frank spoke up from the window seat.

"How do you mean?" asked Van Zandt.

Frank looked at Connie, as if he'd said something he shouldn't have. Connie looked back at him, smiling slightly, and then spoke to the professor.

"What Frank means is that somebody, or something, recently broke into the family crypt where Tessie and some of her kin were buried, and broke open all the coffins."

"That's terrible. I'm very sorry." offered the Professor. "There seems to be an increase in vandalism to crypts and headstones of late; almost like cemeteries, and death, are losing their meaning as sacred ground to more and more people. I presume whoever violated your family's tomb was looking for antique jewelry, and took everything, including the bracelets?"

Connie looked at Frank, silently granting him permission to speak for her.

"Not only the bracelets...." said Frank. "The grave robbers took Tessie's hands as well."

Van Zandt looked horrified. "Good Lord! Who would think there would be people like that out here?"

"We're not entirely convinced it was people," said Frank. "Might have been some kind of animal... we're just not sure what broke into the vault, at this point."

"There are a lot of criminal types actively pursuing Indian artifacts" offered Van Zandt. "The number of collectors in Native American objects is growing, and the demand for genuine artifacts has far outstripped available objects. Prices are soaring, and the types of criminals involved in the illicit procurement of artifacts have changed from amateur opportunists to professional criminals. Could it be possible that someone knew of your great aunt Tessie's bracelets, and hired someone to steal them?"

"I doubt that," countered Connie, "because I didn't know about these bracelets until about a week ago. These papers tell of them."

She picked up the collection of documents from where they were stacked near her feet. "I think I even know where they were from." She opened up the folded map from among the papers, and laid it between the Professor and the end of the sofa. Frank got up from his seat and looked down at the frayed paper.

"'Hendrika's Gift.'" the professor said, following Connie's finger to the small lettering that appeared in the middle of the blank portion of the paper. "Is this water?" he asked, looking at Connie and Frank in turn.

"Yes. At least, it is now," offered Frank. "This purportedly represents the Marsh in Stokes Forest as it looked several hundred years ago. That was a lime pit in the middle of a meadow, back then, before it was dammed up and buried under about a square mile of water."

"A lime pit?" asked the professor. "Do you know that lime is a natural preservative, and that anything non-organic buried in it will last almost indefinitely? Ancient peoples often buried their dead in lime, to preserve their appearance for the afterlife. A 2500 year-old Chinese empress was recently unearthed, and her skin was so well preserved it still had some elasticity.

"It may be that the lime pit that yielded those amulets held other things sacred to the local Indian tribes. It stands to reason that they would have a place to keep important things safe from harm; from weather and time and decomposition, as well as safe from other Indians. When was the Marsh flooded?"

"I've got a newspaper clipping somewhere.... here it is," said Connie, pulling a yellowed square of folded paper from among the other documents, which she carefully unfolded and placed alongside the map.

"This says the Marsh was flooded by some Dutch merchants over three hundred years ago."

The professor scanned the article, then looked back at the map.

"If we could locate that lime pit, I think we'd stand a reasonable chance of finding important clues as to how the early aboriginals lived in this area, thousands of years before Europeans first conceived of a New World." The professor looked at the map, and then up at Connie and her friend.

"My son Bobby found something in the marsh, just a few days ago; a small clay whistle, in the shape of a little animal or person. It's hard to tell which. Would you like to see it?"

"I'd love to see it, yes."

Connie promptly left the room. They could hear her footsteps taking the stairs two at a time, as she went to retrieve the little clay object from Bobby's nightstand. She soon returned, and carefully handed Professor Van Zandt the small figurine.

He gently took it in his hands and held it under the reading lamp beside the couch. The lightly glazed surface looked as if it had been fired only weeks past, rather than centuries ago. The three bands of ochre encircled the round middle section. The finger holes were finely finished; not rough, like a stick had been poked into the one-time pliant clay. A lot of care had been lavished on this graceful sculpture. It must have had great meaning to whoever carried it, thought Van Zandt. A piece of this flawless quality would be a treasured addition to any museum's collection. Smiling slightly, he handed the invaluable artifact back to Connie. He was glad it belonged to a ten year-old boy.

"Thank you for letting me look at your son's figurine. It's very lovely, and I'm sure he is very proud to have found it."

Connie looked at the little figure, then back at Van Zandt. "Do you know who made it?"

Van Zandt sat looking at the object, his left hand idly tapping his elbow as he tried to approximate its age.

"If that isn't the absolute best counterfeit I've ever encountered, I'd guess it to be of Minisink lineage, sculpted and fired right in this neighborhood; perhaps six hundred to a thousand years old, plus or minus another thousand or thereabouts. Specific enough?"

All three laughed at the professor's self-deprecating humor. "So you think it really is an Indian artifact?" asked Connie.

"Yes, Ma'am. From everything I can discern, that is an Indian artifact. A beautiful one, at that."

The three silently looked at the whistle-man, each trying to imagine the world from whence it came.

Chapter 34 — Connie and Bobby Explore the Marsh

The air was cool as Connie and Bobby unloaded the canoe from the rack atop her car. The first few times they'd transported the unwieldy craft after her husband's death had been a little diffi-cult, but she and Bobby had worked out a system, and it wasn't too hard for them anymore. Taking up fishing with Bobby after his fa-ther's death had been a necessary duty at first, but Connie enjoyed the quiet, exclusive time spent gliding over the waters with her son, and she had developed a real appreciation for the beauty of the marsh. She was even relearning to like fishing, not that she had avoided outdoor type activity all her life. As a girl, she had spent many an hour staring into ponds and lakes, trying to see through the sparkling surface to baited hooks beneath, waiting for that big strike. She had just drifted away from all that as she got older, and felt no need to intrude on the mysterious male rituals of father and son. When she had to take on fatherly duties, she just gave it her best effort, and she felt amply rewarded for it.

She and her son had worked out a pretty good paddling routine as well; Bobby sat in the bow, all the better to scout the waters for bass and pickerel, and Connie's "j" stroke contributed enough sta-bility to get them where they wanted to go and back. They always brought along two spinning rods, but hers was mostly for show. She enjoyed the Zen-like ritual of casting the various lures out over the water, but she didn't really care if anything mistook it for food or not. She was just along for the ride and shared moments with her boy.

Bobby had proudly shown her this secret spot where his friend Randy and he spent so much of their time; the canal, their traps, the wooden bridge. It reminded Connie of a poster from an art museum, so perfect were the juxtaposed man-made shapes of wood and stone, set against the profusion of plants and trees and water. It was a prefect launch site for marsh explorations.

Since her discovery of the ancient map, Connie's appreciation for this particular area had increased dramatically. Now, as she looked around, she could almost visualize the damming of the marsh waters, the placing of the stones for the canal and sluice gate. The newspaper article packed away with the map had put the construction of all this around the mid-1600's, over 300 hundred years ago. The Dutch merchants who had first imagined this and made it all happen must have had an iron will, thought Connie. Of course, they had utilized the brute strength of horses and men to give life to their vision, to reshape the wilderness; there had been no bulldozers or motor-driven vehicles to haul all the timber and masonry around.

As they pushed off from the shoreline onto the broad, smooth surface of the marsh, Connie looked down at the weed-covered bottom slipping beneath them.

The waters became deeper as the earth's surface gently sloped downward. Suddenly, Connie had the clearest vision of how all the ground below her had once been cultivated farmland, complete with tilled fields, stonewalls, wooden buildings. Families had lived entire lives tending their crops and livestock, braving the frontier loneliness, right down there, fifteen to twenty feet below her canoe's gliding hull! She even could imagine herself on a summer-dry hillside, looking up from gathering the hay crop to see a thin green wedge with a boy and a woman sitting in it, slipping silently overhead, suspended twenty feet in the air.

"Look, Mom, a heron." Bobby's voice cut her reverie short, and she looked to where he pointed, near the shoreline to their left;

a great blue heron, standing motionless in the water, crouched to minimize his feather-thin shadow as he stalked the small fish near the shoreline.

The sharp prow of the canoe silently cleaved the still waters, and Bobby kept a sharp watch for aquatic shadows among the lily pads. Through mutual consent, the two paddlers kept their talking to a minimum. They both thrilled at the idea of stealing up on the wildlife all around. Once they had seen what they thought was a black bear, feeding at the water's edge. Or at least, a black bear's rump; whatever it was had evidently seen or heard them first, and was crashing through some dense brush when they made their sighting. They never failed to glimpse something; a wild turkey, a snake, a deer.

Today, their objective was to seek out and capture a big pickerel that had revealed itself fleetingly to Bobby a few weeks ago, before he had caught his fever. Bobby and Randy had been trying to hook bluegills from the shore, and Randy had enticed one with a purple rubber worm, dangled from the bridge. As he started to reel it in, a monstrous pickerel rose from the depths and struck at it. The little fish, already terrified at being dragged toward shore by its lip, had seen the predator coming, and miraculously leapt out of the big fish's way.

Unfortunately, the sunfish's heroic efforts were in vain, because Randy was so dumbstruck at the other fish's appearance that he didn't help propel the little fish out of harm's way, and the pickerel twisted around in a flash and attacked again. Randy's line went slack, and he reeled in nothing but nylon line, neatly severed by razor-sharp teeth. Like any fisherman worth his tackle box, Bobby had thought of nothing else since the monster's brief appearance, and his entreaties for a fishing outing to Connie had been ceaseless. After a sufficient recovery time elapsed after his illness, she had relented. Bobby vowed that this day would be the monster pickerel's last.

The consensus had been to paddle to the island about a quarter mile out in the marsh, and ply the weed-choked waters surrounding it. They paddled with steady strokes, a light breeze keeping the insects to a minimum.

"Mom, let's head for that big rock over there." Connie followed her son's outstretched paddle to the southernmost point of their island destination. A large slate grey boulder protruded above the water, surrounded by floating lotus plants. A grove of birch trees, their small leaves rippling in the breeze, marked the island's boundary. "I'll bet that pickerel lives around there."

Amused, Connie did nothing to challenge her son's confident assumption. "Aye-aye, Captain. Full steam ahead."

Somewhere beneath them, Connie realized, was the site noted on the old map as "Hendrika's Gift," as well as the lime pit used by the Indians to prolong the fertility of their tillable soil, and perhaps to hold back the inevitable decay of all living things; to prolong the suppleness of leather, or to sustain the features of their dead. She wished she had brought the map with her, to try and reconcile what she saw today with what was documented then.

As they neared the island, the water changed from a blue-black to a mottled green and brown. The underwater vegetation was visible, and the lily pads were growing closer together, forming shadowed areas for predators to lurk.

"You go ahead and fish, Bobby. I'll just keep us on course."

Bobby shipped his paddle and picked up his spinning rod. A purple rubber worm wiggled at the end of the pole as the boy set up the spinning reel for his first cast. The graphite rod whipped forward and a silvery stream of nylon arced out over the water, shimmering like some spider's silk in the air, before floating down and disappearing into the marsh. Bobby had placed his lure among the protective vegetation around the big boulder, right where he thought the pickerel should be. He sat in the bow, motionless except for the alternating winding and twitching motion of his right wrist, as he did everything he could to make the purple impostor look alive. Slowly, steadily, he reeled in the line, while Connie kept the canoe on course with a minimum of paddling.

Bobby tried another cast, and then another, with no success.

"Maybe its too late in the morning for them," suggested his mother. "I think it's going to be pretty warm today, and perhaps they went to deeper, cooler waters."

"Let's go around the big rock, closer to the island" countered her son, quickly exchanging the rod for his paddle.

They worked together to pull the sleek canoe through the water. As they rounded the large boulder, they could see other, smaller boulders beyond, scattered in the water and on the shoreline. The rocks were all speckled with pale blue-green lichens, darker near the water, and bleached lighter toward the top. There were several large tree limbs protruding from the marsh; mementos of past wind and lightning storms. At the shoreline, erosion revealed how thin the soil's covering was, with pebbles and glacial rubble laying just below the grass and tree-covered surface. The past was never far away out here, thought Connie.

"Hey, look at the turtle!" cried Bobby, pointing to a felled tree that lay toppled between land and water, half of its massive trunk submerged. Connie located a black-shelled turtle, about five inches long, laying on the bark, warming in the sun. What appeared to be another grey-brown rock on the shoreline, right next to the tree, shifted slightly. A pointed head emerged slowly from beneath the "rock," and then Connie perceived the entire object for what it was: a flat, scalloped shell, with a large turtle barely fitting within it. The creature's flat head and long, ridged tail confirmed its identity. It was a snapper, and a big one.

"Bobby, look at that other turtle!"

"Where?"

"To the left of the little one, on the ground. See him? He's starting to move."

Bobby followed his mother's cue, and he saw the big turtle, its ugly head now frozen in mid-swing. They could see its eye watching them. After a moment, it began moving slowly toward the water — backwards. It was trying to sneak away before their very eyes.

"He's a monster!" cried Bobby. "Let's catch him!"

"Oh no you don't, son. We don't want to bother him. For one thing, we have nowhere to put him when we get home. He needs water. And, more importantly, we couldn't pick him up if we tried. He'd bite us!"

The two watched as the big reptile slowly dragged itself toward the safety of the water. Even as they did, Bobby saw another turtle, and then another. There were two more snappers, not quite the size of the first, but big enough to be impressive, on the other side of the log; both were sunning themselves on the bank, practically on top of each other. One had flesh that was almost the orange-yellow of a pumpkin, while the other was closer to the brown-grey of the big bruiser on the other side of the log.

"Wow, I never saw so many snappers in my whole life!" yelled Bobby, practically jumping out of the canoe with excitement.

"Neither have I," confessed Connie, stunned at how the large creatures had blended so perfectly with the narrow border between land and water. It was just like in scary dreams, she thought, where a lifeless landscape slowly reveals camouflaged snakes, or toads, or something equally repulsive.

The biggest of the three snappers had started easing its heavy bulk into the water; in seconds it had slipped beneath the surface without a trace. The other two, sensing the intruders floating beyond the shore, also started a slow motion disappearing act, heading toward the water with a methodical care that bespoke a strategic intelligence; if not for reason, then at least for survival. Connie and Bobby watched in amazement as all three creatures vanished into the environment like prehistoric ghosts: at first they were invisible; then they magically appeared; then they were gone. Now you see them, now you don't.

"Let's explore the island, Mom." Bobby was already paddling toward the birch-lined shore, not even waiting for a response. Connie was content to see Bobby happy, and she quickly acquiesced.

"Okay by me, but let's watch where we step."

They brought the canoe up on the beach and tied the bowline to a small tree. Bobby watched the water for a time, hoping for a return of the snappers. Connie knew they wouldn't surface at this spot for a while, and she finally convinced her eager son to abandon his vigil. The sun was out, and the light breeze stirred the birch leaves enough to provide a pleasant rustling sound. The ground was covered in dried foliage, and Connie was reminded of autumn afternoons as she and Bobby shuffled through them. She guessed the size of the island to be a few acres, at least. Beside the birches, there were maple and oak trees, and some sumac, too. Huge, lichen-covered boulders lay scattered about where they had been left behind by the last retreating ice flows, more than 12,000 years ago.

Connie walked up to a particularly massive one. It had a large, flat surface, and it gradually sloped upward, like a giant wedge. Connie place one sneaker on a part close to the ground and hoisted herself up, and walked on all fours up the incline, until she reached the uppermost portion. She straddled the ridge, placing her palms on its rough surface; it was warm from the sun. She kept her hands there, like some faith healer, trying to absorb all that the rock had been mute witness to during the last 120 centuries. The warmth of the rock and the sun and the light breeze moving through the leaves, all combined to infuse her with a great peace; a sense that all was right, at this moment, in this place. She felt a weight lift off her that had been bearing down ever since—ever since her husband's death. There, she said the word in her mind... death. He was dead, he wasn't coming back, and maybe— just maybe—it was going to be okay.

Enjoying this newfound serenity, she closed her eyes for a few moments, and let her mind disengage from its usual worry. After a time she opened them and looked around. She was on the highest point of elevation for a half-mile or so. The trees and brush that immediately surrounded her gave way to the waters of the marsh. She remembered the name "Flat rock" from the ancient map; she was sitting on that very point depicted. No doubt about it; this was the largest rock on the island, and its vaguely triangular shape was unique to anything else within sight. Connie looked south, toward the dam and the woods beyond. She realized that the other spot noted on the map, the "Lime Pit," had to be straight south about fifty yards out into the marsh, and twenty feet straight down. She thought she could almost see the exact spot on the sun-sparkling waters of the marsh where the spot marked "Hendrika's Gift" was, too. It was practically in the same place as the lime pit. She felt like getting in the canoe and heading out there, right away, lest it disappear for another three hundred years before she could ascertain its exact location, and what it meant to her long-dead relatives.

"Hey Mom, come over here." Bobby's voiced sounded from beyond the big rock, somewhere near the middle of the island.

"I'm coming" she answered, turning her face briefly toward the sun, eyes closed, a quiet smile on her face. "I'm coming, Bobby" as she let herself off the warm boulder and followed its curving surface around, ducking to avoid a branch, then following a narrow path into the brush. Her son was pushing a charred log from where it lay within a circle of round stones, raising a little cloud of white-grey ash as he did so.

"Look Mom. A campfire. Somebody's been living here."

Connie joined her son in the small clearing. She thought it was just about in the center of the island, with dense cover all around. A good place for a camp, protected on all sides from wind, with a few large boulders to hide under in bad weather. Two in particular jutted out from the ground at angles steep enough to form small aboveground shelters. Bobby stood in the center of the clearing, poking at a small mound of charred wood and ash with a stick. A loose circle of stones, also charred, surrounded the burned wood. There had been a small fire, but there was no indication of how long ago. A cardinal called from somewhere among the birch trees that ringed the clearing and hid the area from view.

"Maybe Indians left this fire, Mom." Bobby spoke with an authority that Connie found amusing. Kids always delivered their conjectures with such confidence, she thought. They haven't been beaten down yet, so they still respect their own thinking.

"Well, if they did, I think it was a long time ago, Bobby. Remember how Frank was saying they moved away several hundred years ago?"

"Yeah, but they could come back to visit, you now. Besides, this is a perfect spot for them to camp in."

She didn't have a ready answer to his common-sense response, so she just shrugged her shoulders and gave him a "maybe" look. Scanning the ground, she came across some thin pieces of stone. She stooped to pick one up and examined it. It appeared to be a fractured shard. There were little chips broken out of it, leaving a fairly sharp edge. She ran her thumb over the uneven ridge, and noted the thin white line on her skin where the stone had begun to cut through her flesh.

"Hey Mom, look at this."

She looked over to where her son stood, near the edge of the clearing. The object of his interest appeared to be an inanimate mound of brown, mossy rock.

Connie began walking toward Bobby, who had begun to prod the object with a large stick he had picked up. In what seemed like an instant, the rock had spun around to face Bobby, a prehistoric head protruding from under the mossy covering. A sharp hissing noise, like air escaping from an old tire, filled the clearing.

"Bobby, get away from there!!" The sudden urgency and intensity of her voice cut through her son's excitement, and he drew back.

Connie moved to her son quickly, making a cautious arc around the fierce lump on the ground.

"Holy cow, mom, look at that big turtle!!" cried Bobby, fairly dancing in place with excitement. Connie stood at her son's side and took the large stick from his hand, holding it in front of them both, sweeping it back and forth in a protective arc. The reptile faced them, its mouth open, the flat head tracking back and forth with the movement of the stick.

It looked to be about two feet in length, head to tail. A flat, scalloped shell, mostly covered in moss and mud, barely covered its back. Unlike other turtles, whose shell provided important defensive protection against predators, this thing's carapace seemed to ride on its back like a too-small coat. The big, ugly thing couldn't have drawn its hideous head, sharp-clawed feet, and long, alligator-like tail under the little shell if it had to. But of course, thought Connie; it didn't have to retreat. Something that prehistoric, that mean looking, with its powerful hooked-beak jaws, would rarely find itself in a defensive position. It seemed created to attack. It looked so evil, she thought, the Devil himself wouldn't pick a fight with it!

The turtle's tiny, star-patterned eyes seemed to peer at her malevolently, the partially opened beak ready to strike at anything within reach. Its long claws seemed to dig deeper into the earth, as it positioned itself against the two humans.

It looked absolutely disgusting, thought Connie. There's nothing whatsoever attractive about this slime-covered, moss-backed creature from hell... it was, without a doubt, the closest thing imaginable to a living, breathing dinosaur—No! Dragon!—that Connie had ever seen in her thirty-seven years.

Fascinated, she took the large stick and cautiously approached the creature, circling around it. She had the strange urge to touch it, to test it, to see if something so hideous could be real.

Keeping herself well away from the thing, she gently prodded the back of its shell.....

Suddenly, with a loud hissssss the torpid-looking thing extended its limbs and snapped its shell fully off the ground, like a bizarre jack-in-the-box. It scuttled crab-like around with remarkable agility and speed, clamping its jaws on the extended stick before Connie had a chance to recover it.

She shrieked in surprise, dropping the stick in her alarm. "Good God Almighty!!" she yelled, "That thing's fast!!"

She had no idea something so squat and cumbersome-looking could move like a lizard on a hot rock. It stood there in the clearing, an armored dragon on stilts, serrated mouth gripping the stick like a bear trap. Connie resumed her place by Bobby's side, deciding distance was her best defense for now.

A noise from the perimeter made her look away, just in time to see a large black dog trot forward into the clearing and grab the free end of the stick in its mouth. She grabbed her son protectively and pulled them both away from this sudden intruder.

The big dog gave a sharp tug and jerked the vicious reptile forward, then pushed as hard in the opposite direction. The ugly thing's limbs remained locked in position, and it held its ground. The dog then started to circle around, twisting the long neck of the turtle, but the snapper just tracked the big dog, a hub turning with the spoke of wood, its fierce eyes unblinking. Connie gripped her son tighter, terrified that the canine would tire of the reptile and lunge at her and Bobby. She began looking around for another heavy stick.

"Hey, I know that dog," her son said reassuringly. "That's Blackie, Mr. Van Door's dog!"

A voice from the woods called out. "Blackie! Hold off there!" A grey-bearded man stepped from the woods and stood in a patch of sun, his grizzled face shielded by the long billed cap on his head. "Blackie! Drop the stick!"

The dog stopped it's circling, but it didn't relinquish the stick. The two creatures stood in their tracks, connected by the length of wood. Connie's eyes widened further at this stranger's sudden appearance. She had thought they were completely alone, and she felt even more vulnerable than before.

"Please don't be frightened, Ma'am, Blackie won't do you any harm, will he Bobby?"

Connie looked at her son and back at the stranger who somehow knew his name. "No, Mom, he won't. Mom, this is Mr. Van Door, and that's his dog Blackie."

"How do you do, Ma'am." said Mike, touching the greasy bill of his cap. "Blackie and I had the pleasure of meeting your son a few weeks ago over by the bridge. I'm Mike van Door, and I live a few hundred yards from here. Pleased to make your acquaintance."

Connie was still alarmed, but she somehow believed this old man's reassurances about his dog. She remained cautious, however. No need to fully trust this stranger. She was out of sight of land, and he definitely had the advantage.

"How do you do, Mr. Van Door. I'm Connie Mackay. Bobby and I were just out exploring when we came upon that turtle."

The snapper hadn't moved a muscle. It was still on full alert at the end of the stick, which was held securely by the large dog.

"That's a good-sized one, all right. I'll put him at fifteen pounds, all stinking two feet of him. Do you like turtle stew?" he asked suddenly, looking at the mother and son.

"I don't think I've ever had it." replied Connie.

"Well, you should try it sometime," continued the Old Man. "It's mighty nourishing, and lasts long, too. It's best when you boil them live, of course. Otherwise its a struggle getting them out of their shell."

Connie looked at the heavy creature on the ground, finding it impossible to imagine a pot big enough to hold a dead one, much less one being boiled alive.

"How, exactly, do you get one of those into a pot of boiling water?" she asked incredulously.

"Quickly!" laughed the Old Man. Connie and Bobby laughed with him.

"They're mighty tough critters, and they don't give up for nothing. I dressed one out a few years back, dropped its heart on the ground, and damned if it didn't keep pumping for another 30 minutes, laying there in the dust! Oh yes, they are mighty belligerent creatures, yes indeed. The only way to pick one up is by the tail. Watch."

He walked toward the reptile, which eyed his approach angrily as it gripped the stick. With a swift grab he had the long tail in his hand, and he hoisted the creature off the ground, holding it well away from his body. For a moment the man, the turtle and the dog were all connected, but the stick fell to the ground as the creature extended its obscene neck around and tried to bite at the hand gripping its tail. It couldn't reach that far, and it tried first one way and then another in a futile attempt to free itself from the man's grasp. Its extended legs waved in the air, sunlight flashing off the wicked claws groping for purchase. The dog had also dropped the stick, and stood alertly eyeing the wriggling reptile.

"See how he tries to get a grip on me? Once they get you they never let go. You cut his head off, he'd still hold on; like a rattle-snake. That's the best way to kill them, actually; let 'em get a grip on something, a porch railing, a fence post, let 'em stretch their neck way out, and sssssssss," he made a slicing motion in the air with his free hand, "cut their throats and let 'em bleed to death. You come to my house sometime, I'll show you a snapper's head attached to my railing he's been biting on for two years, now!" Mike laughed out loud, still amused at the dried head whenever he passed it by. Connie didn't join in his laughter, finding the image more disturbing than humorous.

"Will you kill that one?" asked Connie, her arm around Bobby's shoulder.

Seeing the worried look in her eye, Mike decided to let this meal walk. He had traps set out on the marsh, and he liked this woman and her son. He could see they weren't used to death.

"Since this is your first visit to the island, we'll celebrate by letting this fellow rejoin his mates." Mike lowered the turtle to the ground, and dropped his hold just before the front claws found purchase. The thing circled around, trying to face the man and the dog at the same time. Finding it impossible, it backed slowly toward the edge of the clearing, and the protective cover to be found there.

All watched as it disappeared, backwards, into the under-growth, its tiny eyes watching all the time. The dog did not follow, as if it knew this turtle had won a temporary pardon.

"How big can they get?" asked Bobby.

"I've seen them three feet across the carapace. Some say they can get bigger still. If they live to be two years, they'll live to be a hundred. They don't have much to worry about except old fools like me and motor vehicles."

"Motor vehicles?" asked Bobby.

"They get mashed every so often by trucks and cars when they cross the road," answered the old man.

"They certainly are ancient looking; prehistoric, like dinosaurs." said Connie.

"They haven't changed much, not like the rest of us." continued Mike. "No reason to. Besides, who's gonna tell them to?" They all laughed.

"Did the Indians use them for food?" Connie asked.

"They did indeed, even though the people around here worshipped them as well. Turtles were important critters back them. Not like today, where nobody thinks of them at all, except when they run one over. Big snappers like that fellow we just admired were held in high regard. Their shells were used as ornaments, special serving bowls, medicine mixers, anything for important events."

"Where did you learn all this Indian lore from?" asked Connie.

"I just learned it from here and there. You learn a lot living out here on the marsh, you keep your eyes and ears open."

"What was this?" Connie handed the small chipped stone shard to the old man. He took it and held it close to his eyes.

"This is what was left over when somebody formed an arrow head or a spear point. You look closely, you'll find bits of this all over this part of the country. It's shale. It's what everybody's been standing on around here for the last million years or so. Makes a good sharp edge, too." He drew the stone shard along the back of his hand. It cut away a narrow patch of hair effortlessly. "Very sharp indeed."

"Are there any Indians left around here?" asked Bobby, a hopeful look in his eye.

"Hard to tell, son. They were all supposed to have moved on many years ago, or so most folks like to think. There's so much of the past around here though, that sometimes I swear I've seen glimpses of them, moving from one meadow to another, or maybe stalking some animal in the forest, their shadows visible for a second against some big rock or huge old tree. They lived all over these hills and valleys for thousands and thousands of years, you know; too many generations to count. The woods are filled with their memory: flints, clay, copper beads and carved stones, little bits of their lives. Are there any Indians left around here? I couldn't take you to one right now, but I think you'd have to be a blind man, a fool, or both to think they were completely gone from somewhere they called home for so long." He smiled at Bobby. "You found an Indian whistle, looking as fresh as yesterday. What do you think?"

"I guess they might still be around then, huh?" responded Bobby, happy at the thought.

A light breeze riffled the birch leaves on the ground and in the trees, and the shadows danced beyond the sunlight. The big dog raised its muzzle and sniffed the air, its eyes partially closed in contentment.

"Well, I think Blackie and me will leave you people to your pleasure. It was nice meeting you, Mrs. Mackay, and good seeing you again, Bobby."

"Nice to meet you," responded Connie, her arm still around her son.

"Feel free to drop in to my home sometime. If we're not there, make yourself comfortable, it's never locked. We'll be back from wherever by and by."

"Thank you, Mr. Van Door. We'll certainly feel welcome" said Connie.

"Bye, Blackie," said the boy, as the man and dog disappeared silently into the underbrush, and back to their boat moored to the shoreline.

Connie stood in the sun, her arm holding her boy to her side, a feeling of calm as old as the woods enveloping her. She felt curiously at home among these light-dappled birch trees and boulders, with the clean air pushing through her hair and the sun's warmth bathing her body.

"I like it here, Mom."

"I do, too, Bobby. I do, too."

Chapter 35 — At the Trooper Barracks

The air in the State Police Barracks was cool, but stale. A slight trace of cigarette smell lingered, both in the reception area, and the back corridor of offices, where Frank Smith walked now. He had been let through the self-locking door by the desk sergeant with a wave. In his hand was a manila envelope, containing several enlargements of the photos he'd taken at the graveyard, over two weeks ago.

He could see Sergeant Justin's gray hair through the glass partitions that separated the offices, and he tapped on the glass as he passed in front and to the opening.

"Hello, Lawrence, how are the wheels of justice turning today."

"Smoothly, Frank, smoothly. Any major animal arrests lately?" The two men routinely insulted each other's area of authority, belying the genuine mutual respect that had grown from years of working cooperatively. Having to maintain a front of professional seriousness, they enjoyed the chance to loosen up.

Frank sat in the visitor's chair at the side of Justin's gunmetal desk and dropped the manila folder onto the sergeant's cluttered desktop.

"The crypt?"

"Just got around to printing them yesterday."

Larry slid the glossy prints out of the folder, and went through them quickly, looking for something, anything that might set their investigation moving again. There had been no new leads, other than the coroner's report, since Jake Danley had discovered the plundered tomb two weeks ago.

One photo caught his eye, and he sat holding it for a moment, deep in thought. Frank looked to see which photo held his friend's attention. It was one of the close ups of one of the markings in the earth just outside the violated crypt's iron gates. With the harsh shadows and low angle from which it was shot, it looked like one of those unmanned photos from space that NASA periodically released: a clinically-detailed image of some not quite identifiable depression in the ground, with just enough information to intrigue, but not enough to inform.

"A digging tool, with tines, five of them...."

"I'm not so sure, Larry," said Frank, getting up from his seat and coming around to look over the trooper's shoulder. "Look how the sharp grooves end in the depressions. They don't have piles of sediment around them. It's smooth where they end. A digging tool is drawn toward you, leaving a trail of displaced dirt on either side of any point. These marks look more like they were pushed into the ground by something. Do you see what I mean?"

"Yes, I understand, and I agree with you. It looks more like something compressed the earth, rather than dug it out. So, we're looking at the footprint of someone, or something. But what?"

Frank smiled. "I'm glad you asked, because I've been thinking 'footprint' ever since I printed them, though I can't exactly say of what. For starters; something big, and something heavy. The ground in that cemetery is packed down pretty well, and it was bone dry that week.

Sergeant Justin turned to a closely cropped photo of one of the coffin shelves in the crypt wall. Parallel white lines, five in all, were scored into the corner, marking the place where the marble slab covering was broken open.

"Here we are again, same number of tines. But these marks were made by a tool, Frank. You can't tell me an animal popped out four half-inch brass screws from the marble wall, no matter how corroded they were. A sledgehammer could break the vault covering, and a crowbar could pry the screws away from the wall, but I don't buy some curious black bear opening up that crypt like some beekeeper's hive. No way!"

"What about this?" Frank picked up the piece of twisted bronze he'd retrieved from the tomb and handed over to the trooper.

"You mean the marks? Those grooves could be from the same bolt cutter or whatever that was used to snap the hands off the woman. They're sure as hell not teeth marks, Frank. Anything with that strong a bite would have broken their teeth, anyhow. Those marks are a sixteenth inch deep!"

"I don't think we're talking about a bear, Larry," Frank said, looking levelly at his friend.

"Then what exactly are we talking about, Frank? A mountain lion? I mean, what else is there around here that could do that? The Jersey Devil?" Larry was smiling as he offered up the locally famous "Bogeyman of the Bogs". The infamous Jersey Devil was New Jersey's home grown version of the Northwest's "Bigfoot," though all popular myths had him at large in the central portion of the state, gamboling among the vast cranberry bogs.

Frank smiled back at Larry's ludicrous suggestion. He realized his friend's joke illustrated the dead end the available clues left them in.

"I don't know, Larry. The closest animal I can fit into those tracks would be a reptile, and it would have to be a damn big one."

"Why a reptile?" asked Larry, his arms folded across his chest.

"They closely resemble the shape and proportion of a turtle's footprint, though out of all known scale."

Larry looked incredulous. "You mean like a box turtle, or a painted turtle? Those things would run, er, walk away from a tough bunny rabbit!"

198

"No, Larry, I'm thinking of something far more aggressive, and meaner, and bigger... like a snapping turtle."

Sergeant Justin regarded his friend skeptically, not quite ready to give up his comfortable image of shy turtles, retreating into their shells at the first approach of anything bigger than a baseball. But the more he thought about some of the big snappers he'd seen during his life, the less ridiculous Frank's suggestion sounded; at least, not quite as ridiculous as the Jersey Devil. He shook his head slowly, as he looked down at the scored bronze handle, and the glossy photo of the deeply scratched marble beneath it. "I don't know, Frank. I'm ready to believe in anything at this point, just to move forward."

"What about the Coroner's report?" asked Frank.

"Nothing to 'sink your teeth into' if you'll pardon the pun. There were traces of some kind of unusual material where the hands were severed, or bitten off, but Doctor Heckler couldn't identify them exactly. He sent tissue samples to a lab in Atlanta, Georgia for further identification, but he may not get results back for several weeks, if that. We've got to develop our own theories, and follow our own leads. We can't even interest the F.B.I., because the corpses weren't moved interstate. Hell, they hardly moved at all" he laughed. "What about the lady friend of yours, the one related to these people? Anything from her?"

"You mean Connie Mackay. Yes, I visited her, and no, nothing conclusive about who or what would gain from disturbing that crypt."

"What do you mean 'conclusive'?" pressed the Sergeant.

"Well, the woman who lost her hands, Tessie Hardin, had apparently inherited some Indian bracelets from her mother. The jewelry had been passed down through several generations, so, presumably, it had to be the real thing. There's a lot of interest in American Indian artifacts lately, and not just from academics. I've heard stories of some collectors paying thousands of dollars for well-preserved, rare Indian objects, like pottery, clothing, weapons, and jewelry."

"So, maybe we've got something a little higher up the crime ladder than vandalism, but not as exotic as Satanism. But Frank, what about the jewelry that wasn't taken; the pendants, the rings?"

"If whoever broke into the crypt was after those specific bracelets, because they were Indian artifacts, maybe they wouldn't be particularly interested in trying to market conventional antique jewelry."

"You're right. The people trading in stolen Indian artifacts would be dealing in a very select marketplace. They probably have specific people to offer specific items to."

"Exactly," agreed Frank.

"So," continued Sergeant Justin, "we may be dealing with sophisticated burglars from elsewhere, or some local talent that's tapped into some big time Indian artifact network.

The officer regarded the photos again, shuffling them until he got to the close up of Tessie's handless arms and torso. The deceased woman looked more like some discarded horror prop from a "B" grade Hollywood movie than a violated human corpse. Part of one of the mysterious tracks was visible in the corner of the photo, only a foot or so from the corpse's head.

"And what about the marks in the ground outside the crypt, Frank? Did a looter of artifacts make those, or do you want to hold onto your 'Turtle Tomb Invasion' theory?" Larry Justin was only half kidding.

Frank shrugged his shoulders.

"Tell me, Frank, could your turtle tracks yield something big enough to carry off a Hereford cow?"

Frank looked at his friend askance, waiting for a punch line.

"Hey, maybe your theory will explain another mystery we've just been handed." He nodded to two women being interviewed down the hall in another cubicle. Frank followed his gaze and saw the Ellsworth sisters, Ruth and Maudie, dressed in identical polka dot house dresses, with identical cloth coats on, talking to another trooper.

"The Ellsworth girls reported their dog missing a few days ago, and now they're short a cow." Frank knew Ruth and Maudie well, having attended a few of Ruth's school concerts. He stopped in to visit with them occasionally on his rounds through the forest, as much to check on their welfare as to alleviate his own loneliness. They were real characters, and he enjoyed them both. He still had difficulty telling them apart from a distance. They even had similar voices, and would often finish each other's sentences, nodding and agreeing with each other like a two-person tent revival meeting.

"They can't find CJ?" Frank would have seen their irish setter if it was just wandering along the roads, and he hadn't.

"Not a trace. And the cow disappeared yesterday, sometime between 6:30 AM, when they milk them and set them out in the fields, and 5:00 PM, when they wander in for the evening milking."

"Maybe it wandered into the forest. Their fence down by the marsh isn't that secure," Frank offered.

"We checked that out, and everything seems to be where it's supposed to be. No new tire tracks, no funny noises, nothing to suggest wild dogs or cattle rustlers. Unless someone very skilled lured the cow out of the field and into a van. But that big bull of theirs, what's his name?"

"Luther," suggested Frank. "I doubt he'd let someone walk unmolested through his turf."

"You're right, there, Larry. I've seen that bull chase a fox, and he can really move when he gets it all going. I wouldn't bet on anyone sneaking in and walking away with one of his cows... running away, maybe."

"We've put out an alert to all the local butchers and auctioneers. The cow's branded, so if someone tries to trade it within 30 miles or so, we'll hear about it right quick. If it was stolen for private butchering, then we're out of luck. Whoever took it, though, got those old girls pretty spooked. They're sure something peculiar is going on, and they want a man out there patrolling more often than we can spare."

"I'll help you out there, Larry. I've got to go by there at least once a day as it is. I can double up and fill in for your men."

"Thanks, Frank, I was hoping you'd offer. With the number of summer tourists increasing every year, we're going to have to press for either more coverage, or get some official local police departments started out here."

Like most rural areas, the State Police provided local law enforcement for several of the sparsely settled communities.

"Well, I'll keep prowling the forest for anything unusual, be it vegetable, mineral, or 'other,' and you'll be the first to know. I think I'll get back to my rounds for now. I'll stop in with the Ellsworth sisters and reassure them of my extra rounds, and I'll coordinate my schedule with the desk sergeant on my way out."

"Thanks, Frank. We appreciate the help, as always."

"No problem, Larry. I'm glad to know I can radio your troops anytime I need a posse."

"You got it, Ranger!"

Chapter 36 — Visions in the Mist

The temperature had dipped to the mid fifties during the night, cool for this time of year, but not that uncommon, and the morning air around the ranger's cabin was sharp and clear. The sky, visible beyond the dark silhouettes of the trees, was a deep azure blue. Feathered cloud formations, dark gray on top and deep pink where the rising sun illuminated them, sailed close over the time-rounded tops of the Kittatinny Mountains.

The Ranger planned to saddle up Traveler, his Bay quarter horse, and inspect the North Trail, out by Mountain Road. The many hiking trails through Stokes Forest were maintained by Ranger Smith and whatever summer help he could recruit; kids just out of high school with an interest in Forestry, for the most part. Touring by horseback was quicker than by foot, and far less destructive to the trails than by any motorized transport. Besides, riding through the forest in the early dawn was one of the most enjoyable of the ranger's responsibilities. He was always amazed that he was paid for it.

Traveler had been pretty frisky as the Ranger threw the western-style blanket and saddle on him outside his paddock. An even-tempered animal, the big horse could still surprise an unwary rider if he felt like it, and the cool morning air had him wound pretty tight. By the time they were headed up over the mountain behind the cabin, the sun had crested over the low hills to the east, and was painting the tops of the evergreens and maples with its golden light. Looking toward the rising sun, power lines could be seen threading their way over successive hills, and occasional spots of color marked the roofs of suburban split-levels. The view west from atop the mountain, however, gave no hint of the late twentieth century, or any particular time, for that matter; pivoting in his saddle as Traveler carefully placed his big hooves along the trail, Frank could pan the horizon from Culver's Gap to the North, all the way down the western boundary of New Jersey to the Delaware Water Gap, 30 miles south: hundreds of square miles of oak, maple, birch, and pine, rolling like a leafy carpet over mountains as old as the continent, all surveyed in a passing glance. Had he been able to stand up on Traveler's back, he could have peeked over the next mountain and seen fifty miles straight into the heart of Pennsylvania.

The cool night air still hid in the ravines and valleys down below, the gray mists hugging the pockets of shadow. The name of Tillman had been given one of them, a beautiful preserve of waterfalls and wild rhododendron. A popular hiking spot, its trails required frequent maintenance, and Frank headed toward it today.

The air, warming from the sun's first rays on top of the mountain, cooled again as Frank reined his horse slowly down the trail and into the denser woods below. Traveler walked stiffly, bracing himself as he descended the rock-strewn path. Frank angled back in the saddle, holding his reins high to help counter gravity's pull. The saddle leather creaked rhythmically with the horse's swaying movements, and Frank let his mind drift in its hypnotic effect. The lodge pole pine and rocks of the mountain gave way to a meadow at the bottom. Still untouched by the morning sun, clouds of mist clung to the long, golden grasses, undulating slowly as if they had a life of their own.

One area in particular caught Frank's eye. In a corner of meadow, where the earth dipped down to a dense stand of evergreen, the ground was lost beneath a thick layer of fog. Within the mass of gray vapor, darker forms where visible, several of them in a cluster, moving, it seemed, across the meadow.

Or were they pockets of clear air within the swirling moisture? The more Frank looked, the harder it was to decide whether he was seeing forms, or the absence of forms; people moving within a cloud, or a group of beings demarcated by emptiness. The wraiths were suggestive of humans, though they bore no distinct identity. Even as he looked, captivated, the undulating mists changed shape, and the forms within disappeared, one by one, against the dark backdrop of forest beyond.

Frank blinked his eyes, and looked again: he saw only a soft-edged mist in a meadow, dissipating in the warming air. The dreamlike quality the hallucination had induced was also dispelled, and Frank's mind was alert once again. He realized that he was more tired than he had imagined, and that his mind had conspired with the early morning light, the movement of the horse, and the hushed cathedral quality of the forest to bring forth a vision, a waking dream. He noticed that Traveler was also alert, because the big horse's ears were straight up and forward, focused on something beyond the hearing range of humans. Frank rolled his head on his neck and arched his back, stretching in the saddle to dispel any lingering visions from his mind. As horse and man left the meadow and entered the corridors of forest, Frank resolved to focus his mind on the here and now. He hadn't time for visions today.

The trees stood close together beyond the meadow, and the chill of the night still lingered within the tangle of branches above and the leaf-strewn forest floor below. Although sunlight bathed the rock and trees a few hundred feet up the mountain trail, the natural colors were muted down here in the predawn light of the ravine; night hadn't yet yielded to day. Except for the resonant sound of Traveler's hooves crushing dried leaves and clipping against the occasional rock, the deep silence was broken only by the scolding cry of a blue jay, annoyed perhaps at this two-headed, four-legged beast, intruding so early in the morning.

The grass on either side of the trail was long and green, hinting at abundant water nearby. Traveler slowed his walk and tugged at the reins, gaining enough slack to stretch his neck down to gather a mouthful of the tender shoots. Frank allowed him to graze for a few moments, before hauling steadily on the braided leather, bringing the big head back up.

"Okay, big fella, enough breakfast for awhile." He patted Traveler's neck, and kicked the big animal gently to get him moving again.

Even Frank could smell the clean water of the brook that ran across the trail up ahead, and he would allow the horse a few mouthfuls to wash down the well-chewed grass. The ground here formed a plateau, a perfect place of rest, though camping was forbidden due to the inability to get any fire-fighting equipment this deep into the woods. The trail cut a narrow corridor through a grove of birch, and Frank always enjoyed how the stark, white trees looked against the darker hardwoods and evergreens beyond.

As he watched the vertical stripes shift in front of the deep green background, Traveler suddenly lurched to the side, shying from something off to its right. Frank was almost thrown from the saddle, so abruptly had the big animal moved, and he started to pull himself up straight. Traveler was looking in the direction that he'd bolted from, his ears cocked forward to catch any sound, his eyes wide with excitement. He whinnied to the forest, his big legs prancing. Frank held the reins tightly in both hands, and his legs gripped the big animal's sides. He looked in the same direction as the horse, but could see or hear nothing out of the ordinary.

Thinking the worst was over, Frank started to turn Traveler back on the trail, but the animal resisted, turning away from the area it had spooked from.

"Come on, Trav, what's wrong, old boy? Nothing to hurt you out here."

Without warning, the big horse laid its ears back and started spinning and kicking, and it was all Frank could do to hold on. He leaned far out to the left, having lost his grip of the saddle. One foot was halfway out of its stirrup and he grabbed for the saddle horn to right himself, gripping the reins as closely to his chest as he could with the other. The terrified horse started to buck, and Frank had lost his balance by now as his head snapped up and down, forward and back, the forest around him spinning like a bad amusement ride; the blue of the sky shot into view, then the green of the ground, circling crazily, then flashing white birch, and a sharp pain in the shoulder as the horse bucked him into a tree, then sky and leaves above, the spinning, jolting motion crippling his mind's ability to keep his body on the animal's back. The last thing he saw was the mane of the horse's head, coming at him fast, then the dull impact of something hitting him from behind, and black-ness....

The smell of wood smoke was in the air, and something un-yielding was digging into his left shoulder where he lay on the ground, a thin blanket of coarse cloth covering him. His blurred vision revealed a gray dawn or dusk, he couldn't tell which, and figures moving all around, quietly talking, if at all, as they made ready to move somewhere. There was a fire, or fires, burning nearby; he could hear the crackle of the burning sticks, as well as see a pale white-blue canopy of smoke drifting at tree top level, the cold air above holding the smoke hovering like a shroud over eve-ryone below. The figures moving about him weren't anyone he'd seen before, but he didn't feel out of place among them. They were dressed in some sort of dun colored coverings. Although some were speaking, he couldn't make out the words, only the inflection, the tone, which was subdued, sorrowful.

Large wooden poles with nondescript bundles roped atop them were in turn lashed to horses and dogs, which stood patiently as still more paraphernalia was stuffed, hung, or tied on top. These people were moving somewhere, and very soon.

He looked to his immediate left. A person's silhouette was dis-cernible under a similar blanket as he had. A leather thong secured the fabric over the head, and looked to encircle the entire body, down to the feet protruding beyond the frayed edge of the cloth.

The toes and ankles were black with dirt. The person was undoubt-edly dead. Beyond that blanketed corpse lay another, and beyond that another. He looked to his left, and met the dull eyes of a woman; she, too, lay under a blanket on the ground, her arms crossed on her chest, her pockmarked face smeared with dirt. She looked as if she'd once been pretty, but something had aged her face beyond her years; she might have been twenty-five or seventy-five; it was impossible to tell. Her hair was unkempt and matted, her face a blank mask. She didn't register anything when he turned his head to hers. She just lay there, breathing shallowly, like something waiting to die.

He could hear the sounds of animals starting to move off, of voices urging them to pull their burdens of bundles and poles. A dog came close to him and sniffed at his blanket, but a young man kicked the animal savagely, and it moved quickly along. He stopped for a moment and looked down, his face expressionless, his eyes as black as his hair. The young man moved out of view, and the sounds of others passing by continued for a time, then faded into the surrounding forest. After a while, there was no more noise, save for the soft hissing of a burning stick in the dying fire, the heat forcing some trapped moisture to steam through its long dead core, like fever sweat still issuing from a corpse's cold brow.

A tiny spider, unmindful of the troubles of its host, had already attached a sliver of silk from one blanketed form to the other, and was busy extending a third to the ground. When those three tethers were complete, it would begin its concentric dance, going round and round, attaching symmetrical patterns closer and closer to-gether, until it had its own temporary village assembled. When it was finished, it would rest, exhausted, at the center, and wait for the first vibration to rouse it to activity.

The man on the ground would black out before he could wit-ness the inevitable conclusion of the little spider's efforts.

The blue jay's call was the first sound he was aware of. Then the sound of the birch leaves, rustling in a light breeze, which fanned his face as well. He opened his eyes and looked up through sun-dappled green leaves, framing a cloudless patch of blue sky. He was flat on his back, and had no idea where he was. Slowly, he moved his arms and legs, before rolling to his right to rest on an elbow.

There was no campfire, there were no shrouded figures laid out in rows, no sign of a spider's web tethering him to the ground. He must have been dreaming, except... it seemed so real while it was happening... the sounds, smells, colors... that woman's eyes, lying next to him, staring and not seeing... it must have been a dream.

His movement brought pain, especially in his shoulder and the back of his head. He felt slightly dizzy, but nothing seemed to be broken, and he didn't see blood anywhere. He looked around the small clearing he was laying in, and found Traveler grazing contentedly on grass a few yards away. He now remembered the rodeo ride that put him here on the forest floor, and he slowly brought himself to his feet. His hat was crumpled in the grass, and he retrieved it, pushing out and shaping the crown where Traveler had stomped it flat. He felt the back of his aching head, and discovered a good-sized bump under the hair; he must have whacked into an overhanging birch limb. He remembered being ground against a tree, and he rolled his shoulder tentatively. It was sore, but functional. He walked slowly over to the horse, which seemed to have forgotten completely whatever had caused him to spook.

"Well, Trav, did you enjoy yourself?" Frank put a hand on the horse's neck, speaking softly, reassuring the big animal that he had forgotten, too.

"Next time you feel like cutting loose, let's do it with a little more open space around us, okay? I'm not too good at dodging trees and trying to stay on you at the same time, old paint." The horse looked briefly at the man at his side, and then resumed pulling mouthfuls of long, wet grass from the ground.

Frank gathered up the reins, grabbed the saddle horn, put his boot toe into the left stirrup and swung himself up and over the broad back. The horse brought his head up, it's long ears pointed forward.

"Okay, Traveler, let's just continue our rounds and act like nothing happened." He patted the long neck, and combed his fingers soothingly through Traveler's black mane. Turning the horse toward the trail, he sat alert in the saddle, scanning the woods all around. The horse might have smelled a bear or bobcat nearby. Whatever it was, chances were it was long gone by now.

Chapter 37 — Unbroken Bonds

After the excitement of their adventure on the island, and their meeting up with the Old Man and his big dog, Bobby had talked nonstop the entire canoe and car ride home; about Indians, and snappers, and the mysteries of the woods. Back in his room, leaning on his dresser, mesmerized by the ceaseless bubbles pumping in the aquarium, he withdrew into a contemplative trance. Connie figured he was just all tired out. They watched the swimming creatures together in silence. Without taking his eyes from the cool water, Bobby spoke.

"Mom, what did Dad die of?"

Connie was taken aback by his question. He rarely mentioned his late father. She had figured he would start asking sooner or later, and so was relieved somehow that he was beginning to bring things out in the open and, hopefully, process them in some way.

"Your father died of cancer, Bobby; cancer of the lungs."

Bobby kept watching the fish.

"But he didn't smoke, did he? Why did he catch cancer of the lungs?"

"Well, he didn't catch anything, really.... cancer isn't like a cold, exactly; it's something that happens within the tiny cells that you're made up of. At some point, they get sick and don't work right, and instead of doing what they're supposed to do, they just do all kinds of crazy, mixed up things. Does that make any sense?"

"Sort of." Bobby's answer was anything but assured. "What are your cells supposed to do?"

"Oh, they're supposed to generate new cells to replace the cells that die off. You wouldn't think it, Bobby, but your whole body is constantly changing, with little parts gradually disappearing and new ones growing up to take their place. Healthy cells work to re-place those that your body loses." Connie thought of the word that Professor Van Zandt had spoken, that Indian term for things that had gone out of kilter, what was it? ...*Mahtantu*. She marveled that a people could actually have one word that encompassed all that ceased to function appropriately in the world. Maybe the Indians called cancer by that name, she thought, if indeed they lived long enough to die of something so gradual. She supposed the vast ma-jority of primitives perished from more sudden maladies: appendi-citis, food poisoning, infections, animal bites. Perhaps cancer was a modern disease, she thought ruefully, because in a way it was nothing more than cellular parts reaching their break down point; sort of like God's planned obsolescence for all living things.

"Does that mean I might get it someday?"

Connie was at a loss for a response, and she took a moment to answer, watching him observe the creatures in the glass tank.

"No, not necessarily, son." She put her hand on his shoulder reassuringly. "It doesn't mean that at all."

"Then why did he get it?" he persisted, his chin resting on his folded arms, eyes fixed on the aquarium.

"I don't know why your father developed cancer, Bobby. Some people abuse their health their entire lives and live to be a hundred, while others who take good care of their bodies get sick and die at an early age. There just aren't any guarantees, son. I can tell you that your father enjoyed the time he had with us, and that he was very proud to have had a part in making you."

"Am I like him?"

"Yes, Bobby, in some ways you are very much like him. In fact, you are actually made up of parts of him, because his very tiny cells helped to create you. If you think about it, part of him is still living, because in every part of you there's a part of him, and a part of me, and even parts of his father and mother, and of my father and mother. You see, you never ever really stop being... if you have children; you live through them, and through their children, and so forth and so on. You can't help but be like your father, because you are a living legacy of him, and always will be. Isn't that a nice thought, Bobby?"

The boy looked aside at his mother for a few moments; contemplating the ideas she had introduced him to. He didn't say anything; the thoughts were too new for him to comment just yet. His mother continued....

"I remember once, long ago, when I saw my first piano; I was at my grandmother's house, and I couldn't have been more than four or five years old. Anyhow, I just walked right over to that big, dark piece of furniture, climbed up on the padded bench, lifted the keyboard cover, and started playing on those ivory keys like I'd been doing it since birth!"

Bobby showed a keen interest in his mother's childhood memory.

"My mother and grandmother were in the kitchen, getting dinner ready or whatever, and they both came right into the living room, and just stood there in complete amazement, their mouths hanging open and not a word between the two of them. I can see them both as if it happened this morning! Well, I was playing a little song; a nonsense song, I'm sure, but a song nonetheless, with a melody line and a repetitive sort of accompaniment. I'd never even seen a piano, much less had a lesson on one. And yet I just knew what to do with one once I was introduced to one. Where did I learn to do that? And when? Not during my life, that's for sure."

"Well, when did you learn then?" Bobby asked the question fully expecting a logical answer from his mother. After all, adults knew why things were the way they were.

"I have no idea." His mother was looking at him in sincere bewilderment, an amused smile on her face. Bobby looked surprised. He wasn't prepared for his mother's cheerful confession of ignorance. Connie could see her son's confusion, and sought to allay it quickly.

"You know what my grandmother said to me?" Bobby shook his head. "She said that her father had played the piano all his life, and that he just always seemed to have a gift for doing it. She thought that I was showing something I had inherited from him. At that moment I was actually being someone I had never met, who had left this world generations before I was even born. Isn't that remarkable?"

Bobby looked at her in silence for a time, before slowly nodding his head in agreement.

"Yeah, I think I understand... Mom, if you can be a part of someone who helped make you, can you also be part of someone who hasn't been born yet?"

Connie looked at her son in perplexed admiration. His observation was completely reasonable, even though she had never considered his unique idea herself.

So, you are a lot like your father, she thought, touching her son's hair and smiling.

"You know, Bobby, I never ever thought about that possibility. But now that you mention it, I don't see why not."

"Am I like my dad in any way special?"

Connie smiled at him, smoothing his hair with her hand. "Yes, Bobby, special in a whole lot of ways... too many to count. I can see a lot of your father in you."

Bobby resumed gazing at the little watery universe on his dresser top, a small smile gradually replacing the withdrawn look of only moments ago.

"Mom, I think I feel okay now, I mean about Dad. I was getting sad, but I think he's okay. Because he's still with us, isn't he?"

"Yes, that's right, son. He's always with us. Keep that feeling, just the way you have it now. Your father would want you to think of him that way. It would make him happy, too."

They both sat watching the small creatures moving to and fro through the water, as the ceaseless stream of bubbles emerged from the gravel, trembling upward to the dimpled mercury of the water's surface.

Chapter 38 —Van Zandt and Ambrose Search for Signs

The professor and Bob Ambrose got up before dawn, intending to explore the marsh area indicated on Connie's map. At 4:00 a.m., the summer sky was still a canopy of stars, the Milky Way a luminous band stretching north and south from horizon to horizon.

"Wow!" the professor exclaimed, looking heavenward. His friend looked up and nodded in agreement across the car roof, giving the rope a final tug before securing the upside-down canoe fast.

Their headlights formed a yellow path through the darkness, the lush growth seeming to part for them as they drove toward the marsh. A big bird, an owl perhaps, swooped low across the windshield, its mottled white feathers visible for an instant in their light. A small furry form dangled helplessly from its claws.

The sky was still black when they unloaded the canoe and cast off onto the marsh in darkness. Bob was familiar with the area, having fished and explored it for many years, and he guided them through the waters confidently. After what seemed only a little while, there was a slight lightening in the east, indicating the night's retreat. Sitting in the bow, the professor happened to look up just in time to see a white hot speck incinerate to nothingness in the dense perimeter of the upper atmosphere, miles above them; a fiery finish to a journey of who knew how many millions of miles.

"Bob, did you see that shooting star?"

"Yeah… a beauty," he answered. "You really can see a lot more out here in the clear air, can't you?" He continued paddling, but kept his face pointed up at the incredible profusion of stars. Another object streaked across the huge sky above, its light so bright it left an after image on the professor's eye's, like a small thin tear in the black roof of universe.

"Another one, Bob…." the professor whispered in awe, not wanting to break the magic of the moment by speaking too loud. He thought to himself that whatever had just silently immolated in the atmosphere above might have been tumbling through the freezing dark of space since before the first aboriginals camped here, right where he and his friend now paddled. How many night skies had there been to marvel at since the last ice age? Ten thousand years, plus or minus a few centuries... 10,000 times 365 nights equals...what? He juggled the zeros in his head… over three and a half million. All those starry nights, strung end to end, and that little cinder in free-fall, not yet visible to whoever might have looked up from their fire's comforting embers, contemplating the mystery of the prehistoric heavens. How many lifetimes ago was that? What was 10,000 years divided by "three score and ten?" No, better shave a few decades, he thought. Too many statistically valid opportunities to die young back then. Make it 10,000 divided by 40 years... equals... 250 lifetimes, linking us all back to a time of cold, and ever present danger.

The professor tried making some useful scale of time out of the numbers he'd conjured, but failed. He smiled to himself in the darkness, somehow comforted by his inability to neatly encapsulate the past and the present, to reduce it all to something as recognizable and comfortable as mathematics. No matter how much one tried to relate the vastness of time and outer space to one's own life, it just never quite came within conceptual reach.

Daylight was coming on, and with each successive moment there were fewer and fewer stars visible; the frightening vastness of deep space, evidenced by the millions of tiny reference points, was collapsing into the comfortable flatness of the day. Small wonder, thought the professor, that people feel so vulnerable to anxiety and primitive terrors at night, when their insignificance is made so evident by the cold light of stars.

The cool night air was drawing columns of mist up off the water's smooth surface, forming slowly moving shapes. The canoe moved through these figures, its sharp bow cleaving an effortless path. The grey wraiths almost looked like people, thought Van Zandt, dancing on the still, black surface. From along the dark shoreline emerged a huge shadow, gliding close to the water. A rusty croak came from the long beak as it opened and closed, the massive wings moving up and down in seeming slow motion; a great blue heron, mused the professor, posing as a pterodactyl. He pointed his paddle in the bird's direction, silently alerting his friend to the spectacle.

Bob acknowledged the heron, his smile perceptible in the darkness. Both men followed the big creature's graceful passage around a tree-covered point up ahead, until it was lost in the wall of mist and darkness.

In silent agreement, the two shipped their paddles, and allowed the canoe to play out its momentum, gliding noiselessly over the water. There wasn't light enough yet to pierce the depths below, but the men kept their eyes on the water just the same. As they drifted beyond a small peninsula of rocky shoreline, a flock of Canada geese, startled by the canoe's appearance, took noisy flight from their watery roost. The rapid swish-swish-swish of their beating wings, only inches from the mirrored surface of the marsh, gave a measured rhythm to their mournful honking. The two men watched their low, fast passage over the water, their scattershot flight evolving into a tight "V" formation, the great birds suddenly gaining altitude a quarter mile away, swooping up and clearing a stand of dark conifers. As the fitful calls of the geese echoed and faded with the mist, Bob spoke into the silence, his voice barely audible.

"There's something I can't figure about the little whistle found by Connie Mackay's boy."

"What's that?" Van Zandt asked, his eyes still on the tiny dots climbing higher in the sky.

"He found it in the flowing water of the canal, in plain view, and in perfect condition." Bob had shifted himself around on the woven cane seat in the bow, so he could face the professor.

Yes? Go on." The Professor coaxed him.

"Why would something at least several centuries old, be so exposed? I mean, it's not quite as commonplace as finding an old tire, or somebody's watch. Know what I mean?"

"Yes. I do know what you mean. It's almost too good to be true in a way; almost like someone had dropped it there. I can imagine that various artifacts, embedded in the ground for centuries, could be disinterred from their resting places by an underground spring, perhaps; even some animal, burrowing into the marsh bottom for hibernation might dislodge something. But, yes, it is unusual.

"I had a childhood friend who spent summers on a lake in New Hampshire, Lake Sunapee it was, and he and his brothers would dive for hours off their dock. The water was about eight feet deep there, and they had a game of swimming to the bottom and touching an old wooden bathtub. They'd pretend it was a sunken pirate ship or whatever else seemed appropriate to their imaginations back in the early 1950's. It had always been submerged there; just part of the rocks and silt and other discarded things, dropped or thrown into the lake over the years.

"Well, years after my friend grew up and his family had stopped summering at that lake, he happened to read in the local paper how a two thousand year-old dugout canoe had been discovered, waterlogged in eight feet of water, laying in full view for God knows how many years. The 'bathtub' he and his brothers had spent their childhood playing with was actually a prehistoric relic, rare as a frozen mammoth, as casually displayed as a sunken coke bottle or any other discarded object, preserved in the icy waters of a northern fresh water lake for what must have been centuries. So, yes, it is peculiar that we might find antiquities in what we might think of as plain site, but it isn't impossible."

"Do you think the lime pit referenced in that map might be the source of some of the artifacts that have surfaced around here lately?"

"Why not? The Indians did use lime to preserve things; once they'd discovered its value, I'm sure they would camp near enough to it to make it easily available and to protect it from others."

"Why didn't the Dutch exploit it?"

"They probably had other resources, and thought they could realize greater commercial value out of cranberries than quicklime. That would be my guess, anyhow."

A fish jumped a few yards away, concentric rings rippling out from where it splashed through the still surface.

"Let's head for that island over there." said Van Zandt, nodding toward a clump of trees and brush floating on the mist, off to their right. They resumed their measured paddling, in silent appreciation of the early morning solitude, the waters grey and opaque before the daylight.

The bow of the canoe hissed onto a sandy portion of shore, and the two men stepped onto the onetime hill, now island. Stretching their cramped limbs, they climbed through some low shrubs, and were soon within the shelter of the dense foliage all around. Van Zandt was in the lead, and he soon found himself in a small clearing at the island's center. A small area was blackened from fire, a ring of round stones loosely encircling the charcoals and dust. The Professor stooped to feel the fire's remains: cold. Noticing something beside the ashes, he picked up an elongated rock, minute bevels chipped in its surface. Parts of it were smoother than others, almost shiny.

"Look, Bob. A whetstone, fashioned from a river-smoothed pebble. Laying right here, in the open!" He handed the small stone to his friend, who studied it and handed it back.

"Perhaps someone found it somewhere more protected and just dropped it here, not knowing what it was?" suggested Bob.

"Perhaps...." said John, not sounding convinced. "You know, Bob, the more I think about what you said, the more it seems that these objects are unusually exposed.

"But you've said yourself that this whole area has been overlooked in favor of more prominent Indian settlements; the Iroquois camps of upper New York State, settlements further south in Delaware and Maryland," Bob countered.

"Relatively speaking, those other sites have seen a lot more archeological activity; but this region has been pretty well combed over during this century. It's the placement of the artifacts, and their condition that puzzle me; that petroglyph, for instance. There's no record of anything that fantastic being found in this area ever before."

"But it was buried, John, hidden away just like artifacts usually are."

"Yes, it was buried, unlike a lot of the other things popping up of late, but the odds of its being discovered are too outrageous to even consider. I mean, the operator of that backhoe hardly scratched it when he inadvertently unearthed it; that's as improbable as a blind man plucking a single, predetermined piece out of a completed jigsaw puzzle, without having to remove any of the other pieces."

"So what are you saying, John?"

Van Zandt stood contemplating the primitive tool in the palm of his hand, his fingers caressing the polished bevel of its side. "I don't know, exactly; just seems too easy somehow, too obvious. Almost like the things were planted for people to find."

Bob laughed. "You think somebody's tiptoeing around out here in the woods, dropping little prizes for people to stumble across?"

The Professor smiled at his friend, shrugging his shoulders in a bemused way.

"No, nothing quite that benign, Bob." Then the perplexed look came over him again. He looked up at the sloping rock that rose like a submarine conning tower from the island's dry soil. He walked over to it and hitched himself up, scrambling his way nimbly to the top. He stood upright and looked out over the still waters beyond.

"That lime cave should be due south of us, about halfway between here and the canal." His eyes swept the horizon, taking in the waters that encircled the island, and the hills enclosing the marsh in turn. "If the objects recently found are being pushed out of that subterranean repository by an underground creek or something, then there's an explanation for their exposed placement and their pristine condition; a damned odd occurrence, but at least there's a thread of logic to grab onto." He reached in his pocket for the small curio, and looked down at it. "But if that isn't how these presumably ancient things are suddenly materializing in our present..." his voiced dwindled to silence.

"Then?" his friend asked from the base of the boulder. Van Zandt resumed looking out over the land before him. "Then maybe these things are performing some function... for something, or someone..."

Bob shook his head, unable to follow his friend's thinking. "You're losing me, John. You mean these artifacts are pieces in some kind of scavenger hunt?"

His friend looked down at him from the rock, a strange look on his face. "I was thinking more along the lines of bait."

Chapter 39 — Road Kill

The motorcycle's steady whine drowned out the sound of the crickets in the warm night air, its engine sending a numbing vibration up the arms of the helmeted driver. The speedometer needle quivered above the glowing arc of numbers, hovering between sixty and sixty-five, as the solo rider hugged the curving blacktop, the wind blasting past him, sucking the sound of the engine away and into the swirling air behind. The cone of bright headlight lit up the double yellow lines of the road, which snaked far ahead into the blackness on straight-aways, and disappeared abruptly at hillocks and curves. Where ancient oak and maple trees crowded the ribbon of tar, a canopy of pale green leaves flashed overhead, their undersides shuddering as the speeding motorcycle pushed out a wake of turbulent air. In these illuminated tunnels of green, black and yellow, the bike seemed to fly faster, like a bullet in a rifle barrel, before rider and machine shot into the open, starry space of the rolling, open meadows between.

The driver, mindful of the nocturnal meanderings of deer, kept alert for the ruby red reflection of their eyes in his headlight. If blinded by the beam, they would freeze in their tracks, a predictable habit that illegal deer poachers used to unfair advantage. Collisions between vehicles and deer were all too commonplace, given the vast numbers of animals and vehicles occupying the same area. Impact between a one hundred thirty pound animal and a twenty-five hundred pound car was usually fatal for one; between a deer and a motorcycle it would certainly be fatal for two.

Downshifting at a curve, the rider leaned low and twisted back the vibrating handle, opening the throttle wide. The big bike's rear wheel dug into the blacktop and hurtled man and machine forward in a screaming line. The speedometer read seventy, seventy-five, eighty, eighty-five....

Fifty yards ahead on the straightaway, just before a grove of willow trees, the double yellow lines ended suddenly, for no apparent reason. A split second later, the driver saw something ruby-red, glowing in the air a few feet above the middle of the blacktop—an eye. There was something in the road, something large and dark and alive, and the bike was almost upon it.

Hypnotized by the vibration, wind and speed, the driver's reflexes didn't respond to this alarming information quickly enough. With no time to brake or downshift, he could only yank the handlebars to the left, in a desperate attempt to swerve around the living barrier in the road. The front wheel glanced off the sloping shape, launching rider and motorcycle into the air. The engine raced and the man screamed, both sounds becoming one, as the cone of head-light pointed up through the green leaves to the black sky, then arced down to illuminate the columns of trees and a jumble of fieldstone looming up. Cartwheeling crazily, the two objects slammed into the rock wall; both were silenced at impact, save the crunch of metal against stone, and the lingering sound of small bits of glass and chrome scattering along the road.

The two twisted shapes lay still in the high grass just beyond the round rocks of the wall. A chorus of crickets, momentarily startled by the crash, soon resumed their throbbing noise, swallowing the brief silence.

Nearby, in the middle of the road, the dark mound that had launched the motorcycle and man held the same position in which it had braced itself, just before being hit. Slowly, four large limbs stretched outward from the heavy, flat carapace. Two eyes, no longer reflecting ruby red, blinked open, and the large, flat head stretched out, sniffing the night air. Lifting its heavy shell up off the warm tar of the road, it shifted itself around, and moved toward the smell of blood.

Chapter 40 — Hay Baling

The diesel engine of the tractor started slowly, the chug-chug-chug-chug of the engine gradually speeding up, until, with a sudden roar, the engine caught, and the metal disc over the exhaust pipe flipped up and stayed, held there by a column of dirty fumes shooting straight up into the air. The driver, a farm boy in a white tee-shirt and blue jeans, levered the shuddering machine in gear, and started his slow traverse over the big meadow, a kicker-baler and hay wagon following behind. The sun was hot and the dust was rising, but the boy was happy to be driving a big piece of machinery. It would be two years yet before he could legally drive a car.

The meadow, currently sporting twenty-five acres of freshly cut hay, sat atop a gentle ridge, with thirty-five mile views in all directions. Turkey vultures circled lazily on thermals of hot air. Not a bad place to spend your work hours, all things considered, thought the boy, as he steered with one hand on the big wheel of the tractor, and braced himself with his other arm resting on the lip of the metal seat. He alternated peering ahead over the high green cowling of the tractor's engine with looking back at the rusted red hay baler, and the creaking wooden wagon hitched behind.

Every ten seconds, the interlocking gears of the baler would cycle another piston-kick, and a freshly compressed bale of hay, all fifty pounds, would be shot out of the compression chute like a silo missile, a contrail of hay dust and shredded stalks arcing behind. The big bales landed on previously shot bundles accumulating in the wooden wagon, hitched behind the baler. The boy liked to time the projectiles, counting silently after the last grass block emerged from the red tunnel; he very often mouthed "ten!" just as the next bundle popped into the air and landed with a *whump* in the wagon. Matching his mental counting with the unerring cycle of the gears of the baler helped pass the time, and even gave the boy a sense of mastering a skill that might be needed later in life; like counting off seconds before arming an air-to-air missile, or deploying a parachute at the last possible moment before a night landing in enemy territory.

The tractor crawled over the hilltop one row at a time, first north, then south, then north again, gathering up the new mown hay that lay in shorn rows, and packing it all into neat, tied bundles. The first row was the most difficult and the most important because the line had to be driven perfectly without hesitation or wavering: the shape of every row that followed would be determined by the contour of that first row, be it straight or twisted. A two-foot mistake at the western boundary of the meadow would be amplified to a twenty-foot bulge at the eastern edge. The boy prided himself on his near-perfect rows. He loved to look ahead or back at the alternating light and shadow of the furrowed lines. It looked like corduroy, draped over the mountaintop.

The cut hay lay in long rows, awaiting the gathering steel fingers of the baler. As the machine traveled along, turning steel tines scooped up loose growth and forced it into an elongated compartment, where a piston compacted it and forced it into a still smaller compartment. It was then compressed even more and bound with rough twine, and finally set flying with a mighty shove by another gear-driven piston. Like most farm machinery, the baler had been performing its limited function for several decades; the simple genius of its design defied major innovation or improvement. It was a living monument to generations of common sense refinements.

An elongated blur of color appeared before the tractor's wheels and shot out straight ahead, low and fast: a cock pheasant. Flushed from its hiding place, its short wings beat furiously for a few seconds, then froze, straight out, as the bird glided only a few feet from the ground, its red-orange colors flashing and long tail feathers trailing behind, like streamers on a kite. It managed to stay aloft all the way to the brush at the edge of the field, fifty yards or more away. The driver raised an imaginary shotgun and fired, sure he would have dropped the pheasant in a gyrating ball of feathers if he'd had his twenty-gauge —no, better make that a twelve — that bird was doing some serious traveling, and the twenty would have just made it fly faster.

Off to the north and west, rain clouds were forming beyond Culver's Gap. The boy set his mind back on his baling. He wanted to finish before the rains came, because he had other plans for tomorrow, and they didn't include spending all day on an iron tractor seat.

When the hay bales reached to the top of the wooden walls of the wagon, the boy would haul the precarious load to the northwest corner of the field, unhitch the full wagon, connect an empty one to the baler, and continue his traverse of the field. He figured he had only another two wagons' load to go and he'd be done. He looked forward to visiting his girlfriend at Swartswood Lake. She was a lifeguard there at the public beach, and he could cool off and flirt for two hours or more this afternoon, if he finished up here in good time.

He knew he had baleed well over half the field's hay, because he was paralleling route 519. He could see occasional cars and trucks driving by, just beyond the low stone wall separating the eastern edge of the field from that county road.

At one point, there was a notch in the top of the wall. The boy thought of the twisted motorcycle that had been found, just the other day, right over there in the as yet un-mowed tall grass of the meadow. The big bike had clipped the top of the wall, sending fieldstones flying, before impaling itself in the dirt. There was no sign of a driver; no black skid marks on the road to indicate why or how a three hundred-pound motorcycle leapt over a three-foot stone wall. There was a little blood on the ground nearby, but not much. The State Police had figured it as a stolen vehicle, abandoned by a joy rider. The thief survived somehow, they theorized, and had staggered off to sleep off the effects somewhere. The bike's license plates belonged to a different make than the wreck, so there was no way to trace it just yet to its proper owner.

Some kind of peculiar, thought the boy, as he contemplated the spot from his lofty vantage atop the bouncing tractor. He had dumped a bike once, his older brother's, on a rain-slicked road; the hot exhaust had branded a searing mark in his calf, and he'd been sore for a week. He couldn't imagine somebody slamming into a pile of stone and walking away. And the mystery rider must have been doing some fast riding, judging from the condition of the bike. It had been described as a total wreck. The guy must have been completely wasted on booze or pills, and as limber as a microwaved Gumby. That's the only way to survive a wipeout like that, mused the boy.

Every ten seconds another fifty pounds of hay lofted out behind the baler, arcing through the warm air in a brief parody of flight. The wagon filled rapidly, causing the boy to slow the tractor down; the top-heavy wagon threatened to pitch the bales every time its wheels found a rut in the dirt.

He turned the tractor off its repetitive path, and headed for the other full wagons in the far corner of the field. One more to go, and he was gone!

He steered the machine alongside the other stacked loads, and dismounted to unhitch the wagon from the baler. Swatting at the black flies that had sought him out, he noticed something dark brown, like a big leaf or piece of tree bark or something, embedded in one of the outer bales on the wagon.

As he walked toward the pile of bundled hay, his eyes remained on the dark object. He noticed flies. it was at shoulder height on the edge of the pile, and he was able to get right up close to inspect it.

He was only maybe two feet from it when he realized what it was. He peered closer, then staggered back.

It was a hand... a gloved hand... compressed into the wall of shredded yellow hay. Its dark leather fingers curled around the heavy, frayed twine that held it in place, embedded in the bale. It looked almost natural there, like it was trying to help whoever had to hoist the bound clippings, gripping that twisted hemp, ready to haul and away she'd go.... if only there was an arm attached.

Not quite believing what he was seeing, the boy looked closer, some part of him suspecting a prank. But no, it definitely wasn't some rubber novelty gag he was looking at. The bloody, torn flesh protruding from the brown leather glove looked like uncooked chicken skin. It didn't look like rubber, and, besides, there was nowhere for a prankster to hide out here, no place for someone to secretly enjoy their joke.

The boy backed away, heading for the road, his eyes riveted on the glove. Afraid that the hand might release its loose hold on the twine and affix itself somehow to him, he didn't want to turn his back on it; not until he was well on his way down the road. Soon enough, however, panic overtook him, and he broke into a run, the sound of the idling tractor carrying after him.

Chapter 41 — Fight to the Finish

The iridescent color of the green bottle flies looked almost pretty against the subdued lavender of the intestine stretching across the muddied grass. Larry Justin never knew all that stuff could fit in an animal; even a full-grown bull. He prodded the gelatinous tube with his boot toe, and several dozen flies swirled into the air, before immediately resuming their stations all along the thirty feet or thereabouts that trailed from the bull's eviscerated belly, clear down to the blackened water. It looked like the great beast was umbilically connected to the marsh, like some massive stillbirth. The Sergeant had never seen anything like this in his twenty-four years in police work, and he'd seen a lot of everything: car wrecks with decapitated prom kids; frozen drunks, buried in new snow. But the sheer size of the bull made its butchered condition all the more extraordinary.

It looked like the thing had lost a fight with a freight train. One horn was torn from the skull, and lay like a child's loose tooth from the bloody scalp. The beast's jaw was jammed to one side, exposing a lolling tongue and a row of teeth. One of its front legs had been removed, just above the knee. A ragged hole extended from under the bull's thick neck to just in front of where the hind legs met; it looked as if the something had scooped out all the entrails and dragged them down the hill to the water.

The ground surrounding the butchered beast was all torn up from what must have been one hell of a struggle. Deep furrows were dug in the ground, from something pushing or pulling, back and forth. Long, burgundy lines of coagulating blood radiated down the hill, away from the dead bull's broken body.

Larry walked slowly around the huge carcass, studying its wounds. Deep v-shaped gashes notched the animal's side. They reminded Larry of axe cuts in firewood; only these were red within, instead of white. Picking up a broken stick from the ground, the trooper squatted by the stump of the left front leg and looked at it closely. There was no sign of the severed limb, despite the meticulous search carried out by the two other state troopers working their way over the hillside. The protruding bone, though much larger, reminded the officer of the Hardin corpse's wrists, with the same type of compressed marks where the bones had been severed.

He heard the sound of a car, and looked up the hill to see Ranger Smith's green Plymouth rolling to a stop. The driver's door opened, and Frank stepped out, putting his park ranger hat on as he did so. The occasion called for it. He walked directly to the gutted bull, and stood looking down at the huge carcass.

"Good Lord."

"Amen to that." the trooper answered, still squatting by the severed leg.

Frank surveyed the torn earth all around the dead bull. "Any bullet holes?"

"Not that I can see so far," answered Larry, prodding into the cavity beneath the severed leg with his stick. "Of course, we'll have to roll this monster over to check his underside. Might find a hole you could walk through, for all I know."

"I can't imagine anything mauling this animal without it being stone dead first." said Frank, his tone subdued.

"How about a black bear?" queried Larry, his twig probing the area that used to be filled with the huge animal's heart. "Didn't the

Spanish settlers of old California stage fights between bulls and bear?"

"Yes, they did, and no, I don't think a black bear could inflict this kind of damage. Around here, they might run three-fifty, maybe four hundred pounds. Our deceased friend here probably topped two thousand.... maybe more. Not a very sporting match for any bear fool enough to try, least ways a black bear. A good sized grizzly, maybe, but there aren't grizzlies within two thousand miles of here."

"So, what does that leave us with?"

"Either a very athletic lunatic with a hand axe and no fear, or some kind of animal not usually associated with our millennia. Even if this bull was subdued with a sleeping dart, it would have taken a pretty motivated individual to cause so much carnage."

"Maybe it was more than one person, Larry."

"You mean like a gang of kids?"

"I don't really have any idea. I was just thinking it seems a little more plausible for two or more people to bring down an animal this size; unless, of course, somebody blew a hole in it first with a high-powered rifle."

"The Ellsworth sisters were home all yesterday and last night. They claim they didn't hear a thing out of the ordinary. Their dog is still missing, so there was nothing to interfere with whoever, or whatever, attacked this bull."

Frank looked down at the big animal's head, and the one horn that still jutted lethally from its skull. He'd seen rodeo bulls stomp and gore riders unlucky enough to get in front or under them. They moved with a frightening speed and power, whirling their ton of muscle and bone around with uncanny agility and deadly purpose. He couldn't imagine anything that could so thoroughly decimate such a strong and aggressive animal.

"Maybe somebody drugged Luther here, and then butchered him up." offered Frank.

"From the looks of the meadow, I think our friend did not go to his maker quietly, Frank. Somebody or something was all over this bull, but it wasn't too quick. He didn't give up without a struggle. That's for damn sure!" Trooper Justin tapped the dead animal's shoulder, like a conductor tapping a podium, then stood up and tossed the bloodied twig aside. He strode a few feet downhill, and pointed to a depression in the earth.

"Look familiar?" he asked, as Frank walked down to where the trooper stood. He crouched down for a closer look, and beheld an exact duplicate of one of the strange prints he'd photographed in front of the Hardin tomb; the slightly elongated bowl, maybe ten inches in diameter, with five distinct grooves emerging another seven inches out from the front. For a long moment Frank stared at the mark, its identity very familiar to him, and yet unfamiliar at the same time; like looking at a stranger, and thinking you knew them somehow. He was reminded of tracks set in plaster in museum glass cases, of dioramas of prehistoric scenes... prehistoric reptiles.

Suddenly, he realized he was looking at a vastly over-sized footprint of a reptile, a footprint he had seen before; it was a snapping turtle's footprint, though of an impossibly large size.

For a few moments he kept his revelation to himself, still not completely convinced of the possibility of something that large existing here, in the late twentieth century, not four miles from his home.

"Larry, have you ever seen a big snapping turtle, I mean a real whopper, with a shell two, maybe three feet across?" Frank looked from the track in the dirt up at his friend.

"Sure, down on the Paulinskill, every once in awhile I've seen some big bruisers cruising just under the water, or maybe sunning themselves on the bank. My Daddy and I used to hunt them for soup when I was little. Why?"

"Well, either I've completely lost my mind, or we're looking at the footprint of one that must have a shell five, maybe six feet across."

"I've never heard of one getting that big, Frank, not around here." countered Larry, his glance at the track belying his skepticism. "You know how old one even half that size must be? Over a hundred years! And who ever heard of one going twice that long, and twice that size? I'll have to vote for the part where you lost your mind, buddy." The Trooper laughed a short, barking laugh, one that sort of died in his throat.

His friend smiled back at him, but did not return the laughter. He remained crouched in the heat on the hillside, contemplating the footprint in the dirt.

Chapter 42 — Sandra Ely Receives Tissue Sample

Sandra Ely arrived at her cubicle in the Center For Disease Control testing lab after a week of seminars, speeches and presentations. With the threat of bio-terror working its way higher in the Department of Homeland Security's insatiable priorities, her requests for tests on an ever-increasing array of materials seemed to grow by the hour.

And, as always seemed to be the case, the creation of another government agency to combat some previously unforeseen national emergency demanded more from existing agencies under pressure to reduce their own resources.... very likely to help fund the newest Agency and its rapidly metastasizing needs.

Draping her coat over a teetering pile of file folders on her visitor's chair, she surveyed her latest emergency requests, and picked one from the pile.

The letter inside the intercompany envelope had been stamped "PRIORITY" (a onetime useful method of getting to the head of the work line, but rendered completely useless by every incoming package routinely being stamped "PRIORITY"). Sandra noted the date on the enclosed letter was over a week old, so presumably it had lain somewhere in the vast government building since that time, before completing it's interminable journey to her in-basket.

Opening the envelope, Sandra withdrew a flat plastic sleeve, in which a scrap of fabric and what looked like dried parchment were contained. The letter accompanying the material gave a brief description of the contents, from whence they had been retrieved, and a request for testing on the slight grey-green mottling that adhered to both the fabric and the parchment-like material affixed to it.

Holding the contents within the plastic sleeve up to the fluorescent lamp on her desk, Ms. Ely decided that she would make this particular priority among many her first puzzle of the morning. After days inside airless meeting rooms, she welcomed some very intimate and focused project to help dispel the data-drenched fog from her brain.

Uncovering the three-dimensional microscope on the counter top beside her desk, she lay the envelope down and selected a wrapped, sterile slide from a drawer next to the microscope and placed it on a light box.

"Alright, Dearly Departed Ms. Tess Hardin, let's take a look at what's hitched a ride on your burial gown."

Placing a breathing mask over her nose and mouth, Sandra then put on sterile rubber gloves, affixed her lab glasses over the mask, and gently opened the plastic envelope containing the items to be evaluated. Using medical tweezers, she picked up the dried flesh, allowing a few flecks of the desiccated tissue to drop onto the slide. Switching on the light of the microscope, she carefully placed the material and the slide beneath the high-powered twin lenses, lowering her glasses to the viewer as she did so.

The minuscule flecks of skin, illuminated from beneath the glass slide, appeared almost translucent. Several fibers of the burial gown were affixed to the dried flesh, along with what Sandra presumed was a strand of the deceased's hair. "Looks like cotton," she said to herself, noting the frayed tendrils, which branched off the main fibers.

The material that had caused a New Jersey County Coroner concern looked like grey-green pollen; fractals of broccoli-like protrusions, blooming on the surface of the flesh, and clinging to the stray fibers and hair sample as well.

"Interesting," Sandra muttered...... "...doesn't appear to be dead..."

Some decades-old mold, previously inert but reanimated by the corpse's exposure to air? A possible explanation, she thought..... The material had lain out in the warmth of the sun after being disinterred from the fecund tomb. Certainly no shortage of moisture and bacteria-laden air to nurture microbial growth on long-dead tissue.

"Well, Ms. Hardin, late of Sussex County, New Jersey, we need to requisition some time on the electron microscope... Definitely need to make time for your close-up."

While Sandra was able to pick her own priorities once they landed in her in-box, using one the CDC's electron microscopes required coordinating with countless other clinicians' projects. For the most part, booking time was on a "first come, first served" basis. But, like any scheduling system, the orderly progression of work by those already in line was subject to random, completely unscheduled "super priorities" by Administrators beholden to the innumerable political hacks that controlled the entire organization's funding.

No matter the assessed importance by those charged with carrying out the CDC's core mission, or the hours of internal meetings to attend to rapidly evolving needs for finite resources, any number of government overseers, from Committee heads to lower-level staffers, could, and did, demand prioritization for whatever they dropped into the queue. Instances of dueling Senatorial "priorities" were not unheard of, further disrupting any attempts at orderly scheduling of limited resources.

Awareness of the realities of dysfunctional areas of one's organization and how to elude entanglement in them was as important as competence in one's professional skills. Sandra Ely had, by necessity, become proficient at both.

Turning to her computer, she prepared an email request for time on the electron microscope assigned to her area. The scheduler for that resource had lost a bet with Sandra on the outcome of a previous case, and might be willing to forgo a paid dinner out with Sandra for time on the machine.

Chapter 43 — Jake's Fever

Jake had felt a little achy and light headed when he left home on his rounds in the morning, and by lunch time he could tell something was coming on; a summer cold, most likely, though he couldn't remember how long it had been since he was last laid up with anything. He returned home for lunch and parked the truck beside the modest wood frame house provided by the Park Service, and dragged himself up on the porch, where he let himself collapse into the metal porch swing. He suddenly felt too weak to go another step. Besides, the breeze felt good on his hot, clammy skin. The sun was out, but the day wasn't overbearingly hot for August. All the same, he was sweating more than he was used to.

He could usually see clear across the valley to the mountain ridge from his porch. Jake often sat out here of an evening, alone, and enjoyed the fading light of day, as the deep shadow of the Kittatinny mountains, immediately behind his home, marched across the meadow and climbed the hardwood and evergreen-covered ridge that formed the eastern edge of his universe.

Just now his vision was blurring slightly, and he couldn't see clearly the tall rows of summer corn waving in the light wind directly across the road, much less the jagged outlines of the thousands of trees another half mile beyond the cornfield. His limbs felt heavy, and his joints were on fire, aching every time he moved; especially his back. It felt like the vertebrae were welded together in a dull, growing pain. He let himself slide to a prone position on the bench, one leg touching the wooden porch floor, anchoring his swaying body to the earth, or trying to. With one arm thrown across his perspiring brow, the bright sunlight shut out of his aching head, the world around him seemed to be spinning slightly, like a playground ride set low to the ground, rocking on an unsteady axis, gaining and losing speed with no apparent rhythm. Jake sighed out loud, hoping to dispel his growing nausea somehow by vocalizing his discomfort. He couldn't remember feeling quite like this before. There was no question of him going back to work that afternoon. He'd try and call Ranger Smith, after resting for a little while, here in the cool shade of the porch, the breeze his only salvation.

The hard metal surface of the bench began to bother him, and he tried to rally himself to get up and go inside, to fall on the soft bed within the dark coolness of the house, but he couldn't. Despite the promise of comfort, his thoughts wouldn't hold still long enough for him to propel his fevered body up off the swing and into the house. It seemed an impossible task. He rocked back and forth on the metal bench, the repetitive movement at once both annoying and soothing. After awhile he couldn't tell whether his extended leg was causing the rocking motion or limiting it. Images were overtaking his mind, coming and going of their own volition, revolving like a kaleidoscope with increasing frequency. There were moving gears within unknown machines, herds of animals, faces; everything in motion, coming close and moving away, nothing at rest. He fought the blackness that crept in from the edge of his vision for a time....

The sound of crickets, loud all around in the darkness. Shuddering chills swept over his inflamed skin, as the cool night air moved over him, lying there on his darkened porch, the cold metal swing stationary beneath him. Jake's arms were drawn tightly around him, and his legs were pulled up hard against his chest. He felt as if he had become mysteriously drunk during his sleep, and was just awakening to the initial hallucinatory quality of that abrupt recovery from deep slumber. He winced with pain as he unsteadily pulled himself upright, setting the unstable metal swing to sickening motion once again. The black world around him reeled like a ship at sea, and he opened his aching eyes to find a horizon, an object, to anchor himself with.

Beyond his yard, hanging over the silent black road, a street light shone, the only illumination for a half-mile in any direction; its warm yellow cone of light poured out of the silver metal cap and lit up the wooden pole that supported it, the yellow traffic line on the road below, and the first few rows of tall corn stalks just beyond, which were moving fitfully in the evening's cool breeze.

Jake peered through his aching pain at the waving corn, trying to decide what all that rustling activity meant. With the motion of the metal porch swing clashing with the wind-tossed movement of the objects across the black river out in the darkness, he decided he had to get off the swaying porch and move toward whatever was out there, beckoning him.

He got shakily to his feet, hugging himself in a futile attempt to subdue the chills rippling through him. Lurching down the pitching porch steps, he staggered across the darkened lawn, his sense of direction temporarily misguided by flickering fireflies courting in the velvet summer air. He refocused on the wall of wavering green across the road and set off once again, his fevered mind struggling to hold this one important idea for long enough to get him across the black river and then to fulfill this all important mission. His forward momentum was almost lost when his feet moved from the soft grass to the hard pavement. He stumbled, then steadied his swaying body, standing directly below the street light, surrounded by a pool of unexplainable light. He stared down stupidly at the blackness of his shadow, pitching from side to side at his feet, then looked straight up at the blinding star above; he reeled back, and almost fell flat on his back. The light stabbed into his mind with needles of pain, and he pushed himself forward, toward the green wall.

He crashed through the curtain of broad corn leaves, bumping into the thick, hard stalks, grabbing at the rounded, silk-tipped ears for support. He thought he was surrounded by a clattering, chattering group of people, their arms waving softly in excitement, their hands and hair standing in the air, all of them pushing in, bumping up against him, putting their hands on his aching limbs, bringing their shadowed, dry faces up close to his and silently mouthing words he couldn't understand. He tried walking to the edge of the crowd, but there didn't seem to be any outer edge; only more people, and more commotion. Becoming desperate, he pushed harder against those around him, only to feel them push harder back, and he started to strike out blindly among the looming shadowy shapes, vainly trying to smash a space for himself to be free of them and lie down in.

The blackness began to creep in again, and he didn't fight it. It bathed him in heat and cold at the same time, and he let himself be smothered by it.

Chapter 44 — A Compass Found

The area beneath much of Sussex County was riddled with tunnels and water-filled caverns, which were continually replenished by a giant aquifer. Some local folklore had fishermen catching species that were only known to spawn in the Great Lakes, though no taxidermy specimens had ever been seen adorning the wall of any local bar or fishing camp.

Various spelunking groups had explored some of these ancient hollowed leftovers of dissolved lime deposits, and various ores had been extracted over time: first by indigenous Peoples who fashioned copper amulets and other adornments; later by Dutch miners looking for the massive riches their investors back across the sea were certain lay beneath the forests, hillsides and streams; and still later by revolutionary colonists who fashioned musket and cannon balls for their war against the British.

An ancient Indian trail that ran alongside what eventually was named the Delaware River was transformed by Dutch miners and merchants into a travel way suitable for moving ore, mined from the highlands and interior, by oxen-drawn wagon down to ship-friendly deep ports, and Holland.

Known as the Old Mine Road for centuries, it was still very much in use by Mike Van Door and his rustic neighbors, as well as the occasional visitors to the area in search of living history.

It was on a stretch of the Old Mine Road that intersected with the Marsh that Mike and Blackie came upon a seemingly abandoned rucksack and walking stick, laying between the washboarded road and the still waters.

Downshifting the truck to a slow roll, Mike eyed the objects and the surrounding area, looking for the owner. Coming to a stop, he shut off the engine, put the shifter in park, and opened his door. Blackie hopped easily from the open truck bed, marked a nearby bush, and then trotted toward the water.

"Halloooo!" shouted the Old Man, as he stepped from the truck onto the graveled roadway. Cupping his hand to his mouth, he gave another shout, listening as only a faint echo came back from Rattlesnake Ridge out beyond the still waters of the marsh.

The silence following the fading echo was interrupted by the "Caaw, Caaw" of some distant crow, and a solitary cricket's chirping from somewhere in the marsh grass.

At the water's edge, Blackie turned his gaze toward the sound of the crow.

"Something's sure not right, Blackie. Let's patrol the marsh shore and see what we can scare up."

Only a few yards along the shore from Blackie, the Old Man spotted something shining in the mud. Walking toward it, he noticed that the line delineating the water from the shoreline had been mixed around, as if someone had taken a big eraser to it, smudging earth into water and water into earth.

He bent down and retrieved the shining object. It was a compass; a quality one, for sure, with a braided leather lanyard attached. Given all the muck strewn around, Mike looked for footprints; there were none.

Maybe someone met the hiker with a boat," he spoke to the surrounding silence.

"But why leave a compass in the mud?"

"We better alert the State Troopers, Blackie.... This doesn't seem right at all."

Stepping up into the truck's cab, Mike looked around for the big dog, who had disappeared into the surrounding woods.

"Suit yourself, Blackie... I'll see you when I see you." Turning the ignition key brought the old engine to sputtering life, and Mike eased out the clutch to set the truck lurching over the uneven road-bed.

Chapter 45 — Searching for a Hiker

A light rain fell from the low, grey skies, pattering on the equally grey waters of the marsh. The sound of distant thunder muttered in the still, humid air that hung over the group of men standing on the muddy shore. Trooper Justin looked out over the waters, to the divers and skipper working from the wooden boat anchored fifty yards out, and then up at the ominous, low clouds pushing in from the north. From the State Police car parked up on the embankment came a disembodied voice, enveloped in static, as the police radio crackled into the silence, calling him away from two men he was standing with.

"Looks like we'll have to cancel this for awhile, if that storm rolls any closer," said Trooper Justin to Frank Smith and Professor Van Zandt, as he slogged his way through the mud to his cruiser. Frank and John continued to watch the rubber-suited divers, who sat on the boat with legs dangling into the water. They were adjusting their scuba gear in preparation for another underwater search.

Another man, a book bag slung casually from one shoulder, took long, purposeful strides through the clinging clay muck, and nodded his head as he came within speaking distance of the two men.

"John, Frank.... Hell of a day for a swim."

Frank spoke for both when he said, "Hello, Stan. You looking for a Pulitzer Prize today?" Stan Gruber was a reporter for the local

countywide paper, *The Herald,* and had been forever as far as anyone could tell. Stan unfailingly showed up at any accident scene,
fire or brewing political squabble, as if he had single handedly in-
stigated each event. While Stan would never, in all probability, win
a Pulitzer Prize for reporting, he was as good a reporter as any
county paper had a right to expect on their staff. He truly loved his
work.

Stan smiled at Frank's gentle gibe, and looked out at the divers,
one of whom had just flipped himself backwards into the marsh.

"Who're the divers?"

Frank replied, "I think they're from a diving club down by
Lake Hopatcong... freelancers. Justin said they've worked for Sussex and Morris counties in the past. Can't say as I'd enjoy that kind
of work." The three men looked on silently for a few moments, as
the remaining diver on the boat peered over the side, following the
groups of bubbles that occasionally broke the rain-dimpled surface
of the marsh.

Trooper Justin returned from his radio. "Afternoon, Stan."

"Afternoon, Justin. What's up?"

"Mike Van Door found some abandoned hiking equipment are
at the marsh's edge, so he called us in."

"What was found?" asked Stan, sliding his book bag off his
shoulder and pulling out a small steno pad and pen.

"A rucksack, a compass and a walking stick."

Stan nodded as he scribbled some notes in his pad.

"You thinking suicide?" Stan asked, still writing.

Frank brought his hand up, pointing to a shiny black sphere
with a facemask that had just emerged several yards from the boat.

"Looks like one of them found something."

All three men followed his pointing hand, and watched as one
of the divers side stroked his way to the side of the wooden boat,
and swung something over the gunwale and into the stern. Stopping only long enough to adjust his mouthpiece, the diver quickly
disappeared beneath the water. The other diver, who had been sitting with his legs dangling in the water, reached down to inspect

whatever his partner had brought up from the marsh's bottom, then cupped his hands to his mouth, and shouted to the three men on shore…

"Do you think this hiker had a dog with him?"

Trooper Justin yelled back. " Don't know… What did you find?"

"We found a dog's head," he called back, a dripping, shaggy ball hanging from the end of his upraised arm.

The three men on shore stood motionless, as if waiting for some indication from the man in the boat that it was a gag, served up to break the tension of searching for a possible drowning victim. After a few moments, he lowered his arm, and placed the severed dog head back on the deck, looking down at it with a mixture of curiosity and distaste.

"That looked light-colored, didn't it, sort of red-brown?" asked Frank of the other two men.

"Yes, maybe so," answered Justin. "Why do you ask?"

The trooper looked at Frank in silence, then out toward the boat. "What the ..." he began, before cupping his hands and yelling "Mike! What kind of dog is that?"

The man on the boat looked in their direction, then down at the severed head. He looked closely for a moment, turning it slightly with his hand, before announcing… "Looks like a retriever, or a setter or something. Pointy nose, long ears, reddish coat. Yeah, I'd say its a setter... maybe an Irish setter."

"Okay, Mike. Thanks!" called Trooper Justin.

"What is a dog's head doing in the marsh?"" asked Stan, as if one of the other men might provide a logical explanation.

Before either could reply, the other diver drew their attentions out onto the marsh waters again by surfacing down stream from the boat about 30 yards and waving his arms excitedly. The skipper on the boat sat down facing the stern, put oars into the oarlocks, and after a few well executed strokes delivered the bow of the wooden craft into the outstretched grasp of the diver, who was holding something underwater with his submerged arm. Shipping the oars, the boatman carefully walked to the bow and, joined by the topside diver, struggled to hoist this latest find into the boat.

Whatever the diver had brought up, it seemed to be fairly large, and quite heavy. The two struggled for a bit with the cumbersome thing before they had it fully out of the water.

Half of a large ribcage, attached to a long section of still intact vertebrae, hung precariously over the side for a moment, before flopping into the boat. The three men on shore stared incredulously at the boat, before looking at each other.

"I think they've found him," offered Stan, a grim look on his face.

"Too big" responded Trooper Justin

"What's too big?" asked Stan.

"That ribcage is too big to belong to a human. Unless our missing hiker stands 8 feet tall or more, I'm afraid that belongs to something else."

Stan and the Ranger resumed looking at the bobbing tableau on the grey marsh waters.

The skies above were darkening by the moment, and banks of swirling white storm clouds were slipping beneath the higher, darker cloud cover, gliding in over the marsh waters like torn cotton candy. The rain began to fall steadily, and the flat, tearing sound of distant thunder boomed in the dead air.

"That'll do for today!" the Trooper called out to those on the water. Turning to walk back to his car, he said to Stan and the Ranger, "Best get out of the rain, Fellas. We don't want to have to call in any deaths by lightning."

Twenty feet below the hull of the search boat, the other diver had continued his groping examination of the marsh bottom, and he was drawn toward a flash of light, nestled among the dark green marsh grass. With a kick of his flippers, he brought himself over the area, and reached down to discover a small disc. Bringing the object close to his mask, he saw that it was ceramic; a beige colored plate, with dull red imagery glazed into it. Looking up at the hull of the boat above, he unzipped his wet suit and slid the small artifact against his chest, then zipped his suit closed. He noted that it was barely perceptible beneath his wetsuit. He kicked off from the bottom, slowly following the column of bubbles up toward the surface above. It looked like their work here was done for today, but he knew he'd be back.

Chapter 46 — Feeding Frenzy

The earth warmed as the summer progressed. Millions of tiny forms, secreted within dirt, wood, and water, mutated predictably as they had done uncountable times before. Under cover of decaying tree bark and leaves, standing water, and cocoons, single cells split, little spheres elongated, portions bulged outward and took distinct shape. Clumps of darkness grew beneath translucent, protective coverings; respiratory, digestive and reproductive systems, appearing in all their complexity as if out of thin air. In every stream, pond and lake, floating islands of gelatinous eggs sprouted tails, then legs and eyes, mouths and lungs; from tadpole to croaking bullfrog, millions of years of planetary evolution compressed into a few weeks, the story retold again and again, for anyone who cared to see.

The green growth of spring provided food for the later births of summer. The larvae deposits ate their way to midsummer freedom, burrowing and tunneling out of the profusion of new growth that fed the land with each season's passing. The advent of crickets, katydids, and cicadas ended the silence of summer night, like the chiming of a grandfather clock announcing the passage of time. Wave after wave of birds arrived, reproduced, and moved on, their distinctive songs following the warming of the earth, and the things that grew out of it.

Maudie Ellsworth got up from her reading chair on the screened-in porch and went to the kitchen to turn on the new outdoor lamp. The daylight was fading, and ever since the mutilation of their bull, she and her sister Ruth put the yard light on as soon as the sun dropped behind the western trees. The events of the last few weeks had so unnerved them that they had even discussed selling the farm and moving down near their cousin Betty in Sarasota, Florida. The prospect of selling off land that had been in their family for upwards of three hundred years, and that they had spent their entire lives tending and working on, brought them alternately to tears and anger. Torn between fear and resolve, they had contracted a local electrician to install a sodium vapor light over their barn door, in an attempt to hold back the darkness and give them time to sort out their reactions to all that had disrupted their lives.

The state troopers now drove right onto their property with each tour through their area, and the ranger made a comforting point of stopping and checking on them at least once a day. But after the reassuring police cars drove off into the night, and their lights were swallowed by the darkness, the sisters' unease returned, their sense of isolation and vulnerability to whatever was out there only heightened.

To spread a reassuring glare of white light around the property between the house, the barn and the rolling hill down to the marsh was some comfort, but not enough. The sisters possessed an old deer rifle, a lever action Winchester .30/.30. It had belonged to their father, and he had taught them both how to use it when they were girls. Maudie had gotten pretty good at making tin cans hop on the water of the marsh after practicing one entire autumn, long ago. Ruth hadn't cared for the recoil or noise, and never spent much time trying to master it.

After cleaning and oiling the rifle for the first time in over thirty years, Maudie bought a new box of bullets for it. She had even propped a two by four up against a stump down by the water, and test-fired the weapon to make sure all was in working order. Walking back about twenty-five feet, she carefully slipped a shiny new round into the side chamber, and levered the bullet into the breech. Bringing the old wooden stock to her shoulder, she laid her cheek along the wood, carefully took aim, and squeezed the trigger.

She had forgotten how sharp the kick was and how deafening the sound! The weathered two by four did a back flip over the stump and into the marsh, a splintered hole a foot from its top. A column of muck shot up thirty yards beyond, where the bullet slapped into the water. Maudie's ears were ringing for an hour. She had warned her sister of her experiment, but not the cows, and when the rifle went off, the Herefords stampeded around the meadow like a bolt of lightning had dropped from the sun. They stopped running after a few minutes, but remained unusually attentive to Maudie's activities for the rest of that day. Although Ruth didn't like it, the rifle remained within ready reach, propped by the fireplace, the new package of bullets on the mantle.

As night fell, the symphony of nocturnal insects warmed up, their polyrhythmic messages filling the soft night air. Finished with putting the cows to rest, Ruth joined her sister on the porch, a shared lamp between their two chairs. While Maudie read, Ruth worked on yet another needle point design which, when complete, would join its predecessors in a neat pile in a drawer, next to the formal place settings that never saw the light of day.

A soft bumping occurred whenever a flying insect, trying to get to the glowing reading lamp, was stopped by the screen. Neither sister paid attention at first. Gradually, the bumping became more frequent, like beginning rain; sporadic, but heavier than usual. At one point, Maudie even looked up and commented, saying "Certainly a lot of moths trying to join us tonight."

Ruth, looking up, nodded agreement, then peered outside at the barn light.

"Look out there, will you! It looks like a snow storm." Maudie looked out at the colorless light of their barnyard, and noted the swirling white flecks randomly careening through the air, coming into the area of light and then disappearing back into the black night, just outside the lamp's reach.

"You're right, Ruth, it does look like snow." She hadn't noticed this many moths and other flying insects lately. Perhaps it was all the rain they'd gotten during the spring that would account for the profusion of insects in their yard. The ladies resumed their activities, but were soon distracted again by the incessant thumping of the soft bodies on the fine mesh of the porch screens.

"Do we have any bug spray?" asked Ruth. "Maybe if we spray the screens they won't be so apt to bang into them." Without waiting for an answer, she got up and disappeared into the pantry. She returned in a moment with an old fashioned hand sprayer, its dark green metal coated with old insecticide and dust.

"Stand back, Maudie, while I spray the screens." Her sister vacated her seat only moments before Ruth vigorously pumped atomized insecticide onto and through all the porch screen panels. The mist smelled like a spearmint disinfectant; a nostalgic smell, thought Ruth, evocative of long-lost times, like burning leaves in autumn. Decades old, the chemical in the sprayer had probably been banned from commercial use years ago, and so, like the eye-watering fumes of fired leaf piles, was now an outlawed sensory pleasure. Ruth missed a lot of things from the past.

After lacing the humid night air with the deadly perfume, Ruth returned the sprayer to the pantry, and took her chair next to her sister. The light-hungry insects had retreated for the time being, and the sisters resumed their silent pleasures.

The bright light on the barn continued to draw all manner of flying insects, and their lighted and shadowed forms danced through the air. Now and then larger shapes would join the swirl of aerial activity, fluttering into the pool of harsh light, their shadows flickering between the lamp and the house. At one point, Maudie looked out toward the barn, her reading interrupted by the strobe-like flickering of the flying shapes outside, and the shadows they cast on the porch screens.

She was startled at the profusion of flying insects in the barn-yard; there seemed to be millions of them! It really did resemble a blizzard out there, she thought, mesmerized by the movement. She'd have sworn it was mid-winter, except for the contradictory warmth of the air, and the steady buzz and hum of the crickets and katydids. Some of the insects had even resumed trying to penetrate the mesh of the screen, their little bodies pinging off the wires, leaving fine pollen residue at each point of impact. The effects of the insecticide must have dissipated, thought Maudie, because there seemed to be more of them pounding against the screens than before. And where their collisions had appeared to be haphazard, they now seemed frenzied. Maudie looked beyond the twitching bodies pressed against the wire to the maelstrom out between the barn and the house. The larger shadows that had drawn her atten-tion had been cast by bigger shapes careening through the air, flut-tering and squeaking with excitement amidst the profusion of food on the wing....

Bats.

Maudie looked with apprehension at the flickering shadows. There seemed to be a lot of them, although their darting move-ments made it impossible to accurately count them. Swooping in and out of the circle of light, their tiny cries audible above the ca-cophony of insects, they formed a swirling mass of terror and vio-lent death.

There were so many insects crushing against the barn light that they were actually covering it up with their writhing bodies. The night's darkness was enveloping the barnyard, dimming the slaughter outside. As the yard lamp's luminescence decreased, more insects became drawn to the single 100-watt bulb illuminat-ing the screen porch and the sisters within. Ruth looked up as more moths and other unrecognizable flying insects hit the screens, their incessant impact now making an almost steady noise, thump - thump - thumping like dusty raindrops.

"Ruth, you'd better see if we have any more insect spray in the basement..." Maudie stopped in mid-sentence, as she and her sister

watched in growing alarm at the porch screens: the bats had followed the moths to the light, and were now joining the frenzied
insects immediately outside the porch, throwing themselves at the
screens! The sisters stood, transfixed, as the little rodents spread
themselves over moths, hooking their claws through the mesh and
crushing the insects as they bit into them with their tiny, white
teeth. All this only served to spur on the frantic activity of the
moths, which tried harder and harder to push through the unyielding woven barrier.

The sisters had gotten out of their chairs and were wordlessly
backing away from the crush of pursued and pursuers. It looked
like a rippling wall of dried ivy, undulating under its own, writhing
weight; a living, breathing nightmare.

One panel of mesh started to tear, and a wiggling lump of insects and bats fell onto the porch floor, exploding in a hundred directions. Maudie and Ruth rushed into the house and slammed the
door shut between the porch and living room. Ruth ran for the
phone and Maudie grabbed the .30/.30 and the cardboard box of
bullets, shaking the heavy brass cylinders out onto the sofa, and
feeding a handful into the side chamber. She threw the lever forward and back, chambering a live round, and brought the stock to
her shoulder, pointing it at the glass panes of the porch door. She
was sighting down the barrel, with her finger pressed against the
trigger, only a few ounces of pressure away from firing the bullet,
when she realized how useless the .30/.30 was to her situation; like
throwing a rock at a landslide, she thought. All it would do would
be to give them a hole in the glass to come through.

She stood in the living room, her faced pressed against the
wooden stock, her eyes fixed on the swarming shapes fluttering on
the porch and bumping against the glass panes of the door.

"Hurry Ruth!" she cried, as her arms began to shake with fear.

The porch light exploded, and the feeding frenzy beyond the
closed door continued in darkness.

Chapter 47 — Microbial Persisters

"Frank, this is Dr. Heckler. I'm calling to see if you had any new information regarding Tessie Hardin."

Silently holding his phone to his ear, Frank realized he hadn't gotten back to the doctor with any updated instructions from the local descendants of Tessie Hardin.

"I've been meaning to call you for the last several days, Doc, but a few other things came up in the meantime. I spoke with Connie Mackay, the deceased's closest relative, and asked her for any information she might share with us. I also told her you needed disposition on the re-internment or cremation of the corpses.

"Thanks Frank. Any decisions yet?"

"Nothing at this time, Doctor, although she's aware that she'll have to decide on something within the next few days."

"It may have to be sooner than that, Frank. I just received a human hand today. A left one, to be precise. And while it doesn't take up much space, it's going to require a fair amount of my time."

"A hand?" Frank was confused. "It wouldn't look like it belongs to someone dead for over a century, would it?"

"No, Frank, unfortunately it doesn't belong to Tessie Mackay. At best its been severed from someone for three or four days. It had a tight-fitting leather glove on, which kept external putrefaction at bay somewhat, only making it more difficult to pinpoint exactly when it was separated from whoever it belongs to."

"Pardon me, Doc, but I don't understand how you can find a hand without hearing from whoever lost it, or having a missing person to tag it to. You did say three or four days, correct?"

"Yes, that's right. It does seem peculiar, unless the rest of its owner is scattered somewhere else, waiting to be discovered."

"Where was this hand found?"

"It was laying in the meadow up on the ridge that 519 runs along, just south of the forest boundary. It turned up in a bale of hay, without so much as a button from the rest of whomever it came from. I've already had the troopers over here with their traveling fingerprint lab. We Fed-Xed a set of prints to the F.B.I., and should have some feedback by a week or two, assuming this mysterious person's prints are on record".

"This hand was found near where the wrecked motorcycle landed, right?"

"That's correct, Frank, and we don't have much to go on. The person the bike is registered to reported it stolen a few days ago. We'll just hope to get lucky with the F.B.I."

Frank marveled to himself at how bizarre the summer had been. And it was only half over.

"I haven't been able to shed much light on our Tessie's past, Doc, other than to ascertain that she was apparently wearing some antique Indian bracelets when she was buried.

"You're thinking grave robbers?"

"I really don't know what I suspect, Doc. Some of those corpses were wearing jewelry they had been buried in. Anyone going to all the trouble to break into their crypt wouldn't leave valuables behind.

"I've got to suppose that the Indian bracelets had special significance for someone. Either that or Tessie had some valuable rings on both hands that wouldn't come off, and our crypt-cracker decided to make a quick job of it in the field and worry about removing them later. At this point, I'm looking for somebody in the antique Indian jewelry trade. That's the only thing remotely reasonable to pursue at this time."

"What can you tell me that's not so reasonable?" The Doctor's tone suggested Frank had more theories to share..

"Well,... " Frank began, "there were some prints outside of the vault, and some marks within the marble chamber as well."

"Correct" agreed the Doctor.

"I think those prints might have been made by a very big reptile."

There was no sound at the other end of the phone. "Doctor Heckler? You still with me?"

"Yes, Frank, I'm sorry, I was just thinking..."

"Thinking I'm out of my mind, or just over tired?" joked Frank.

"No, no Frank... on the contrary, I was applying your admittedly eccentric theory to the types of wounds inflicted on the Hardin corpse.

"And...?" asked Frank.

"And, although I can't imagine a reptile that size existing in this area beyond the late Paleolithic era, I see a disturbing logic to your idea. Any fairly sharp implement would have been adequate to remove her hands. Yet Tessie Hardin's wrists were crushed and severed... might as well as smashed them off with a mallet."

"Yes, Doctor, I can visualize those marks quite well. Matter of fact, I saw some very similar ones all over the Ellsworth Sisters' field-butchered bull."

"You're kidding!" Doctor Heckler sounded genuinely surprised.

"After seeing that big bull strewn all over the Ellsworth's meadow, I'm no longer capable of kidding. Same type of bites, same foot prints as I photographed outside the Hardin crypt. I even proposed to Sergeant Justin that our culprit might be a monster snapper, but he wouldn't buy it."

"He might buy it now." said Heckler.

"He might at that," agreed Frank. "Did your disease center ever respond to those tissue samples from our Miss Tessie?"

"Oh, I'd almost forgotten to tell you. This is even stranger than the latest little addition to my case load."

"They didn't want to stand behind their first battery of tests, so they insisted on running them again, gratis. At first they couldn't identify some microbial persisters found in the tissues from Tessie Hardin's severed wrists—"

"Excuse me, Doctor, but what was that term you just used?"

"Microbial persisters: latent germs, like AIDS virii that exist inactively in host carriers, without infecting surrounding tissues and initiating gross symptoms of the disease."

"Okay, thanks for the translation."

"Anyhow, we would expect latent germs of varying diseases to show up; the same type that exist among every human population.

"What baffled the disease center were the presence of some partially unfamiliar persisters."

"Uh, you're losing me again, Doc… how can something be "partially unfamiliar"?

"Well, ….according to our friends at CDC, these bore a passing resemblance to smallpox microbial persisters."

"Smallpox? Wow, that's serious, isn't it, Doc?"

"It would be serious, Frank, if it were theoretically possible. According to all accepted medical knowledge, smallpox has been effectively extinct from our part of the world for over one hundred years.

"Didn't smallpox ravage parts of the western U.S. during the nineteenth century?"

"Actually, it was first introduced to the American southwest by the Spaniards in the 1500's, and later by the Dutch and German immigrants to our area. It flared up most famously during the 1800's, decimating the Plains Indian tribes, but it had already wiped out many natives before those more famous pandemics. It wasn't until Native Americans were induced to be vaccinated did the scourge end and finally die out completely."

"So how can a disease last heard from over a century ago reappear on a long-buried woman?"

"Either the microbes survived in latent form on the corpse's wrists since her burial in 1912, which I find highly unlikely, or they were deposited there by whoever or whatever severed her hands within the last few weeks."

"And if they were recently deposited on the corpse?" Frank didn't follow the Doctor's logic.

"Then I still can't figure out where they came from. Again, as far as anyone can tell, there are no remaining microbes of smallpox anywhere in the world. And nobody back then had the technology to store and preserve smallpox microbes, other than in an active, virulent state."

"Doctor, you said smallpox was introduced in this area by the Dutch?"

"Yes, there are medical records from the very early European settlement of northwestern New Jersey and surrounding New York and Pennsylvania areas that document outbreaks of smallpox among some of the Native American tribes of Minisink and Mandan Indians. Unlike the European settlers who introduced the microbes, the Indians had no acquired immunity to the virus, and it swept through some of their settlements like wild fire. Whole villages were wiped out. With no one left to bury the infected corpses, roving packs of wild dogs and other animals would carry off parts of those stricken, spreading the disease further. For any survivors, not being able to properly care for their dead must have been almost as tragic as actually losing so many of their people to a mysterious, seemingly invincible evil."

"So, when will the disease center have a positive fix on whether or not we've got to worry about an outbreak of smallpox or whatever these microbes are in Sussex County?" Frank's voice betrayed his worry. Given the summer influx of tourists from all over the heavily populated tri state area, the possibility of widespread infection from a highly contagious disease like smallpox was all too real. One visitor from Paterson, or New York City, or

Philadelphia unwittingly transports an invisible germ bomb home and…..

"They promised to resubmit their report on the Hardin tissue samples within forty-eight hours, and I sent along additional samples from the gloved hand. You can't ask for a better response than that."

"I'll have to take your word on that, Doctor. I'll do what I can to help on my end. Like I said, I'm still going on the assumption that there are Indian artifact hunters coming into the area, looking for easy money."

"Well, I'll certainly let you know as soon as we get some positive feedback from the CDC."

"I hope to God they're wrong, Doctor. You know better than I that we're just not set up to deal with something like that."

"Nobody is, Frank, believe me."

Chapter 48 — News of Interest At the Barbershop

Early Saturday morning was the best time to get a haircut at 'Robbie's Barber Shop' in Branchville. The tiny town's main street hadn't yet filled up with tourists, looking for rural bric-a-brac bargains; pieces of America's small town past to take back to their suburban dwellings. To many people, Branchville was a living embodiment of what Norman Rockwell had deified in the previous century; a Lionel train town of small-scale commerce.

One of several commercial establishments in Branchville, 'Robbie's' had been on the same spot for over seventy years. A freestanding wood building with only two barber chairs, the compact business had been in the same family for fifty-five of those years. Robbie had been shearing the heads of Sussex county citizenry for a quarter century; he maneuvered a barber's electric clippers like a surgeon used a scalpel, with unerring accuracy, speed, and assurance, all the while providing just enough pleasant banter to calm a customer's thoughts. A haircut at Robbie's was just what a haircut should be: a comforting ritual, free of any outside stressful interference.

The paneled walls of Robbie's were spotted with photographs: little league photos from 1952, a volunteer fire picnic, the Kodak colors shifting away from their original richer-than-life vibrancy, toward a more subdued, sun-bleached hue. A large black-and-white photo featured the bank building, looking exactly as it did in the present, the only clue to its age being the rounded contours of the early 1950's automobiles parked diagonally in front. In the fore-ground, in the middle of Main Street, two smiling men posed, one holding an iron-rimmed wheelbarrow, the other propped inside, legs and arms dangling beyond the iron bucket, brushing the long-buried tar of the street. The picture was an archival record of a bet made on the 1955 World Series, between the Brooklyn Dodgers and the New York Yankees; the winner, Robbie's father, rode, and the loser, his friend, pushed. According to Robbie, his father would subsequently regret winning. The iron wheels of the wheelbarrow did not make for a comfortable victory tour around the town square.

Frank Smith parked his car in the space directly in front of the small building, and let himself into the air-conditioned room. He nodded to the stranger in the far barber chair, and said hello to the barber at work on the man's beard, Robbie's assistant, Pete.

"What do you say, Pete."

"Good morning, Frank, how's things."

"No complaints, partner. Where's Robbie?"

"He just stepped across to the diner. He'll be back directly." Even as Pete spoke, Frank could see Robbie waiting on the curb across the street. A tractor, hauling a full load of hay bales, was bouncing slowly up the street, the only traffic this early in the morning. After it had passed, Robbie walked briskly across the empty street, and let himself into the cool room.

"Hey there, Frank, long time no see. Have yourself a seat, old timer."

"Thanks, Robbie, how are you doing?"

"Happy to be alive and have somewhere to go everyday."

Frank took a seat in the chair, and Robbie wrapped his neck in tissue and threw a shroud over Frank's shoulders. Robbie needed no direction about how to cut Frank's hair. They'd been perform-ing this monthly ritual for several decades.

"So what's been going on out at the Ellsworth Sisters'?" asked Robbie, referring to their missing setter and Hereford. "Any clues yet?"

"Nothing really substantial. The dog might have suffered a heart attack and drowned; it wasn't averse to going in the water. Or maybe it just wandered into some tourist's car, although people are more likely to steal a puppy or a show dog for breeding. The sisters' dog was fairly old; five or six, at least."

"The cow, though.... that's something different altogether. No obvious tire tracks, or anything else to indicate modern rustlers. Besides, who would steal a milk cow for beef?"

"Maybe something spooked her into the water, and she drowned?" Robbie speculated. "Like a black bear, or a coyote, even. I hear they're making a come back around here." For the last few years, eastern coyotes, smaller cousins to their more famous western kin, had been migrating down from New Brunswick and Maine, repopulating areas they'd abandoned over a hundred years ago. Like raccoons and skunks, larger animals were finding ways to scavenge abundant human refuse, finding cohabiting with shopping malls preferable to starving in the wilderness.

"Maybe...." Frank looked thoughtfully at the mirror image of his friend expertly shearing his hair with the humming electric clippers. "But that big corpse would have gassed up by now, and it'd be bobbing on the marsh like a polka dot raft. You'd figure somebody would see it, a fisherman, someone flying low over the marsh." Sussex County was home to three private airports, and innumerable commercial airline pilots; there always seemed to be some type of small aircraft up in the clear blue Sussex sky, Piper cubs, and vintage biplanes, home made ultra lights.

"It's been about a week. Anyhow, needless to say, the Ellsworth girls are plenty spooked. The troopers and I alternate driving in front of their house twice or more a day, just to keep them calm."

"Can't say as I blame them, living alone out there, right up against the marsh. On an overcast night, you can't see your own hand in front of you. When the stars are out, though, you can read a book by the light from the Milky Way. Unbelievable."

Robbie continued…."Charlie Miller told me about some big rock found out that way, with writing, or pictures on it. Maybe its haunted!" Robbie laughed at his joke, as he hung the large electric clipper from a hook below the mirror, and picked up a smaller, cordless one, to work around Frank's ears and neck.

The eyes of the bearded stranger in the other barber chair shifted from vacant disinterest to a clear attentiveness, and he shot the two men a covert glance, before locking his gaze on his own reflection, the better to attend to the ensuing conversation.

"Yeah. A county road worker popped it out of the ground with a backhoe, and the county called Ben Haubrich and Bob Ambrose, and they hauled it back to the college. Even had some expert from New York come out and take a look at it. Nice guy. I met him a few days ago. He knows a lot about Indians, the ones that lived here before us newcomers."

At this point, Pete had finished with the man in the other chair, and started to remove the cover from him. The stranger, silent thus far, spoke up.

"Say, I think I'd like you to give my beard a trim. Maybe shape it a bit."

"Sure thing." Pete agreed, re-pinning the cover around the man's neck, and reaching for a wet, warm towel. "Nobody's hurrying you out of here. Make yourself comfortable." The man laid his head back against the headrest, as Pete tilted the seat back a few degrees.

"So" Robbie continued, "what did the New York guy say about the rock?"

"He said that it was very old, that it was probably made by Indians, and that it told a story; about something that happened long ago."

"Remember when we'd go out drinking and necking in the marsh, back in high school, and everybody said it was haunted, and everybody said they'd seen a ghost, or monsters, or such and such... remember? Jeez, seems like that was so long ago."

"It was long ago, old timer." Both men laughed, and Pete joined in the laughter. The stranger sat impassively beneath Pete's deftly working razor, his eyes revealing nothing.

"You know, I always got the feeling it was haunted out there, sort of..." mused Robbie, as he moved the buzzing clippers along the base of Frank's neck. "We were always finding arrowheads, pieces of pottery, all sorts of stuff out there. Must have been a popular place for the Indians, that marsh."

"Must have...." continued Frank. "Hey, here's a fun fact I'll bet you didn't know. The marsh wasn't always as big as it is today."

"Oh, how so?"

"According to a map that a friend of mine found in her attic, the marsh was dammed up several hundred years ago by some Dutch settlers, and extended almost a mile on its south end."

"You know, I'd heard something about that from my dad when I was a kid, but I forgot about it." Joe had stopped his meticulous work, and stood looking at Frank in the mirror, the silent clippers held aloft as he reconstructed a moment from thirty years ago, lost until now. "Yeah, he'd told me that the southern part of the marsh had once been a big meadow, and in the middle of the meadow, hidden among some large glacial boulders, was a lime pit. And the old time farmers still remembered stories of the earliest settlers to the area, using the lime to make the soil less acidic, and more productive for crops. Apparently, the local Minisinks used the lime for their crops, and taught the white settlers to do the same."

The stranger sat silently, not wanting to do anything to encourage Pete to talk, or to stop the flow of information from the two men at his side.

"The map my friend found—you know her, Connie Mackay—shows an area in the southern part of the marsh that must be what your father was referring to. It looks to be about a quarter of a mile from the Vorsted Road, not far from the island where Mike Van Door hunts for turtles."

268

"Say, how is Connie?" asked Joe. "I haven't seen her since the funeral. How's she getting along?" Joe was referring to her husband's funeral, four years ago. Connie was well liked, as had been her deceased husband, and the turnout for the funeral had turned into an impromptu reunion for many locals who hadn't been together in years.

"She's doing well, Joe. Her son Bobby is growing like a weed. Looks just like his father; a really nice kid. I think she's just about ready to move out from under the past."

"Good for her. Glad to hear that."

Pete had finished with trimming the stranger's beard, and was pulling the cover away and shaking it out. The man stood up, and wordlessly opened his wallet and withdrew a ten-dollar bill. Pete took it, and counted out three-dollar bills from the register. The stranger handed one back.

"Thank you, and please come back. Have a nice day."

"Thank you," the man mumbled, and he headed out the door.

Robbie watched him casually walk across the street, and swing himself up into the cab of a blue 4x4 truck parked outside the Diner.

Pete checked his watch and said "Think I'll head home for lunch, Joe."

"Okay, Pete. See you in an hour."

"See you later, Frank."

"Have a good one, Pete." Frank answered, as the barber let himself out into the sunlit morning.

"Hey, maybe the marsh *is* haunted, and some Indian spook got the Ellsworth Sisters' cow!" laughed Robbie.

"Maybe, Robbie, maybe...." Frank was silent for a moment. Suddenly, he smiled at his friend's reflection. "Hey, all I ever did out in the marsh was get drunk with a bunch of guys and howl at the moon. Hell, I could never get anybody to go out there with me necking!" laughed Frank. "All the girls I knew were too scared. At least that's what they told me."

"I think you were asking the wrong girls, Frank." said Robbie, a sly grin on his face.

"Well, then, who went out with you?"

"My lips are sealed. The secrets of the past shall remain secrets. We're talking about several of our prominent citizens here, buddy; pillars of the community, members of local government and all that. Lives could be ruined, Frank!"

"Okay, enough already! You got more back then because of that '52 convertible. It was a Chevy, wasn't it?

"Yup, a Chevy. Cherry red, grey top, velour interior, bench seats front and back. They made cars wide enough to lay down in, back in them days."

The two men laughed, enjoying the purified images of their high school past, all the youthful, adolescent uncertainty filtered out by time, the convoluted reality of then made simple and fun, the miracle of memory rewriting their personal history each time they convened for a haircut, and talk, and laughter.

Chapter 49 — Connie at the Library

The main branch of the Sussex County Library was situated among rolling cornfields and pastureland. For a semi-rural system, it boasted a professional staff that kept the offerings of recent best sellers and periodicals on a par with any library in the state. One corner of the vast open room was devoted to non-circulating documents having to do with the history of the county. The files were well organized and scrupulously maintained by the staff, being comprised of various scholarly works devoted to the development of the county, burial records from the various cemeteries, maps, and microfiched newspaper articles dating back to the early 1800's.

Connie had come to try and deduce what further information concerning the disappearance of Tessie's father she could cull beyond that already noted in the scrap of newspaper from her family's mementos. With only an antiquated schedule of full moons to go on, she had enlisted the help of the research librarian to narrow the possible dates of John W. Hardin's disappearance. Since his will was dated 1838, she began looking at that year.

Meteorological records, available from a compilation published locally in 1884, listed all phases of the moon for the previous seventy-five years. Connie matched the information listed on the scrap of newspaper from her family's collection with that in the farming journal; the three full moons listed in her clipping fell on the same dates as those for the summer and autumn of 1839.

With March of 1839 as a starting point, she then began reviewing the microfiched copies of the defunct Sussex County Register, which the library had dating back to 1834. As she reeled the illuminated scrolls forward, scanning the articles for further news of the disappearance of Mr. John W. Hardin of Layton, New Jersey, she realized the enormity of her task. The wealth of information available back to that point was amazing: the daily news items concerning bake sales, local crop yields, new businesses opening up and old ones closing down; birth announcements, engagements, weddings, funerals, public auctions, special events such as club outings, church picnics, trials of ne'er-do-wells and tramps; the detail of daily life of a rural American county was almost overwhelming, as the backlit procession of hand-set typography flowed upward and off the screen, lost again to the past after so brief a resurrection.

One article concerning the annual arrival of a traveling circus to Newton in the summer of 1839 caught Connie's eye. A particularly ancient member of the touring menagerie, an Indian elephant named "Empress Cleopatra," had given her all, apparently, and died during a performance. The huge carcass was buried, with all respect and ceremony required of such an occasion, right were she fell, amid the summer daisies of the unused farmland on the outskirts of town, where the circus and other traveling attractions traditionally set up. Connie was familiar with the locality, now a neatly subdivided neighborhood of manicured lawns and outdoor gas grills. How curious, she thought; somebody out there has an elephant buried beneath their split level! The idea of the huge skeleton, resting inches beneath someone's game room, intrigued her. Perhaps the restless spirit of "Empress Cleopatra" roams that suburban terrain, thought Connie, periodically rousing sleeping dogs and children with her ghostly footsteps and trumpeting?

But then the idea of elephant bones buried beneath the topsoil of the county wasn't that bizarre, she realized. Only a few decades ago, the petrified remains of a mastodon had been unearthed near Franklin; a dramatic reminder of how thin the physical boundary between modern and prehistoric was in this province.

The rich paper trail of life in Sussex county and its environs petered out fairly quickly beyond the 1830's. Except for certain government and church documents, such as census records, lists of the births, baptisms and deaths of church parishioners, and other "official" tabulations of human lives, farm produce, and livestock, the written record of what life was like back then pretty much evaporated. One had to rely on the written reminiscences of people in Philadelphia, New York, and the other major population areas, and from them infer what the daily lives and worries of the unlettered people scattered throughout the hinterlands and wilderness of western New Jersey may have been like. The past seemed so very close, so palpable, and yet so opaque, unreadable and mysterious, thought Connie. Bones of then were buried inches from now, occupying the same space and time, yet inconceivably apart.

She caught herself from drifting further from the text immediately in front of her on the microfiche screen, and refocused her attention on the slowly rolling type. An article on the front page of the July 21st edition of the Register noted an outbreak of smallpox among a few elderly citizens of Walpack. The account described how one woman died of fever before the frightening scourge played itself out, apparently confining its deadly symptoms to those few residents of that isolated rural community. A related story recounted the last documented outbreak of the disease in the area, during the summer of 1788, near the Dingmans Ferry crossing of the Delaware River. A tiny community had been stricken with the infectious plague, killing all but two.

A flash of something went off in Connie's memory, something related to isolated people, living off in the wilderness, alone for most of their lives. She couldn't visualize exactly what was just beyond the periphery of her mind's eye, but she knew it was rooted in the past; of Sussex County and of her forebears. Connie focused on memories of her Aunt Netta, seated graciously on a blanket in front of the Hardin crypt in Stokes Forest, telling stories of long ago, of the people resting within the hand-cut stone of the tomb.

Fever. She had spoken of fever. The pioneer girl's Indian lover, her young prince, who defied his family as she defied hers, who sired her child and then died soon after... of fever.

A fever, thought Connie.... contracted from someone of European descent.... contracted from the girl.

Of course.

Connie sat perfectly still in the blue plastic chair, the 1839 newspaper projected on the screen before her a meaningless jumble of vertical and horizontal lines. The connection just envisioned seemed so perfectly logical and irrefutable; it was so clear to her she might as well have read it off the microfiche before her, if only one existed for whatever passed for a newspaper back in the 1600's....

Youngsters Defy Elders, Conceive half-breed!

God Metes out Puritan Justice... Girl gives Fatal Pox to Boy!

As she had recently been made aware, there was ample documentation of the spread of smallpox throughout the local Indians during that time of colonization of the northwestern hill country of New Netherlands. Connie had read how early Dutch explorers—shown trinkets of raw copper ore by native aboriginals—sailed back to their homeland with shiny treasure and procured the funding and grants to begin large scale mining operations, leading to the rapid settlement of the interior wilderness along the Delaware River.

An Indian trail, as old as time and running the sinuous length of the river, was enlarged and upgraded to accommodate the heavy wooden ore wagons that moved the precious metal back to European markets. Known variously ever after as The Old Dutch Road, The Old Mine Road, and The River Road, it survived into the present as the oldest known highway on the North American continent. Eerily unchanged during three hundred years, its untended boundaries were still marked by rotting Dutch barns, crumbling stone graveyards and shadows of ghosts long dead. By showing the

274

Dutch explorers their copper, the Indians had hastened their inevitable expulsion from their Eden. The Dutch settlers who followed the miners laid claim to the fenceless land of the Minisinks, introducing them to the concept of private ownership of land, along with liquor, Christianity, and smallpox.

The map from the attic appeared then to Connie, the finely penned words "Hendrika's Gift" taking on a new and sinister meaning. Did the words merely signify the receipt of a pair of copper bracelets, a token of love, albeit forbidden, from the Indian to the Dutch girl? Or did they insinuate the evil transmittal of a viral microbe from new culture to old, benign to one and deadly to the other? Indeed, the phrase could even be interpreted as an omen for the future; an open-ended curse, periodically visiting itself upon those biologically descended from those two innocents of the primeval forest.

Connie had started this journey into her past only meaning to speculate on the mysterious disappearance of Tessie's father. Instead she had seemingly fallen into an entirely new dimension of her family's tortured history, spinning past John W. Hardin, far back to those who preceded him. Did Tessie's father die of smallpox, randomly transmitted as he rode through an isolated rural community, or was he the victim of some viral curse, set unwittingly in motion hundreds of years before by a couple of frontier children?

According to family legend, at least as much as Connie had ever heard, no remains ascribed to John Hardin had ever been recovered. He had simply vanished into the wilderness, along with his horse and whatever he had on his back. That in itself was not hard to understand. Back then, the Stokes-Walpack area was sparsely settled, the woods dense and filled with wildcats, wolves and bears. A man suffering a merely inconvenient accident in more civilized surroundings, like a bone-breaking fall from a horse, might easily perish alone and untended in the wilderness, to be later devoured by any of the innumerable predators, down to the tiniest remaining bone. After a few months, there needn't be a trace of human remaining, with the possible exception of the rusted barrel of a rifle, or the tarnished buckles of a saddle, its rotted leather returned to the rich loam of the forest floor.

So it was conceivable that John Hardin had suffered such an undocumented end, as did scores of others back then. Whole generations of families had burrowed in, cleared the forest, farmed for a few decades, then died off; forgotten, only to have the woods close back over their transient piles of logs and bones. Connie had heard of isolated individuals and families—as recently as the early 1960's—living far back in the untraveled ravines and hills of the Kittatinnies, with only CB radios linking them to the world beyond their immediate horizon.

The ultimate fate of John W. Hardin, like so many of his forgotten contemporaries, was probably lost for all time. Any possible clues or connections between his disappearance and his daughter Tessie's eventual disinterment and mutilation were seemingly lost as well.

The fate of Hendrika's Indian lover, however, seemed all too clear to Connie. Furthermore, she sensed this unexpected revelation into the far distant past might possibly be more directly related to the violation of Tessie's corpse than anything of the more luridly documented present.

Chapter 50 — Nick Searches for Treasure

Nick slowed the truck as he reached the top of the hill. He knew the turn off was close, he just wasn't sure exactly where it was. He'd only tried this access road to the marsh during the day, and that had been in the early spring, before the greenery had sprouted and camouflaged the recognizable landmarks. He hunched forward, peering over the steering wheel, scanning the jungle of shrubbery and trees to the left of the road. Up ahead, a flash of fluorescent yellow; his headlights reflected off a strip of reflective material, nailed to a heavy wooden pole. This was it, he thought, downshifting and easing the truck off the tar and onto a bumpy dirt path into the woods. The lush summer growth closed all around the narrow dirt path, scraping the sides and undercarriage of the truck. Through the passing pine boughs, Nick caught an occasional glimpse of the blue gray blanket of mist rising from the waters. Another half mile or so into the forest, and the expanse of marsh came into view, only a few yards through the leafy barrier of woods. The equipment bundled in the bed of the truck shifted slightly as he rolled up over the drainage lip on the side of the road, and then over ferns to a secluded spot off the fire road. He'd have to leave his truck unattended for several hours, and he didn't want to make things easy for anyone who happened upon it.

Satisfied that he was hidden from all but the most inquisitive travelers, he stopped the truck's engine and hopped down from the cab. Walking quickly to the rear, he opened up the wooden chest behind the cab and hauled out his diving tank and duffel bag. Checking the ground for an area free from sharp twigs or stones, he lifted an inflated rubber raft off the truck bed and onto the ground. Scanning the area all around one more time, he shrugged off the mechanic's coveralls and removed the black wetsuit from the duffel. Stuffing the coveralls into the duffel, he then dragged on the rubber pants, top, and belted on the knife and flashlight. After checking the tank and regulator, he hoisted them into the rubber raft, along with diving flippers, a mask, and an open mesh bag.

He hauled the raft the remaining seven feet or so to the water's edge, and slid the black inflatable onto the still water, keeping a hold on a braided yellow nylon line attached to a heavy rubber ring on the raft's bow. Tying the yellow lanyard to a stout willow, he back tracked to the truck and pitched the duffel into the truck's cab, locking the door. He walked back to the dingy, released the painter line and shoved off, hopping in as soon as the rubber hull had cleared the sandy soil.

The air was silent and still at that early hour. The dawn hadn't illuminated the colors of things yet, leaving everything a ghostly gray, with the far shores cloaked in black. A few stars were visible still, although the sky was lightening to the east. The cerulean blue was fading slightly at the horizon to an aquamarine, with streaks of lavender-pink appearing at the base of some otherwise charcoal-gray clouds above the dark silhouette of the pine trees. The early morning mist clung to the waters, obscuring the features of the shoreline as it receded into the distance.

The island that he was using as a reference point stood out like the prow of a low ship, a few hundred yards dead ahead. Placing the aluminum oars in the rubber oarlocks, he rowed with short, choppy strokes, pausing every so often to look over his shoulder, checking his progress. The air was still cool enough to keep him from sweating in the tight-fitting rubber skin of the wetsuit.

As he neared the island, he shipped the oars and peered down into the dark green of the marsh. He was looking for the pale round shape of the rocks, supposedly 50 yards due south of the island. He thought he must be near there. Without ample sunlight to illuminate the depths, he'd just have to go by dead reckoning from the shore of the island. Replacing the oars in their locks, he headed for the western side of the mound of earth and trees. The boat would be undetectable there, at least to anyone driving along the fire road to the east.

Gliding up to the round rocks of the shoreline, Nick hopped quietly from the raft and pulled the boat out of the water. He made the rope fast onto a birch tree, and made ready to dive. He wanted to be underwater before the sun cleared the horizon; the sight of a skin diver out here would get people talking in a hurry. He'd just have to risk the bubbles from his regulator. If there was a slight breeze, the surface of the water would be riffled enough to give him good cover.

He slipped the heavy tank on, then his mask, stepping into the shallow water before putting on his flippers. Encumbered by the diving gear, he walked awkwardly, following the rapidly dropping bottom of the lake bed straight out from the shore. A few yards out and he was chest-deep. He ducked his head underwater to wet his hair and skin, rinsed the inside of the mask, and secured it tightly around his face. He fitted the breathing piece in his mouth, inhaled and exhaled rapidly a few times to test the regulator, and dropped underwater. The early morning bird sounds were abruptly replaced by the strong hissing sound of his breathing. Satisfied that his scuba gear was functioning perfectly, he kicked off from the bottom, and proceeded, fully submerged, in the direction of the rocks.

Without the benefit of the sun, it was almost impossible to see under the waters of the marsh. Faint outlines appeared after his eyes became adjusted to the murk, the early morning light not strong enough yet to penetrate the darkness. He didn't want to risk an underwater light; after several more minutes the rising sun's light would render it unnecessary. The sound of his breathing was choppy and rapid, so he took a moment to control it, letting himself draw in slowly, hold a half-second, then exhale gradually. He didn't want to use up his air too quickly, not after he'd come this far. He had plenty of time, he reminded himself. This part of the marsh wasn't visited that often, especially during weekdays. He could afford to pace himself, and do the job thoroughly. If he rushed, he might swim right over something valuable. No sense in missing any opportunities, now that he was so close.

He kicked his fins slowly and steadily, letting his arms hang loosely at his sides, following the gently sloping floor of the marsh bottom down as he moved away from the island. The world above the water was lightening as the sun rose in the sky, and some of that light was beginning to illuminate the shadows and shapes around the diver. He was about 10 feet below the mercurial surface of the marsh, and 5 feet or so above the silt covered vegetation at the bottom. The grasses below waved gently, revealing unseen currents and movement within the great marsh. Small fish darted through the waters, appearing suddenly in his mask's limited field of vision, before disappearing with a few flicks of their silvery tails. Vertical tangles of aquatic growth closed in from the sides, then opened up, then closed in again, like aisles in a green maze. At times a claustrophobic fear began tingling in his belly. He never liked to feel closed in, or not have a clear vision of what was all around him, front, side and behind. The corridors of plants that held the night's lingering darkness gave him an eerie sensation of vulnerability that he didn't enjoy. He reflexively touched the rubber handle of the diving knife strapped to his belt, even though the biggest thing he was likely to encounter was a largemouth bass. The light of day above was penetrating the water more with each minute, and he could start to discern browns from green, and light green from dark. He looked at his diving watch; 7:15 a.m. The sun would be over the trees in a few minutes.

The silted floor of the marsh passed beneath him, a mat of dead vegetation and obscure shapes. There were rocks, some boulder-sized... glacial litter, strewn about thousands of years before. Some of the stones were laid out in crumbling lines, leftovers from fields cleared and delineated long ago. There was younger refuse as well:

bald tires, a rusted radiator, a sunken rowboat, its wooden planks waterlogged and rotten. A discarded glass coca cola bottle twinkled from the mud. Must be an old one, he thought, noting the still-visible white lettering on its green sculpted side as his large shadow drifted over it. Even glass coke bottles were worth something these days, he thought, amused at the idea of people paying money for yesterday's garbage. Of course, he was searching for junk, too. His garbage was just older, and was fire-hardened clay rather than green glass. But it was just garbage to him; expensive garbage, he smiled to himself, a relaxed feeling coming over him for the first time that morning.

He realized the significance of his shadow's appearance, and why he was letting himself lighten up a bit. At last, the sun was in the sky, and the darkness gone, at least for a few hours. He scanned the bottom for other telltale shapes and colors that would might signify greater treasures beneath the mud. Anything round or circular caught his eye, and he would descend with the weight of his leaded belt, and probe the sediment with his fingers, delicately waving away the settled earth, hoping for the glazed appearance of pottery. Of the first dozen or so investigations, three proved to be crockery of some sort, a small bowl and two plates, dull red in color, with simple geometric designs fired into their surfaces. He couldn't tell if they were real Indian curios or not; he wouldn't concern himself with that right now. He would gather up everything in his mesh bag, and sort out the treasures from the trash later, in the world of air above.

He had moved along a fairly straight path from the island due south, toward where he had been during the dive for the missing hiker last week. He could discern a grouping of large, pale boulders maybe thirty yards dead ahead. Keeping his eyes on the marsh bottom, he kicked his fins with increasing power and proceeded toward the big rocks. The columns of green plant growth wavered in the water, with rippling curtains of sunlight flashing among them. Schools of bluegills played in and out of the walls of vegetation, providing hues of red and sky blue to the muted tones of the waterscape. The diver occasionally caught a fleeting glimpse of larger fish swimming slowly in and out of the corridors all around: bass and pickerel, lazily choosing their prey from among the smaller fish.

He sighted another odd shape on the bottom a dozen yards up ahead, among a congregation of large boulders. He kicked a few strokes, angling himself down toward the mud. Waving away the silted covering and giving a gentle tug, he was holding a pot, a large one, perfectly formed and fired, unscarred by time, as if re-gurgitated up from the earth after lying in obscurity for centuries. The sunlight from above refracted off the bands of soft colors en-circling the glazed sides. This was an important one, he could tell, judging from the interest shown in the earlier, smaller pieces al-ready delivered and paid for. He was excited, and carefully added the weighty vessel to his collection, depending on the water's buoyancy to cushion the ancient clay from harm. He realized that these objects must have been laying practically in the open before the marsh was dammed up and expanded. That puzzled him, since the people who walked on and tilled this land when it was dry would have presumably come across the pottery. Maybe it did come from beneath the earth, he mused, released periodically by some underground force; a spring, perhaps.

Realizing that the day would leave him exposed, he proceeded to collect several more silt-covered vessels, carefully adding them to his mesh bag. As soon as thought he had enough from this pre-liminary dive, he headed back the way he came, holding the pre-cious bounty in his arms as his legs propelled him toward dry land.

Chapter 51 — Ray and Nick At the Pine Cone Café

The Pine Cone Cafe on Route 206 was a mini version of a classic roadside truck stop. Its clean, airy interior held several booths, and big picture windows let patrons enjoy the mountain views from all sides.

A mix of courting teenagers and weekend day-trippers provided an anonymous cover for the two men in the corner booth, farthest from the front door. One had a freshly-trimmed beard, and sported a heavy diving watch on his right wrist. There was a small knapsack at his feet beneath the Formica table. The man sitting across from him had on a light blue windbreaker. Both spoke in low tones, letting the general din of the place mask their talk. The man with the windbreaker spoke.

"My friend assured me that whatever I can provide will be appreciated. My last offering was well received, and he's ready for more, the sooner the better."

"That's good, because I think we're very close to uncovering a new opportunity" Nick answered.

"How so?"

They stopped talking as the middle-aged waitress came over, delivering their hamburgers and coffee.

"Medium-well?" she asked, a plate in either hand.

"Here's the medium-well," said Nick, motioning to the place in front of him.

The waitress smiled, placed the orders on the table, and asked, "Will you gentlemen have some of our blueberry pie today? It's fresh and very good."

"Ahh, sure, we'll both have a piece," said the bearded man, handing her their menus, anxious for her to be gone.

"Very well. I'll bring the pie over after you're done with your hamburgers."

After she had walked away, Nick resumed his talk.

"Two things. I was hired by the Smokies last week to find a floater out at the marsh. We didn't find the stiff, but I found something else of interest." He reached beneath the table and hauled the rucksack up on the bench beside him. Looking around briefly, he opened the drawstring on top and reached in. He withdrew a small ceramic plate, about 4 inches in diameter, and placed it on the table in front of the other man. "Interested?" he asked, smiling in anticipation of the other man's assured reaction.

Keeping his hands folded on the table in front of him, Ray spoke in a quiet but firm voice. "Put that away."

The other man slipped the plate off the table and into the rucksack in one smooth, effortless motion, like a magician palming a coin. One moment it was there, the next it had never existed.

"Is there more?" asked Ray, slowly lifting the steaming coffee to his mouth.

"You can bet on it." Nick's voice was assured, his smile cocky.

After sipping his coffee, the man in the windbreaker put the cup carefully on the tabletop. He lifted his eyes and looked levelly at the smiling man. "What was the other thing you wanted to discuss?"

Nick sat back in the booth, putting his arm up along the back of his bench. "I overheard some locals talking about an old map." He was enjoying his little moment of power; savoring the potentially valuable information he alone had access to.

Ray was quickly tiring of this jail yard game, but he hid his impatience and contempt. He needed what this small-timer had, and they both knew it.

"Oh? What kind of map?" He picked up his hamburger, took a bite, and waited for the other to respond.

Nick now leaned forward conspiratorially, pushing his own plate aside. Taking a pen from his pocket, he drew a large oval on his paper place mat, marking an x near its center.

"A map of buried treasure," he answered dramatically, replacing his pen and sitting back against the booth seat. He slid his platter onto the drawing, hiding it, and picked up his hamburger and took a self-satisfied bite.

Ray continued eating in silence, his face a mask of indifference. He wasn't sure if Nick was out of his mind, or actually might have something.

"Where did you get your information?"

"Where does anybody get their gossip? I overheard some locals talking in a barbershop. They were going on about a local woman, and her map of a certain local area. They mentioned Indian artifacts a couple times."

The other man finished his hamburger, wiped his mouth, and picked up his cup of coffee.

"Where is the map?"

"This local woman has it. For now." He smiled when he said the last.

"Why do you think the map has any value?" asked Ray.

"Because these people don't know what they've got a hold of...," the bearded man continued, his voice low and excited. "They think the only thing you can do with old Indian stuff is put it in a glass case, next to the pickled two-headed rattlesnake, and charge tourists a couple bucks to look at it. Christ, they might not even have the smarts to do that much!" Laughing, he picked up his burger and finished it.

Ray was silent, weighing the information he had just been given. If Nick was right, and there was an undiscovered cache of Indian artifacts, then he wouldn't want to spend time haggling with this fool over royalties. Better to find them himself. All he needed was the local lady's name, and he'd find his way to the cache without anybody else's help. He might even go around Mr. Sacks this time. After all, those Museum types looked to economize whenever possible. Their pockets weren't bottomless, and too many middlemen resulted in too little profit for all concerned. If, on the other hand, Nick was wrong, and there was no map, or treasure, then there would be no reason to risk an arrest creeping around some strange broad's house for a piece of paper that didn't even exist. All things considered, better to let the guy produce the paper, and evaluate the risk and rewards at that point.

So, Nick, you've got yourself a partner, he decided silently.

"Okay, so you get that map, and I'll make sure you can unload whatever you come up with quickly, and at a fair market price."

"That's pretty much what I had in mind," said the bearded man, his smile returning.

Just then the waitress came around with their pie.

"I'll take the check, please." said the bearded man.

"Certainly, I'll be right back," answered the waitress.

The man in the windbreaker had no further reason to stay, and he had several things he had to attend to. "Thanks for the lunch," he said, sliding out of the booth and standing up. "What about the pie?" said the other, his teeth already a light blue from the berry juice.

"Help yourself. Call me when you need anything."

Without waiting for an answer, the man with the windbreaker strode out of the cafe, and into the afternoon sunlight.

Chapter 52 — Price Increase

The air on 40th street was hot and foul with exhaust fumes and the smell of burnt pretzels as Ray shouldered his way through the crowd of people pouring into and out of the Port Authority Bus terminal. The city's frenzied activity used to excite him, but now it just annoyed him; too many stupid people in too little space. And a pig wouldn't live on the sidewalks, for all the urine, spit, and other unrecognizable stains. Seemed like it got uglier and dirtier each time he came in. Twenty, even ten years ago, there was still a little class shining through the crud, but not anymore. Used to be you avoided certain spots at certain times and you were okay. Now anything could happen, anywhere, at any time. People got iced in broad daylight, regardless of race, creed, or color. Only last month Ray had witnessed a murder, right in the middle of 10th avenue, between 30th and 31st street. A black guy in a business suit, carrying a briefcase and an umbrella, had gotten stabbed in the neck by a vermin like little creep in a sleeveless parka and sweat-pants. One minute the black dude was marching along, and the next he's on the ground, trying to hold down the fountain of blood spraying from his severed neck artery, crying out like a baby. The little rodent that stuck him grabbed the guy's briefcase and ran, bloody stiletto still in hand.

Ray had seen dying men before, so he didn't wait around to be interviewed by some eyewitness news team. He did what any sensible person would do; he stepped around the writhing, blood-spewing man, and kept walking.

Ray only came in when he had to, and when he did he packed a compact 9mm semi-auto, tucked in the small of his back. With his loose-fitting shirt, it didn't show, and he could grab it whenever he needed to. He'd had plenty of situations come up where, just knowing he had it, he'd avoided things getting out of hand. One thing you had to do in NYC was, if somebody crowded you, you better crowd them right back. Having the piece gave him a real ba-dass aura, and other badasses sensed that and left him alone. Most of the jostlers and loudmouths were cowards, anyhow: they'd only target the weak. If they sensed you were strong, they wouldn't even look at you.

He checked his watch, and saw it was later than he'd realized. Looking up 9th avenue, he saw a break in the onslaught of delivery trucks, limos and cabs, and sprinted across the street against the light. He had to be at the meet in fifteen minutes, and he still had ten blocks to go. His mirrored sunglasses allowed him to sweep each block that he entered, assessing the players, the working stiffs, and the tourists. He never walked into anything without be-ing prepared; it was a lifelong habit. His pace was just shy of being a trot, but he called so little attention to himself that he didn't really look hurried. He gracefully cut around, behind and through everyone walking ahead or coming at him, like a barracuda through a school of mackerel, covering ground quicker than the congested vehicles along 42nd Street could.

A disheveled drug addict saw him coming, walked out onto the sidewalk and, flowing alongside him, one predator to another, hissed "pcp, my man, some nice dust for you, only a dime today." But Ray just maintained his speed, his right arm limber at his side, ready to fill his hand with his 9mm. The dealer lost interest after a few seconds, and peeled off to intercept a group of white teens walking from the other direction. Ray heard him pitching his wares, his evil voice merging with the noise of midtown Manhat-tan on a hot, summer day. A few months ago one of these clowns had pressed Ray too much, and he'd whipped his fist into the man's ear, dropping him right on the street. For all he knew the guy might be laying there yet; he hadn't bothered to look back.

At 5th Avenue, he headed north, only five more blocks to go. The pedestrians took a turn for the better here, he noted. Career girls, dressed to kill, cruised the streets on lunch break, their entire incomes either on their backs or tied up in some two-thousand-a-month walk-up studio. Everybody in Manhattan under thirty looked like they made three hundred grand a year, and most over sixty-five looked like they couldn't afford a shoeshine and didn't give a shit if you knew. Those in between looked to fit somewhere between the two extremes, either going up or coming down. As far as Ray cared to think about it, you were either getting better or getting worse, a winner or a loser, and nobody gave a rat's ass how you ended up.

He could see the green awning of "The Silver Spoon" up ahead. He checked his watch. One minute to go. Just right, as usual. No matter what sidesteps he might encounter, Ray always arrived exactly where he was headed precisely when he planned to get there. He had once guessed his arrival time to within five minutes, on a seven hundred-mile car ride to a place he'd never been. His partner hadn't believed him, so he'd done it again on the return trip, winning a bet worth a dollar a mile.

Andrew Sacks was sitting at a table on the sidewalk, the arm of his cream linen sport coat draped over the wrought iron railing like a farmer in a pick up truck. He was wearing his summer uniform of brushed leather loafers with no socks.

A purple paisley handkerchief flowed out of his jacket pocket. A real fop, thought Ray, as he walked directly to the empty chair across from him and sat down.

"Ray, you're here! And right on time, as usual." Andy smiled, looking at his Presidential Rolex watch. "Please do have a drink, it's so frightfully hot out. How are you, Ray. You look fit."

The young waitress, dressed in mandatory black dancing leotards, materialized at Andy's side, but Ray waved her away. He rarely drank during the day, and never when conducting business.

Andy arched his brows quizzically at the hand motion, but an easy insouciant grin spread across his face, as he recovered from Ray's silence.

"Perhaps some salad? Or a napoleon! You must have a napoleon, Ray. They are absolutely out of this world!" Andy was one of those people who's pampered lives revolved around their feeding time, like a peacock in a zoo, thought Ray. Why was it that these upper class twits always carried on about tiny little bits of food? He felt like kicking the white metal chair out from under Andy's powdered ass, but he let the thought run its course, his face impassive behind the mirrored sunglasses.

"No thanks, I just ate. Tell you what, on second thought, I'll have a glass of ice tea."

"Fabulous!" the man said, beckoning the waitress back.

"An iced tea for my friend, and I'll have another of these delicious little crème de menthes, please." He talked to the waitress like she was doing him the biggest damn favor, standing there, just waiting to take his order. They all did that shit, Ray observed. These people never ceased to amaze him.

Just then a fire engine's siren whooped two blocks south, as the big truck turned onto 5th avenue and headed in their direction. Pushing its way through the sluggish, apathetic traffic, it blasted a piercing air horn every few seconds, but with little apparent effect. A few pedestrians along the sidewalk stopped to see where the noise was coming from, but most didn't break their stride. A woman directly in front of Andy and Ray put her hands to her ears and mouthed a curse, hurrying along as if to outdistance the noisy intrusion. Both men watched as the red and chrome machine rumbled past their sidewalk seats.

"So, I take it your friends liked your presents?" Ray said. Andy paused, a spoon of pastry midway to his mouth.

"Oh, the presents. Yes, of course they were pleased, Ray, very happy indeed." He put the bit of food in his mouth and grinned happily at Ray, chewing like a contented rabbit.

Ray looked back at him without expression.

"Have you anything else in the style of the last items?" Andy asked, toying with the remaining crumbs of his dessert, his eyes on the place setting.

"I have access to more." Ray's reply was flat, assured.

Andy looked up at the mirrored sunglasses, smiled slightly, and looked down at his plate again. His usual confidence, his innate ability to charm most anyone and thereby gain control of almost any situation, wasn't working here. Ever the salesman, he ignored Ray's impenetrable barrier and pressed on.

"I'd be interested in other things, provided they are commensurate with the quality of the last. Same price range, naturally." Andy leaned back in his chair, arms folded, legs crossed, and looked assuredly at the man across from him. Ray thought he was posing for some invisible photographer.

"The quality is four-star, and the prices will reflect that."

Andy's bemused grin didn't change a millimeter, but his insides tightened at Ray's comments about price. Before this moment, price had rarely been an issue; Ray was fairly new to the antiquities market, and had always seemed satisfied with the money offered.

"I see no support for increased prices at this point, Ray. My clients have their parameters for certain acquisitions; these people have diversified portfolios. They're not limited to just one commodity. If I don't have the right investment at the right price, they simply look elsewhere. Really, my hands are tied, Ray."

The thought of Andy's hands tied behind his back brought all kinds of associations to Ray's mind.

"Then I'll have to go elsewhere." Ray started to rise from the table, and Andy looked as if he'd been slapped.

"Whoa!... hold on there, Ray! I'm merely stating the economic realities of my clients' considerations." Andy hadn't figured at all on this reaction. He had supposed that Ray considered this antiquities business almost like found money, and thus wouldn't become so greedy so quickly. "What prices are we discussing here, Ray, and for what type of objects?"

Settling back into his seat, Ray folded his hands on the table, and spoke in a quiet, level voice.

"I can deliver various sized objects, in excellent condition, within the next two weeks. The difficulty in acquiring these objects necessitates a general price increase of from twenty-five to fifty percent above those recently negotiated."

Andy had enjoyed a substantial profit margin on items delivered thus far, and he didn't want to cut into that. Although he had no staff, no inventory to carry, and worked out of his upper east side townhouse, his living expenses were high: the boarding schools for his two children, the house in the Hamptons, the payments on the Bentley, club dues, the antiques his wife and he furnished their home with. His line of work necessitated moving in certain social circles, and maintaining access to those circles required a particular standard of living. How much money one had socked away wasn't anybody's business, but where and how one lived, well, that was another matter entirely. Unlike most of his clients, Andy only looked like a millionaire. In truth, he spent a lot to look like he had a lot to spend, and lately he was wildly overextended. He needed cash; a lot of it, and soon.

He couldn't afford to lose this supply line, no matter how much margin he had to give up.

"Suppose we leave it at this, Ray: you let me know what you are prepared to deliver, and at what price, and I will do my best to convince my clients of the inherent value they are getting. I may be able to pass these increases along, but only if I can be assured of exclusivity." He had no idea who else, if anyone, Ray had approached with previous objects. He suspected no one, since Ray had been introduced to him through a mutual acquaintance that served the entertainment needs of celebrities and socialites craving anonymity. The professional world of prehistoric collectibles was very select; everybody knew everyone else, at least by reputation, if not socially. He was fairly confident that he was Ray's only outlet, but there was no harm in reinforcing that arrangement.

"You give me my price, and I have no need to go anywhere else." The logic of Ray's reply was irrefutable. Andy could discern his own fish-eyed image reflected in the mirrored sunglasses across from him. He realized there was no room for further negotiation at this point.

"Please give me a call when you have some specifics you'd like to discuss" Andy said, motioning for the waitress with one hand while he reached for his wallet with the other. "I'll be delighted to help you place them with those that will appreciate them the most."

"I'll call." So saying, Ray got up from the table, stepped around the railing and soon disappeared in the river of people that flowed in either direction.

Chapter 53 — Looking for Blackie

"Blackie!"

Mike Van Door listened to his call echo once in the cool ravine. He had been searching the woods below Rattlesnake Ridge since early morning, hoping to find Blackie. It wasn't unusual for the self-sufficient dog to disappear for a day now and then.

But it had been close to five days since he last saw him, back near the marsh where the missing hiker's items were found.

"Blackie!" he called again. The soft splashing of the stream, following the descent of Tillman's Ravine to the ancient cemetery below, underscored the quiet. The trees on either side of the stream formed a moist canopy, returning drops of water onto the slippery exposed rocks.

Mike carefully picked his way along the stream, occasionally using an overhanging branch as a support. He knew that Blackie followed this and other streams in his rambles, lapping up water as he explored the submerged hiding places and pools for delicacies like crayfish and frogs.

Knowing that the big dog was self-sufficient didn't allay Mike's concerns, though. There were plenty of black bears in the vast area, some with cubs. While Blackie wouldn't engage one, a mama bear was dangerously unpredictable, as ready to fight as to retreat.

Out of season hunters posed an equal threat, as they would blast away at anything resembling wild game.

Mike stopped on a small promontory to catch his breath; while in good shape, he had felt out of sorts since that morning; a slight fever, some minor aches. Hell, he wasn't in his prime, he thought… could be arthritis… his hands and arms had spent who knows how much time laboring in frigid waters, under all kinds of conditions and weather. Sometimes he was surprised at how he'd lasted so long.

He would make a point of taking a rest at the bottom of the ravine, maybe stretch out on the grass of the Walpack cemetery between the headstones of long gone denizens, left behind after their most recent descendents were forced off their land holdings by the Federal Government in the early 1960s. No matter that some had farmed in the valley for generations, a few as far back as before the Revolutionary war. With the stated goal of eliminating the periodic flooding of the Delaware downriver, The Army Corps of Engineers decided that building a dam and making a reservoir of this entire valley would do the trick. Declaring eminent domain for the project (known as the Tocks Island Dam Project) allowed for getting rid of the private landowners in preparation for submerging every house, barn, garden and pasture, ultimately making way for thousands of campers and pleasure-boating day-trippers, who might water-ski over history without a glance at the watery ghosts beneath them.

While there were a few holdouts, most took the offered compensation and left. Even as the Feds began bulldozing centuries-old dwellings, barns and paddocks, environmentalists fought the project and, ultimately, won.

So the U.S. Parks claimed all the seized land and remaining buildings as their own.

As efficient a human eradicator as a hydrogen bomb, thought the Old Man, but without poisoning the ground and surviving buildings for thousands of years.

Almost at the bottom of the Ravine, the feverish Mike slipped on a mossy rock. His left boot, jammed between two rocks, twisted painfully, as his outstretched hands cushioned the fall, sparing the rest of him from serious injury.

"Bloody Hell!" He muttered, stretched full length, his head downstream from his feet.

He pried himself up onto his elbows and knees, the one ankle throbbing with pain.

He tried getting to his feet, but his legs wouldn't cooperate. He swayed woozily on all fours, testing the limited range of movement with his damaged ankle. He couldn't tell if it was broken or just sprained. He knew he couldn't put his full weight on it just yet.

He looked around and spied a broken tree limb, imprisoned between two submerged rocks just a yard or so from his position. It would serve as a crutch if he could free it from the rocks and flowing water.

On his elbows and knees, he gingerly moved toward it, his entire front soaked, his limbs trembling from the shock of the fall, the cold of the water and the odd fever.

Reaching under the rushing water, he grabbed the limb and moved it to and fro, eventually wresting it from the rocks.

Holding it upright against a moss-covered boulder, he pulled himself upright, slowly and with effort, holding onto it with both hands.

Finally, he was on his feet, or at least on one, his staff supporting half of him, as he tried to hold the other off the wet ground.

Whoa there, Pard, he thought.... That exertion alone had taken a lot of energy, and he stood still, his heart pumping, his head woozy. I've got to get myself down to that grass between the headstones, someplace with shade from the oaks that share the ground.

With great care, he picked his one-legged way down toward the gravel road that marked the bottom of the ravine, and just beyond where the stream disappeared beneath a gathering of boulders and fiddlehead ferns.

Painfully hobbling across the sun-drenched gravel road, he made for the nearest patch of shade in the small cemetery.

Reaching a lichen-pocked headstone beneath an ancient oak tree, he gripped the cool stone with one hand to steady himself. His makeshift walking stick trembled in his other hand, both from his exertions and from the fever that seemed to increase by the moment.

He dropped to his knees, lay down on the shaded grass, and surrendered to the velvet black.

Chapter 54 — Dr Heckler and Sandra Ely

The phone on Sandra Ely's desk had already been ringing before she unlocked her office door, picked up the receiver and shrugged off her coat.

"Doctor Ely speaking..," she said, tossing her coat onto its usual place on the guest chair.

"Yes, Doctor Ely, this is Dr Heckler of the Sussex County, NJ Coroner's office calling. How are things with you?"

Taking her seat behind her cluttered desk, Sandra collected her thoughts, knowing that what she had to report would not be welcomed by the Coroner.

"Dr. Heckler, my apologies for not contacting you sooner. I only received our additional lab report on your sample recently. We have been very busy of late and I pushed things along as expeditiously as I could."

"I appreciate your efforts, Doctor. Everyone seems to be called on to do more, and with far less resources these days."

"Certainly the case here at CDC, Dr. Heckler." Sandra Ely took a breath and proceeded....

"Okay, our second test *did* seem to confirm my original suspicions, in that what *seemed* to be traces of anomalies on your tissue sample were evident...."

She paused, searching for her next words....

"Yes?" asked Heckler

"While the results did suggest possible anomalies," Sandra continued, "the margin for erroneous readings by the equipment cannot be ignored..."

"Forgive me, Dr Ely, but just what are you attempting to say here? They ARE or they AREN'T.... yes? I mean to say, what IS this margin for error? Eighty percent? Ninety-nine? Thirty?"

"The problem here, Dr Heckler, at least as explained to me by our Public Outreach Department Head, is this. With such a potential for an overreaction by the media and, subsequently, the public, to any official announcement on this matter by the CDC, it would be irresponsible, indeed, reckless on our part to make a positive determination of any contagious disease without 100% certainty of our findings." Sandra Ely practically winced as she listened to herself speaking the words prepared by her PR Department. While she understood the requirement for scientific accuracy and caution, she knew it must sound like so much government speak to the Coroner.

A profound silence on the other end of the line seemed to confirm her thoughts.

"Dr Heckler, are you still there?"

"Yes, Dr. Ely, I am still here. And, while I understand the gravity of our topic, as well as the caution you and your Organization must weigh in coming down on a positive identification for existence of anything like smallpox in this or any instance, please understand MY position. I have a person with an undiagnosed ailment in isolation up here at our county hospital. I have several other residents who may have exhibited some form of a similar fever. And, while we are less densely populated than many other counties, we ARE about a two hour bus ride from over 12 million people, with another 5 million or so not much further in all directions."

"Dr. Heckler, please believe me when I say that I fully understand what is at stake here... for ALL of us.

"Will you trust me to keep pressing for some resolution of this on my end?" Sandra asked. "I mean, before letting this take on a life of its own?"

Dr Heckler knew she was powerless to do anything other than what she proposed. He would just have to trust that Dr. Ely would do everything in her power to carry through on her word.

"Alright, Dr Ely. I will keep you updated on anything further on my end. I thank you for your help with whatever you are able to accomplish with the resources at your disposal."

"I couldn't ask for more, Dr. Heckler. Thank you. I'll certainly be in touch with any developments." Sandra Ely placed the receiver back on her desk phone, her mind processing a myriad of concerns.

Chapter 55 — A Cornucopia of Riches

Nick had decided to celebrate his successful treasure hunt and subsequent negotiation with Ray by getting thoroughly drunk at one of the local bars. By the time he awoke the next morning with a hangover, a blackened eye and a bruised hand, he had no memory of much beyond buying several rounds for a woman he chatted up, and who took exception to some things he might have said or done. He figured the large guy she was with must have taken exception as well, but he could only speculate. He didn't even remember how he had gotten back to his motel room.

He berated himself for acting without considering consequences, but he had never been much on self-control. What concerned him most was any possibility that he might have compromised his and Ray's mission. One thing to get in a bar fight, but drawing undo attention to himself could threaten their ultimate success; and screwing up a money-making opportunity that involved Ray wasn't something Nick wanted to dwell on.

Motivated to amend any possible fallout from his previous night's misadventures, Nick decided to revisit the marsh that very day. With his knowledge of the underwater spring's location, he could avoid using the rubber raft entirely, and enter the marsh from where he had previously concealed his truck.

The sun was well up by the time he turned onto the dirt road leading to the water. No one was about, so he proceeded slowly until he had once again secreted his vehicle among the dense foliage beside the marsh. As he donned his wetsuit, the only sounds were the ticking of his truck's cooling engine and a call of a blue jay somewhere in the pines. Hoisting the scuba tank onto his back and putting on his flippers, he waded into the still waters of the marsh. In a few moments he had slipped silently beneath the surface, and was following the gentle drop off of the marsh floor.

He used dead reckoning to head for the island, noting various submerged boulders and waterlogged tree trunks from his first trip. A few lost fishing lures occasionally flashed reflected sunlight from above. At one point, an unusual form on the bottom caught Nick's attention, and he hovered briefly above it; a smart phone of some make, and a fairly recent one from the lack of sediment on it... Maybe belonged to that missing hiker? Well, no time to bother retrieving and, besides, that wasn't Nick's concern anymore.

Continuing on, the shafts of sunlight illuminated a profusion of submerged rocks several meters ahead. This was the shoreline of the island where he had stashed his rubber raft before, Nick realized. It was time to alter course for the underwater spring, and the secrets it might offer up.

Once again, corridors of swaying underwater plants formed passageways, some wide, others narrow, an aquatic maze that seemed to lead in all directions, and none in particular. Schools of minnows shimmered in the sunken sunlight, moving as one into and out of the undulating vegetation. Larger predators swam lazily among the green corridors, their apparent torpor masking the reserves of speed and attack on call, should a victim swim too near.

Nick scanned the bottom closely now, and his attentions were soon rewarded. Down amongst the smaller boulders and effluvia, unnaturally shaped objects stood out in contrast; oblong tubular forms, squat round spheres, some tiny, others large enough to hide a pumpkin in.

His forward motion stalled, the lead-weighted dive belt allowed Nick to drift slowly down, where he could inspect these treasures.

Fanning any sediment away with his hands, he carefully lifted a small pot from its resting spot and brought it close to his diving mask. Its glazed surface was fairly smooth, and the reddish bands of color that encircled its upper half stood in sharp contrast to the muted beige of the fire-hardened clay.

He gently placed the pot into his bag and resumed his collecting.

As he examined and added succeeding vessels to his trove, thoughts of new found wealth competed with his need for calm precision, and he let one medium-sized pot slip from his grasp before stowing; it sank in slow motion before landing on a sharp rock. Nick cursed his carelessness, and turned the vessel in his hands to reveal a new crack running vertically along its side.

No room for seconds, he thought, letting it drift to the bottom, as he refocused his concentration and claimed another one.

There seemed such abundance and variety of objects that Nick, despite his excitement, couldn't help wondering how all these objects had been overlooked for so long. Didn't the guy in the barbershop say this had been open meadow a few centuries ago? Impossible to imagine all these things exposed for so long without being observed, collected, broken. Even covered by water, anyone fishing could have looked down and seen some of these oddments.

The profusion reminded Nick of photos of historical wrecks, untouched for centuries, their cargo spilled all around after tragedy scuttled the ship and crew.

Letting the mystery go for the time being, he refocused his attention on finding more treasure to add to his mesh bag. He moved among the big sunlit rocks, sure that more was near. Another circular shape beckoned him from between two rocks, and he reached toward it as a shadow passed over him. He absently thought it curious that a cloud in the sky, passing beneath the sun, could actually be detected underwater.

But the cloud didn't move on; the shadow remained.

He looked up toward the water's surface, and froze dead in his place. Above him, suspended in the water, was a very large shape, something oblong, with things protruding from the edges.

He'd been spotted! Possibly by some fishermen, he thought, cursing his decision to explore the treasure littering the bottom of the marsh in the full light of day.

The obscured sunlight streamed from behind the dark mass, radiating out in thousands of shimmering lines through the water. The shape dipped slightly, and the sun reappeared, temporarily blinding the diver as its light pierced the marsh's surface. Backing away, the diver shielded his mask with one hand, to discern whatever the large shape was and, more importantly, to ascertain if he had indeed been discovered.

Suspended in the water, not 10 feet above and looking directly at him, was a huge reptilian head, connected to a massive body. It was almost on top of him, and Nick kicked furiously, swimming backwards as fast as he could, while still keeping a terrified watch on the giant creature.

Slowly, the thing descended in the water, moving its extended limbs in an unhurried paddling motion....

It started moving toward him.

All was still silent, save for his very rapid breathing, as he continued to kick backwards, twisting around to make better use of his arms. The mesh bag of crockery smashed into a large boulder, and Nick didn't even register the loss of his treasure, so intent was he on escape. In his haste, the mesh got caught on some protrusion of the rock, and he was stopped cold. He had to tear furiously at the nylon, trying to release it from his belt. He finally unsheathed his knife and hacked the tangled fiber away from him.

He was just regaining his forward momentum when he was stopped again, suddenly and painfully. His left leg was being gripped —crushed— by something! He couldn't budge, despite all his thrashing and contorting, and he twisted around in horror to see his lower leg encased in the hooked jaws of the huge demonic head, which was extended out from a large, moss-covered carapace. He screamed silently in fright and slashed downward with his knife, clumsily hacking at the gruesome thing that held his leg like a dog gripping a bone. The sharp point of the blade pierced the leathery head covering, but wouldn't plunge through what must have been the thing's skull, despite the terrified diver's frenzied efforts. The wounds seemed to have no effect on the creature, other than to annoy it, causing it to clamp down harder on the man's leg and sever it completely, allowing the thing to withdraw from the slashing attacks of the knife.

The man's eyes bulged in terror as he looked in disbelief at clouds of his warm blood billowing out into the cold waters of the marsh, his left thigh ending in a ragged white tear, the severed leg now part of the hideous head before him.

He began thrashing with his remaining leg and arms, trying to move up and away from the monster as quickly as possible. With only one remaining leg and flipper, his movements weren't coordinated or balanced, and he shuddered through the water like a fish with a broken back.

It didn't take the creature long to catch up with him again, clamp down on the other kicking leg, and jerk him to a stop. Biting him sideways, where the pelvis and upper leg joined, the creature didn't wait for the stinging blade again. A quick snap of its head and the right limb joined the left, leaving the legless man dangling midway between the surface and the bottom, his arms ineffectually moving in circles, his life pumping out of his ruined groin and legs like a ballooning red hula skirt. His remaining limbs became weak and tingly, and he dropped the bloodied knife, losing all ability to cope or reason out his thoroughly unreasonable situation.

The eyes behind the diving mask were no longer wide with terror; they stared apathetically out at the mixture of blood and water swirling in front of them, incapable of connecting recent events with any semblance of reality.

The partial man was suddenly and violently sick, vomiting into his respirator and fouling his oxygen supply. Choking and gagging, he knocked away the mouthpiece with his left arm, inhaled blood and marsh water, and twitched a few times. At last he was still, and sank slowly through the dull red cloud of his blood, his arms outstretched like a crucifix, his masked face bowed, a stream of crystalline bubbles streaming upward toward the surface and the blue sky above.

The thing gulped down the two legs, and leisurely descended onto the inert meal on the marsh floor.

Chapter 56 — Ray Questions Bobby at the Bridge

The tinny ringing sound of the unanswered telephone was lost as a semi roared by on the wet road. Ray put his free hand over his ear and strained to hear the muted noise coming through the pay phone receiver, hunching his large frame into the ineffectual plastic bubble.

"Dammit!" he swore, as the accumulated rainwater in his hair traveled down his neck and found its way under the collar of his windbreaker. The faint ringing continued to trill from the receiver pressed to his ear. He'd lost count by now, but it must be over twenty times, and this was the third payphone call he'd placed in as many hours. His cell had proven useless out here among the interfering mountains, no matter where he had tried using it.

Something was definitely not right. Nick never missed an opportunity to turn a minimum of expended energy into cash, and this had been as sure a thing as they'd ever worked on together. He slammed the receiver into the wet cradle and traversed the accumulating puddles of water in the parking lot of the motel, leaping into the front seat of the rented car and shutting out the driving rain.

He stared through the water-beaded windshield in frustration. "Damn!" he yelled in the stuffy interior of the car, punching the padded dashboard with his closed fist. He'd driven out here after a day and a half of unsuccessful attempts at making contact, and as of that minute he was through sitting around waiting for something to happen. He decided to make direct contact with the girl with the map. What was her name?

Carol, Carla, something starting with a 'C'....

Connie.

Yes, that was it.... Connie. Connie, Connie, Connie.... What did Nick say was her last name? Mackay... that's what he said. Connie Mackay. She had a kid, a boy about ten or eleven. She was single; had to be divorced or widowed. She had to be local because the barber and that other guy knew her from way back, from high school Nick said. The kid's name was Bobby, he remembered that, too. He had to find a single parent named Connie who had a kid named Bobby, ten or eleven years old. Piece of cake, he thought, turning the ignition key and slipping the car into gear. If he hurried, he could be back on schedule by nightfall. He headed for the Pine Cone Cafe. They had a dry phone book he could look through there, and he could use a cup of tea anyhow. All he needed was about three minutes and he'd have everything he needed. To hell with Nick.

Mackay, C. 35 Love's Lane Hainesville 886-1337

He stared at the address, committing it to memory. Love's Lane had been easy enough to find on the map of Sussex County Ray picked up at a 7-11. The road marked the hundred year-old western boundary of the town, running north-south along a ridge. In fact, the road had been called Ridge Road for over a century, before some depression-era developer decided it needed a snazzier name to draw prospective homebuyers.

Ray slowed the car down as he passed number thirty on the lower side of the street. A row of old wooden houses, typical for this part of the country, lined the shaded right hand side. There were a half dozen all in a row, with identical slate roofs, clapboard siding, and front porches with side entryways. Only two had garages; 1920's-style outbuildings, with double doors that swung out, parallel cement runners, clipped grass in the center strip running from the garage doors to the sidewalk. The few cars that were parked were modest; a working class neighborhood, the only kind there seemed to be in Hainesville.

There, number thirty-five: white vinyl siding, screened in porch, dark wicker furniture, chrysanthemums, two huge old lilac bushes, passed their early summer bloom.

A small two-wheeled bike lay on its side near the porch steps. No car in the driveway. Ray pulled his vehicle over to the side of the road and unfolded his new map to look like he belonged there, albeit a stranger. Anybody could see he was lost, and people out this way were more than likely to walk up to a stopped motorist and offer their advise on how to get where one needed to get to.

He spread the accordion map out on the front seat and pre-tended to study it, all the while glancing at the white home across the way, looking for signs of activity. He didn't want to risk enter-ing the house in broad daylight.

He'd have to return well after dark and take his chances with whatever was inside the house. He was confident he could handle anything he encountered; it was those silent calls to cruising police that made for unpleasant surprises.

As he was preparing to fold up the map and move on, he heard the front door of number thirty-five slam shut. A dark-haired boy came flying through the screen porch door and pummeled down the front steps, snatching up the bike and pedaling along the side-walk, toward the woods beyond the neatly arranged wooden houses.

There goes my meal ticket, thought Ray, his eyes following the boy's exuberant progress over the buckled slate sidewalk. Feigning disinterest, he finished putting his map away, checked the rearview for traffic, and put the car in gear. Slowly, he moved away from the curb and began driving down the road, in the direction the boy had taken only moments before.

Bobby was oblivious to anything not immediately in the way of his bike, and didn't notice the sedan pacing itself behind him for a while. Jumping his favorite bumps and out-running the neighbor-hood dogs that ran snarling to the limits of their property lines kept his attention, until the fences and cement regularity of the town gradually diminished to the sparse quiet of the countryside. The sounds of summer cicadas broke the hot midday silence, and their loud buzzing rang into the air from hedgerows and thickets along the way.

At one point, Bobby stopped his bike to witness a fierce, noisy dual between a cicada and a hornet, locked in mortal combat, spinning and hopping about the dusty, cracked road like some exotic windup toy. The dry rattling of the cicada and the enraged buzzing of the hornet combined to form a unique noise that sounded far nastier than either insect could voice on its own.

Bobby watched, arms draped over his handlebars, ready to stomp the two contestants if they brawled too close to his feet. The brightly colored abdomen of the wasp plunged repeatedly into the armored thorax of the cicada, which skittered along the concrete in a blind, futile parody of upside down flight. Finally, with no apparent victor, the two broke apart, each shooting up and away in opposite directions, presumably none the worse for their violent encounter. Bobby pedaled on, imagining his efforts capable of lifting him off the hard, uneven ground and up into the soft weightlessness of the air, following the insects' careening flight. So involved was he that the sedan passed unnoticed by him; just another nondescript vehicle, driven by another faceless adult.

The cement road dipped downward as it moved away from the town, toward the low wetlands and the marsh. Fields cultivated in dark green stalks of corn alternated with thin windbreaks of trees and brush, the heat of the open spaces dropping a few degrees with the shaded leafy bands of darkness between. Up ahead, a light green sedan was parked alongside the ditch where the black and white Herefords gathered to drink during their pasture time. Bobby saw the silhouette of the driver, a man, as he pedaled quickly by, and he gave him a wide berth. It wasn't far now until the bridge and the canal. His progress was effortless as the land dropped quickly to the plateau of water. Bobby lifted his hands from the bars and stretched out his arms like hawk wings, his weightless imagination soaring free, high above the rolling land below.

At last he came to the bridge, and swung one leg off the bike like a pony express rider dismounting at a gallop. He tromped down on the brakes, and the rear tire fishtailed neatly, coming to a skidding stop. Bobby dropped his bike and ran down to the mossy rock wall, attentive to any peripheral movement, aquatic or otherwise. He thought he detected the silvery flash of something beneath the sun-speckled water, but he wasn't sure; whatever had been there was gone by the time he focused directly at where it had been.

Bobby noticed the sound of a vehicle stopping, and heard the metallic sound of a door slamming shut moments before he saw the reflection of someone in the shadowed water below the archway of the wooden bridge: it was a man, a stranger. Bobby looked back to the water, not wanting to meet the eyes of a grownup unknown to him or his family.

"Caught anything lately?" the stranger asked in a voice both friendly and demanding; a typical teacher-type voice. Bobby let himself glance furtively up at the man leaning on the railing of the bridge. He didn't answer, but looked quickly back down into the comfort of the cool flowing waters of the canal. The stranger on the bridge looked down into the dark water and spoke more to it than to the boy.

"I haven't fished this part yet, but I imagine you could find some mighty big bass in here. I usually fish the northern edge of the marsh myself. I like to work the lily pads from the shore; usually get a strike or two from some big bruiser lurking in the shadows." The stranger flipped a pebble into the gently flowing water. The stone made a plopping sound as it disappeared into the canal.

"I'm sorry, I suppose you never talk to strangers, and you're right not to" said the man. "So let me introduce myself. My name is Ted McLoughlin, and I live in Sussex. I'm a teacher at the high school; shop class. Ever build anything?"

Taking the person at his word, Bobby relaxed a bit.

"I built a birdhouse last winter; I mean, my Mom helped, but I did most of the sawing and hammering."

"Oh yeah? That's great. I build birdhouses, too. I like purple martin houses the best, because they take the most planning. Have you ever seen a purple martin house?"

"Sure, everybody's seen them around here." Bobby spoke assuredly. This teacher wasn't so smart, he thought to himself confidently.

"Have you ever seen one made out of gourds?" asked the man.

"Gourds?" asked the boy, a puzzled look on his face.

"You know, those yellow and green vegetables people buy along with pumpkins for Halloween decoration. Down south they dry out gourds, carve a hole in them, and then hang a bunch of them off a pole or on a clothesline. The martins love them so much, they return to them year after year, and they bring their young ones back, too. After a few seasons you have maybe a dozen gourd houses, and so many birds flying around you wonder how they avoid colliding with each other. Besides their beauty, they catch any bugs with wings smaller than them."

"I can make a sound like a purple martin" Bobby boasted, having relinquished all suspicions toward the teacher on the bridge.

"You can? I'm not so sure I believe you," the man laughed. "A purple martin squeaks more than sings, and its pretty tricky to imitate them."

The boy had pulled a small pale object from his shirt pocket, and put it to his mouth, cupping it with both hands. He took a deep breath, and blew his cheeks out; a piercing trill sounded above the low gurgle of the canal, warbling between two or three octaves rapidly. It didn't sound like a purple martin, but it was an intriguing noise just the same.

The stranger watched the recital carefully, his eyes locked onto the object cradled in the boy's hands. Bobby finished after a few seconds, and lowered the clay instrument from his face. He stared at the whistle as he turned it in his hands.

312

"Not bad, not too bad at all. Where did you ever learn to do that?"

"I taught myself." His answer came a little too quickly, and he modified his message slightly. "Well, I taught myself mostly. I had some help from some friends."

"Sure, of course. Where did you get the whistle?" The man's voice had lost some of its easy warmth. It was more authoritarian now.

"I found it in the canal; right here." The boy walked to the edge of the stone wall and pointed straight down into the water moving past his feet. The man stared in silence, seeming to look at the boy and the things beneath the water at the same time. He knew the kid would never hand over a found treasure to a stranger, so he didn't ask to look at the whistle closely; he could tell it was real from his perch on the bridge. He didn't want to jeopardize the rapport he'd achieved with the kid just yet. He could take the artifact any time he decided to. That wasn't his objective. Finding the place out in the marsh where that whistle flowed from, that was the main event.

"You figure somebody dropped it there by mistake?" The man's voice had lost a fraction of its edge and was taking on a little warmth again.

Bobby studied his prize in silence.

"Well, I think somebody misplaced it while they were swimming maybe, or they dropped it off the bridge by mistake. Everybody loses stuff once in awhile."

"You maybe have something there. I'll put my money on somebody accidentally dropping it into the water, from the bridge maybe?"

Bobby looked at the water below the bridge, then up at the balustrade where the man rested.

"Yeah, I'd say it was the bridge, too."

The man turned around, hands still on the railing, and looked behind him to the watery expanse of the marsh. Somewhere out there, he knew, was the limestone pit Nick had heard talk of. Something seemed extremely logical about the pit being a main source for various recently unearthed pottery mementos from the past. He was back on schedule, although searching the vast green mirror of the marsh would cut into his allotted time considerably. He really couldn't explore all that water by himself; if it wasn't the correct area, he would have wasted too much limited time on this effort. He looked from the empty wetness back to the boy, who was currently fiddling with a fishing line on the wet bank of stone next to the water. The stranger would probably have to move things along quicker than he'd be comfortable with; but what the hell, if he'd wanted comfort, he'd be tucked away in an office somewhere, moving paper from one part of a building to another for a few decades. But now was not the time. Not just yet. He might as well probe a little deeper, with the mother. That would be fun.

"Hey, you have a good day now, son. And don't fall in that water!" The man laughed as he walked off the bridge, toward the invisible car that had deposited him up there on the embankment.

Bobby didn't wave back. Something in the man's voice had changed, and the boy didn't like the way it sounded.

Chapter 57 — An Abandoned Truck

Ranger Smith had come across Mike Van Door's pickup truck about a half mile from where Tillman's Ravine began its descent from the mountain. It was parked just a few yards off the fire road, the driver's door ajar. Frank pulled up beside it, turned off his engine, and stepped out of his car.

Listening to the silence for a moment, he yelled out "Mike!"

His voice echoed back to him from the lodge pole pines and boulders.

"Mike Van Door!" he called again. Nothing.

Stepping to Mike's truck, he put his hand on the hood, checking for engine heat. Stone cold, he thought, as he walked around the open driver side door to look inside the truck's cab.

A set of keys rested on the worn fabric of the bench seat.

Growing concerned, Frank stepped back, scanning the ground at his feet for... what? Anything at all would do, he thought, hoping his own footprints hadn't destroyed any useful signs to be read in the dirt.

He soon realized the gravel from the road made any tracking pointless. The woods beyond, littered with pine needles and all manner of windfall, wouldn't yield much, either.

It was late in the afternoon, and shadows were already deepening amongst the trees. Accepting that it was too late to start randomly searching such a large area by himself, he decided to call in the truck to the Trooper Barracks, and then drive to Mike's cabin.

After clearing his visit with Sergeant Justin, Frank arrived at Mike's yard. The years of neglect and casual decay of the Old Man's house and outbuilding blended naturally with the surrounding trees and undergrowth, despite the profusion of junk and the general dishevelment of the place.

Frank stepped from his car and walked up on the porch, turning to look down to the water from that elevated vantage. The setting sun was reflecting directly up into his eyes; he couldn't make out anything other than the rippling surface and the vague tree line across the marsh.

Except for the screeching of a blue jay and the soft hiss of a breeze in the pine trees, the place had that dead, final quiet of many empty and abandoned dwellings.

While it was too soon to draw conclusions from a driverless truck parked in the forest, Mike's place seemed forlorn, lonely. All the energy and activity that imbue a building with life, that somehow make a place a home, seemed gone, like the spirit out of a deceased body.

Frank unlatched the door and let himself in. Aside from a window on the sidewall, he couldn't make out any details in the gloom. Gradually his eyes adjusted, and he was able to discern the rumpled form of a bed, a few chairs and a table; every surface seemingly littered with papers, cans and who knew what else.

Something unseen scurried in the dark corners, and Frank instinctively put his hand on the oversized grips of his revolver. He'd taken to wearing the gun since the Ellsworths' bull was mauled, having substituted the high-velocity .357 copper-jacketed hollow points for the standard-issue .38 caliber rounds.

A tiny shape, barely visible, scurried from beneath the bed to a crack in the far wall. He released his grip and relaxed, smiling at his tense overreaction. The sound of his gun blasting a field mouse to a bloody mist would have brought every neighbor running for miles around.

He'd only been in Mike's house once before, when the Old Man had asked him in for a drink to help celebrate the dog Blackie's birthday. He hadn't bothered to pursue how anyone could ascertain a stray dog's actual birth date, but had graciously accepted a shot of rye and toasted the dog's health and long life. Actually, he thought, the place didn't look much worse than any recluse's sanctuary. Unlike most middle class people, who used impending company as a recurring excuse to put their things in order, folks like Mike never needed to make of their dwelling anything beyond a comfortable place to sleep, eat, and retreat from the world.

As his eyes adjusted to the interior of the cabin, minute details of clutter became more apparent: a corner hutch crammed with old magazines, several wooden boxes along a wall, filled with what looked like an assortment of old car parts, rusting tools, and books. Frank lifted a volume out, holding it near the window to read the cover:

"LIFE ALONG THE DELAWARE - Early Dutch Settlers"

Frank opened the thick book to the frontispiece, adorned with an intricately rendered engraving of a pastoral landscape, presumably of the New Jersey/Pennsylvania border, circa 1645 or thereabouts, according to the brief legend printed below. There were several other romantic depictions of the earliest white settlements throughout the book, which Frank leafed through, standing there in the dust-filtered light.

"So, Mr. Michael Van Door, you are more of a scholar than you would have led anyone to believe," Frank said aloud, his voice sounding strange in the silence of the deserted house. He turned to the table of contents and looked down the chapter headings, his finger stopping at one entry in particular-

"Copper Mining and the Lenape"

Frank turned to the chapter and scanned the closely printed text, which was a compressed history of the exploitation of the native ore by the earliest permanent Europeans to the North American continent. According to this account, the indigenous Lenape Indians rarely used copper for anything other than decoration, since they hadn't invented or acquired the technology to meld the metal into anything else useful to their hard existence.

An illustration of some primitive copper bracelets was etched into the thick paper. Frank thought of the handless corpse of Tessie Hardin, and of the legacy she purportedly wore into her grave; the bracelets handed down form the Dutch girl, the wedding gifts from the Indian.

There was a connection between the violation of Tessie Hardin, the bracelets and Mike Van Door, but he didn't have enough to link them together. The Old Man had always been a rich repository for bits of local history. A lot of useful knowledge would disappear forever with him, thought Frank, looking at the book held open in his hands. Wonder if Mike had any relatives? mused Frank, looking around at the eclectic collection of paraphernalia amassed during one man's lifetime. Who would disperse all this stuff, if its temporary caretaker were, in fact, gone for good? If no relatives surfaced after a public notice was made, Frank supposed there would be an auction.

No, more like a county-sponsored dumpster, he thought ruefully.

Nothing in here to interest the kind of people who were moving into the county now. They didn't seem to care for history, whether in antiquated books or shadows of the past; they only wanted what was new, what was of the here and now, and the future...

He closed the covers and dropped the book into the box with the others. Perhaps he'd bid on these books. He'd rather they sat unread in his storage shed than have them become landfill for some housing development yet unnamed.

Along the solitary window ledge, two small figurines stood on uneven limbs, supported by the dusty panes of the glass; one rudely formed to resemble a tortoise, the other some kind of bird, its clay wings outstretched. Cobwebs connected the figures to the wooden sill, the fine silk moving gently in the close air of the cabin.

Frank pulled the tortoise away from the dried wood, turning it in the light. It looked childlike in its simplicity; he couldn't tell if it was one year old or a thousand. The features were detailed enough to claim its resemblance to a reptile, but not enough to classify it as any particular type. Frank thought about what the professor had said regarding turtles and the native Americans of this region. This little benign figure didn't resemble anything powerful or wise to him, but he realized he was looking at it from a modern perspective, merely as a little clay model on a dusty windowsill, illuminated by the comforting light of day. Perhaps it would appear more as its creators intended if viewed by firelight, embellished with the magic of song or chanting, empowered by darkness.

Frank carefully replaced the little totem from exactly where he'd taken it, not wanting to disturb anything else in this seemingly haunted place. The afternoon light was fading, making it increasingly difficult to see within the dark shack.

There didn't seem to be anything to glean from Mike's meager possessions to cast any further light on his mysterious disappearance, so Frank decided he'd seen enough. Besides, he had a growing feeling he didn't belong here, poking around among the Old Man's things.

He walked to the open door, turned and looked around briefly, then shut the door behind him. He looked out over the water down past the weed-choked yard once again, marveling at the thought that the view was in all likelihood little changed from how it had appeared for thousands of years. A sense of the local past was very strong just then; it actually felt physically close, like you could reach just beyond your peripheral vision and grab it, and hold it in your hand. Frank couldn't shake the feeling that there was a special resonance, a configuration of some kind of special energy to this whole area, and that Mike's disappearance was very much connected to whatever that presence was.

He walked down the wooden porch steps and across the yard, wanting to move away from this place. He hoped to find answers to Mike's disappearance elsewhere. The signals from this place were strong, but he couldn't decipher them. Not yet.

Chapter 58 — Mike Awakens in the Cemetery

Blanketed whiteness, broken by dark forms here and there.... in the distance, low hills forming a rose-tinted horizon as a cold dusk descended......

Newly sealed pots, arraigned at the entrance to a lime pit, awaiting the words to ensure their purposeful burial.

Keening of the dying, hidden in skin-covered structures a hundred meters or so from the clay offerings...

The few standing figures huddled around the pit, after listening to and repeating words spoken by the Sachem, prepared to lower the pots into the entrance, with one of their group poised below to receive them, one by one, and carry them to a carved niche well below ground.

A light breeze came up, though it was warm and moist instead of cold and dry...

Mike opened his eyes, which were level with the grass on which he lay. His body ached where it contacted the ground, and his joints were stiff. He had no idea where he was, and, for several moments, who he was. The powerful images from his dream refused to yield to his current sensory input, intensifying his disorientation.

Except for the discomfort in his limbs, it was almost like he had no body at all, and his being resided somewhere between the images from his eyes and the images from his dream... not an unpleasant reality... just... different.

From the grass only inches from his face, his gaze shifted up and outward, to a pitted grey surface a few feet away.... his mind eventually supplied a name for the shape; a headstone, he thought.

This initial recognition initiated a cascade of realizations, and the Dream reality yielded to his waking sense of who he was, where he found himself, and how he came to be there.

Reclaiming his body, Mike tentatively moved his arms and legs..... Except for soreness in one of his ankles, and the low ache from his joints, everything seemed to be in working order. He pushed himself to a sitting position using his arms, exhaling slowly as he did so. He was very groggy, and he shook his head reflexively, as though he might rearrange his scattered senses into some semblance of order.

Unlike his dream, the air WAS warm. Judging by the fading sunlight and the movement of the air, Mike decided it must be dusk... though what day or how long from his last waking he hadn't a clue.

Eyeing the stick he had used to guide him before, he took hold of it and, with great effort, brought himself up right. His joints were very stiff, so he judged he might have been unconscious for a day or more. He had apparently sweated a lot during his slumber, given the rank of his clothes, and he recalled the feverishness he had experienced before his blackout. Indeed, he still felt a slight fever, which caused him to shiver slightly as the warm breeze helped to evaporate his sweat-soaked clothing and body.

"Well old-timer, best get to walking before night completely falls," he spoke aloud, the sound of his voice comforting to him among the silent gravestones.

He knew that the Old Mine Road lay within a hundred yards of the cemetery, and he could follow it easily enough towards his home a few miles north. With luck, some one might be traveling and give him a lift.

Chapter 59 — Bobby Called Into the Night

At night, when the late summer light was rapidly fading, Bobby liked to look out his window onto the garden, and watch the slowly rocking forms of the sunflowers and the corn; you could almost hear them talking in hushed tones to each other, the evening breeze sounding among their leafy shapes like whispered secrets, the great, shaggy heads bowing and coming close together in murmured discussion. It scared him a little, but he couldn't keep from looking at them. It was like they had some strange power over him. Often enough, this bedtime ritual would end with him drowsing off to sleep, with a seamless transition from the actual world beyond his window to a similar dreamscape behind his closed eyes.

Awakened by a loud clap of thunder, Bobby opened his eyes to the dark shadow of his bedroom ceiling. He had been dreaming strange dreams again; of a place outdoors, a field of some kind, ringed with low mountains. He had been playing with other children his age, and a yellow dog, or were there several dogs? There was a loud noise, and a dog had flopped onto the dusty earth, dead. The other children had run away, leaving Bobby alone in the field with the still form.

Thunder again. Bobby propped himself up on his elbow and looked out his bedroom window, feeling the approaching rain in the wind that pushed through his curtains and on into the darkened hall of the house. Dark grey clouds, barely visible against the night sky, were rolling in behind the tossing branches of the trees in the backyard. A brilliant flash of lightning illuminated the garden below, and Bobby looked to the tall sunflowers, moving in the night. The thrashing stalks were strobed into a frieze, their bright yellow pods in various attitudes of repose or supplication, their trembling leaves uplifted, it seemed, in thanks or thirst, Bobby couldn't decide which.

After another blinding bolt, the separate tall plants reverted to a single dark mass, whose outline changed slightly with each moment. As the crackling roar of thunder followed, Bobby thought he saw smaller shapes scurrying among the vertical shadows of the sunflowers. His eyes, wide with wonder and riveted to the garden below, looked intensely at the plants with each successive lightning flash, seeking those smaller shapes among the swaying green stalks.

There! He thought he saw something scamper, hunched low to the ground, feet shuffling, from one line of growth to another, a spooky apparition coyly revealing itself for only a split second. He looked as hard as he could, little stars of after-image obscuring any details or movement. There was none.

What had he seen? Was it an actual thing, sneaking among the growth, or some storm-induced hallucination, flowering in Bobby's mind from a seed of suggested shape.

At one point, a heavy gust of wind threw his curtains wide, and a tributary of air funneled somehow through the little whistle beside his bed, giving birth to a short burst of sound. The disembodied note was cut short when the open bedroom door slammed shut in the wind, sealing him off from the rest of the house. Bobby sat bolt upright in his bed, more excited than scared by these events. There was an electrical tension in the air, a tingling; he could feel his hair lifting up at the back of his neck. The black silhouettes of the trees outside were tossing violently in the warm wind. He could actually feel the storm moving closer, as the trees and shrubs and plants registered the increasing movement of air with their thrashing and leaf-shaking.

Bobby got out of his bed and stood at the window. He felt fear, but something else as well. He wanted to be outside, among the moving shapes and shadows. He wanted to feel the storm all around him.

He groped for his discarded clothes and hurriedly put them on. Not wanting to disturb his mother, he quietly opened his bedroom door and slipped down the back stairs to the darkened kitchen. The quiet hum of the refrigerator sounded above the wind outside, as Bobby stood in silence, listening. Satisfied he hadn't awakened his mother, he let himself out the back door, and crept down the wooden stairs and onto the lawn.

The warm wind gusted around him, pushing first this way then that. The tall stalks of the sunflowers rustled against one another, their low sound and movement drawing the boy closer to them and further from the house. Another flash of lightning, and Bobby was sure he saw a form, a person, no taller than himself, standing perfectly still between two stalks. Another flash of light, less intense than the first, and there was nothing. He walked forward, stepping between the tall dry stalks of sunflower, their huge leaves tossing about, brushing his face and arms, rustling in the night, welcoming him.

On the far side of the garden, a glimpse of someone, something moving, away and toward the wall of trees. A seeming backward glance, a round face looking back over a shoulder, then nothing.

Bobby followed.

The headlights of Ray's car swept the dark road as he rounded the curve. Suddenly, there, in the middle of the road, a person, a small boy, running ahead of the truck, but not fast enough.

Ray slammed on his brakes, almost throwing himself into the windshield. The boy had disappeared beneath the hood of the truck, but he couldn't tell if he had hit him or not. He threw the gearshift into park and jumped from the cab

The boy was lying prone on the road, face down. Ray knelt down and gently turned him over. A bloody bruise covered the small forehead. The eyes were closed. Ray recognized him as the kid on the bike, the one he'd followed out of the house earlier that day.... Connie Mackay's kid.

Ray smiled at his good fortune.

He lifted the unconscious body into his arms and carried Bobby back to the truck, placing him in the passenger side of the cab. He'd passed by one of the abandoned houses left from the Federal takeover of years long past.

Though unoccupied for years, most of the seized properties and their outbuildings were kept up by the Parks Service, inherited wards of eminent domain.

The house Ray had passed, just several yards off the Old Mine Road, bordered the marsh. He headed there now.

Chapter 60 — Ray's Plan Moves Ahead

Connie had awakened during the storm, and had lain in her bed, watching the lightning-induced shadows of the trees flash along her bedroom wall. She usually enjoyed summer storms, but something propelled her from her cozy bed. She felt compelled to check on her son. She discovered his empty bed and quickly made a search of the house, floor by floor. At first her alarm was controlled, restrained. But by the time she had thrown on all the lights and had even searched the basement, in vain, she was panicking.

"Bobby!" she called into the warm night air, stepping out the back door and down onto the lawn, the wind tossing her loose hair across her face.

"Bobby!!" No answer, save for the rustling of the sunflowers and corn in the garden.

She ran inside and got dressed. She wasn't sure exactly what she was going to do, but she wanted to search further from the house, at first on foot, then with the car. She'd only been asleep an hour or so. He couldn't have gone far, assuming he'd left on his own, alone.

But how else could he have disappeared? Might he be sleep-walking, somewhere out there in his bare feet? Wouldn't he awaken? Tugging on a pair of hiking boots, she ran back downstairs, looking for a large flashlight usually kept by the back porch. The sound of a car in her driveway made her stop her frantic activity, and she looked out her kitchen window, trying to see who might be calling this late at night.

A loud knocking on the door sounded in the stillness.

She walked quickly through the hall and looked out the side panes of glass to see a stranger, a man, standing on her front porch.

She quickly drew back but realized, too late, she'd revealed herself. She couldn't hide now.

"Who is it?" she called, trying to mask the fear in her voice.

"Ma'am, I've got to use a telephone! I found a little boy down the road, and I think he's hurt!," the stranger called from beyond the closed wooden door.

Connie unlatched the door and threw it wide open, her fear suspended by the man's words.

"Where is he?" she demanded, looking beyond him to the headlights of a truck idling in her driveway.

"I left him by the side of the road.... I didn't want to move him. I think he needs medical attention, lady." The man looked concerned. Connie decided then and there she'd just have to trust him.

"Take me to him, now. My son is missing." She'd already started down the stairs past the stranger, and was heading for his truck. He followed quickly after her.

He backed the truck out into the dark road and gunned it forward, throwing her back. She clenched the door handle tightly, so much so that it hurt her hand, but she couldn't let it go. She kept her eyes straight ahead, not looking at the dark profile of the stranger she had just entrusted in the middle of the night. She struggled to make sense of things, but gave up. No matter that she was flying down a dark road in the middle of the night, in a truck with a man she never saw before in her life, searching for her boy.

Things were moving too fast for her, but she had no choice but to go with whatever happened. At least until she found Bobby.

The truck's headlights knifed straight down the black road, the wind-tossed trees fanning in and out as they raced through the dark corridor.

"How much farther?" she asked, her voice tight with tension.

"Just a little ways more." the stranger answered back, his voice colder than before. Connie thought the distance too great for her boy to have traveled, alone and on foot. Her focus on finding her boy had suppressed all the initial warning cues, but now they were flooding in on her, and she felt very vulnerable. Her heart sank as she realized she had been duped in a moment of panic and confusion.

"Where is my boy?!"

The sudden change in her tone made Ray look over at her. She was staring straight ahead, afraid to look at him, but he could tell the charade was up. He'd have to hurry things along now, before she got out of hand.

"Your boy is up ahead, he's resting near an abandoned house, and he's alright. We'll be there in a few more minutes."

"Who are you?" she looked at him now, her eyes blazing more with hatred than fear, her hands frozen at her sides.

"Makes no never mind who I am. I need your help, lady. I'll make it worth your while."

"What are you talking about?" she asked, her teeth clenched in growing fury. "What are you doing with my boy?!"

"I found your kid on the road, just like I said. Now listen up, lady. I need to know where your old map of the marsh is, and I need to know quickly. You'll be okay, your kid will be okay, but I need that map, and I need it now!"

He looked at her as he turned the wheel into a darkened driveway. A "For Sale" sign flashed briefly into view. Connie looked around and thought she recognized the place... it was the Ellsworth Twins' farm. But what were they doing here? The Ellsworth Sisters had moved away two weeks ago, with hardly a word to anybody.

"What in God's name are you talking about?" Connie demanded. Her fear was gone, replaced by a wild anger. The truck was slowing and she flung the door open, jumping from the still rolling vehicle. Ray jammed on the breaks and jumped from the cab, scrambling around in front of the headlights, chasing after the fleeing woman. Connie ran for the house, screaming "Bobby! Bobby, where are you?!"

She yanked open the screen porch door and tried to open the front door. It was locked. She felt for a latch below the knob, and flicked the mechanism first one way, then another. She jerked on the doorknob, but nothing happened.

She slammed back through the screen door and almost ran into Ray, who made a grab for her but missed. She eluded his grasp and fled around the side of the dark house, seeking the back door and safety. She rounded the back corner of the house and caught her hip on the handle of a water pump. Spinning around, she sprawled to the ground face first. Before she could recover, Ray was on top of her, grabbing her hair and yanking her to her feet.

A sudden, stinging pain covered the side of her face as he slapped her head with something hard and heavy. She tried to cover her face with her hands but he hit her again, twice, once on either side of her head. She dropped to the ground again, stunned, her limbs useless. Once more he grabbed her by the hair and dragged her to her knees, the barrel of a gun pushed painfully between her eyes. The man's face was inches from hers, his breath ragged and gasping from his brief chase.

"If you don't stop fighting I will kill you and your boy." He pulled on her hair and shook her violently, knocking her head into the barrel of the gun. "Got it?!"

She winced with pain, but managed to shake her head affirmatively. He continued his tight grip on her hair for a moment longer, then slowly released her. She started to weave and almost lost her balance, but he gripped her shoulder and pulled her slowly to her feet.

"Your boy is down this way, by the water. Let's go." He prodded her in the small of her back with the gun, and she walked unsteadily before him, her hands cradling her numb face. She tasted blood filling her mouth, and spit it on the ground. She couldn't see if her hands were bloody. They both felt wet, so she figured she was bleeding from several places on her head. She strained her eyes to see ahead of her in the dark, looking for her boy. All she could make out was the gently sloping ground going down to vague shapes. There seemed to be a large, dark mass out there, just beyond her vision. She smelled something beside her blood; water. They were near the marsh.

"We're here" he said, grabbing her arm and stopping her stumbling walk. "Your boy is right over here." He turned Connie and shoved her forward. She stumbled over something at her feet. It made a moaning noise.

"Bobby! Bobby are you hurt? Talk to me, Bobby, please..."

She fell to the ground and grabbed the small form to her, embracing her son and rocking gently. He responded by lifting his arms up and holding her head in his hands. His eyes fluttered open, then closed, as he put his head against her chest.

Ray was piling several sticks and dried bulrushes together. He struck a match, probing the tinder with the flame. His face glowed orange in the mounting light, and he looked over at the woman and boy across the fire. He crouched comfortably, one hand prodding the growing fire with a stick, the other resting on his knee, a shiny gun still in his grasp. Behind him a broken wall of bulrushes and beyond them, the dark waters of the marsh.

"So, let's talk about the map, and the limestone pit, and everything else concerning antique Indian pottery found around here."

"I haven't got the map with me." Connie's voice was slurred. The beating had clouded her mind, making thinking difficult.

"We don't really need the map, so long as you can describe it to me."

"What part should I describe?" asked Connie, holding her boy in her arms.

"Tell me about the limestone pit. Let's start with that."

"My boy needs help."

"We'll get help for your boy. Here, let's make him comfortable." The man stood up and came around the fire. Connie flinched as he came near her, gripping Bobby tightly to her.

"Don't worry, I'm not going to bother your boy.

"Here, lay him down. I've made a nice little bunk for him."

Ray guided Connie and the unconscious form a few feet away to a sleeping bag unrolled on the ground. Connie gently placed Bobby on the lumpy cover and moved away slightly, trying to draw the man away from her boy. She figured if he was going to do any more hurting, she didn't want him to take anything out on Bobby. Better he take his anger out on her. Ray had resumed his place back across the fire, and he reached for a rucksack at his feet, opening the top. He carefully withdrew several wrapped bundles, and placed them on the ground in front of him. He lifted one and carefully unwrapped it, revealing a small, round piece of pottery.

"This is what I want from the limestone pit. I have a general idea about where it is out there," he motioned over his shoulder at the wide, dark area of marsh waters behind him, "But I need to know exactly where it is, and I need to know very soon. You are going to help me, and I will let you and your boy go home just as soon as you do." Thunder rolled somewhere beyond the mountains, and the air moved fitfully through the bulrushes.

Connie stared dully at the fire. Ray could tell she was still punch drunk from the blows to her head. He'd give her a few minutes to find her senses, get the information, and get rid of her and her boy. He'd do it with his hands, quickly and quietly. The marsh was a big body of water, and they wouldn't be found for a long time; long enough, anyhow.

Chapter 61 — Walking with Ghosts on the Old Mine Road

Mike Van Door had traveled about a half mile on the Old Mine Road before dusk had given way to darkness. His progress was slowed by the discomfort in his ankle, but he knew the area well enough to keep pushing on, and his walking stick helped greatly. There was a moon out, but some clouds had come over the Kittatinny Mountains, accompanied by intermittent flashes of cloud-to-cloud heat lightning.

Mike's fever had increased with the coming of night, and his exertions added to the slightly hallucinatory effect it had on his vision. The sky was still a few shades lighter than the black of the wind-tossed foliage lining the road edge and the hilltops beyond, and all conspired to conjure phantoms along the ancient byway.

The shuffling noises of his own progress magnified in the darkness, especially where occasional outcroppings of shale and low rock walls of abandoned farms crowded in close to the road.

At times he thought he might well be among others, all traversing this ancient valley and place at night, partaking of a journey hundreds, possibly thousands of years old.

The sporadic flashes of heat lightning caught all in set tableau; the tunnel of darkness along the road suddenly expanding to illuminate the entire valley... millions of moving leaves caught in freeze frame... dark forms in fields revealed as abandoned silos and homes, barns still wearing their last faded coat of red paint.

After each lightning flash, these brief moments of vastness collapsed to the dark tunnel of road again, leaving after images on the Old Man's eyes and mind. Similar to his transition from dream to wakefulness in the cemetery, fleeting glimpses of all manner of things blossomed. The magnified sounds of his footfalls were joined by images of fellow travelers, ox-drawn wagons bearing chunks of mined ore, their drivers cracking whips over the massive, harnessed shoulders of the laboring beasts. Family groups, dogs laden of packs, occasional people on horseback, a milk cow or pig in tow...

With so much history packed into so close an area, it didn't take much to summon such wraiths to a lonely traveler at night.

Topping a low rise in the road about an hour into his walk, the Old Man thought he saw a bright flicker of some kind up ahead, perhaps a half mile or so. Still well within the boundaries of the State Park, no commercial venture or known campground could account for it.

Not completely convinced it wasn't just a hallucination, Mike picked up his pace a little. Should whatever it was not be close to the road, he decided to make a detour toward it as he got nearer. If it *was* a campfire, whoever tending it might well be cooking something, and Mike was suddenly very hungry.

Chapter 62 — Firelight Rendezvous

The wind was picking up, and the flashes of lightning came at closer intervals as Mike made his way toward the area where he thought the flickering ground light might be. Soon he came upon a dirt drive to his left, leading into a property he was familiar with; a For Sale sign confirmed that he was at the Ellsworth Sister's farm. He could see the undersides of some trees back beyond the dark shape of the house, aglow from what must be a campfire beneath them. The wind tossed night air caused the fire light to cast moving shadows, though he couldn't make anything distinct out from where he stood in the darkness.

Aware that the sisters had abandoned their home several weeks past, Mike decided that whoever had started the fire didn't mind trespassing.

Two figures.... no... three figures, were gathered around the campfire. The two facing his position across the fire were familiar to Mike. It was the mother and boy he and Blackie had met on the marsh several weeks before. The boy appeared to be sleeping on a blanket... Bobby is his name, Mike thought... The mother was sitting about a yard away from her boy... he couldn't recall her name....

Across from them, a man crouched, moving some objects between himself and the fire.

"Can't do myself or anyone any good just standing in the shadows," thought Mike, and he stepped ahead to make his presence known.

Connie saw the Old Man first. Alarmed at his sudden appearance out from the dark, she instinctively moved closer to her sleeping son.

Ray looked at this movement, then noticed Connie's eyes, staring beyond and behind him.

Pivoting on the balls of his feet, Ray whipped around, gun in hand, to face whatever had caused Connie's alarm.

Recognizing the man with the gun as one of the uninvited trespassers on his property, Mike realized, too late, that he should have assessed the situation more carefully before revealing himself.

For his part, Ray slowly stood up, the shiny gun aimed at the figure just emerged from the blackness.

"Hold it right there!" Ray commanded. "Drop that stick and hold your hands above your head!"

His thoughts racing, Mike realized he had to act; there would be no other opportunities for him.

Securing his grasp on the walking stick, he flung under hand with all his might at the outstretched gun, which seemed to go off at the same time.

Mike was knocked off his feet, his right leg crumbling beneath him. The thrown stick had glanced off Ray's right shoulder, causing some damage but failing to stop the bullet that was now lodged painfully in Mike's thigh.

Transferring the gun to his left hand, Ray tested his right shoulder, checking its range of motion as he grimaced in pain.

Shifting the gun back to his right hand, Ray leveled it once again, saying, "I ought to finish you right now, Old timer. But I have more important things to do, so be sure you lay right were you are."

Keeping the gun trained on the prostrate Mike, Ray turned to Connie and her boy.

"That didn't have to happen, Lady. But you know I don't mind doing what I have to, so let's you and me get back to our discussion about that lime pit."

The firelight flickered off the leaves hanging down from the close trees, and Connie thought she might use the dancing shadows to her advantage. With Ray focused on the Old Man, now seemed as good a time as any to make a move.

"My boy doesn't look good," she said aloud, shifting her weight slightly as she motioned to the sleeping form at her side. Ray looked up at her, and then at the boy. "I'd like to give him some water to cool him off." Ray nodded his assent and reached down to retrieve a canteen from the ground at his feet. He lobbed it toward Connie, where it landed just beyond the embers of the fire. Connie reached for it slowly, not wanting to spook Ray into a repeat of his pistol-whipping. The thought of the pain made her wince, but it didn't overrule the dread of what must inevitably follow, once he had organized everything and was ready to move out. Neither she nor her boy was necessary to him anymore, and she held no illusions about their fate.

She slowly dragged the heavy metal container toward her, keeping a steady tension on the extended canvas webbing. She figured she'd have only a split second after she swung the canteen back at him to dive for the burning log in the fire. For a moment her short term fear almost paralyzed her, but she blocked it from her mind and pulled hard on the cord, swinging the water-heavy container up and around in a back-handed circle over her head. The canteen gathered speed sharply as she whipped it around, and it hurtled back over the flames, crashing into Ray's face. She lunged for the end of the burning log and grabbed it with both hands, awkwardly lifting the flaming wood from her kneeling position, struggling to get herself upright before the startled man could re-

337

gain his balance. Obviously stunned with pain, he was already raising his gun. Moving quickly to the side of the fire, she swung the
heavy stick across Ray's face, knocking him back off his heels and
eliciting a howl of enraged pain. Sparks exploded upon impact, as
if they had burst from within his head. The gun discharged as he
rolled away from the fire, both hands clutching his charcoal-
smeared face. His hair ignited in a halo of fire, flaring briefly like
an old time photographer's flash pan.

Following the moving form, Connie put both hands solidly
around the stick, pulled back and swung forward with all her
might, catching him across the other side of his face. There was a
sharp, hollow sound as the wood met his skull, spraying still more
sparks into the dark.

"Bobby! *Run!!*" she screamed, as she stalked the writhing man,
looking for another opening to vent her fury. He had rolled further
back from the light of the fire, toward the green wall of bulrushes.
Another white-blue flash exploded in the darkness, and she fell
backward onto the hard ground. Her breath had been knocked out
of her, and her head was ringing like a hammered bell. Stunned
senseless for the moment, she lay paralyzed on the ground, having
dropped the smoldering log. She had no idea where Bobby was,
whether he had slipped away into the safety of the darkness or was
still lying exposed in the firelight. The injured man was staggering
to his feet, one hand to his burned head, the other hanging limp, the
shiny blob of lethal metal attached to it. He was trying to raise his
arm, the gun weaving to and fro in the firelight, seeking its target.

"Bobby, where are you?!" Connie cried, trying to lift herself
from the ground.

The lurching man across the way seemed to focus on her voice,
as he lifted his hand away from his scorched face long enough to
find and shoot her. Connie scrambled, trying to wriggle out of the
way of the next bullet. Dreading the inevitable impact, she clung to
the hope that her son was by now safely hidden in darkness.

The man's red mask of rage turned to a look of wide-eyed wonder, as if he were suddenly witnessing a miracle. His mouth opened wide, like he was trying to vomit up something impossibly large from his guts, and he leaned forward, eyebrows arched in surprise, gun still outstretched before him, the barrel pointing at Connie. He held that incredible pose for what seemed like an eternity. He lowered his head slowly, and a shrill scream of terror came from his sneering lips, as he looked down to his crotch and the strange pointed jaw that now encased his loins like some reptilian breech-cloth.

Connie watched in dull incomprehension as Ray was lifted up like a puppet on a stick, his legs kicking out ineffectually on either side of the nameless dark form, dancing on air. Slowly he pitched forward, magically floating a few feet off the ground, his screams negating the obscene comedy of his jerking limbs and ludicrous position. Stretched out horizontally, the man twisted his head forward and up, his eyes now pleading across the firelight, arms reaching out as if to embrace the woman he'd intended to kill only moments before.

Suddenly he was slammed to the ground, his head bouncing violently as his jaw banged shut, his prolonged scream ending as an abrupt grunt as all the air flew out of him. Something clattered off the rock at Connie's back, landing somewhere on her side of the fire: his gun.

He was silent now, though his eyes were still open, looking at her from ground level, like a bearskin rug, the firelight dancing in the glazed, uncomprehending eyes, the lower jaw thrust forward, pouting.

Whatever had lifted him up and thrown him down was still attached; there seemed to be eyes and a snout, merging with the small of his back, and beyond that a large mass. The prone man's rear end arched up, and his head and arms, flat on the ground, were being slowly dragged backwards.

He looked like someone prostrated in prayer, thought Connie.

There was a loud crunching sound, and the body flopped back onto the ground, revealing to Connie a face that looked like a blackened Halloween pumpkin — a living one; serrated lips mouthing some grisly portion of the man's lower body, red eyes expressionless in the flickering light. It stretched what must have been its neck, extending its head above the still form on the ground, swallowing a large lump of meat it had ripped from the dead body. With what only seemed a passing interest in the form across the fire, it bent to its meal, shoveling its lower jaw into the lower back of the man and raising him, a disemboweled Lazarus, once again. There he stood, slack-jawed in the firelight, briefly resurrected before being slammed down again, this time directly into the campfire, sending showering sparks swirling upward into the green canopy above and the black sky beyond. The corpse jerked as the beast tore ribs from the back, then lay smoldering in the flames, the vaporizing blood hissing on the coals.

Connie's dumbfounded reaction to Ray's end turned quickly from disbelief to terror. She realized she would next if she didn't get away from this man-eating demon.

Where was Bobby?!

Putting one huge, clawed paw on the carcass's legs, the beast tore another long piece out of its back, the almost dismembered head flopping doll-like on the end of the thin strip of flesh tethering it to what remained of the torso.

"Mom, are you alright?" Her son's terrified voice, coming from somewhere to the left of her, sounded in the darkness.

"Bobby, stay back! Run away!"

The beast looked up, its red eyes searching beyond the flames for the source of noise.

Food.

She saw her son spring forward into the firelight, moving toward the shiny metal in the dirt, Ray's gun. The huge beast stepped toward the small form, its head shooting forward on the extended neck, reaching....

A black missile flew suddenly between her and the thing, hitting the hideous neck and head with enough force to halt its forward movement. Loud snarling accompanied furious commotion as the beast recoiled from the impact of its attacker, which was still attached to it, big jaws clamped to the thing's neck, just behind its fierce jaws.

Dust and sparks flew as the two shapes fought, the big creature whipping its huge carapace and tail around, scattering the half-eaten corpse from among the burning logs.

Connie recognized the thing for what it was; a huge turtle. The beast that had just hurtled out of the darkness was a large animal with black, matted fur... A bear?

But whatever had affixed itself to the turtle's head had a long black tail... it was a big dog!

Bobby scurried backward just as the turtle gripped its attacker's back and shook it viciously, slamming the animal to the ground. The dog yelped a horrible cry, but scrambled to its feet and launched itself again at the exposed neck.

With its windpipe constricted by the clamped teeth of the dog, the reptile tried to spin around, looking like a rodeo bull trying to dislodge its rider. The dog did not loosen its grip, but it had lost its footing, and was being whipped to and fro.

The hooked jaws of the turtle caught the dragging body once again, and with a powerful twisting motion, ripped the dog's jaws from its neck, and sent the black form crashing into the wall of bulrushes.

"BOOM! BOOM!"

Two loud explosions sounded right by Connie's head, accompanied by two intense flashes of white light.

The Old Man, lying on his back, held Ray's discarded gun with both hands.

"BOOM! BOOM! BOOM!"

Three more shots pulled off in rapid succession, and the big beast hissed foully, scuttling backwards toward the bulrushes. Its movements seemed confused and uncoordinated, and it shook its head as if trying to rid itself of some annoying insect. It's jaws snapped open and closed several times rapidly as it bit at the darkness, trying to tear at the shredded metal inside its brain. It kept worrying the air, backing through the green wall behind it, seeking the cool protective dark of the marsh. It was shuddering now, as if from some deep cold. It withdrew behind the curtain of weed, and Connie heard the sound of splashing water, a guttural wheezing, and then silence.

The burning logs popped. The dead man's spilled blood sizzled among the coals.

"Bobby!! Where are you?!"

"Here Mom, I'm right here...." She peered into the blackness beyond the fire. Her son was crouching between her and Mike Van Door.

Thank God, she thought....

She looked back at the litter before her, but quickly averted her eyes from the torn husk of the man, seeking instead the dog that had saved her son's life.

It was lying where the sloping yard of the Ellsworth Sisters ended and the bulrushes began. Its mouth was open, exposing bloodied teeth. A ragged gash along its side seeped blood.

Mike Van Door laid back, the gun released from his hands. The soft popping of the fire and the gentle rustle of the wind-tossed leaves were the only sounds to be heard.

Chapter 63 — Renewal

Several weeks after the events at the Ellsworth Sisters' property, Bobby and Connie made ready for another visit to Mike Van Door at his home. Bedridden since his encounter with Ray, the Old Man was recovering, but slowly, and was unable to prepare his own meals. Every other day or so, Connie would cook and bake double whatever she made for Bobby and herself, and deliver the overage to the cabin, retrieving the empty containers and utensils from the last.

She and Bobby knew that Blackie's absence must have been difficult for Mike; even more so with the enforced idleness of his recovery. Their visits were as much for their own healings as for his, of course. The trauma they had all experienced would take time to dissipate, and visiting with each other helped the process.

As Connie's car slowly lurched over the rutted road that led into the clearing in front of Mike's cabin, they saw the Ranger's official vehicle parked in front. Pulling up next it, Connie shut the engine, and she and Bobbie removed plastic food containers from the back seat, the road dust raised by their tires hanging in the sun-filled air.

"Hello the House!" Connie called, as she and Bobby ascended the wooden steps to the porch.

The smiling Ranger appeared at the screen door, swinging it wide to welcome their entrance to the cool shadow of the interior.

Mike, propped up on an easy chair, waved them in.

"Ah, my meals on wheels has arrived" he called cheerily, motioning to the several mismatched folding chairs that served his guests.

"Connie, that broiled chicken was tasty, and I presume the vegetables were grown by you and Bobby?"

"Yes," answered Bobby, "we picked them before we delivered them, same as this bunch."

As he said that, he hoisted a basket laden with tomatoes, corn and peppers onto the cluttered table in the center of the room.

"And we've brought you some lasagna this time. Mike. Bobby rolled the dough and we both made the meat sauce."

"We used our own fresh tomatoes, too.," added Bobby.

Mike smiled at them both, then gave a brief look at Blackie's empty water dish under the dining table.

Everyone in the room followed his gaze, observing a respectful silence at the big dog's absence in the cluttered, dark room.

The Ranger spoke up, breaking the somberness that had crept into the gathering.

"Mike, how about sharing some uplifting news with your friends here."

"Yes, please, Mike," seconded Connie. "We'd love to hear some good news!"

The Ranger looked at Mike, who still seemed lost in wistful thought.

Turning to Bobby, the Ranger spoke quietly "Bobby, there is something you might be interested in the back seat of my car. The windows are open. Go outside and take a peek... but walk softly as you approach, OK?

Puzzled by these instructions, Bobby looked at Connie, then at the Ranger.

"Come along, Bobby... I'll go with you" said Connie.

Gently opening the screen door, Bobby and his Mother stepped off the porch and made their way, as instructed, toward the Ranger's car.

All the windows were open, and a gentle breeze moved across the yard and through the parked vehicle.

Looking through the open back window on the passenger side, both beheld a brindle-colored dog; of exactly what type they couldn't be sure; a working breed, or mix of some kind, given her large bones and well muscled limbs. She lay at length along the entire back seat, her head resting on an outstretched foreleg. She raised her head slowly at the intruders; not with alarm or fear... more like a calm interest. Apparently satisfied that the two people outside the car posed no threat (or at least nothing she felt intimidated by), she lowered her head once again onto her foreleg, shifting her body slightly as she did so.

It was then that Bobby said in wonder "Mom! Puppies!"

Sure enough, there, in the shadowed interior of the car, several small bundles of fur were attached to the bitch's teats, blissfully feeding.

The Ranger had joined them by this time, and all gazed at the resting mother and her pups.

"I found them in an outbuilding on the Ellsworth Sisters' property. While we were completing our investigation with the State Police, one of them called me over to a small gardening type shed, pointing out this dog and her pups."

"She didn't seem afraid of us, and I have no idea who's she is or where she came from. I only knew of the one dog, CJ, who the Ellsworths had lost recently, so I figured this one had just moved in between CJ's going missing and the night you all ended up there."

"She's quite beautiful" said Connie softly, not wanting to disturb the little group occupying the Ranger's back seat. "How on earth did you coax her into your car?"

"When we discovered her, she was quite emaciated," said the Ranger. "Looked like she hadn't eaten in awhile, and with all those little pups at her teats, she was pretty exhausted. So I bought some cooked meat and bowls, and put them right near her in the shed. I left her alone, and the next time I put the bowl of food halfway between my car and the shed. Took her an afternoon to get up the courage to leave her little ones and come out to eat, but once she saw I meant no harm, she proceeded to eat and drink heartily. I left her alone, and came back with refills for a few days, until I had moved all to the backseat with the door left open. Yesterday she had moved her pups into my car; certainly more comfortable than the ground inside the shed."

"And today, here she and her pups are, happily living in style!" He smiled at Bobby.

"Cute little devils, aren't they?" He said to Bobby.

"Oh, yeah!" agreed Bobby. "And their fur is so soft looking... and so many different shades!"

"Look closer!" a voice said from the porch.

All turned, and there, one hand on the porch railing and the other gripping a cane, stood Mike.

"Look closer at those pups, Bobby, and tell me what you see."

His face just outside the open window, Bobby surveyed the small beings. Their heads were fairly big in relation to their tiny bodies; some were brindle-colored, like the mother. Bobby looked at one in the middle... slightly larger than the others, its fur was jet black, from its nose to the end of its short tail.

Bobby looked over them all again, but his eyes came back to the one in the middle.

He looked up at Connie, then the Ranger, then at the smiling old man on the porch.

"Looks like Blackie had himself a family" Mike said to Bobby. "No wonder I couldn't find him those past days... he had more important things to take care of than this old coot."

Bobby turned his eyes back to the black pup. His expression was one of wonder... and sadness.

"Oh, Blackie," he said softly, thinking of the big dog he had befriended, the being that had saved him and his mother; the friend he had lost.

Connie put her arm around his shoulders, recognizing the mix of feelings Bobby was experiencing, perhaps for the first time in his life.

"We are lucky to make new friends, aren't we, Bobby? Even though we sometimes lose some of them, we always find ways to continue their memory, and our love for them. That way they are always with us; in the way they influenced us, the things they taught us, shared with us. They are forever in our hearts, and forever part of us."

Bobby looked silently at the little pup, and those on either side, all part of this one tiny family, just starting out on whatever adventures lay ahead for them.

"In a few days, after they're strong enough, if you'd like one, you can take one home," said the Old Man…

"I mean, of course, if it'd be ok with your Mom," he quickly added..

Bobby looked up at Connie, his eyes bright..

"Oh, we'd be most honored to have it join our family," said Connie, beaming at her son and pulling him close.

Chapter 64 — Andy's Big Night

The warm sound of cocktail chatter filtered through the heavy plastered walls and thickly carpeted floors of Andy Sack's brownstone.

From the ground floor living room, the indistinguishable voices of the assembled guests carried out into the open vestibule and up the spiral stairs, to the fourth floor. Occasional bursts of loud laughter broke over the murmur as well-heeled guests amused each other with clever witticisms and rejoinders.

The furnishings, immaculately polished and placed, looked even more jewel-like than usual, as the Sacks' had been preparing for this party for weeks in advance. All of Andy's friends were there, along with most of his clients: Antiquity collectors, institutional investors, and a smattering of scholarly museum types. He'd even managed to lure a curator of a prominent museum that he'd been prospecting for years. When he'd greeted the man and his male companion at the door, he'd barely been able to conceal his glee, and he'd quickly steered the two into the living room and introduced them to an investment banker friend who wanted to move a few million out of antiquities and into precious metals. He knew the museum represented by the curator was looking to embark on an acquisition drive for Native American pottery, and their funding was about to be approved. Andy had placed himself indispensably between the buyer and the seller. If just these two alone got together, he'd pay for the party and make enough to take the family to Switzerland for several weeks.

In a converted maid's quarters upstairs on the fourth floor, a cozy silence contrasted with the crowded noise of the party down below; a gentleman's reading room, complete with antique brass-railed library ladder, green-shaded reading lamps and red leather chairs. A polished coal grate, laden with shiny black lumps of ancient life, waited for a winter's match to be struck. Among the leather-bound first editions and signed limited edition prints were other treasures purloined from the river of time: things older than the written word; pots and small figures, smoking pipes and braided leather ornaments, things of antler, bone and hair. Prominently displayed on one deep shelf, their rounded, granular contours softly illuminated by recessed pin-point lighting, their matte buff color accentuated by the warm dark mahogany all around, stood four matched pots. Each was encircled by crude renditions of living things: a turtle, a wolf, and a bird.

They weren't a permanent part of that room's decor. They were on temporary display, arrayed in their quiet elegance to ensure maximum visual impact on the selected individuals who would later be led, one by one, to view these exclusively offered treasures. Each potential buyer would think that he or she was the only person even being offered the opportunity to own these unique pieces of history.

The participants in this cryptic bidding war would, in fact, establish the ultimate selling price among themselves, without ever knowing so. Andy would merely present the matched pottery and consider any interested offers. If none of his assembled guests thought the pots were worth what Andy expected, he'd merely tell each individual that "another party" had exceeded their offer. He would then have to market them somewhere else in the world, at a higher cost, but assured of a higher price.

The largest vessel, the one with a sealed lid, rocked slightly. So brief was its movement that its shadow wavered on the recessed shelf for only a second. The sound of the party below filtered into the silent room. After a few moments, the sealed vessel shuddered again. Its rough clay base vibrated against the smoothly polished surface of the wood shelf, making a slight scratching sound.

Downstairs, the echoing noise of several dozen people all talking at once was punctuated by the faint popping noise of something breaking, high up somewhere in the upper floors of the townhouse. Several people stopped in mid-sentence, their conversations temporarily halted by the mysterious noise from above.

"Did you hear something just now?" asked a young man of his companion.

"I'm not sure... thought I heard something breaking....maybe it was a backfire from outside..."

Shrugging his shoulders, the man plunged ahead with his ribald story of a certain society lady's exploits with a noted downtown artist. The noise level soon regained its slightly drunken boisterousness, and the brief interruption was forgotten.

Meanwhile, a time capsule from the far distant past had been opened, unheralded and unacknowledged, into the quiet warmth of the study.

Chapter 65 — Dioramas

The last of schoolchildren were working their way toward the museum gift shop, and their random shouts and laughter echoed through the cavernous halls of the upper museum floor. The sharp squeak of sneakers on the polished marble floors below made their tour sound more recreational than educational.

As the boisterous group moved further and further away from the Indian exhibits, a crypt-like silence reclaimed the glass-cased treasures from the past, a small, warm light glowing on each isolated object; suspended in airless time, out of context, without any seeming connection with living events.

One person remained, a girl, her braided hair held in place by a bright yellow bow, tied that morning by her mother. Shy by nature, she had lingered behind her classmates throughout their guided walk through the myriad displays of bones, artifacts, and taxidermy. Initially afraid of the varnished remains of dinosaurs and other extinct monsters, she was drawn to the miniature dioramas of American Indian life, set into the darkened marble walls like magical holograms of the past.

The little doll-sized figures, frozen in mid-motion, depicted the daily rituals of their lost civilization; a woman stooping to pluck ripened corn from a stalk, another kneeling before a miniature woven mat of straw, tiny hands on button-sized sunflower heads laid out to dry in the electric sunlight of the display. The girl leaned closer, forehead against the thick glass case, imagining herself a member of that little family, carrying bundles of autumn crops, trodding the red-brown dirt paths between the basket-like buildings of woven sticks and animal skins. It all looked so familiar and inviting, this little world of perpetual, airless sunlight and peaceful industry.

The girl walked to the next diorama, and looked into a frozen landscape of blue-shadowed snow drifts and ice; a floundering mammoth, fiercely curving tusks and trunk in the air, up to its shaggy shoulders in a pit, surrounded by tiny hunters brandishing weapons of flint and bone. There was no sunlight to warm this scene; only the dim cast of an endless winter, grey clouds hiding even the cold stars from view.

She moved a few feet along the wall, and peeked into the curved warmth of a lodge, the smoke-darkened walls absorbing the meager light from the ruby-red coals of a cooking fire. A family group of four, two adults and two children, huddled around the burning wood. All were busy at some task; a woman was mending an animal skin, her hand in mid-air, a microscopic porcupine quill needle poised to pierce the leather in her lap. The man was fashioning something from clay; a pot, for storage perhaps, or cooking. The two children were each working on similar clay implements. The scene reminded the girl of pictures she'd seen of the igloos of Eskimos, only this shelter was darker, more confined. She figured this group to be living in the world of winter depicted in the previous diorama, and not the one of the earlier, sunny scene.

She moved on to the next glass case, this one holding actual artifacts, as real as anything in her world: a blue-green necklace of hammered metal, a few parts of it coppery colored; a small square of woven porcupine quills, the black and ivory portions alternating in pleasing patterns; and a sealed clay cooking vessel, its bottom blackened by ancient fires, the shadows of beasts long extinct galloping around its outer rim. After peering into the miniature views of the dioramas, and imagining so vividly the lives of those people, the girl was startled when confronted with actual things from that time; full-sized, textured, close enough to touch, were it not for the flat barrier of glass.

Bathed in the subdued light of the exhibit case, the objects took on a hallucinatory quality, seeming to glow from within, their edges shimmering, almost breathing with life. The girl stood in the darkness of the hall, transfixed by their eerie luminescence and vibrancy, like a mouse caught in the gaze of a cobra. As she stared unblinking at the artifacts, the outline of the cooking pot seemed to resonate at a different rate than the quills or the copper necklace. The curved edges were vibrating, even beyond the strange pulsating quality of the light, causing the stoneware to dance slightly on the cloth-covered pedestal, like something moving from a subterranean disturbance; a small earthquake, perhaps, or a subway train thundering through the ancient rock below the museum.

The girl stepped back in alarm, looking down at her feet to see if she, too, were being rocked by some unseen force. The polished marble beneath her was still; there was no other vibration. She looked back at the illuminated display... the pot moved again, like some invisible hand was nudging it from without, or something unseen was trying to escape from within.

Suddenly afraid, the girl looked all around the dark, vast space of the hall. There was no sound of her classmates anywhere in the cavernous room. She realized she was completely alone.

She'd seen enough; too much, in fact. She ran, terrified, out of the room and bounded down the wide stone stairs, the round brass handrails guiding her down and away from the scurrying fear of the empty exhibit hall. On the ground floor, the sound of the fire door slamming wide open as she ran outside to join her classmates, already lined up and ready to walk through the autumn leaves back to their school, echoed through the cavernous museum.

The soft lights of the entombed exhibits spilled out onto the dark floor of the hall, forming pools of yellow warmth on the cold marble. The distant sounds of city traffic, muffled by the massive stone walls of the old building, occasionally broke the silence: a faint car horn; a bus accelerating away on the street four stories below.

A faint scratching sound could be heard, fitful, random; the sound of something awakening and moving tentatively within its clay shell; something seeking light and air, after many years of cold interment and darkness.

Acknowledgements

As this is obviously a work of fiction, any resemblance to any names, occurrences, persons, living or dead, is purely coincidental.

When I started this story over 20 years ago, there wasn't much "internet" to seek out historical notes, names, etc., regarding the first recorded People of the northeastern coastal United States. A book I borrowed from my wife's family, The Lenape: Archaeology, History, and Ethnography by Herbert C. Kraft (Jan 1987), gave me a wonderful introduction to the subject. Anyone with an interest in these fascinating People would do well to start with the late Professor Kraft's several books. Of course, now there is an abundance of information on the web, so there are many "entry ways" to pursue one's interest.

Like any self-induced project, there are plenty of times when the effort seems pointless, a fool's errand (fill in your favorite name for personal doubt here….) So, I want to thank all those who inspired me, cheered me on, challenged me to try something new. A toast to all those in our lives who say "Do it!!" "Cheers!" While I am lucky to have been encouraged/influenced positively by too many to name here, I must acknowledge a few…

Carla Brunelle, for teaching me to be a father,

My brother John, for showing me that anything is possible,

My lovely sisters, Linda, Janet and Barbara,

Our wonderful Mom, Margie Jenkins, who survived all her kids! XXX

My wife Monica, for her wit, wisdom and calm forbearance. While she doesn't generally suffer fools, I am extremely thankful she occasionally suffers this one.

My longtime Amigo-in-Minor Crimes, Jack Hobson-Dupont… for encouragement, for laughs, and for helping me avoid a life of misguided mediocrity.

www.ingramcontent.com/pod-product-compliance
Lightning Source LLC
Chambersburg PA
CBHW022148010726
47493CB00002B/393